As soon as he heard the deadbolt thrown and saw the knob turn, Billy hit the door with a force that recalled his playing days as a fullback at The Citadel. The panel exploded inward to hit Dillingham flush in the face, hard enough to poleax him. Dressed only in his jockey shorts, Dillingham straightened, eyes rolling back in his head. Then his knees buckled. The impact sent him toppling backward to sprawl onto the entry foyer parquet. The back of his head hit with the sickening thud of a melon falling off a truck. Billy moved to slip inside as the fallen man's body began to thrash spasmodically. He stared in surprise. These deadbeat artist types were fragile.

Also by Christopher Newman
Published by Fawcett Books:

NINETEENTH PRECINCT
MIDTOWN NORTH
MIDTOWN SOUTH
MAÑANA MAN
KNOCK-OFF
SIXTH PRECINCT
BACKFIRE

PRECINCT COMMAND

Christopher Newman

FAWCETT GOLD MEDAL • NEW YORK

A Fawcett Gold Medal Book
Published by Ballantine Books
Copyright © 1993 by Christopher Newman

All rights reserved under International and Pan-American Copyright Conventions. Published in the United States by Ballantine Books, a division of Random House, Inc., New York, and simultaneously in Canada by Random House of Canada Limited, Toronto.

Library of Congress Catalog Card Number: 93-90084

ISBN 0-449-14795-9

Manufactured in the United States of America

First Edition: June 1993

For Ann and Bill Newman,
    my long-suffering mom and pop,
    with love.

"For where the virtue of intelligence
Is added to malevolence and power
'Tis then no human recourse may avail."
Dante's *Inferno*
Canto XXXI

PROLOGUE

The moment Troy Brooks saw her, the tall, perfectly groomed blonde looked familiar. Familiar but out of place; as though she were wearing a disguise. His interest piqued, Brooks watched her. She sat in the front row, flanked by several painfully thin matrons with facial skin stretched tight like hide over bone. Her conservative designer suit was exactly appropriate for that company. With it she wore a pale gray silk blouse buttoned to the throat and a single strand of pearls. What *was* it? She didn't seem at all out of sync here, but neither did he think himself mistaken. His memory for faces and ability to place them rarely failed.

Today's event was a well-publicized debate held at Manhattan's elegant Park View hotel. Sponsored by the League of Women Voters, it sought to address the issue of censoring rock and roll record content via legislation. Brooks and his camera were prowling the perimeter of the seated observers—a throng of mixed origins. An assortment of New York's glitterati had turned out, some intent on making their own political statements and others just curious. They were joined by men and women of social standing and political prominence. For any and all, a chance to glimpse the rabble-rousing Cora Davis was almost as appealing as an opportunity to share the limelight. With her penchant for ultraright rhetoric wrapped in yards of American-flag cloth, Tennessee's eight-term Republican congresswoman had become a celebrity, too.

The blonde looked to be in her mid-thirties; thirty-five playing forty-five. She listened with rapt attention as Cora Davis squared off against the surprisingly articulate Randy Logan, lead singer of the heavy metal band Crucifixion. After apologizing to the audience for its offensive nature, the congresswoman had just finished quoting an excerpt from a Crucifixion lyric.

"These 'gates of ecstasy' are an obvious metaphorical reference to a woman's intimate area, Mr. Logan. And 'the price is right when love is free'? These are the values you and others like you are feeding our children."

Troy Brooks watched some of the audience squirm in its seats while others shot amused smiles at their neighbors. Logan also smiled, but not in amusement. His expression was patronizing.

"Choose to bury your head in the sand if you like, Mrs. Davis. I'm not encouraging kids to have sex, I'm acknowledging the fact that they do; that for most of them, their sexuality is the most important aspect of their existence. Why? Because your God and my Mother Nature *made* them that way."

"No, Mr. Logan," she retorted. "*We've* made them that way. By *we* I am referring to the television and movies we as parents let them see; the music we allow them to listen to. Our value system is a shambles. Decency has become a dirty word."

Rather than come right back at her, Logan stared thoughtfully out over the audience for a moment. When his eyes returned to her his expression was puzzled. "What is it you're afraid of here, Mrs. Davis? That in their uncertain world, faced with bigotry and hatred and a million health and environmental crises just over the horizon . . . that our kids might experience a little pleasure? Have a little *fun*? I'm not inciting anyone to rape or murder, Mrs. Davis. I'm inciting them to love."

2

"Nonsense!" the congresswoman shot back. "You are inciting them to fornication, Mr. Logan, and fornication is *not* love."

Forty minutes later, as Brooks prowled the post-debate reception, he found himself once again observing that mystery blonde. She moved easily within the congresswoman's circle, but as Troy watched her she occasionally separated herself from it by casting quick, furtive glances into the crowd. To his eye she seemed tense, like a dog about to steal a steak off the kitchen counter.

He was still wracking his memory as she separated from the congresswoman with a gesture toward her empty glass. She'd been younger—and not dressed like this. The face was the same, only a bit more mature. Her tall, angular stature was also very familiar. He was sure now that their paths had crossed somewhere. Brooks had never lived anywhere near the circle she was moving so comfortably within now. No, they had met somewhere in *his* world.

He watched her move past the hors d'oeuvres buffet to the refreshment bar. No white wine or Scotch and soda for her. She collected a refill of sparkling water. In the process she paused to dig into her handbag, extracting a pen and what looked like a business card. She scribbled something on the card and dropped the pen back into her purse. After a glance back in the direction of the congresswoman, she started into the crowd.

Randy Logan was holding court at the opposite end of the hotel ballroom. There were no tight-faced matrons there. Instead, he'd surrounded himself with a number of his celebrity peers. Troy spotted a popular actress—and that dancer who defected from the Bolshoi Ballet. The dancer had a wide-eyed little redhead clinging like moss to one arm.

Brooks watched the blonde move past the rock singer and catch his eye. Then memory hit him like an Alpine avalanche. He watched her drift around the rocker's circle and saw the man drop a hand to one side, palm backward. The buff-colored business card caught the light as she pressed it into the singer's hand.

Damn! No wonder it took him this long to place her. It was the downtown club scene, at least a decade ago. He'd stumbled into her and spilled beer all over the front of her skintight black leather jumpsuit. Her hair was cut short and set spiky with gel. Logan had been there, too; just another struggling nobody in those days.

Troy's pulse rate skyrocketed. As the singer slipped the card into his pocket the blonde headed for an exit into the hotel lobby. Brooks was certain the singer would extricate himself from his conversation and follow. If Troy played it right, this could be the bonanza every paparazzo dreams about. He knew who the blonde was now, and who she'd been. He had to hurry. If she was with the congresswoman's party, she was staying here at this hotel. He'd get her room number from the front desk and pray there was enough light in the hallway upstairs. He was an expert at pushing a film to its limits. All he needed was one good, clear image of the singer at the blonde woman's door.

ONE

Chief of Detectives Gus Lieberman received a call from the Operations Desk at quarter past eleven that Tuesday night. The Manhattan North Homicide Squad was on the scene of a nasty one. *Real* Nasty. A conservative United States congresswoman, in New York campaigning to see the content of rock and roll records labeled by law, had been found bludgeoned and strangled in her Park View hotel suite. High visibility victim; prestige location. A homicide like this could turn into a nightmare not only for the department, but for the entire city. Gus and his wife had just returned from the Metropolitan Opera's production of *Rigoletto*, and Gus was bushed. He had his feet up in front of the fire, had just lit a cigar, and was savoring the taste of an Armagnac considerably older than his own fifty-five years. He was in no mood for a trip from Queens back into Manhattan. But that was his life. In the face of a high-profile homicide the chief of detectives doesn't sit home.

It was close to midnight when Captain Wayne McKillip met Gus upstairs at the scene. Still dressed in his evening clothes, the chief followed the Homicide Squad whip into the living room of the suite. A small army of Crime Scene Unit technicians had just arrived and were busy unpacking equipment. Two EMS attendants stood by with their rolling stretcher at the ready, looking bored. Gus knew that both the mayor and Police Commissioner Anton Mintoff would be arriving momentarily. Before they did, he needed to get an overview, to begin formulating an immediate plan of action.

"Two bedrooms?" he asked McKillip.

"That's right. She's in this one on the right." The captain led the way. "A pathologist is with her now. The 19th got the call at ten thirty-five. They had uniformed personnel on the scene within five minutes. We got the call from their squad about twenty minutes later. As soon as I heard what was involved I had the Op Desk call you."

"Her husband found her?"

As McKillip entered the bedroom he nodded. "The way he tells it, he took a seven o'clock train here from D.C. Arrived at the hotel at quarter past ten. When his wife didn't answer the door, he picked up a second key from the desk downstairs. He's pretty shook up. The management found another room to put him in, down the hall."

Gus paused on the threshold to observe the room's interior. Queen-size bed, a settee and chair with matching upholstery, powder blue carpeting, and the open door of a bath beyond. There at one side of the bed the corpse of the victim lay sprawled on her side, her panty hose down around her knees as the pathologist took body temperature with a rectal thermometer. Otherwise, the congresswoman was still fully dressed in a cream-colored suit trimmed with navy piping. One of her navy and cream spectator pumps lay on the carpet alongside. The other was still on her left foot.

"Took me a minute to put the husband's face together with his name," McKillip continued. "Then I remember. Sunday morning television. Early. That character who quit congress ten-fifteen years ago to become a preacher. The husband is Jerry Davis, the televangelist."

As Lieberman groaned inwardly, he kept his face impassive. No, he didn't know much about early-morning television, but he had heard of the Reverend Jerry Davis. The man's quitting politics was news back in 1975. Two years ago when the Reverend Davis was in New York to speak to the Congress of Christian Businessmen, a large group of homosexual-rights activists had nearly turned the lobby of the Pierre Hotel into a war zone. For some reason he hadn't connected the good reverend to Congresswoman Cora Davis, but it made sense. Ideologically, the pair were two sardines from the same tin.

"That's wonderful," he murmured. "Tell me this ain't as bad as it's starting to sound, Wayne."

McKillip shook his head. "It's worse, Chief. There's no sign of forced entry. It looks like the perp hit her with that bedside lamp on the floor over there. Then he finished her off with a pair of panty hose."

The medical examiner's man was examining the dead woman's scalp laceration and the bruises around her neck as Gus stepped closer to watch. Gus tried to recall what he knew about Cora Davis and realized it wasn't much. She hailed from the Bible Belt and had surfaced over the last three or four years as an ardent advocate of several controversial causes. The legislation of decency was the basis of her crusade: the banning of certain fictional works from the classroom, the control of rock and roll record content, and the closer supervision of who received National Endowment grants. She was also very active in the so-called pro-life movement and in the effort aimed at putting prayer back in public schools. For the most part these were the same positions her husband championed from the pulpit.

"And get this," McKillip was saying. "There was some sorta booking screwup between her office and the hotel. Somebody got their wires crossed and didn't realize the reverend was planning to join her. The congresswoman was put into this suite here with another member of her party. Mrs. Lyle Mitchell."

Tennessee's Lyle Mitchell was somebody Gus *did* know a lot about. Mitchell was the United States Senate's loudest and most bombastic patron of the same platform Cora Davis supported in the House. A widower until just recently, the senator made a different sort of news by marrying a woman more than twenty years his junior. An ex-beauty queen. Gus remembered the press coverage at the time. Lyle Mitchell was the liberal's scourge. As the ranking Republican member of the Senate Appropriations Committee he led a one-man crusade to cut federal support for inner-city infrastructure repair. He vigorously opposed any new civil rights legislation and was a staunch adversary of handgun control.

"I'm sinking fast, Wayne. Throw me some good news. Tell me somebody threatened her; some heavy metal wacko with a bone in his nose. Tell me anything to kill the attack of heartburn I feel coming on." Gus patted his pockets for his smokes, found them, and dug them out. "The Reverend Jerry Davis? Lyle fucking Mitchell? This can't get worse."

"If there's a wacko, he hasn't surfaced right off," McKillip reported. "From what we've been able to piece together, Cora Davis arrived at the hotel at ten this morning after a shuttle flight from Washington. This afternoon she participated in a debate here at the hotel. 'Censorship and the Constitution' or some such; sponsored by the League of Women Voters. After the debate there was a reception in one of the ballrooms downstairs. A real star-studded shindig by the sound of it."

Both men watched the pathologist remove the rectal thermometer and hold it up, squinting. He then consulted his watch, punched numbers into a credit-card–size calculator, and made an entry in his notebook.

"You got an estimated T.O.D. on her?" Gus pressed him.

The man looked up, recognized the chief of detectives and shrugged noncommittally. "It's *only* an estimate, sir. The longer they have to cool off the harder it is to pinpoint. I'd say sometime between three and five this afternoon. No *later* than five. The one constant we have is the temperature here inside the room. I'm told by Captain McKillip that it's been a steady seventy-four all day."

"What killed her?" Gus asked.

Another shrug. "Can't say with any precision. Not yet, anyway. It looks like the blow to the head fractured the skull. There's very little bruising where the stocking was wrapped around her neck. It's possible that the blow killed her and the strangulation was wasted effort.''

Upstairs, Detective Lieutenant Joe Dante could hear the revelry of the party he'd recently left continuing full tilt. Down here in his own bed he was enjoying the way the warmth of Rosa Losada's alluring backside radiated into his loins. Still, there was confusion accompanying his pleasure, and he was at a loss to disentangle them. He was having trouble figuring out just how she'd come to be here.

''You're awfully quiet,'' she murmured.

He let his right hand glide up along the silky texture of her thigh and hip, savoring the delicious drop-off encountered beyond her hip bone. As his fingers moved on to caress her waist, he could feel the breath in her, belly rising and falling.

''Just thinking,'' he replied. God knew how often he'd thought about this happening; the only woman he'd ever been marriage-serious about—an ex-lover of three years now—becoming his lover again. ''Thinking about how much the two of us have changed.''

When Rosa left him, Joe was forced to examine many of his directions. He'd been devastated at first. Too soon after the split she'd taken up with another man. He was forced to confront old-world notions inherited from his parents—about marriage and family, about ambitions and how they could poison the soul. One of the sticking points in his relationship with Rosa had been her ambition. She'd wanted to be the Job's first female commissioner. In pursuit of that ambition, she'd quit the street and gone to work as a high-profile press liaison officer in the Public Information Bureau.

Rosa eased over onto her back, her eyes meeting his. ''Have we? I'm still clawing my way up the brass ladder, and you're still kicking and bucking every time they try to put you in harness. So what's changed, Dante?''

If Rosa's recent promotion to lieutenant was any indicator, she wasn't just clawing, she was making rapid progress.

Dante chuckled. "Touché. I'm still a fuckup and you're still a rising star. I guess I'm talking more subtle changes."

"Okay," she allowed. "I've got to admit you seem more relaxed lately. You're still at odds with half the Job most of the time, but it doesn't seem to bother you anymore. You work under a commissioner who hates your guts, and that doesn't bother you either. In that sense, you *have* changed. It used to eat at you."

"Just like your ambitions used to eat at me, Rosa. The idea of your someday outranking me was anathema. Now? I couldn't give a fuck. In another two or three years you'll make captain. Me? As long as Tony Mintoff remains our esteemed P.C., I'll retire right where I am."

"But not to worry, huh? You've mellowed?"

At that, he chuckled again. "Mellowed? I don't think so. Just gotten smarter. I don't beat my head against walls just for the hell of it anymore."

As he spoke, Dante met the intent gaze of those huge brown eyes. Square on. Rosa Losada was the best-looking cop the Job had ever seen. Hell, she could hold her own in *any* walk of life. She joined straight out of college. Bennington, of all places. To many, her motivations had seemed obvious. Her parents were victims of a brutal double homicide. She'd made detective in five short years. Joe, fresh from a five-year deep cover assignment, was her first partner in plainclothes.

"So what happened here tonight, Rosa? Something we can wake up tomorrow and blame on a full moon?"

She shook her head. "No good. Last week."

"What?"

"The full moon. Friday, I think."

Dante had been too busy the past month to pay any attention. He'd had a war between Hong Kong and Taiwanese Chinese factions on his hands. He'd also been too busy to spend much time on a costume for tonight's Mardi Gras party. He'd dressed in black, donned a dime store Zorro mask, and gone as a cat burglar. The minute Rosa stepped off the elevator every male head in the place turned. It was no mystery to Joe whose face was hidden behind the cat mask. That black body suit with its tail and pointed-ear hood did little to disguise a body that only a eunuch could forget. He knew she recognized him, too, and yet they'd pretended. He asked her to dance, and as they moved to the raucous rhythms of three different live bands, they'd flirted. The collapse of all defenses came during a slow number. Rosa's costume was glued to her sweat-damp body like a second skin. She'd come easily into his arms to pick up the beat of a fluid Latin ballad.

"Are you as surprised as I am?" she asked.

"You kidding? When I kissed you I half expected a knee in the balls."

Her eyes twinkled with amusement in the stray light leaking into the room from the hall. "Don't bullshit me, Dante. You knew I wanted you."

He nodded. "You *did* ask me to show you my place."

Dante's residence was a half-finished warehouse loft. He'd moved there recently when the apartment he and Rosa once shared was destroyed by fire.

"So we both wanted it, and it's nothing we can blame on a full moon. So what's all this about, Rosa?"

"Can't we just lie here and feel good about the moment?"

In considering her question, Joe realized he had no idea who this woman was anymore. Three years was a long time. Most of the pain they'd inflicted on each other was just dim memory now. Maybe it would be best to leave it buried, to shrug off tonight's lovemaking as a roll in the hay for old times' sake.

The bedside phone rang, startling them both. Joe could tell by the pitch of the ring that it wasn't his buddy Brian upstairs, wondering where he'd gone. No, this was the special line dedicated to Job business. That phone rarely rang after midnight unless he was being summoned to a crime scene.

This one sounded ugly. Gus Lieberman was requesting Joe join him at a Park View hotel homicide scene. A prominent politician had been found on the floor of her suite, her skull crushed.

Rosa sat up as Dante hurried to his closet, yanked a shirt off a hanger, and started to dress.

"Wham, bam, huh?"

"Gus is sitting on a nasty one. Wants me to have a look. There's an extra key to the elevator hanging by the phone in the kitchen."

Gun and shield case from his top dresser drawer. Sneakers from last night's costume. As Joe shrugged into his jacket, he hurried around the end of the bed to kiss Rosa quickly before starting away. She was already burrowing back beneath the covers by the time Dante reached the bedroom door. "Watch for the cat when you're leaving," he said. "Little bastard loves that goddamn elevator."

On reaching his parking garage the next block over, Dante conned the attendant out of a cup of coffee and gulped most of it while the man brought his car to the curb. It wasn't late by New York standards, but this being a Tuesday, there wasn't much traffic on the streets as Joe started across town on 28th toward Madison Avenue. It was chilly, with the night sky overcast and temperatures hovering in the mid-thirties. Dante hated February in New York. He was happy that this one had now run two-thirds of its course.

The Park View was located on Central Park at the corner of Fifth Avenue and 61st Street. The city was even quieter in the lower reaches of the Upper East Side than it had been in midtown and further south. The curb outside the hotel was jammed with police vehicles, and Joe had to find an empty hydrant half a block downtown on the park side of Fifth. As he crossed the avenue on foot and entered the main lobby he saw that the news hounds were already encamped. Several spotted his approach, with a Channel 5 beat reporter leading the charge.

"Lieutenant Dante. What can you tell us about events upstairs?"

Dante's face became a mask, his expression pleasant but

impenetrable. "You know the drill by now, Ms. Campbell. The chief of detectives is here on the scene, and when he's got something to say to you I'm sure he'll let you know." As he spoke, Joe shouldered past, nodded to the uniforms monitoring traffic in front of the elevators, and gave them a look at his shield. Before anyone could ask a follow-up, the doors to the car before him parted. Dante dodged inside.

Out on the street Joe had spotted two vans from the Crime Scene Unit, an EMS wagon, at least a dozen unmarked sedans, and another ten blue and whites. Upstairs on the seventeenth floor, the scene reflected that street crowding. The hall outside the elevators was jammed with Job personnel, most of them loitering in groups of four or five. While the noise level was subdued, the smoke level was high enough to warrant issuing respirator masks.

Dante found Gus in the living room of the homicide suite, huddled in conference with the mayor and P.C. Anton Mintoff. The chief had his back to him as he entered, but Mintoff spotted him right off. Instantly, the P.C.'s face hardened. Eyes narrowing, Mintoff stopped midsentence to shoot an accusing scowl at the chief.

"What the hell is *he* doing here?"

TWO

Commissioner Anton Mintoff, known to the rank and file of the Job as "Big Tony," was not quite five feet eight inches tall. He was generally acknowledged to have a short-man complex, a short memory, short attention span, and short fuse. He hadn't brought Gus Lieberman aboard as his chief of detectives in a gesture of friendship. Gus had a reputation as a hard-nosed, get-the-job-done administrator. There were other senior cops who could fill the position adequately enough, but the exemplary record Gus had compiled since assuming control of Detective Bureau commanded Mintoff's respect, albeit grudgingly. As Big Tony bristled at Dante's arrival, Gus asked the mayor to excuse them and took the P.C. to one side.

"He's here because I asked him here," Gus growled. "This mess is gonna send shock waves clear to the Gulf of Mexico and back. I've got Joey fresh off that Chinese trouble. There ain't any doubt in my mind that McKillip and his people can conduct a competent investigation, but I want a guy on this that I know can hit a curve. He ain't gonna be taking anything over, just working parallel."

Mintoff went through the routine he always did when he got wound up tight as a clock spring: the adjustment of the perfectly knotted tie, the inspection of the jacket sleeves for lint. He paused to pick at something invisible to Lieberman's eye and then shot his cuffs before returning to meet the chief's gaze.

"It's no secret that Dante and McKillip don't get along. Your scenario creates undue friction. I don't like it."

"Wayne McKillip's a big boy," Gus scoffed. "My scenario might wind up saving the city of New York a lot of embarrassment. Our homicide victim was bunking in with the wife of Lyle Mitchell, for Christ's sake. That man *hates* this town. Cora Davis was his political protégée. We don't find us a perp, and *fast*, we could be up to our asses in fallout from this shit storm."

Mintoff considered himself an astute political animal, but not in quite the same league as his C of D. Gustav Lieberman, a blue-collar Jew, was married to the former Lydia Cox, an heir to one of the most powerful specialty brokerage houses on Wall Street. A *WASP* brokerage house. Because he was tapped into worlds Mintoff was barely able to fathom, Gus had different insights. It often paid to listen to him.

"I *still* don't like it," Mintoff muttered. "You keep that son of a bitch on a short leash. I'm not going to tell you how to do your job, but the way that pet goon of yours operates scares me."

"Pet *goon*?" Gus asked with raised eyebrows. "Two department medals of honor. Six bronze commendation stars and a medal for merit. A fucking *masters* degree in criminal psychology from John Jay. He's the best investigative cop in the Job, Tony. You count the times he's saved *both* our fannies, you need the fingers of more'n one hand."

Mintoff turned abruptly to collect the mayor and escort him away into the outside hall. As he passed Dante he took pains to avoid eye contact. Joe smirked as he advanced on the chief's position. Lieberman shook another butt out of his pack, muttering to himself.

"Just when I was beginning to think he liked me," Dante murmured. "What is it? My aftershave?"

Gus shot Joe a scowl and started across the living room toward the location of their corpse. As he moved, he hurried to bring Dante up to speed. After detailing the particulars of the bludgeoning, he moved on to the peripheral players. "The Reverend Davis is pretty shook up, Joey. Understandable. The hotel has him in another room up the hall. Likewise with Senator Mitchell's wife. She was away having dinner with friends and only returned half an hour ago."

Dante stopped him. "Let me get this straight. The senator's wife was sharing this suite with the congresswoman. The guy from the medical examiner's is putting the time of death sometime between three and five this past afternoon. Mrs. Mitchell went out to dinner this evening . . . so where did she dress?"

Lieberman jerked a thumb at the other bedroom door. "Right there. She attended the reception downstairs after the debate and left around two-thirty to take a shower and dress early for her evening out."

"At two-thirty?"

"Yep. Claims she had a fitting appointment at Bergdorf's and was going from there to meet an old friend for drinks at the 21 Club."

"And what about the congresswoman? When did she leave the reception?"

"About an hour after Mrs. Mitchell. They say it was winding down then, and that she was paged to take a phone call. Never returned. Three-thirty is about the time Mrs. Mitchell says she left the suite. If that's accurate, it narrows the time of death down a little."

"Unless it was Mrs. Mitchell who killed her."

"Jesus, Joey. I don't even want to *think* it."

"Of course not, but her name's in the hat along with everyone else's, right? Can anyone confirm her departure time?"

Gus shook his head. "Not yet. None of the elevator operators who worked that shift are in the hotel right now. We'll have to wait until tomorrow and hit them all then. Maybe they can help us pin the T.O.D. even tighter, especially if one of them remembers the congresswoman riding upstairs with him.''

"Do we know who placed that call? The one to the congresswoman?''

"Same deal there. The switchboard operator who took the call and placed the page ain't here either.''

"And no sign of forced entry.''

"Not a scratch.''

Dante continued forward, slipping between two detectives from the Homicide Task Force to enter Cora Davis's bedroom. "Let's have a look.''

The corpse was still on the carpet, and as a photographer from the Crime Scene Unit was busy packing his equipment, two EMS attendants stood by with a body bag. The dead woman looked to be in her late forties. Not a particularly attractive woman, but well dressed and groomed. Her hair, gone entirely gray, was cut in a neat, businesslike bob. She didn't appear to be much more than five foot one or two and her build was heavy through the legs and hips. Dante squatted to examine the gash in the back of her head and the bruises on her neck. Just as Gus had reported, the strangulation marks weren't pronounced. Then again, she'd lost a fair amount of blood through that head wound. It indicated the heart had continued to beat at least briefly after she sustained that blow.

Joe was sitting back on his heels to survey the surrounding room when Crime Scene Unit commander Chip Donnelly entered. The moment Donnelly saw Dante his face registered confusion.

"What's up, Joe? I thought McKillip and his guys'd caught this one.''

Dante glanced to Gus, and Lieberman hurried to clarify Joey's position. "The lieutenant's here on special assignment, attached directly to my office, Chip. It's still Homicide's case.''

As if on cue, the florid-faced Wayne McKillip stormed onto the scene, his big hands balled up into fists and shoulders hunched forward as though set for combat. The instant he spotted Dante he pulled up short, his jaw set with grim determination.

"What's going on, Gus?" he demanded.

Lieberman repeated what he'd just told Donnelly. "I don't imagine I've gotta elaborate on what kinda problem this can become for us, Captain. Ideally, the P.C. and mayor would like to see it wrapped quickly. We know it don't always work out that way, but they've authorized all the overtime needed to chase it hard. I want Lieutenant Dante kept abreast. Access to your squad meetings, forensic evidence developments as they come in, the works."

Gus watched McKillip open his mouth to protest and then close it again. There was no way the Homicide commander could mistake the chief's mood. Lieberman was the boss, and the boss had spoken.

Dante pointed to the overturned lamp presumably used as the murder weapon. "No evidence of forced entry, but there must be plenty of master keys floating around a hotel this size. Maids, maintenance, all the usuals."

"We've thought of that," McKillip growled. "The possibility it was a burglar caught in the act. I'm inclined to doubt it. Outside the dead broad and that lamp on the floor, there's nothing disturbed in here. The senator's wife had a look around her room and don't report nothing missing in there either."

Dante shrugged. "Unlikely or not, it's still gotta be considered a possibility." He turned to Donnelly. "How about your guys, Chip? What've they come up with?"

"The pickings are slim, Joe. The panty hose used to strangle her? Same brand as the pair she's wearing, and six more pairs in the top dresser drawer. There must be fifteen different partials on that lamp, and I'm betting none of them are the perp's. We'll do all the usual hair and fiber workups, but I wouldn't hold my breath. A hotel ain't your ideal closed environment."

Dante stepped away from the corpse, and Donnelly waved

the two EMS men ahead. They sprang into action none too delicately. Spreading their bag on the floor, they shoved the dead congresswoman into it with little ceremony. This wasn't a human being anymore; it was garbage. Zip it up, sling it onto the stretcher, and strap it down. A man didn't last long working corpse removal if he couldn't learn to dehumanize the dead.

Wayne McKillip lingered just long enough to inform Dante that he and his squad would be meeting at Manhattan North's 119th Street station house at eight in the morning. Once the corpse was gone and Chip Donnelly left to supervise his unit's withdrawal from the scene, Gus was left alone with Dante in the dead congresswoman's bedroom.

"It's too late for me to accomplish much tonight," Joe told him. "I'd rather have some preliminary lab results to start chewing on . . . and that list of hotel personnel. Once I can sit down with them I'll begin to get a picture of what went on here this past afternoon."

"I've put a rush on the autopsy," Gus reported. "And requested Rocky Conklin do it. You should have his results by noon."

Dante nodded. "We'll also want to look into any threats. If our dead lady was anything, she was controversial. You've always got to scour the lunatic fringe in a case like this."

Lieberman was inclined to agree. "The husband may be able to help you there. They say he's in pretty bad shape right now. A doctor the hospital called put him under sedation. He'll probably be more use to you come morning."

"How about the senator's wife?"

The mere mention of Senator Lyle Mitchell made Gus nervous. "I'm gonna ask you outright to tread very lightly there, Joey. Lyle Mitchell ain't the kind of adversary any of us wants to rile. This lady is his blushing bride of less than two years. By all accounts, he's fucking nuts over her."

"Duly noted, boss."

"She's in room 1706. Just up the hall." The chief peered

at his watch and rubbed his face with an open hand. "What else? Anything?"

"Yeah. I want Jumbo."

Sergeant Beasley "Jumbo" Richardson had partnered often with Dante and was currently assigned to duty with Detective Bureau's Major Case Squad. Gus doubted his Major Case whip was going to be happy about losing Richardson, but Dante and Richardson were a unique combination. Over the years they'd become close personal friends. Gus would swear at times that they could read each other's minds.

"Consider him yours. And let's watch whose toes we step on, huh? McKillip's already worked up and we're hardly outta the blocks."

Dante winked at him. "Worry not, boss. I've been watching old black and white musicals in my spare time; taking tips from Fred and Ginger."

Eager to solidify this year's campaign strategies, Tennessee State Republican Chairwoman Nancy Hillman had accompanied the Reverend Jerry Davis to New York from Washington Tuesday night. When they arrived at the Park View hotel and Jerry discovered his wife dead, he was so overwhelmed with shock and grief that he'd required sedation. Senator Mitchell's wife Lyndelle was badly shaken, too. She wasn't particularly close to Congresswoman Davis, but learning that murder had been committed in the suite they shared sent her into near hysterics. Nancy was forced to take control. The Reverend Davis was asleep across the hall now. She and Lyndelle were at least temporarily sharing a suite. Right now Lyndelle was showering and getting ready for bed while Nancy was making another of a million phone calls.

The noise of police activity could still be heard outside in the hall. When a knock came at the door, Nancy was just hanging up after her conversation with Lyle Mitchell's chief of staff in Washington. She could hear the water of Lyndelle's shower still running as she answered.

Tall, at well over six feet, the man on the threshold was

unfamiliar to her. Casually dressed in sneakers, black jeans, and a bulky tweed overcoat, he held identification and a gold shield in his right hand.

"Mrs. Mitchell? Detective Lieutenant Joe Dante. I know it's late but I need a moment of your time."

Nancy shook her head. "Not Mrs. Mitchell, Lieutenant. Nancy Hillman. Maybe I can help you."

The detective glanced at the number on the door in confusion and Nancy hurried to explain. "This *is* the correct room. Mrs. Mitchell is indisposed at the moment. I'm the Tennessee State Republican chair. I traveled here with the Reverend Davis this evening."

"You and Mrs. Mitchell are sharing a room?" he asked.

"A suite. It's all the hotel had available. Come in please, Lieutenant." As he entered and slipped out of his overcoat, Nancy was impressed by what she saw. His jacket hid a lot of his build, but she could see that he was broad-chested, wide through the shoulders, and lean in the hips. A shock of unruly, dirty blond hair and slate blue eyes seemed to belie his Italian surname. The high forehead lent an intelligence to an otherwise rugged appearance. "Your chief of detectives couldn't tell us anything an hour ago. Has there been a new development?"

Her visitor shook off anything so optimistic. "I'm afraid it's early yet, ma'am. We're still getting this investigation organized. I've got a few routine questions I wanted to ask Mrs. Mitchell."

Nancy pointed to Lyndelle's closed bedroom door. "I'll tell her you're here, Lieutenant. I expect she'll be a few minutes. Please, have a seat."

The detective smiled, thanked her, and sat. Nancy emerged from Lyndelle's room a moment later to relay Lyndelle's apology for making him wait. In return, he flashed her a disarming grin and nodded to her open briefcase and the paperwork spread on the sofa opposite.

"It's possible I lucked out, finding you here, Miss Hillman. Can you tell me what your connection to the congresswoman was? You mentioned you traveled here from Washington with her husband.''

Nancy reached to straighten up and stuff those scattered papers back into her case before she sat. ''That's correct, Lieutenant. Congresswoman Davis was seeking statewide party backing for a gubernatorial run. I flew east this week to deliver it and came north with Reverend Davis to plan our immediate strategy.''

''It sounds like you and the congresswoman were close.''

She smiled. ''Republicans in the state of Tennessee are *all* close, Lieutenant. The Democratic Party is deeply entrenched in our politics. Any gains we make are the result of tight, close-knit cooperation.''

The detective mulled that over a moment before asking his next question. ''What kind of shot did she have? Realistically?''

''Of winning the governor's job?''

''Right.''

Nancy leaned forward a bit, forearms on her knees and hands clasped. ''A very *good* shot. The incumbent Democrat is embroiled in a banking scandal. The polls show him to be extremely vulnerable. Still, unseating him will require careful, painstaking planning.''

''And now all your best laid plans are up in smoke.''

She sighed, her cheeks puffing out as she got a far-off look in her eye and nodded. ''I'm afraid so. February is none too early to get the ball rolling, and the only way you do that is to prepare the playing field first. Groom it. Make sure the conditions are ideal. Now I'm faced with the task of finding a new Republican champion, and frankly, it won't be easy.''

The cop eased one ankle up over a knee and adjusted his sock. His relaxed demeanor put Nancy at ease. ''We're looking for motive right now, Miss Hillman. I know that Tennessee is a long way from New York, but what are the chances a political rival may have gotten to her? Somebody else who's got designs on the party's endorsement.''

Nancy didn't have to think about that one for long. ''Cora

Davis had no real rival, Lieutenant. Not in the primary race. Outside of Lyle Mitchell there isn't another Republican on the state scene who has Cora's visibility; or who embodies her same decent, Christian values. The Reverend Davis is extremely popular with our constituency, and she was married to him. Cora's decency campaign was something she collaborated with her husband to launch.''

Lieutenant Dante digested this and frowned as something else entered his train of thought. ''Why New York for this strategy planning session? Was there something that couldn't wait until the congresswoman returned to Washington?''

Nancy shook her head. ''Part of the strategy involved the publicity which would accompany a meeting Cora was scheduled to take here in New York tomorrow evening. Senator Mitchell recently conducted negotiations with a Japanese electronics manufacturer to bring a state-of-the-art production facility to Tennessee. He wanted to see Cora win the governor's race and arranged for her to share some of the spotlight by helping conclude those negotiations.''

''Here. In New York.''

''That's correct. Mr. Kagoshima is flying in tomorrow at five o'clock.''

''So who will carry the ball now? The senator himself?''

''That's one of the dilemmas I've been working to unscramble since I got here,'' Nancy replied. ''Senator Mitchell is away on an Armed Services Committee inspection of U.S. bases on Guam. Fortunately, his chief of staff William Beaumont is available. I just got off the phone with him when you knocked.''

Before the lieutenant could ask any more questions about Lyle Mitchell's pending deal with the Japanese, Lyndelle Mitchell emerged from her room cinching the sash of a silk robe tight around her waist. Her face was devoid of all but the slightest hint of makeup, and she had combed her wet hair straight back, tying it with a black ribbon.

''Lyndelle, honey,'' Nancy moved to introduce her. ''This is Lieutenant Dante.''

The detective rose to shake the tall, elegant blonde's hand. Nancy was amused to see the surprise he was trying to suppress. She knew exactly what he was thinking, too. This woman couldn't possibly be Lyle Mitchell's wife. She's young enough to be his daughter. And she's beautiful; not at all what the lieutenant had expected.

"Is there anything you can tell us?" Lyndelle asked. "We're all just sick with shock."

The detective replied as he had to Nancy's earlier query and moved on to explain why he was paying this call. "I understand you were sharing that suite with Congresswoman Davis, Mrs. Mitchell. There are a few routine questions I need to ask."

Lyndelle nodded and moved toward the hospitality bar. "Certainly. I'm afraid we don't have much to offer you, but we did have room service deliver a carafe of coffee about an hour ago. I'm not sure how warm it is anymore."

"I'd love a cup. Thanks." Dante turned back to Nancy. "I'm sorry, Miss Hillman, but would you mind excusing us for a few minutes?"

Lyndelle looked up from pouring coffee to wave away any privacy concerns. "That really isn't necessary, Lieutenant. Nancy and I have been friends since college. Sorority sisters, United Daughters of the Confederacy, you name it. We don't have any secrets."

THREE

Paparazzo Troy Bendix Brooks and glitter novelist Terry Dillingham could barely hear themselves speak over the din of woofer-shredding rock and roll. It was Mardi Gras night at the Big City Diner and the place was jammed with wee-hour partygoers. Not an ideal setting for conversation, but perfect for people watching. Many of the patrons were costumed to shock. In just the past ten minutes, three different bare-breasted women had paraded past. One, otherwise dressed as the Egyptian goddess Isis, was caught midstrut by the strobe of Troy's camera. The others he ogled but otherwise ignored. Their costumes were less artfully contrived, the intended outrageousness too obvious. Generally, Brooks would be hard at work in a scene like this, but tonight he was content to lay back. He had much bigger fish to fry. For the first time in months of chasing hostile entertainment celebrities all over New York, he'd finally hit pay dirt.

". . . a fucking First Amendment censorship debate, right?" He screamed it into his buddy Dillingham's ear. "I mean I've got to be desperate for sure. But Randy fucking Logan was gonna be up there on that stage, arguing the rock and roll side of it against Cora fucking Davis, and this I've *gotta* see."

Randy Logan was the well-spoken but otherwise reprobate lead guitarist/singer for the heavy metal band Crucifixion. A man of many contradictions, he was known to possess an exemplary collection of contemporary artwork and to breed thoroughbred racing stock at his upstate New York farm. Onstage he was liable to do anything to incite his legions of teenybopper fans, from wearing codpieces and setting them aflame with lighter fluid to using his guitar to drive spikes through the hands and feet of inflatable dolls. Brooks had been desperate for nearly a month now to find a story hot enough to pay his back rent. This looked like just the ticket; something guaranteed to set off a bidding war between *People*, *Premiere*, and the Florida-based tabloids.

"So there I am at the reception, hanging around like maybe I've actually been *invited*, when I see something that goddamn near makes my eyes pop." Brooks backed a few inches away from Dillingham's head to make sure he had his pal's full attention. "You remember reading or seeing anything about the bimbo Senator Lyle Mitchell married last year?"

Dillingham nodded. "Some former beauty queen, isn't she?"

"You got it. An ex–Miss Tennessee. She's there at this debate, too, and at the reception I'm watching Logan when I see her pass so close she brushes right up against him . . . and then I see her hand him something that looks like a business card. I'm thinking to myself I *recognize* this bitch; from way back when Logan was just another downtown dream-chaser. A nobody. I'd never made the connection, but this bitch used to be Randy Logan's *girlfriend*!"

Dillingham sat up a bit straighter as he absorbed this news. "You're shitting me. Lyle Mitchell's *wife*?"

"I shit you *not*. I'm standing there with my chin on the floor, watching the way Logan palms that note she delivered. Him? He's watching the way her ass moves as she minces her way through that crowd and out a side door." Brooks paused to snatch up his beer and take a huge swallow. All that hollering above the deafening music was making his throat sore, and the cool liquid felt good going down.

Dillingham was excited now, too. "Jesus. Can you *prove* this?"

Troy smirked, his eyebrows wiggling up and down. "Hang onto your hat, compadre. I haven't gotten to the good part yet. I see Logan sneak a peek at that note and start for the door when a couple of Junior League types waylay him. I figure I've sniffed out something major here; I've got to gamble. Two minutes later I've got Mrs. Mitchell's room number from the front desk and I'm heading up to the seventeenth floor. It's as quiet as a church up there. Once I find that room, I slip around a corner down the hall. First I make sure I've got good focus and then I push some already-fast film to 2000 ASA. Five minutes later my bet pays off. Logan steps off the elevator, walks straight to the Mitchell broad's door and knocks. I trigger my motor drive and pray to God he don't hear the shutter clicking as she opens up. No problem there. He was otherwise preoccupied. You should have *seen* them, Terry! I thought she was gonna fuck him right there in the hall!"

Dillingham continued to stare at Brooks with a mixture of incredulity and disbelief. "You got all this on film?"

"You got it, amigo." Brooks patted the breast pocket of his aging Armani jacket. "Soon as I get this roll home and into the developing tank, the world won't have Troy Brooks to kick around anymore. I'm *back*!"

Dante accepted the cup of coffee from Lyndelle Mitchell and watched her appreciatively as she sat opposite. It was difficult to ignore how handsome both of these two women were, but while Nancy Hillman was attractive, Lyndelle Mitchell was in an altogether different league. Senator Lyle Mitchell had better taste in women than Joe would have imagined. As Mrs. Mitchell addressed him, she tugged at her robe to make sure it was covering her knees. Joe wouldn't have minded if she hadn't bothered.

"I can't imagine anything being routine about an investigation like this, Lieutenant. None of us can believe this has really happened. What is it you wanted to ask me?"

Dante lifted the cup to his lips, sipped, and found the

27

coffee tepid. As long as he wasn't drinking decaf, it didn't much matter. "The medical examiner is putting the time of death at sometime between three and five yesterday afternoon, Mrs. Mitchell. We know the congresswoman was called away from the reception by a phone call sometime around three-thirty. That narrows it down for us a bit more. I'm wondering where you were between three-thirty and five o'clock. Did you have occasion to visit your suite?"

"Not between those hours, but I must have just missed her."

Dante drank off half the liquid in his cup and replaced it on his saucer. "Oh? How so?"

He imagined that the quick, wan smile those big green eyes conveyed had disarmed many before him. "My schedule was pretty tight from four o'clock on. I had a fitting appointment at Bergdorf's, and from there I went directly to the 21 Club . . . for drinks with an old friend. We were meeting other friends for dinner—a sort of reunion, you might call it—so I left the reception early to run upstairs, take a bath, and dress for my evening out."

It occurred to Dante that this girl must bathe a lot. "A reunion. Old school friends?"

That quick smile again, and a shake of the head. "No, Lieutenant. Old friends from the fashion world. I worked here as a model for a few years after college."

"Lyndelle was in *Vogue*," Nancy Hillman interjected.

The senator's wife blushed, and Dante questioned the ease with which she accomplished it. He was finding it difficult to get a read here. So much about the woman seemed facade. Was the blush genuine or something she'd trained herself to do?

"You said you must have just missed her. So you left the suite when?"

"It was right around three-fifteen. Certainly no later than three-thirty. I like to walk as much as I can, and Bergdorf Goodman isn't very far, I know, but I wanted to stop into Harry Winston before my appointment. I saw a fire opal bracelet in his window this morning that I just fell in *love* with."

"You wouldn't happen to remember whether Mrs. Davis's bedroom door was open or closed when you left?"

She thought a moment before shaking her head. "Not specifically. No. Cora was a very private person, Lieutenant. It was probably closed."

"Were you two friendly?"

No smile this time. "With Cora? Not really. My husband thought it appropriate that I attend her debate and show support. He regretted being unable to attend himself."

It sounded to Dante like this woman was more interested in shopping than demonstrations of solidarity. He turned to make contact once again with Nancy Hillman. "I'll ask you both this next question. What about any threats Mrs. Davis might have received?"

Nancy fielded that one. "Threats were part of the territory, Lieutenant. Most of them were routinely passed along to the FBI. Most came from crackpots. Of course, some were investigated more thoroughly."

"Was the FBI taking any current threat seriously?"

"Not that I'm aware of. You'll have to check with them. I was in touch with her as recently as this morning, and she mentioned nothing new."

Dante placed his cup and saucer on the table before him and started to stand. "I know it's late, ladies, and I thank you for your time. Once we get a better overview of the whole picture I'm sure I'll want to talk with you both again. We may want to explore those negotiations with the Japanese in more depth, Miss Hillman. Give what you know in that regard some serious thought. It sounds like there's a lot of money at stake." He reached for his coat and started for the door.

Nancy Hillman had risen with him and now moved to follow. "My schedule's crazy tomorrow, Lieutenant. And I'm sure Mrs. Mitchell has other obligations. What time would you be talking about?"

He shook his head and smiled apologetically while reaching for the door knob. "I'm afraid I don't know that yet, ma'am. Sometime tomorrow; probably in the morning. Don't worry, I'll find you."

Most nights when the club scene remained this hot, this late, Troy Brooks would stick around. The prospect of insinuating himself into the bed of some attractive morsel looked unusually good. It was too bad that he had that roll of film burning to be processed. All hot prospects had to be measured by degrees. If he drank any more tonight he ran the risk of screwing up the processing.

"Where the hell do you think you're going?"

Brooks stood with the strap of his trusty Nikon slung over his shoulder and Dillingham jerking at his sleeve. Terry was half in the bag but had managed to lure a pair of beautiful wannabe models to their table. A blonde for you and a brunette for me; or vice versa. For the past fifteen minutes Terry had been leveling the full power of his famous-personage charm at them and plying them with drink.

"Duty calls, compadre."

Terry pulled him close, his breath hot in Troy's ear. "Stick around, for Christ's sake. This blonde's so hot for me I can *smell* it on her. A man's best buddy doesn't leave him in the lurch; not at a moment like this."

Brooks grinned while prying Dillingham's fingers loose from his sleeve. "Got my eyes on a different sorta prize tonight, Dill. Somebody scoops me on this one and I'll never forgive myself. A man's gotta make certain sacrifices."

"You're crazy. Look at them!"

Brooks began backing away. "I've *been* looking. I look any longer I'm gonna want just the tiniest taste. I'll be in touch." And before Dillingham could argue further, Troy was gone.

Out on the street the February night was bitter cold. Troy turned his collar up against a biting breeze coming off the Hudson and flagged a cab. He guessed it was more the

weather than the wee hours of Wednesday that had turned
this stretch of Eleventh Avenue so quiet. When the wind
started to blow in the dead of winter, even the hookers called
it quits early.

Troy's cabbie had an all-news station tuned in and playing
at low volume as they started south for the East Village.
Brooks snuggled back in his seat, eyes scanning randomly
over scenes outside, as he listened to how two small Newark
children had burned to death when a bedroom kerosene heater
ignited; how the mayor was calling for job cuts in city-run
hospitals; how another of the Mets pitching staff was threatening to declare his free agency at the end of the upcoming
season if the front office didn't renegotiate his contract. All
this guy was asking was 5.5 million per year over the next
four years. Peanuts.

''And now to repeat the story we've been following since
it broke just before midnight. Four hours ago, at ten-thirty
P.M., Tennessee congresswoman Cora Davis was found mur-
dered in the Park View hotel suite she shared with the wife
of Tennessee senator Lyle Mitchell. It is believed the congresswoman was killed sometime late Tuesday afternoon after leaving a reception held downstairs in one of the hotel
ballrooms. Cora Davis, wife of televangelist Jerry Davis,
was known nationwide as an outspoken crusader for legis-
lated restrictions on the content of rock and roll recordings.
Mrs. Davis was here in New York to participate in a debate
on rock censorship. At this time the police have established
no motive for the slaying and have taken no suspects into
custody. And now for all-news weather at the top . . .''

Brooks could feel the adrenaline hit his bloodstream. He
was still a touch drunk but was having no trouble absorbing
what he'd just heard. Late Tuesday afternoon. In a suite
shared with the wife of Senator Lyle Mitchell. His heart was
hammering in his chest. By the time he arrived home on St.
Mark's Place he was a lot more sober than when he had left
the Big City Diner fifteen minutes before.

The downstairs bathroom of his duplex apartment was

rigged as a compact darkroom. Because of the delicate nature of his work, Troy refused to trust his raw stock to any of the custom labs twenty blocks uptown. Fearing possible compromise, he'd educated himself in the processing of films pushed to extreme high speeds and did the processing here at home. He'd logged hundreds of hours working in this cramped space, and his fingers didn't often fumble. He didn't customarily drink six beers before immersing himself in the necessary gloom and was frustrated trying to thread the film onto the tank reel. Nearly ten minutes elapsed before he could switch on the overheads and mix his chemicals. The most critical phase was over now. No matter how badly he screwed up his concentrations and timing he would no doubt get an image. He breathed easier as he mixed and poured developer into the tank.

Half an hour later he had his first frame mounted in the enlarger. The image it threw onto the focus board clearly revealed two figures embracing in an open doorway. An adjustment of the bellows increased the focal length between negative image and lens. Features emerged as the two heads grew larger. A twist of the focus ring brought them up sharp and clear.

By the time Joe Dante arrived home it was nearly three-thirty. Instead of finding Rosa in his bed, he found his cat Toby curled up where he'd left his recent lover. There was a note for him atop his dresser, weighted by his penknife. In it Rosa said she doubted her cat costume would pass the deputy commissioner's muster downtown. She would give him a call.

Dante set his clock and prepared for bed, trying to ignore the monster day that lay ahead. This was the second time he'd crawled between those sheets tonight, but this time his agenda was less complex. Soon he would be forced to push those few hours with Rosa from his mind; forced to focus on the how and why of another nasty homicide. All the homicides he investigated now were complicated and nasty. He never caught the upshots of simple turf disputes, street crimes gone awry, and family quarrels anymore. No, he got the handiwork of the clever ones; the devious and the desperate. For a few moments tonight he'd lain face to face with a beautiful, intelligent woman. The next moment he was hunkered down on his heels, face-to-face with death.

Eyes closed, Joe reached within and tried to warm himself with the image of Rosa's body, now gone from his bed. The glow of her warmth was faint now, the memory of it growing dim too quickly.

FOUR

Heavy metal rocker Randy Logan was troubled by dreams through the early hours of Wednesday morning. In them he was on a stage in an arena somewhere in mid-America, and a throng of screaming, faceless fans was suddenly surging past security and up over the apron. They came at him like surf crashing onto a beach, and rather than run, he was petrified. He searched desperately for something to cling to and found himself alone against this tide, forsaken by his sidemen and technical crew. When the fans, all of them barely pubescent girls, reached him, they began tearing his clothes from his body and then tearing his limbs. Horrified, he stood rooted, watching his legs and arms being plucked away. Only when their clawing, bright-painted nails slashed at his face and eyes did he awaken.

Logan sat bolt upright in his bed, rivulets of cold sweat soaking the sheets twisted around him. He stared at his still-intact hands, struggling to understand. A month had passed since his wife Lisa had left on assignment to chronicle the continuing effort to identify MIA remains in Vietnam. Two months earlier he'd been on the road with Crucifixion's Christmas tour. In fact, over the past two years he and Lisa had spent very little time together in New York, but right now he wished she were there. He didn't pretend really to understand his dream, but he knew what some of it was about. While that horde of screaming girls was busy tearing him limb from limb, he'd gotten the distinct impression that those weren't *his* body parts. They were someone else's; someone he didn't know. He'd experienced the same feeling about his own body yesterday while lying in Lyndelle Jennings's arms.

Lyndelle Jennings was Lyndelle Mitchell now, married to that ogre senator from Tennessee. Eight years ago, when Randy last saw her, she was an actress/model living two buildings down from his own East Village loft on Great Jones Street. For three years, Randy spent many nights at her place, and she at his. Then she got homesick, or so she claimed, and moved back to her native Memphis. In truth, she couldn't handle the pressure cooker of her chosen profession. Life in her rich-doctor daddy's world looked much more appealing after four years in New York. She'd promised to stay in touch and hadn't. Meanwhile, Randy sold out any integrity his early music had for fame and money.

Seeing her again yesterday had driven a jolt of pure sexual electricity from his groin clear down to the soles of his Tony Lamas. In her arms he was Randy Logan again, a younger, less self-absorbed version of his current self. Now, in his mind's eye, he watched his latest music video and wondered who that oil-rubbed, gyrating and prancing other was.

He was surrounded by the trappings of wealth, this new Randy Logan, with a thriving thoroughbred horse farm upstate, six platinum albums, an art collection worth millions, and a wife he knew no better than he knew himself. He'd become someone else. *That* was who those screaming girls— with their crude makeup, teased hair, and feeding-frenzy desires—were tearing apart. Perhaps if he'd let them finish the job, he might have discovered who was beneath that veneer.

Exhausted, Randy peered at his clock radio. Four fifty-eight. He rose to pad barefoot into the bath and towel himself dry. When he crawled back into bed and eventually fell asleep, the dream did not return.

* * *

35

Troy Brooks had catnapped, setting his alarm for seven. When it woke him, the light of the new day flooded through the south-facing front windows of his bedroom. A new day and a new life. Troy had a couple of precariously positioned but economically secure entities by the short hairs today. After less than three hours sleep he climbed from bed feeling rested and self-satisfied. He took his time shaving, showering, and setting his coffee to drip. While waiting for the carafe in the machine to fill, he placed a call to the *New York Post*, identified himself, and confirmed the one last item he needed to put the screws to his unsuspecting victims. Last night, when talking with Terry Dillingham, he had visions of squeezing some nice bucks out of an editor for a truly juicy exposé. Troy Brooks, vanquished bad-boy novelist of yesteryear, would rise phoenixlike from the ashes of catastrophe, gloriously transformed into Troy Brooks, fear-instilling muckraker. There would be no more grubbing around the slimy leavings of the glitterati for crumbs. Once again, Troy would be the toast of the avant-garde. Editors would fight over him, vying for his services with *real* money now.

Today, Brooks entertained no such pedantic fantasies. Any thought of work was out the window. He wouldn't have to. He was going to be rich.

At ten minutes of eight Brooks placed the call to Randy Logan. The rock star answered on the seventh ring, sounding groggy with sleep.

''Wha? Unh—hello?''

''Forgot to switch on your answering machine, didn't you, amigo?''

''Who's this?''

''Your worst nightmare. You may not remember me, but we met at the Mudd Club once. You gave me a lot of lip about kicking my ass but wouldn't back it up. Remember any better now? I'm the guy who spilled his beer on your girlfriend.''

There was a pause on the line. ''Listen, pal. I don't know

how you got this number and I don't know who you are or what the fuck you're talking about. It isn't even eight o'clock in the morning so why don't you fuck the hell . . ."

"Lyndelle Mitchell, Randy. Only I believe her name was Jennings back when I dumped that drink. You're not the only one who's come a long way."

Another pause, this one more drawn out. "Am I supposed to know you, Mr. . . . ?"

"Not really material, Randy. Do yourself a favor, turn on your radio and listen to the news. There's an item you might find interesting. I know I did. And don't worry about you and me losing touch. I'll be sure and get back."

Before Logan could say another word, Brooks broke the connection and carried his coffee upstairs to his guest bedroom/office. His approach to Lyndelle Mitchell would have to be handled differently. He needed to determine where the hotel was housing her now. Then there was the hotel switchboard. Could someone else have access to their conversation? No, he would make this approach in writing and deliver it to the hotel by hand.

For the next ten minutes Troy executed several different drafts of his communication on his word processor and then printed the final on clean white copy bond. He took care to wipe any trace from the computer's memory and sealed the note along with three eight-by-ten enlargements into a manila envelope. It was time to place his second call by the time he finished.

Logan had switched on his answering machine. Brooks listened to the message and endured the beep. "That's cute, Randy, but I know you're there and I know you're listening. No matter, amigo, I think it's more than coincidence that they're putting the congresswoman's time of death at sometime between three and five. Let's see; I watched you walk in the door to that suite at what? Two-thirty? And don't worry about me having the suite number right. I checked. I've also got pictures of you where it's clearly visible on the door." Troy let that bit of news hang out there awhile, punctuating his pause with an exaggerated sigh. "So just how long does it take a stud like you to fuck an old flame, Randy? Forty-five, fifty minutes? An hour?"

Logan snatched up the phone, his tone harsh with threat. "Just who do you think you are, making allegations like that, asshole? Pictures my ass! You don't have shit!"

Brooks chuckled and clucked his tongue. "Oh but I *do*, Randy. And I'll show them to you. They're good enough to get you arrested for suspicion of murder unless you and I reach some sort of agreement. You want to talk about it, I'll be at Blanco Boys, Avenue A, ten o'clock. If you've still got an appetite you'll really dig their huevos rancheros."

The site of Manhattan North Operations, 120 East 119th Street, was in the heart of Harlem. Marcus Garvey Park interrupted Fifth Avenue just a block north and another block west. The building Dante parked out front of also housed the 25th Precinct. With all that concentration of police activity, the street was jammed with radio units, unmarked sedans and double-parked personal vehicles of Job personnel.

Jumbo Richardson was waiting for Dante on the sidewalk outside the building's main entrance. An imposing specimen at a touch over six foot and weighing close to two and a quarter, Richardson now weighed a hundred pounds less than when he and Joe first met. Nicknames had a way of sticking, even in the face of significant weight loss. Jumbo could shed the weight but not the handle. Now, the big black detective sergeant broke into a broad grin as Dante approached and reached to shake hands.

"All I know is what Op Desk could tell me and what I heard on the news. How late they have you up, Joey? You don't look too much the worse for wear."

Dante gripped that meaty paw and clapped Richardson on the shoulder. "Late enough. I was just getting comfortable when they hauled my ass outta bed. Any problems cutting you loose?"

Jumbo gave it a waggle of the hand. "We been buried in

that joint-task-force op with Central Robbery. The diamond courier rip-offs on 47th Street. Captain Costanza didn't exactly dance a jig when Gus gave him the word.''

"Us guineas don't generally dance jigs,'' Dante reminded him.

Richardson chuckled. "Neither do us jigs. So what're we doing here? Ain't this a straight Homicide matter?''

As he responded, Dante mounted the front stoop, leading the way inside. "That's sure how Wayne McKillip sees it. But Gus is worried. He thinks the politics could get ugly if the file isn't closed on this in a hurry. Lyle Mitchell is one mean son of a bitch when he's got his back up.'' Dante held up two fingers, intertwined. "He and the dead congresswoman were like this. His *wife* was sharing that suite at the Park View with the victim. He's the guy fond of characterizing New York and L.A. as modern-day Sodom and Gomorrahs. He's also the ranking Republican member of the Senate Appropriations Committee. He can make a lot of trouble for this town.''

The two detectives found Captain McKillip and his five-man unit already assembled around the central table in the Homicide Squad upstairs. Coffee had been poured and donuts were being passed around. McKillip looked just ready to get started. His casual demeanor tightened up visibly as his guests circled the table to pull up chairs.

"All right. Listen up. Some of you probably know Lieutenant Dante there, and Sergeant Richardson. They've been attached to the Davis investigation by the C of D but won't affect how we conduct it. Let's get down to business. We've caught us a hot one and we're gonna try and close the book on it before it reaches critical mass. That means getting a jackrabbit start. You know the drill.''

He went on to detail everything they already knew about the case and summed up by handing out assignments. Two of his people got forensics—visits to the labs and the medical examiner. Another pair would work up the congresswoman's background.

39

". . . up and down, inside and out. I want her enemies, her network of associations here in the city, workups on all the people in her organization and the husband's organization. Talk to this broad who came up with the husband on the train. While we was scrambling to find them rooms, she mentioned being some sorta politico from down there. Let's see what she can tell us about the down-home side of it. I wanna develop the bigger picture. Bucky and me'll take the immediate homicide scene, hotel staff and management, anyone else we can think of." He stopped to turn his attention to Dante and Richardson. "What about you two, Lou? We wanna avoid stepping on each other's toes, we need to know which way you're headed."

Dante hadn't been offered a cup of coffee or a donut. None of the others around the table had even nodded acknowledgment to either him or Richardson. "Don't worry about us, Cap. We'll stay out of your way; just poke around and head where our noses take us. You find yourselves short in any particular area, we'll be happy to shag anything you toss our way."

Dante watched the way the captain's nostrils flared slightly and fingers began to drum.

"Thanks, Lieutenant. We'll all be sure to keep that in mind."

It was midmorning by the time Lyndelle Mitchell awoke. She was still exhausted from being up half the night but knew she couldn't afford to tarry longer. She and Randy needed to talk, to get their stories straight. Randy Logan had become a famous personality. He was too damned noticeable. Somebody may have seen him leaving the suite or boarding an elevator.

As Lyndelle showered and dressed she repeatedly asked herself the same question. Had she meant it to happen, or was it, as she'd so artfully feigned, just fate? Since meeting and marrying Lyle, she'd rediscovered how chameleonic her psychology really was. It was almost as though she had no control over it. Grind those hips so subtly the judges wouldn't consciously register it, but sure as hell wouldn't miss it where the fire burned. Strip away who *she* thought she was and become who they wanted her to be. It was a strategy that demanded cleverness, and it worked just as well in the realm of Washington politics as it had in the worlds of beauty pageants and fashion modeling. It was eight years since she'd left Randy Logan and quit the dog-eat-dog hustle of New York. She'd known he would be debating Cora and had come along anyway. Why? Curiosity, or a perverse desire to tempt fate?

The bedside clock read nine-fifty when she dialed the number Randy gave her yesterday afternoon. She got a message machine in a woman's voice and a surge of ridiculous jealousy swept over her. The wife. Lyndelle had seen the woman interviewed on ''20/20'' and couldn't imagine what Randy saw in her. Lisa Dodd was a globe-trotting photojournalist who'd shot dozens of covers for *Time* and *Newsweek*. She looked tough, almost dykey. Yesterday when Randy invited Lyndelle to give him a call, he mentioned Lisa was out of town on assignment. Still, Lyndelle wasn't going to risk leaving a recorded message for him. The surge of jealousy passed. Where the hell was he? Hadn't he listened to the news?

Troy Brooks had named the location. He now sat reading the new edition of the *Village Voice* in the back of Blanco Boys, a hip little Tex-Mex eatery on Avenue A. It was a number of years since Brooks had basked in the fleeting light of fame, and the unmolested solitude he was enjoying spoke volumes about how quickly New Yorkers forget. Ten years ago when he'd dumped that drink on Randy Logan's girlfriend, Logan was a struggling nobody and Brooks was a bona fide star in the downtown firmament. His first novel took the club scene and college campuses across America by storm. A movie was made from it. He was the toast of trustfund babies who partied late, slept late, and straggled in for breakfast at three in the afternoon. That was then and this was now. Now he couldn't get a contract to clean toilets from any of the major publishing houses.

When Logan entered at five minutes past ten, the few somnambulant patrons just perceptibly stirred. Brooks felt a rush of jealousy burn at his ears as the rock star made his way toward the booth. That night at the Mudd Club ten years ago, Logan had backed down when Troy challenged him to back *up* some pretty hot words. Today he had Randy up against the ropes, and this time he would enjoy pummeling him.

"You're late," Brooks observed.

Logan slid into the banquette across the table and leaned forward, his hands spread flat. "I'm *here*, fuckhead. And now that I can see you I *still* don't know who the fuck you are. Some asshole from the Mudd Club ten years ago isn't much of a clue. Give me another."

Brooks smiled, ice frosting the edges of it. "I take pictures now."

Randy scowled as he studied the face. "You said that much on the phone. You're acting like I should know you. If this is your idea of a game, you're the only one playing."

Troy removed a five-by-seven enlargement from the side pocket of his jacket and slid it in Logan's direction. "You're the one's been playing games, amigo. With a United States senator's wife. I can make trouble for her and I can make trouble for you. And better than that, I can make a different kind of trouble for both of you together if I send a copy of that picture, and the time I took it, to the cops."

Logan glanced for an instant at the obviously compromising situation depicted in the shot. He and Lyndelle Mitchell embraced on the threshold of her suite, the number clearly readable on the door behind. He then pushed it back across the table at Brooks.

"I didn't kill anybody."

Troy shrugged. "Maybe. Maybe not. How do you know your girlfriend didn't, after you left?"

"I don't."

"And you'd rather not have to explain anything to anyone, right compadre?" Brooks picked the photo back up and returned it to his pocket. "Don't worry. I think *that* route would be an awful waste of potential. You see, I've caught a prominent, married man in the arms of a prominent, married woman—only they aren't married to each *other*. Now I ask myself how their respective spouses would react to that picture. I think I know how Lyle Mitchell would react." Troy paused to look Logan directly in the eye. "How about your wife, Randy? How would she react? You're a rich man now."

"Just as slick as snot, aren't you, fuckhead?"

Brooks clucked his tongue and grinned. "Gotcha."

Logan eased back from the table to slouch against his seat back. Brooks was mystified by the look he encountered in his adversary's eyes.

"Like I told you, shit-bird, I didn't kill anybody. I'll tell the cops the same thing, and it's up to them to prove different. They won't because they can't."

Troy tried to match him cool for cool. "Like I said, that route would be an awful waste of potential."

The rocker snapped his fingers. "Right. You want to slip it to me yourself. Grease me up good and watch me wince while you ream me. Well, you've got nothing to stick me *with*, fuckhead." Logan slid to the edge of his seat and started to rise. "Bummer, huh? Your fun's over already."

Brooks felt the icy grip of panic wrap fingers around his bowels. The son of a bitch was leaving. He was bluffing. He *had* to be bluffing. Troy dug deep to summon more of his initial bravado. "Your old girlfriend's gonna love you for this. You walk out that door and I send this picture and the others to her husband."

Logan was on his feet and looming over the taller, heavier-set Brooks. "I doubt that. Think of the awful waste of potential. You'll take a stab at her, too."

Brooks shrugged. "Either way, *your* wife gets them. I guarantee it."

Logan laughed outright, loud enough to draw the attention of every patron in the place. "You don't quite get the picture, fuckhead. I don't *care*! My wife decides to file for divorce, I doubt I'll starve. So take your best shot. Hell, if you don't go to the cops with this, maybe I'll tell them myself."

Stunned, Brooks watched Logan saunter past the front counter and out onto the sidewalk. The rocker, dressed in a ratty old overcoat, jeans, bulky sweater, and scuffed boots was recognizable to anyone looking closely, but wasn't the prancing prince of outrage he played on stage. Troy wondered if he'd misjudged the man. He hoped Lyndelle Mitchell didn't feel the same way about *her* marriage.

FIVE

High-profile homicides tended to set One Police Plaza buzzing from basement to belfry. As the deputy commissioner of public information's executive officer, Lieutenant Rosa Losada had a lot on her plate this morning. The news stringers downstairs in the police department press pool were clamoring to be fed, and it was her job to organize a press conference. Unfortunately, there were very few bones to throw them. Short of manufacturing facts out of whole cloth, Public Information was collecting every scrap of noncompromising news on the Cora Davis case that they could find. Rosa was on her way to the office of the chief of detectives on the Big Building's thirteenth floor when Joe and his partner Jumbo Richardson emerged into the hall outside.

Dante turned to his partner and indicated the elevator bank just ahead. "Give me a minute, Beasley. You dig the wheels out and I'll meet you at the street entrance to the garage."

Richardson shrugged and wandered off as Joe took Rosa aside. "I'm sorry I had to rush away last night," he apologized.

Rosa wasn't sorry. His departure had spared her an awkward exit scene. "Not a problem, Joe. Workday and all, I wasn't expecting to stay the night."

That uncomfortably frank gaze of his met hers with its typical intensity. "Yeah. Diana told me you'd been so busy lately you probably wouldn't come. I was thinking about skipping it myself but figured the noise would keep me up half the night anyway. What are the chances of us having dinner tonight?''

"Tonight? Not tonight, Joe. Prior commitment.''

His expression betrayed his disappointment before he could cover it with a quick smile. She'd said it too quickly.

"Another time then. It was just a spur-of-the-moment idea.''

Even after two and a half years, making love to this man sparked intense memories of their other time together. There had been so much Joe didn't understand. Why she didn't want to be a street cop anymore. Why she wouldn't marry him and have his kids. Now she had climbed back into his bed. She didn't have all *that* much to drink, so why had she done it?

Dante was turning away when Rosa reached to touch his sleeve. "Joe. Listen. I need a little time, to sort my feelings through. I'm not trying to push you away. I'm just a little scared by this.'' She stopped to think about what she'd said. "You want the truth? I'm scared about how good it felt.''

Dante took her hand, gave it a squeeze, and began to back-pedal toward the elevators. "Me too. Scared shitless.''

Randy Logan sat alone behind the wheel of his Mercedes 560 roadster, peering intently at the front door of the restaurant he'd just left. "Who the fuck *is* this guy?''

Up and down the Avenue A sidewalk, pedestrians were slipping and stutter-stepping through the icy residue of a weekend snowstorm while Logan enjoyed the warmth of his leather-wrapped cocoon. He'd surprised the man. By virtue of it, he'd won the first round. That was all well and good, but the first round would surely not be the last. He'd learned a few things about his opponent but needed to know more.

The door to the restaurant swung open and Logan's would-be extortionist emerged to start up the avenue. At the corner of St. Mark's Place he turned west. Auto traffic on St. Mark's ran one way in the wrong direction, and Randy cursed his luck. He wrapped his coat tight around him and got out of the car, feeding another quarter into the meter in passing. He reached the corner just as his tormentor mounted the stoop of a building three doors down.

There was no way, on a bright day like this, that Logan was going to determine which apartment the man entered by watching for lights in the upstairs windows. He had no desire to loiter out here on this sidewalk for any length of time. He gave the guy five minutes to get settled before mounting that stoop and scanning the intercom directory. There were five apartments on the first and third floors. None of the names did anything for him: O'Sullivan, Jagielski, Hutchings, Brooks, and Devore. Logan began pressing buzzer buttons.

Neither O'Sullivan in apartment 1 or Jagielski in apartment 2 answered. When a woman's voice responded from apartment 3, he quickly moved on to four.

"Who is it?" The pitch and inflections were still fresh in Randy's memory. Bingo.

"Just me, fuckhead. I know your name now, and where you live. That makes us a bit more even, don't you think?"

If Jumbo stared, it was justified. Any preconceived notions about the state Republican chairwoman from Tennessee had just been torpedoed. Nancy Hillman wasn't just unexpectedly young for someone in her position, she was very good looking. He guessed her to be in her early to midthirties. A conservatively cut black worsted wool suit and white silk blouse hid all the curves of her petite and nicely distributed stature, but he had input adequate to feed his imagination.

The chairwoman glanced at her watch as she invited Richardson and Dante into the living room of her suite. "I don't mean to seem uncooperative or rude, but like I told you last night, Lieutenant, I've got a purely maddening day ahead."

"How about fifteen minutes?" Dante asked. "That should be all we'll need right now."

She nodded her acquiescence and gestured to the coffee

carafe on the hospitality bar. "If either of you would like a cup of coffee, please help yourselves. I hope you don't mind if I shuffle some paperwork together while we talk."

"Not at all," Dante replied. "I've had some additional thoughts on that meeting you told me about last night—the one Mrs. Davis was scheduled to have with the Japanese manufacturer."

"Mr. Kagoshima. Yes."

"You mentioned that Senator Mitchell had already concluded his negotiations. Have any contracts actually been signed?"

Jumbo was at the bar, pouring the two of them some of the offered coffee. He watched as the chairwoman straightened from collecting her papers on the sofa.

"I believe that is the purpose of the meeting tonight. Not to sign an actual contract, but some sort of letter of agreement. I'm afraid I don't know as much about the particulars as you're probably hoping. Senator Mitchell and Congresswoman Davis kept security pretty tight on this deal."

Dante accepted the coffee Richardson handed to him and took a tentative sip. Jumbo hadn't tasted his yet, but judging from the way Joe tipped the cup back a second time and gulped, he guessed it was better than the mud brewed in the C of D's office.

"We've got to consider burglary as a possible motive," Joe explained. "Nothing appears to be missing from either Mrs. Mitchell's or the congresswoman's rooms, but appearances are often misleading. What would Mrs. Davis have had in her possession regarding this meeting tonight?"

Nancy Hillman's expression turned troubled. "I've really no idea, Lieutenant. I understand what you're getting at; some other party with an interest in landing that deal. It will be extremely lucrative for the state that gets it, both in jobs and in tax revenues."

"Care to hazard a guess about who that party might be?"

She shook her head. "Like I said, I've been left pretty much in the dark there. I believe I mentioned that Mr. Beaumont will be handling tonight's meeting now. Senator Mitchell's chief of staff. He's due here from Washington at three-thirty, and you might want to speak with him about this.''

Dante scribbled a note to himself in his book and forged ahead. ''I asked you to think about any enemies Mrs. Davis might have had. Did anything occur to you?''

Nancy turned thoughtful. ''I *have* given it some thought. All you need do is dig through back issues of newspapers and magazines to find accounts of bitter confrontations with hecklers. It happened wherever Cora spoke. Lyndelle tells me there was a crowd of them out front of this hotel, yesterday afternoon. How do you sort through that kind of hatred?''

''It's a good question, Miss Hillman. We're hoping the Bureau can help us isolate the dangerous ones.''

Now Jumbo eased his way into the conversation. ''I've seen the Reverend Davis on television a few times. He seems to be—how do I say this?—less confrontational than the congresswoman was. He and Mrs. Davis got along all right?''

Nancy smiled indulgently. ''You'd be chasing your tail if you waste much time in that direction, Sergeant. They had different temperaments but were very close on the issues. Cora was a city councilwoman in Nashville when they met. Back then it was the Reverend Davis who held the congressional seat. They were very much in sync politically, even then.''

''How is the reverend this morning?'' Dante asked.

''We had breakfast together about an hour ago. He's extremely upset. And angry.''

Richardson found that understandable. He wasn't looking forward to interviewing the grieving widower. Family grief always bothered him, even after twenty-six years on the job.

''I see Mrs. Mitchell's door is closed,'' Dante observed. ''Is she still sleeping or has she gone out?''

''She's at breakfast.''

''You get a chance to talk to her any further?''

She shook her head. ''I've been pretty busy.''

"Could Mrs. Davis have mentioned any fears she was harboring to Mrs. Mitchell? Were they close enough to have a conversation like that?"

"I doubt that very much, Lieutenant. They were sharing a suite, but Cora and Lyndelle weren't particularly close. Cora was private. She kept her fears, if any, to herself."

Joe drained his coffee cup, nodded to Jumbo, and started for the hospitality bar. Once he set his empty cup there he turned back to their hostess. "We appreciate your frankness, Miss Hillman. And thanks for your time. You're sticking around until after this meeting tonight?"

She nodded. "Until at least tomorrow morning. Maybe longer. In light of these developments and the fact that Senator Mitchell won't be back stateside for another four days, Mr. Beaumont and I have quite a few things to discuss."

Lyndelle Mitchell heard voices as she was about to put her key into the door of her suite. She still hadn't reached Randy, and the last thing she needed was Nancy tying up the phone. There were privacy booths in the lobby downstairs. She turned and hurried back toward the elevators.

Lyndelle finally reached Logan and not his machine. He barely had time to say hello before she let fly with her fears in a manic rush. "Have you heard the news? We've got to talk. Get our stories straight. The police have already asked me questions, Randy. They find out you were here yesterday, we'd better have a damned good reason why. What if someone *saw* you? It isn't like you're just another . . ."

"Lynnie. Slow down."

". . . face in a crowd, for godsake. You're a *some*—"

"Lynnie! *Stop!*"

She quit as suddenly as she'd started. Short of breath, she sucked deep.

"What the hell happened up there, anyway?"

"You're asking *me*? I don't know what happened. Once you left I took a shower, dressed, and walked to my appointment at Bergdorf's. Then I had dinner with Angie and the others. When I got back the whole floor was alive with cops. You remember my sorority sister Nancy Hillman? The one who came to visit and was disgusted with how I was living?''

"We never met, remember? You thought I was a bit much for her delicate sensibilities.''

Lyndelle absorbed the lingering bitterness in his tone and moved on. ''Well she and Cora's husband found her. We've got to get together and talk, Randy.''

"You don't know the half of it. Something's come up that you won't be too happy about. How soon can you get here?''

"What are you talking about?''

"Not right now, Lynnie. There are a couple calls I've gotta make. I want you to come down here to my place. I should have more I can tell you by the time you get here.''

Lyndelle checked the time. It was ten forty-five, and she had to be back at the hotel no later than two-thirty. ''Where?'' she asked.

"Corner of Duane and Staple. In Tribeca.''

"It's going to be tight, Randy. Lyle's chief of staff is flying up on the shuttle. He's arriving at three-thirty. I told Nancy I'd ride out to LaGuardia with her to pick him up.''

"So put a whip to it. You'll have plenty of time.''

Dante was surprised to discover how short the Reverend Davis was. He was by no means a regular viewer but had caught the preacher's act once or twice while running through the channels on a Sunday morning. On television he appeared to be a man of medium stature. Hence, in his hotel room, the top of his head was level with Joe's chin. Looking down on it now, Dante could see at least as much shiny scalp as he could sandy, thinning hair. Davis was one of those guys who parted what he had left way down low over one ear and combed it straight across the top. The face beneath that vanished hairline was drawn with lines of grief and exhaustion.

Dante also remembered being surprised by the tone of the man's Sunday morning show. It had none of the showmanship, the piled-on piety, or the fire and brimstone he expected from a televangelist. Davis seemed more fatherly than Jimmy Swaggart or Oral Roberts.

"What can you tell me, officers? I've had the mayor's assurance that you people are doing everything in your power to see my wife's killer brought swiftly to justice." There was no particular agitation in his tone. Dante wondered about the impact of last night's sedation—how much residual effect the drugs were having.

"It's early yet, sir," Jumbo replied. "We're putting a lot of manpower on it. Right now, we're hoping you might be able to help us."

Davis's puzzled gaze moved from Richardson to Dante and back again. "Me? How?"

"By giving us an idea of who your wife's enemies were," Jumbo told him. "Whether she discussed any particular fears with you, any threats she might not have reported to her staff. You knew her better than anyone."

The reverend nodded. "You'd think the majority of people in this country would want the same things for America that Cora wanted, wouldn't you?"

"What would those things be, sir?" Jumbo prodded.

Davis seemed surprised. His expression suggested he didn't believe Richardson wouldn't know. "Good jobs, Sergeant. Decent schools for our children. The airwaves free of smut. A strong sense of basic, Golden Rule ethics. That's all Cora fought for, and yet she had enemies everywhere."

"Can you be more specific?" Richardson asked. "We need the names of persons or organizations."

Davis shook his head, his eyes closed now. "I know it isn't popular to talk about Satan up here, Sergeant. You people are too sophisticated for him. Every day I see his hand at work. If Cora had one enemy, it was him." The preacher sighed, rose from his perch on the edge of his bed, and stood staring out his window at Central Park. "How can I be specific, officers? We're a nation whose youth is poisoned, by violence in our streets, violence in their entertainment. Any one of those poor, lost souls could have done something like this.''

Dante saw them getting mired and didn't want to encourage the man any further. As long as he was in this state of mind, Davis was useless to them. Joe hurried to change the subject. ''We understand your wife was scheduled to finalize negotiations with a Japanese manufacturer this evening, Reverend Davis. A deal that would bring new jobs and tax revenues to Tennessee. What do you know about those negotiations? Anything that might have bearing on this case?''

Davis seemed to have trouble changing directions. He struggled to focus, and Joe was sure now that it was the drugs. ''Cora was preparing to announce her candidacy for governor, Lieutenant. Lyle Mitchell thought that bringing her on board with this deal would enhance her image with voters. But . . .'' He stopped, his eyes clearly focused now. ''I can't imagine it having anything to do with her murder. The deal is all but signed and sealed. Tonight's meeting is a mere formality; the dotting of i's and crossing of t's.''

Nancy Hillman hadn't described the situation in quite such confident terms, and Dante wondered whose version was more accurate. ''So you can't see the sabotage of those negotiations as a possible motive?''

Davis was vehement now. ''Utter nonsense. There *is* nothing to sabotage.''

Richardson had his notebook out and consulted it before asking his next question. ''You left Washington at what hour yesterday, sir?''

''Seven o'clock. On the Metroliner. I hate to fly. Miss Hillman and I arrived here in New York at ten.''

''And could you tell us what you did yesterday, sir? What you had on your schedule?''

Dante watched Davis's face appear to twitch. His jaw tightened and eyes flashed for an instant. Then he was just as cool and slightly spacey as before. ''What *my* schedule entailed? What a curious question, Sergeant. I was home at our apartment in the Watergate complex for most of the day. I did go out to lunch with a friend at Jean-Louis. I spent most of the rest of my time either on the phone or editing my monthly newsletter.'' He pronounced the name of the restaurant *gene-lewis*.

SIX

The switchboard operator who'd been on duty Tuesday when Congresswoman Davis received her call was a tall, painfully thin middle-aged woman with a soft, velvety voice. Right now Joe and Jumbo sat with her in the spacious hotel manager's office, her station being covered by a coworker. Management was bending over backward to be of assistance this morning. The publicity this homicide would generate could mean a drop-off in reservations, and nobody wanted that. The Park View treasured its reputation and would go to great lengths to protect it.

"In truth, Lieutenant? Ronnie, the fellow who's there at the board right now, was out sick with laryngitis yesterday. The place was a madhouse. Our bookings are generally lighter, midwinter, but with that debate and three different foreign delegations attending UN trade talks, I never had a chance to catch my breath. I can hardly remember having lunch yesterday, let alone the calls I took."

"Any recollection of placing the page?" Jumbo asked. "The assistance desk says you called them at three twenty-three."

"It's vague, Sergeant. I remember it took nearly five minutes to locate a bellman. That means the caller was on hold all that time. By the time I could put the call through, my board was backed up from here to Hoboken. With Ronnie out, I was at wit's end."

55

"Anything about the caller?" Jumbo persisted. "Male or female? An accent, maybe? Something?"

She shook her head. "Complete blank. I sit down at that board, I'm a machine. Ask me about the two dozen calls I took in the ten minutes before *you* arrived. It's a blank slate. If I pay attention to any one call, I lose my overall concentration. Those calls aren't for me. I'm just a conduit."

Randy Logan descended in the elevator to bring Lyndelle upstairs when she arrived. Today her perfect makeup and hair were offset by a high-strung nervousness. The instant she saw him, her hands began opening and closing uncontrollably. There was no mistaking the look in her eyes. Pure panic.

"How the hell did it happen, Lynnie?"

Lyndelle's jaw dropped, her fingers freezing. "How did *what* happen, Randy?"

Logan didn't know if he was surprised by her denial or not. What else would she say? "Take it easy. No matter what happened, it isn't the end of the world. It's handleable."

Her head jerked from side to side, eyes searching the walls of the elevator like a trapped animal inspecting the bars of its cage. "What do you *mean*, whatever happened?" she hissed. "What are you implying, Randy Logan?"

He stopped her there, a finger pressed to her lips. "Not here, Lynnie. Let it wait until we get inside."

She was still fidgeting as the car arrived at his floor. When the door opened, they stepped into the huge living room of his loft and Lyndelle stopped. Logan knew this must seem odd to her, this place. The last she'd seen him he was living in a one bedroom, fourth floor walk-up. Here the floors were strewn with expensive Orientals in a chaos of colors and designs. Some walls were hung with contemporary art. Another featured Crucifixion's half-dozen platinum records and the poster from the film in which Randy had a supporting role. Off to one side a separate, white-painted gallery held enlarged selections from his wife Lisa's body of work: starving African children, combat infantrymen consoling a wounded buddy, earthquake devastation in Armenia. As Lyndelle absorbed her surroundings, Randy led her to a furniture group fronting a glass case loaded with pre-Columbian ceramics. He asked if she'd like something to drink.

"Diet Coke?" She said it distractedly, still hanging on to what he'd said earlier. "You haven't answered my question."

He waved it off as he turned to open the door of a tiny refrigerator in a wet bar. "I'm not sure I *want* to know what happened, Lynnie. Cora Davis was a zealot and now she's dead. Life's a bitch. Ice?"

"Please! I can't believe you think I killed her."

Logan chuckled as he filled her glass with cubes. "I didn't say I did. I said I don't really give a fuck whether you did or not. You've *still* got problems."

She was barely able to stay in one place; the tension hummed through her like voltage through power lines. "On the phone—what did you mean? *What's* come up? All I did was take a nice, casual stroll down memory lane and all of a sudden my whole world's coming apart."

Randy topped up her glass and handed it to her. "I gather you haven't been contacted yet."

All remaining color drained from her cheeks. She faltered as she tried to speak. "C-contacted?"

"We were followed yesterday, Lynnie. By a guy who took pictures of us at the door to your suite. He contacted me this morning and threatened to send copies of those pictures to my wife, your husband, and the police if we don't pay him not to. Considering what's happened, I'd say the next move is your call."

Lyndelle sat clutching her glass without drinking from it. "Oh my God. If what happened yesterday ever gets back to Lyle, he'll have me burned at the stake. What did you tell this man?"

Randy winked at her. "The stake, huh? You might want to hide your beloved gasbag's rope and matches. I told this guy to eat shit and die. I'm not paying him dick-all."

She was on her feet so quickly she spilled her drink. "You told him *what*?!"

"Relax, Lynnie. He was too fucking stupid to cover his trail when he left me. I followed him. His name's Troy Brooks. He's got a chip on his shoulder over something that happened at the Mudd Club ten years ago. Him spilling a beer on you, and me chewing his ass for it. Truth is, I've got no idea what the fuck he's talking about."

Lyndelle's agitation slackened a notch as her face registered a hint of recollection. "I remember," she murmured. "Troy Brooks. The writer."

Logan nodded. "That's right. I learned that much about him by making a few calls . . ."

"The one who wrote that horrible book," she interrupted. "It's been quite awhile now. Five or six years."

Randy only knew what a staff writer at *Rolling Stone* had told him. He didn't read much himself. "Yeah. Lived pretty high before his fall. Went broke when he couldn't get another contract. Lost his beach place in Quogue and his boat. His wife left him. The whole sorry shot."

"You must remember that night," she insisted. "He was drunk and abusive. You called him an asshole and he tried to get you to step outside. I remember how big he was and how scared *I* was. But you just told him where to go and dragged me away. He was furious you wouldn't fight."

"He remembers it, too," Logan growled. "I guess it's been eating at him. He hates my guts."

Some of the color had returned to Lyndelle's face. Logan watched her take a tentative sip from her glass and then a gulp.

"This guy's threat can be nipped in the bud with one phone call, Lynnie. I've got friends in some pretty strange places now. People don't call me out into the street anymore. I'm *protected* from shit like that."

Lyndelle started to pace, her fingers at work on the dewy surface of her glass and her brow knit in consternation. "Are you asking me if I want to have this man *killed*? For godsake, Randy. I'm a United States senator's wife."

Logan grabbed himself a beer from the box, twisted the cap off, and shot it at that movie poster across the room. "Did I say anything about killing? Hell, babe, I don't even want to know what happened in that room yesterday, let alone what happens to this guy if I make that call." He advanced into the room behind Lyndelle and stopped to face her, ten feet away. "What I *am* saying is that we can handle it any way you want, Lynnie. The one thing you've gotta know, right here, is that I'm not paying this prick a nickel. I've already told him that."

Backlit by windows in the photo gallery, she had an aura of vitality that belied her current distressed state. Her simple wool-knit dress hugged that long, lean physique with an honesty that most women wouldn't risk.

"I won't stand by and let this man destroy my life, Randy. If the police find out you were there and even *think* I killed Cora, my marriage is destroyed."

"So . . . ?"

She threw back the remaining contents of her glass and shook her head in frustration. "I don't know what I want to do. I need time to think. Maybe there's some other way."

Randy shrugged. "Brooks won't do anything too dangerous until you blow him off, too. You're safe as long as you can stall him. But let's not wait too long, huh? He's got an itch that wants scratched *bad*."

Lyndelle set her empty glass on a side table and straightened to meet Randy's gaze. Logan felt her eyes probing as though she were still hoping to find some simpler answer, the unseen easy way out. There was none, and she knew it.

"Hold me?" she begged.

He advanced to take her into his arms and was surprised by the fierceness with which she suddenly clung to him. It was the same surprise he'd experienced yesterday at that embrace on her threshold. The senator's beautiful wife was a trapped animal whether she knew it or not.

He let his hands glide down along her waist to cup her hips. Instead of pulling away, she responded by pressing one thigh into his groin. When he bent his head to kiss her he felt her fingers grip his ass. She rotated her pelvis, grinding hard against him.

Traffic was snarled on First Avenue as Dante and Richardson crept the ten blocks between the police labs on East 20th Street and the morgue. The two of them tended to split the driving when they worked together, and right now Jumbo was behind the wheel. His irritation at being trapped in traffic was evident in his tone.

"I hope Conklin's got more for us than those guys had," he complained. They'd just completed a brief stop-by at the labs to make sure nobody was dragging tail on the Davis forensics results. "They vacuum, scrape, dust, and shoot up God knows how many rolls of film and still can't tell us jack shit. That was a flesh and blood perp did her, not a ghost, Joey."

"In a *hotel* room."

"I know that," Beasley snapped. "And they've got enough hair and fiber evidence from it to be a month just cataloging it all."

"I think he knew her."

Richardson turned slightly to contemplate his partner. "Say what?"

"I think our guy knew her. Either that or he was someone who had access and knew something that we don't *about* her. If anything's missing it isn't obvious, Beasley. That means he was either after something specific or only after her."

"Not necessarily. She coulda surprised the guy. He coulda just been getting started."

"He had access."

"Okay. Granted."

Dante shook his head. "I don't like that angle. Most burglars who kill people are psychologically unstable—jacked up on drugs or hurting for *more* drugs. Guys like that use

crowbars, not keys. They'll accost a victim, face-to-face, but
only when it's out in the open somewhere. Gives them an
avenue of escape if the thing goes sour.''

Richardson picked up his drift. "Or break in some place
where there's little danger of being caught. You're right. A
hotel like the Park View sure ain't a place a junkie hits."

Dante nodded. "Nope. Doesn't fit the M.O."

"Okay," Jumbo theorized. "So she opened the door to
our guy. How many people check the peep hole when a maid
or maintenance knocks?"

"And walked with him clear into the bedroom before he
did her? There was little or no evidence of struggle. I still
say she knew him."

Richardson pointed to the morgue building, dead ahead.
"Let's let our friend Rocky be the judge of that."

Pathologist Rocky Conklin was Dante's ghoul of prefer-
ence and had been for the past half decade. Conklin was
quick, precise, and rarely missed anything of importance.
He was in his office and relaxing in a familiar pose when the
two detectives found him. Feet up on the blotter, he had one
of his ever-present cigars going and a file open in his lap.
Neither Dante nor Richardson was a connoisseur of such
things, but today's smoke smelled smoother and less pungent
than usual.

"New brand?" Dante asked.

Conklin held the cigar at arm's length, wedged between
the first and middle fingers of his left hand. "Matter of fact
it is, Cowboy. Cuban. Buddy of mine on the money side of
this business brought me a box back from Holland."

"Mortician?" Jumbo wondered.

"*Medical* doctor, asshole."

"C'mon, Rock," Dante protested. "Think of all the dough
you save on malpractice premiums."

"Spare me the wit. I'm a busy man and you want the
lowdown on your congresswoman. It's swell the way your
boss requested my services specifically; dragged my ass outta

61

bed at four-thirty this morning. You be sure to thank him for me.''

Jumbo beamed, his hands spread. ''What are friends for, Doc?''

''Congresswoman Cora Davis.'' The pathologist pushed a pair of half glasses back up his nose and read from the file before him. ''Female Caucasian, age fifty-one, five foot three inches tall, one hundred forty-two pounds. Cause of death? Depressed fracture of the skull in the occipital region and extensive laceration of the soft brain tissue. There is little evidence of bruising in the area of strangulation, though there is some. It's my judgment that respiratory function ceased at the time she suffered the blow to the head. The heart no doubt continued to beat for an undetermined but certainly very short period of time. Strangulation was, as you two clowns might term it, overkill.''

''Clowns?'' There was amusement in Dante's tone.

''There is no evidence of struggle. Based on the temperature readings our man took at the scene prior to midnight, I'm fixing the time of death at somewhere between three-thirty and four-thirty yesterday afternoon. That's also based on an ambient room temperature of seventy-four degrees.''

The two cops eased back in their chairs, considering what they'd just heard.

''We were talking about whether or not she knew the perp on the way over,'' Dante told the pathologist. ''I think she did, and you've just given me another reason to feel that way. I'm inclined to rule out activist nut cases. Crazies who kill are making statements. The Squeaky Frommes and Mark David Chapmans go for their targets in the open. They need people to see them and probably even to catch them.''

''Either that or he had access to the room and got the dead drop on her,'' Jumbo offered. ''Caught her cold.''

Conklin was busy relighting his smoke as he listened. He paused now to examine the glow of the lit end. ''Your conclusions are your business, gents. But you're right about one thing, Sarge. Your perp did get the drop on her. From behind. There is no evidence of struggle; nothing beneath the nails, no bruising outside the areas of impact and strangulation.''

"Another thing," Dante added. "If I'm a burglar who's just been surprised in the middle of a sneak job, am I gonna have the presence of mind to first whack her and then make *sure* she's dead? Those panty hose didn't come off the body. She was still wearing hers when I saw her. First our perp hit her, hard, and then he goes rummaging through her lingerie drawer? Bullshit. This guy definitely wanted her dead.''

Photojournalist Lisa Dodd was bone weary. She'd departed New York three weeks ago to chronicle the discovery of three B-52 crash sites in the jungles of Vietnam. She'd spent her nights since in a sleeping bag, on a cot, in a tent. She'd showered on average of once a week and spent any free time spreading bug repellent on those few areas of exposed flesh. Because of the conditions she'd worked as quickly as possible, but of course she couldn't run roughshod over a situation where politics were still quite delicate. Once the last of the recovered remains was bagged and cataloged, Lisa was out of there. It took her the next thirty-six hours to reach Ho Chi Minh City, catch a flight to Hong Kong, and connect to San Francisco and JFK. She was home early, nearly a week ahead of the schedule proposed by *Newsweek*. She was seriously considering not advising them of her return for another day. She needed that much time to soak clean, catch up on her sleep, and eat some decent food. In the time she was gone, Lisa had lost nine pounds.

As her cab pulled up before her Tribeca building, she fervently hoped that Randy was away at the horse farm upstate. After a Jacuzzi she wanted to crawl between the sheets, take the phone off the hook, and sleep clear through into tomorrow. After that she would start making reservations at all her favorite restaurants. Somewhere in there she'd get her hundred-plus rolls of film delivered to the lab. Meanwhile, she summoned the strength to lug her equipment cases and single garment bag to the door of the elevator.

Randy Logan was too excited to pay much attention to the whir of the elevator motor. Lyndelle was a woman of healthy appetites, and she made love with the unstoppable intensity of a runaway freight train. He'd briefly considered carrying her to his bed but abandoned the idea when she began pawing at his belt buckle. The wool knit dress came away like the peel from a banana. His hands roved, remembering every inch of her as she lay atop him now, her whole body moving eagerly against him. Like it had yesterday, the smell of her triggered an avalanche of long-buried memories.

Randy was brought around abruptly when the elevator car stopped at his floor.

"What?!" Lyndelle gasped.

Randy struggled to sit upright, his forearm pushing her aside. "Shhhh!"

His head rose above the back of the sofa just in time to see the elevator door roll back and his wife Lisa emerge lugging two aluminum equipment cases and a garment bag. Lyndelle's head came up, too, and the moment she saw Lisa standing on the elevator threshold she screamed and dove for the floor. Randy and Lisa stared at each other, not a word passing between them. Lisa sighed and dropped her things, shaking her head. Then she turned and disappeared behind the closing elevator door.

There was panic in Lyndelle's voice as she rose on her knees. "Who was *that*?"

Randy reached to pull a strand of sweat-dampened hair from his lover's cheek. He let his fingers ride down her neck and across her shoulder, stroking her. "*That* was my wife."

SEVEN

Captain Wayne McKillip was fielding this one personally. An unidentified male caller to one of the popular morning radio shows had claimed credit for the Cora Davis homicide. The station's offices were located on Fifth Avenue at 34th Street. McKillip and his investigative partner, Sergeant Dennis Roscoe, were seated in the reception area, waiting to interview the station's program director. McKillip was using the downtime to soak up atmosphere. Most of the support staff here was female, and in the five minutes since he arrived the captain had watched a parade of them pass by the receptionist's desk; half were dressed like Madonna and the other half like Paula Abdul. Overhead, the station's raucous rock programming poured from a pair of speakers.

"No wonder the youth of America's all fucked up, listening to shit like this," Roscoe complained. Dennis didn't have much patience for music trends more recent than the Beatles. Nor did he have much patience for New York and the Job anymore. Five years McKillip's senior, Dennis would have his thirty in soon. He'd already put in for retirement and put a down payment on a condo in South Carolina.

McKillip grunted. His sixteen-year-old daughter Maureen listened to a lot of rock and roll radio, and he'd recognized this station's call letters immediately. Wayne wasn't a lot more tolerant than Roscoe, and this station played the type of format he found most grating.

"Can't understand a single fucking word of the lyrics," Dennis continued. "Sounds like two cats fighting in an alley. And that screaming-guitar shit? Jesus."

A door down the way opened and a youngish, curly-haired man with his tie hanging loose and sleeves rolled back emerged. As he advanced, one of his hands disappeared into a pocket while the other remained available for pressing flesh. His cautious approach told both cops he wasn't accustomed to dealing with policemen.

"Captain McKillip?" The program director's gaze roved between his two visitors.

Wayne eased both hands into his pockets as he stood, not offering to shake. Always keep them a little off guard. "Mr. Posner? This is Sergeant Roscoe, my second in command."

Posner jerked his head toward the door through which he'd just passed. "My office all right?"

Minutes later the three men were seated around Posner's desk, the director behind it and the two cops out front. McKillip reached into the inside pocket of his jacket and extracted a pack of cigarettes. There was no ashtray in evidence.

"Mind if I smoke?"

Posner *did* mind, but quickly masked his displeasure. Before he could reply, McKillip was spinning the wheel of his Zippo. A small plastic plate came out of the director's desk drawer and was pushed across the surface in McKillip's direction. Wayne nodded his thanks. His ground rules established, McKillip was ready to dig in.

"Our Operations Desk tells us you've got this guy on tape. The one who made the call."

Posner nodded and reached to pick up a cassette tape from his blotter. His office had an elaborate sound system installed in a rack on the credenza behind the desk. As he spoke he kicked around in his chair to face it. "Real head case by the sound of him. Frankly, we didn't know how serious we should take him but figured we should let you know any-

66

way." Once the tape was inserted into the cassette deck, Posner depressed the "play" button.

McKillip listened as the voice came at him through a pair of bookshelf speakers.

"Yeah. Rad Man here. From Jersey. Like I'm the one whacked the congress bitch. I mean, like who the fuck she think she was? I'm *into* my tunes and she wants t' fuck with my fuckin' *rights*. Like, ain't *no* body like her gonna take 'em away. No way. I mean, like this is America, right? Anybody can say whatever the fuck he *wants*. You know what *I* say? I say the uptight bitch took it up the butt from dogs. Long live rock and roll, dudes. Anybody else tries t' fuck with it, we'll kill them, too."

The fidelity was good. If it weren't for the distortion natural to any phone conversation, the kid could have been right there in the room with them. McKillip peered closer at the face grilles, trying to read a brand name.

"That's it," Posner reported. "He said his piece and hung up."

"You got the time that call came in?" Roscoe asked. "Some kinda log?"

Posner consulted the legal pad before him. "Nine forty-three this morning."

Dennis turned to McKillip. "He said he was from Jersey. That'd make it a toll call and easy enough to trace."

"Maybe not," Posner cautioned. "During our morning show we get as many as two hundred calls from New Jersey. All come in on the same line and are routed to our six switchboard operators via computer."

"So we trace out six instead of one," McKillip murmured. "If the call itself is any more than a lotta wiseass bullshit, it ain't no big deal."

Back outside on Fifth Avenue, McKillip and Roscoe sat a moment in the front seat of their company car. McKillip, riding shotgun, stared ahead down the sidewalk.

"Just another jerk-off, Denny," Wayne growled. "We ain't got any choice but to track this mutt down, but did you listen to that shit? Makes you wonder what the fuck's happening to this world.''

Roscoe's fingers drummed idly on the steering wheel, his eyes following the progress of a pretty young woman as she crossed the Avenue in front of them. She was carrying a portfolio case, and her skirt ended at least eight inches above the knee. Wayne watched, too. She was wearing tights, but in this weather he figured she was freezing her ass off.

"One thing I know for sure, Cap. That call came too late. They generally make 'em before it hits the news; prove *they* did it. This is some kinda hoax. Kids just fucking around.''

"It ain't like we ain't got enough other avenues to chase down,'' McKillip agreed. "They had five hundred hecklers on the sidewalk outside the hotel yesterday. Pack of little shitheads, most of them. Nothing better to do with their time. Still, a nutcase could blend into a crowd like that, no problem. We ain't got much choice but to go through the motions with this Rad Man asshole, but that's *all* he's gonna get. We got plenty of other fish in the pan.''

Several Park View hotel employees on duty Tuesday afternoon had worked split shifts. They hadn't yet reported when Dante and Richardson visited the premises earlier. After lunch, the partners returned to interview them. The first was a desk clerk, middle-aged and meticulously groomed. He reported having worked at the Park View for twelve years, with five years prior experience in reservations at the Plaza. Dante hoped the man's memory for detail was better than the switchboard operator's.

"We're curious about keys to that suite,'' Joe explained. "How many were in circulation yesterday? There's no evidence of forced entry.''

The clerk, thoughtful, glanced back toward the array of cubbies behind him. Each was labeled with a room number and appeared to contain several duplicate keys on individual rings. Some also contained mail and message slips. "In addition to master keys? Yes, I'm sure you've already considered that. Let me see. Seventeen hundred five. Oh yes.'' His face lit up. ''We did issue Mrs. Mitchell a duplicate. You see, she lost hers.''

Dante stopped him there. ''Mrs. Mitchell *lost* her key?''

''That's correct, Lieutenant. Within an hour or two of her arrival.''

Dante absorbed this as he let his eyes drift along the array of room boxes. They came to rest at the murder suite's. There appeared to be one key in it now. Three boxes down, he saw that Reverend Davis's box contained a number of telephone-message slips. The next box, for the suite shared by Nancy Hillman and Mrs. Mitchell, contained an envelope.

''Could you ring Mrs. Mitchell's suite for us and let her know we're on our way up?'' he asked the clerk. Earlier, when Lyndelle Mitchell hadn't returned from breakfast, Nancy Hillman voiced the assumption that her friend had most likely gone shopping. That was several hours ago now.

The clerk started to reach for the phone and stopped. ''I'm afraid you won't find her in, Lieutenant. She and Ms. Hillman left in one of the hotel limousines fifteen minutes ago. I believe there's someone flying into LaGuardia whom they plan to meet.''

It took the driver a quarter hour of fighting midtown traffic just to get Lyndelle and Nancy to the mouth of the Queens Midtown Tunnel. At this rate Billy Beaumont would be waiting for them on the sidewalk outside the terminal when they arrived. The soundproof partition was up, and as Nancy completed a call to the airline to check the flight's arrival time, Lyndelle was busy summoning her courage. When Nancy cradled the cellular handset, Lyndelle cleared her throat.

''Nancy?''

Her old college chum turned, head cocked to one side. ''I'm trying to decide if I should have Billy paged; let him know we're hung up in traffic.''

Lyndelle checked the time and rolled her eyes. ''Relax.

We've got forty-five minutes. That's plenty of time.'' She let a hint of peevishness into her tone. "We need to talk."

Nancy frowned, finally bringing herself into full focus. "What about?"

"I may have a problem." Lyndelle knew she had to pick her way carefully across this terrain, and she paused to formulate her thoughts. "With something that happened yesterday afternoon." Another pause. "Maybe I should have used better judgment, but I could see the headlines if it got leaked to the media. I just *couldn't* tell the police."

Nancy was no longer worried about marooning Billy Beaumont on the airport sidewalk. She came clear around in her seat to face her friend. Eyes blazing, she waved a finger quickly back and forth in the air between them. "Stop. Right there. Headlines? Better judgment? Out with it, Lyn. *What* problem?"

The senator's wife took a deep breath and spewed words in a rush. "I didn't go upstairs alone when I left the reception, Nance. That is, I did, but I had a visitor a few minutes later. We'd gotten into a conversation about horse breeding and he was interested in Daddy's syndicate. I didn't have the syndicate secretary's number with me, but it's in my little book. He came upstairs to get it."

Commensurate with her increased concern, the creases of Nancy's frown deepened. "He?"

Lyndelle nodded. "That's why I didn't say anything about it." She squeezed her eyes shut, set her jaw, and shook her head. "I can't believe I was so *stupid.*"

"Who?" Nancy insisted.

"The rock singer Cora debated. Randy Logan." There. It was out.

The anticipated explosion didn't come. Instead, Nancy sat there, stricken. When she did speak it came out as a tight, near-strangled whisper. "I don't believe this. Please, Lyn. Tell me I didn't hear you right."

Lyndelle averted her gaze to stare out at traffic and the tiled interior of the tunnel. The driver of the cab in the next lane was squinting to see into the limousine's interior but was being thwarted by the tinted glass. His passenger leaned forward to point at his watch. The cabbie gave up on the limo and lifted his hands from the wheel in a gesture of helplessness.

"That's not all of it, Nance. I wouldn't be sitting here spilling my guts if it was. Logan was followed . . . by one of those guys who photographs celebrities. He took pictures when I answered the door."

Nancy was beside herself. In a gesture fueled by anger and impatience, she grabbed Lyndelle's sleeve and jerked her back around. "You *saw* this man? Why didn't you call security? Make a scene right on the spot?"

Facing Nancy now, Lyndelle shook her head. "Nance, I *didn't* see him."

Nancy was confused. "If you didn't see him, how do you know it happened?"

Lyndelle looked down at the fingers still gripping her sleeve. Her gaze lingered there until Nancy removed her hand. "The photographer contacted Mr. Logan, making all sorts of allegations that simply aren't true. He's demanding money, Nance. Mr. Logan called me with this news, right before breakfast."

Nancy had stiffened. "Money for what?"

"To prevent him from going to the papers and the police with his pictures. I've got no idea what he wants. He's only spoken to Mr. Logan. I expect he'll contact me next."

Nancy thought quickly and suddenly shifted gears. "We could . . ." She stopped and shook her head. "No, that would change your story to the police, and we can't do that. The media would have a field day." She turned to look directly into Lyndelle's fear-filled eyes. "I need time to consider how best to handle this, Lyn. If he does contact you, you're going to have to stall him."

"What if I can't?"

Nancy waved it away. "What's he going to do instead? Kill the golden goose? He'll take a certain amount of runaround if

71

he can smell money at the end of it. You can make some sort of excuse about needing time to get access to funds.'' She stopped to nod, liking that angle. ''So what did Logan tell this gutter crawler?''

''He's refusing to pay him a dime.''

''Darn! Right off the bat like that? Why?''

''Claims he has nothing to lose. But he's assured me he'll say nothing to the police, at least for now.''

''Good. I heard from one of the detectives on the Homicide Squad that a man called a radio station. He's claiming responsibility for killing Cora. They think it won't be more than a day before they have this crazy in custody. That will defuse a lot of your extortionist's power.''

''Unless this *crazy* is just somebody looking for attention. That happens all the time.''

Nancy scowled at her old friend, her eyes narrowing. ''Why even think that, Lyn? You didn't do it, did you?''

Lyndelle reared as though she'd been slapped. ''That hurts, Nance. Especially coming from you. Don't be ridiculous.''

Nancy hurried beyond. ''I don't think it's wise to tell Billy about this. At least until we've exhausted our other options.''

Lyndelle was relieved. Billy Beaumont's loyalty to her husband was legend. He'd served as Colonel Lyle Mitchell's adjutant during the Vietnam conflict and followed Lyle into political life. Both men shared the same political philosophy. Indeed, if it weren't for the fact that Lyle Mitchell came from a monied background and Beaumont did not, there were many in Washington who guessed their roles might be reversed.

''But please, Lyn.'' Nancy's tone was pleading now. ''This sort of indiscretion has got to stop. People are starting to talk, and not just in Washington. Back home, too.''

Lyndelle bristled. ''Just what the hell are you trying to say, Nance?''

''You don't have to curse, Lyn. And you know *exactly* what I'm saying. The word is trickling back to the constituency that Lyle went and married a Margaret Trudeau–type.

If it didn't play well in Canada, it sure as heck won't play in Tennessee.''

"And you believe it. All the backbiting gossip. I thought you were on my side, Nance.''

Nancy was clearly torn. She bit at her lower lip, her eyelids dropped to seal in the internal conflict. "I *am* on your side. But I don't think you're hearing what I'm trying to tell you.'' Her eyes opened, meeting Lyndelle's with an unsettling directness. "If you want to continue being a senator's wife, you'd better start using your head. There's nothing worse in the eyes of a Tennessee voter than an old fool being led down the garden path by his privates.''

The two elevator operators who ran the cars servicing the homicide-scene floor were the last hotel personnel on Dante's list. In all, he and Jumbo had interviewed an even dozen management, desk, security, housekeeping, and communications people. It was frustrating work. They felt like two ball players who'd gone a combined zero for twelve at the plate.

Management provided relief for the two operators as the partners interviewed them, one at a time. They struck out with the first, a detached, introspective man who was pleasant mannered but inclined to loiter off in his own world.

"What I said on the way to the morgue this morning?'' Beasley grumbled. "I take it all back. Maybe it *was* a ghost did her.'' He rolled his shoulders to work some of the tension out and rubbed his face with the open palms of his two huge mitts.

Dante pushed his weariness aside with effort and smiled. "Slim pickings, all right. But there's one thing I've learned from all this. It's unlikely it was one of that rabble out on the street. Nobody sneaks anywhere in this hotel, let alone into one of the rooms. It was somebody who knew how to play the game. I can feel it. They fit right in; knew how to dress, how to walk. Could have been another guest. As soon as registration finishes printing out that list, we'll ask Gus to have it researched.''

"Be a good way to do it," Jumbo agreed. "Check in. Stay a few days. Get people used to you. Somebody sees you on seventeen and your room's on sixteen, you weren't thinking; got off on the wrong floor."

A knock came at the door and Richardson moved to answer it. The uniformed man he invited to enter had a tough, roguish demeanor that belied his neat, tailored dress. A bushy, gray-flecked mustache enlivened the slightly fleshy face. He was Jumbo's height and a few pounds heavier.

"Didn't mean to hang you up, officers. Kid relieving me was late. Can't remember when he was on time."

Jumbo indicated a seat. When the elevator operator took it, the cops introduced themselves. The operator's eyes brightened at Dante's surname. He pointed to the name tag on his uniform jacket.

"Ricci. Dom Ricci. Pleased to meet you both. The boss says this is about that congresswoman got it upstairs yesterday. Damn shame."

"You remember her?" Jumbo asked.

Ricci nodded. "Oh sure. Came into my car all in a rush yesterday afternoon. Must've been around three-thirty. There was nobody else riding upstairs with us so I looked to make a little friendly conversation. I do that whenever I can, y'know; make the guests feel at home." He paused, thinking about what he'd just said. "But only if they *look* like they might want to talk, you understand. I ain't one of them guys always trying to *insinuate* himself."

"Understood," Jumbo assured him. "What did you talk about?"

"Me'n the congresswoman? You understand I didn't *know* she was a congresswoman then. Just another guest about my age, dressed like most of them here. She seemed sorta nervous so I asked her if there's anything I can do. I got a house phone right there in my car. Somebody forgets their key or whatever, I can save them a trip back downstairs; have one of the desk staff send it right up.''

"Was that it?" Jumbo asked. "She'd forgotten her key?''

"Naw. Somebody from security'd called her. Asked her to come upstairs to her room. I guess they weren't real specific because she didn't know what the problem was. She thanked me for asking, though. When we arrived on seventeen I waited until she got down the hall to her door. She seemed to think somebody was s'posed to meet her there. When they didn't, we figured it was some sorta mix-up. She used her own key to enter and I headed back for the lobby.''

"There was no one else in the hall?" Jumbo pressed.

"Not that I saw. Nope.''

"What about other traffic up to her floor?" Dante asked. "In the hour or so before the congresswoman made her trip and in the hour after.''

Dom Ricci frowned. "I can only speak for my car, but I'd say there was 'bout half dozen or so. You already talked to Melvin, so it was his traffic plus mine. I mighta handled a guest on the way up and he mighta handled the same guest on the way back down.'' Then he brightened. "There was two, though. One was this blond woman. Young. A real looker, but cold. I didn't even *try* to make conversation with this one. Tall, y'know. Tall as me almost, and I'm six even.''

Dante glanced to Jumbo and saw the question in his eyes. Beasley hadn't seen Mrs. Mitchell yet. "And the other?" he asked. "You said there were two people who stuck out.''

"Yeah. I wouldn't know him if my little girl didn't have a poster of him on her bedroom wall. I guess everyone her age does. Remy almost killed me last night when she found out he rode in my elevator and I didn't get her his autograph.''

"Who?" Dante prodded.

"Oh.'' Ricci grinned sheepishly. "Guy's name is Randy Logan. Lead singer of a rock band calls itself Crucifixion.''

Jumbo eased himself back into the exchange. "You said he rode with you twice.''

"That's right. First time must've been around two-thirty. He rode back down again about an hour later."

"What about the blonde?" Jumbo asked. "You see her again?"

Ricci shook his head. "Not in my car. Just my luck, she prob'ly took her next ride with Melvin."

Five minutes later, Dante and Richardson found themselves alone again.

"What am I missing?" Jumbo wondered. "You remember the security chief mentioning a call made to the congresswoman?"

"I doubt he or anyone on his staff made one," Dante replied. "But somebody did."

"A setup."

A slow nod. "Be my guess, too."

EIGHT

William "Billy" Beaumont liked to see himself as a new-school politician with an old pol's heart. When Washington took up jogging, Billy ran. When Washington embraced avid participation in competitive sports, Billy unveiled a vicious backhand and developed a reputation for tenacious net play. He worked the old Capitol Hill watering holes cautiously, drinking just enough to be sociable. In back rooms he drank rye, straight, and could hold his own with the best. He was a confirmed bachelor, heavyset but fit enough to look a decade younger than his fifty-seven years.

Beaumont's principal job now was to handle damage control. Cora Davis was dead, throwing the political picture in his home state of Tennessee out of focus. He needed to determine the extent of damage done to the party's position—to ensure that Senator Mitchell escaped the crisis unscathed and perhaps even turn the tragedy to the senator's advantage. Meanwhile, the wheels of commerce still turned. Mr. Kagoshima would no doubt express deep regret, but he still had his own agenda. Billy was determined to make short work of these final dealings with the Japanese industrialist's money people before getting on with the more crucial business at hand. Because the Japanese preferred working with men, Billy believed this assignment should have fallen to him initially. Lyle Mitchell, in the interest of seeing Cora Davis elected governor, chose to forgo Beaumont's talents as a natural born deal-closer in favor of political expedience.

Right now Beaumont was seated in the back of a limousine with Nancy Hillman and Lyle's wife Lyndelle. They were traveling along the Brooklyn-Queens Expressway somewhere above Long Island City. Billy had just poured himself a whiskey.

"I spoke with the senator in Guam just before I got on the airplane," he told the two women. "It was late, his time; right around midnight." Billy and Lyndelle occupied the backseat while Nancy sat on the jump seat facing rearward. "He's alarmed and saddened, of course, but I've assured him that everything is under control. He mentioned that you spoke with him earlier, Lyndelle."

She nodded. "I told him what happened and that Nancy had already spoken with you."

"That she had." Billy lifted his glass to his lips and took a sip. He thought his boss crazy to have married Lyndelle. She was a bauble, and baubles were pure liability. The marriage wasn't eighteen months old and already the rumors were coming back to him; the shopping extravagances, the late nights in fast-lane Georgetown haunts. Memphis born and bred or not, Lyndelle Jennings wasn't quite down-home enough for the Tennessee constituency. She'd spent a few years in New York awhile back, trying to be a fashion model. It had affected her the way New York affects everyone seduced by its bright lights and promises. "I'm glad to hear you haven't been dragged into this," he told her. "The fact that you and Cora were sharing that suite could have created problems."

That said, Beaumont quickly shifted his attention to Nancy Hillman. "How about that threat angle we talked about this morning? I'm having trouble believing there isn't something we or the FBI have overlooked." Truth was, Billy didn't have much use for Nancy Hillman either. Yes, she was driven and even smart, but he didn't trust her gender or her breed. Washington was crammed with her type nowadays, all of them too full of personal ambition to be good team players and too soft to be good infighters. In truth, the new crop of smart-boys wasn't any tougher or more astute than the girls. Surely, Nancy had run some pretty effective campaigns, and Billy gave her credit for that, but he doubted her skills as an overall party organizer. Women were a distraction in the back rooms. It was hard for a man to keep his mind on the business at hand with a woman present.

"Cora's staff, the Bureau, and the New York police are all digging as hard as they can," Nancy reported. "A man called a local radio station, claiming credit. They're following it up."

Until Beaumont could do a little digging on his own and talk to some of these people, he would have to accept her assessment as the status quo. Right now it was going on four o'clock. He was scheduled to meet Kagoshima's team for drinks at six-thirty.

"Okay. I want to sit down and talk, first thing in the morning; make sure we're all aimed at the same target. I've got no idea how much time this Jap business is going to take up, but I'll make time for Jerry, see what kind of help he needs. Have they released the body yet?"

"Not yet," Nancy replied. "They're holding it for autopsy. I'm told it won't be released until all the toxicology tests are completed and they hold a coroner's inquiry; probably Friday morning."

"What about arrangements for having her shipped home?"

"A funeral director was recommended to us," Nancy replied. "The Reverend Davis and I have an appointment to meet with them tomorrow morning. They've assured me they can handle everything."

For the moment, Beaumont couldn't think of anything else to ask. He finished his drink in a gulp, ran a hand through his short-cropped gray hair, and nodded his satisfaction. "Breakfast, then." He said it rather than asked it. "Let's shoot for eight sharp."

* * *

Randy Logan couldn't find his wife anywhere. He checked her studio on West 25th Street and found it empty. Then he tried a series of bars frequented by the journalist crowd: Costello's midtown near Grand Central and the *Daily News*, then the Lion's Head on Sheridan Square in Greenwich Village. When he failed to find her in either of those places, he played his hole card. There was one more place she frequented, also in the Village, on Washington Place.

The bartender at the Stoned Crow was an old friend of Lisa's from the days she used to spend her spare time stateside drinking beers with the boys and watching ball games on gin mill televisions. It was still an hour before the post-work crowd would hit, and Randy found the joint all but empty. The barkeep, taking advantage of the lull, had the *Times* open to the crossword and half the blanks inked in. An empty soup bowl and spoon at his elbow were half-obscured by a crumpled paper napkin. He looked up as Randy entered and wandered his way.

"Well, if it ain't the cocksman himself."

"Where is she?"

The barkeep straightened, hands planted palms down on the mahogany. The slow shake of his head said everything his eyes failed to convey. "No can do. She knew you'd come looking for her. Said she's—and I quote—'too tired for his bullshit right now.' I believe her. She was almost forty-eight hours getting home. Looked like hell when she walked in here."

Logan pulled up a stool. "Give me a pint of Newcastle, will you?"

A tug of the stick sent ale cascading into the regulation British bar glass. "This gal you were shagging—anything serious?"

Logan scowled as he shook the notion off. "Old girlfriend from a couple years before Lisa. Hadn't seen her for ages. Married now, too. In from out of town for a few days."

"She knows it's not the first time, you know."

Logan lifted his drink and sipped. "It's hard to expect that two people who spend more than half the year apart wouldn't get a little on the side, here and there.''

"She says she doesn't," the barkeep contended. "I don't think she's jiving me."

Randy set his glass down and fixed his wife's buddy with a sad smile. "Oh, I believe it, too. But what the fuck difference does it make? She's faithful because it's convenient to be. Everybody knows who she married. She can still be one of the guys, hang out, do her work without being hassled."

The barkeep chuckled as he stepped away to retrieve his own glass and refill it with soda. "The politics are for you and her to work out, pal. It sounds to me like you're someplace you don't want to be. Okay. That's why they invented divorce." He paused to grab up his pen and fill in another of the crossword blanks.

This was Billy Beaumont's first time at the Park View. While he loitered at check-in he surveyed the lobby and liked what he saw. The place embodied a kind of old-world elegance that was just too expensive to replicate in newer construction: heavy columns, plenty of ornamental plasterwork, ceilings high enough to give even the tighter spaces a nice, airy feel.

"You're all set, Mr. Beaumont," the clerk informed him. A key and two telephone-message slips were pushed at him across the front desk. "Room seventeen-eleven."

Beaumont pointed to the cubby a few down the way from his own. "Is that a message for Miss Hillman?"

The clerk reached for the envelope indicated and read the typewritten address. "Mrs. Mitchell, sir."

Beaumont beckoned for it. "I've got to stop by there on the way to my room."

As Billy started for the elevators, he glanced over the two telephone messages, both from the office in Washington, and then at the sealed envelope for Lyndelle Mitchell. He noticed the absence of a stamp or postmark and realized it must have been delivered by hand. Interest piqued, he tore the flap.

* * *

It was early evening, and darkness was descending when Randy Logan returned to his Tribeca loft. He had little hope that Lisa might have arrived in his absence and wasn't too disappointed to discover she hadn't. The place was the same as he'd left it; Lynnie's soda glass removed to the dishwasher but the memory of her presence still strong. Lisa was going to want blood. Troy Brooks definitely wanted money. Right now, what Randy wanted more than anything else was another drink.

He didn't notice the single message blink on his answering machine until he was in his bedroom and changing from his street clothes into his robe. Having moved from beer to bourbon, he retrieved his tumbler from the dresser top before crossing to rewind the tape.

"Mr. Logan? Detective Lieutenant Dante. NYPD. Give me a call, please. I'm conducting an investigation and would like to ask you a couple of questions." The cop left a phone number.

Randy was shaken. He couldn't imagine that Brooks would give up his extortion scheme so readily. The photographer had shown himself an opportunity-driven animal. There was no way he'd fold his hand after one minor tongue-lashing. So what the hell was this?

There was only one way to get an answer, but Randy waited until the thundering in his chest subsided before picking up the phone. He wasn't sure that more alcohol would help but took a stiff belt anyway. The searing warmth of it felt good in his throat but felt like hell on hitting bottom; a wave of nausea washed over him. As he punched the cop's number out on the keypad, he reminded himself that he'd done nothing wrong.

"Sergeant Richardson. What can I do for you?" The answering voice was deep and confident, the way Logan expected a cop's voice should sound.

"This is Randall Logan, Sergeant. A Lieutenant Dante

left a message on my machine, asking me to get back to him.''

The sergeant asked him to hold, and less than fifteen seconds later another confident voice came on the line.

"Lieutenant Dante. Thanks for getting back to me so soon, Mr. Logan."

"No problem, Lieutenant. What's this about?" Logan struggled to keep his tone compliant, cooperative.

"I'd rather speak to you face-to-face," Dante replied. "It involves a somewhat delicate matter. If you're gonna be home for the next hour or so, I can explain when I get there."

What choice did Randy have? "An hour? Sure. I'll be here. You know where here is, I expect?"

"I do, Mr. Logan. I'm sorry about all the mystery, but I think you'll understand once I explain."

Randy saw his hand tremble as he replaced the receiver. Damn. Maybe something had happened to Lisa; something this lieutenant thought too delicate to discuss over the phone. He immediately ruled out suicide. Lisa didn't have a suicidal bone in her body. An accident? Something so recent that even the bartender hadn't heard of it yet?

The Park View hotel wasn't any more on Richardson's way home than it was on Dante's. This end-of-shift stop-by fell to Beasley by default. Joey had more experience with people like Randy Logan. His upstairs neighbors and landlords were both bona fide members of the same glitter club to which Logan belonged. Brian Brennan was a sculptor and a fixed star in the contemporary art world firmament. Brennan's wife, Diana Webster, was lead singer of the popular rock band Queen of Beasts. They considered Dante one of their closest friends. So while Joey drew Logan, Jumbo got Mrs. Lyle Mitchell. The fact that she'd reported her room key missing just hours before the Cora Davis homicide was something that troubled him. A good investigator learns to hate coincidence.

Lyndelle Mitchell was finally in residence when Jumbo

knocked. She answered her door clad in a dressing gown, her hair tied atop her head and most of the makeup scrubbed from her face. The discovery of the big black detective on her threshold obviously startled her.

"Sorry to drop in unannounced, Mrs. Mitchell. We've had a heck of a time finding you in today." As he said it, Richardson dangled his shield case and identification.

She frowned. "I don't understand. I spoke with two detectives last night and a Captain McKillip for a second time again this morning. If this isn't urgent, I wonder if it can't wait until tomorrow. It's been a trying day."

"I'm sure it has, but I'm afraid it *is* urgent. It'll only take a few minutes." Jumbo gestured past her toward the interior of the suite. "May I?"

She sighed and stood back from the door. Richardson entered, his eyes sweeping the familiar surroundings of that morning's interview with Nancy Hillman. The state chairwoman's bedroom door was closed while Mrs. Mitchell's own door hung open. The interior of her room was a mess, with clothes thrown over chairs, shoes strewn across the carpet, and shopping bags bearing all the right store logos burdening the bed.

"You said urgent, officer."

It was warm in there, and Jumbo would rather have shrugged out of his heavy topcoat. He chose, instead, to leave it on. "We understand from the front desk that you reported losing your room key yesterday. We're curious to know where you might have lost it and why you didn't mention it to the investigating detectives when you spoke to them."

"Oh." She waved a casual, dismissive hand at the air between them. "You had me *truly* concerned for a moment. You suspect some sort of *connection*." She punctuated it with a relieved chuckle. "I dropped my handbag outside the Chanel boutique on 57th Street. I only had two hours to do some shopping after we arrived and I was in a rush. I was standing with one foot in the street, trying to hail a cab, when

84

one of those bicycle messengers brushed me back. I tripped and dropped my bag while trying to catch my balance. Half the contents ended up in the gutter, and a few items fell through a storm grate.''

''And that's where you're saying you lost your key?''

She started to take offense with the way he asked it but stopped herself. Instead, she forced a smile. ''I can't be certain, of course, but it seems the most likely place. I had no idea I'd lost it until I arrived back here at the hotel. When I wanted to get into the suite, Cora had already left for downstairs . . . to meet with the debate organizers.''

Richardson thought back over what he knew of Joey's interview with the woman last night. ''I understand you did some shopping on Fifth Avenue, too—or at least you mentioned a bracelet you'd seen in a jeweler's window yesterday morning. Is there any chance you were followed? That the key was stolen while you were in a dressing room somewhere?''

She smiled outright while shaking her head. ''I seriously doubt it, officer. I lived in New York for four years. Whenever I'm on the street or in a store here, I'm extra vigilant about my bag. Then again, you asked if it is *possible*.'' She stopped to shrug.

She wasn't acting quite so guarded now. Jumbo knew some subjects to be naturally suspicious, habitually protective of their inner feelings. It often took longer for those people to get in sync with a particular investigator's line of inquiry. His misgivings weren't as strong as they were initially. She seemed less defensive, more available.

''I hear a man made a call to a radio station, officer. Has anything come of that?''

''Not as far as I've heard, no. Captain McKillip and his squad are investigating. Maybe they'll get lucky there. Nobody hopes it more than me.'' He thanked her for her time, said good night, and started for the door. Mrs. Mitchell followed, and while Jumbo was reaching for the knob she shifted gears again, becoming solicitous.

"The spot where I dropped my purse is at least five, maybe six blocks from this hotel, officer. I can't see how it's possible, but I hope I didn't inadvertently help a murderer gain access to Cora."

Jumbo gave her a consoling look as he shook his head. "It's too early to start losing any sleep over it. I think you're right. It *is* unlikely."

NINE

The first thing Dante noticed on entering Randy Logan's Tribeca loft was the art collection. Through his own associations outside the Job, Joe knew a thing or two about the artists on display there. He was impressed. He hadn't imagined a heavy metal singer would have such tastes. Then again, people were surprised to discover similar sensibilities in a certain New York City cop.

Logan looked less contrived than the image his posters projected, plastered above the bins at Tower Records and Sam Goody stores. He wore his shoulder-length hair pulled back and tied at the nape of his neck; no glitter, no sequins. He watched the way Dante cast an appreciative glance at a Blechner hung near the elevator and frowned, studying his guest.

"I'm bad with names, but I remember faces. We met once, didn't we, Lieutenant?"

Dante turned to face him. "Did we?"

"Yeah. Sorta in passing. A party or an opening or something. You're a friend of Diana Webster's."

"You *do* have a good memory."

"It sticks out in my recollection; probably because somebody mentioned Diana's got this friend who's a cop. I haven't seen her in months. You?"

"Just last night. We're neighbors. This is quite a collection."

"Thanks. We've had some good advice."

When Dante shrugged out of his coat, Logan offered to hang it.

"Just toss it over the back of a chair. Thanks." Joe stepped further into the vast living room. Outside west-facing windows the Hudson gleamed beneath the lights of Hoboken. Directly south, the twin towers of the World Trade Center seemed close enough to touch. The surrounding art, the view, and the prospect of dinner and sleep put Dante in a more relaxed state of mind than he'd been in all day.

"Tell me this isn't about my wife, Lieutenant."

Dante turned back to the singer, a frown knitting his brow. "Your wife? No. Why?"

Relief was evident in Logan's expression. "We had an, uh, incident here this afternoon. She left and I can't find her. I'm a little worried."

Dante resisted the temptation to pry. "Nothing about your wife, Mr. Logan. It's about the debate you participated in, yesterday afternoon. At the Park View."

"Oh Christ. Right. Cora Davis. I heard about it on the news. Real screw loose, that one. You got any idea what the hell happened?"

Rather than favor the rocker's query with a reply, Dante let the other shoe drop. "An elevator operator says you rode to the same floor the congresswoman was killed on. Sometime around two-thirty. You rode back down to the lobby right around the time she's believed to have left the reception for her room.

Just for an instant, Joe saw panic in the rocker's eyes. "When was that?"

"Sometime between three-fifteen and three-thirty. Is my information accurate?"

A shrug. "Sure. I mean, I guess."

"Someone you know staying on that floor?"

"That's right."

"You mind me asking who?"

Dante never let his eyes waver from his subject's during

this exchange. There was something unexpected going on here. Logan *knew* something.

"I'm wondering if I shouldn't have my attorney present, Lieutenant. Before this goes any further."

While maintaining his best, rock-steady poker face, Dante marvelled at how quickly an incidental bit of information could change the direction of an investigation. "Did you kill the congresswoman, Mr. Logan?"

The singer registered abrupt, shocked surprise. "Did *I*? Not hardly. We shook hands up there on the podium and that's the last I ever saw of her. Not even at the reception."

"Then why would you need an attorney?"

"Because it's maybe a little less clean-cut than it sounds."

"How?" Dante bore in. "If you know something material about a homicide, it's your duty as a citizen to reveal it. You *do* know something, don't you?"

Logan continued to look uneasy but was still determined to stand off. "About the murder? No. Not specifically."

"C'mon, Mr. Logan. One minute you're asking me if you should have your attorney present. The next, you're telling me you've got no cause to need him. Make up your mind."

Logan was having trouble maintaining his cool. Backed into a corner, he searched fruitlessly for an avenue of escape. "I suppose I could try to bullshit you . . ."

"*Don't*, Randy."

The last of the air in the singer's balloon seemed to come out as he sighed. "What the fuck?" he asked the ceiling. Then, with eyes lowered to his shoe tops, he shook his head in surrender. "The truth's bound to come out anyway, sooner or later. I'll wind up looking guilty of something I'm not."

Dante listened, fascinated, as Logan began relating some of the background behind his visit to Mrs. Mitchell's suite the day before. It was awhile before Randy got to the part about the two of them ending up in her bed. Joe stopped him there.

"Hold it a sec, Randy. You had no *idea* your old girlfriend would be there?"

"Complete surprise, Lieutenant. I swear. I didn't see her in the audience, probably because I showed a few minutes late. It blew me away when she wandered over and stuffed that note into my hand." He wore a pleading look now. "I know this can't look good, but I swear I never saw Cora Davis once the debate ended. A lot of my friends were at that reception. I imagine she had friends there, too. It was a big room."

"What about Mrs. Mitchell? Did she see Cora Davis again?"

"How would I know that, Lieutenant?"

For the few minutes it took Logan to relate the history of his romance with Mrs. Lyle Mitchell, he loosened up, spoke freely. Now Dante watched him retreat again. "You wake up this morning and hear about the murder of the woman you debated yesterday, killed in the same suite where you and your old flame were . . . uh, reunited. But you and Mrs. Mitchell haven't said 'boo' to each other since? C'mon, Mr. Logan. I'm a student of human nature on permanent fellowship. I thought you weren't gonna bullshit me."

Once again, Joe watched Logan make a decision. Randy took his time coming to it, mentally hitting all the dead ends before finally admitting defeat. "I guess I might as well give you everything."

"That would be wise."

"It's not like it sounds. It's just that I promised Lynnie I'd keep a lid on it long enough to give her time to think. You see, I'm being blackmailed."

He went on to reveal how a paparazzo named Brooks had followed him upstairs at the Park View and photographed him on the threshold of the homicide-scene suite. Brooks, on hearing the news of the murder, realized the potential value of what he had on film. He was turning the screws.

"I know Lynnie's already lied to you about where she was and who was with her," Logan concluded. "But that's pretty understandable. She's a senator's wife. When the shit hits the fan like that, self-preservation's a natural instinct."

"She's being squeezed by this guy, too?" Dante asked.

"Probably. He hadn't made his approach when I saw her today, but I expect he has by now."

"And you're sticking with your story that you left her behind in her suite?"

"It's the truth."

"Fine. It also means you've got nothing but her word for what transpired afterward, correct?"

Logan saw where Joe was headed and didn't like it. "Listen. She's changed since we used to hang out together, but I don't think she's changed *that* much. She's ambitious, sure. Always was. There's no doubt she wants to go *on* being a senator's wife. That's who she is now. But she wouldn't kill for it. No way."

"Maybe she didn't have time to think about it," Dante theorized. "Maybe Cora Davis saw you leaving and confronted her. Maybe your old girlfriend just reacted."

Logan snorted in derision. "Reacted, Lieutenant? Lyn Jennings has never *just reacted* in her life. She's way too calculating."

Dante thought back over his career and the lessons he'd learned concerning who is capable of what. He guessed that Logan would be surprised. On his arrival here he'd noticed two aluminum equipment cases and a garment bag stacked by the elevator. He gestured toward them now. "You planning a trip?"

"Those belong to my wife."

"Ah." Dante eased his hands into his pockets and sauntered over to stare out across the river. When he turned back from the view, Logan was idly sorting through a stack of CDs left out next to the sound system. "Looks like she left in a hurry."

"Uh-huh." Logan kept it neutral, his eyes averted. "I've probably got no right to ask it, but until you've got something concrete, could you go easy on Lynnie?" He looked up to make contact again. "I doubt she can avoid her husband finding out about all this, and that puts her up against it. A man like that is sure to throw her out. When he does, it's gonna be a long, hard fall.''

Dante nodded. ''If she's as innocent as you think, it's possible you can help us blunt this photographer's threat. Tell me what you know about him.''

Logan revealed what little he'd been able to ascertain by following the man that morning and later making a few phone calls. Dante jotted down the address on St. Mark's Place.

''I'm going to request a search warrant. It'd be nice if Brooks wasn't home when I got there. Too much opportunity to destroy evidence if he is.''

''What can I do to help, Lieutenant? Name it.''

''You told him to go fuck himself this morning, right? Well, after having some time to think about it, you could be having a change of heart.''

The instant he heard Randy Logan's voice on the phone, Troy Brooks knew he shouldn't have smoked that joint. He'd rolled it and absentmindedly smoked it more out of habit than anything else, but now the shit was making his mind do back flips. Cannabis didn't mix well with surprises, and this had been a day full of them.

Logan called to say he was having second thoughts. Troy couldn't put his finger on why, but right now he didn't trust Logan any further than he could see in a monsoon rain. All day he'd been plagued by the notion that Logan was out there digging to undermine him. When he delivered his extortion demand to the front desk at the Park View, it failed to supply the expected jolt of fresh optimism. Logan's showing up on his stoop that morning had set the day's tone. His voice had been full of challenge then, but now the man wanted to talk. Why this sudden shift?

The paranoia gripping Troy told him it was time to take precautionary measures. Logan wanted to meet at his place in Tribeca, but Troy didn't trust leaving the treasure behind at home. He needed to get those negatives hidden away in safekeeping. He caught a cab just fifteen minutes after breaking off with Logan, rode it to the south entrance of the Helmsley Building on 45th Street, and hurried through to 46th on foot. Ten minutes later he emerged from a second cab out front of Terry Dillingham's building on East 36th Street. Though the night was once again bitter cold, Troy hardly noticed. Inside his head the cannabis continued to distract him with its own agenda. A figure looming from behind a row of garbage cans all but stopped Troy's heart before he realized it was the same ornamental cedar he'd seen at least a hundred times. A cold sweat soaked the shirt beneath his sweater and overcoat as he depressed Terry's bell button.

On being admitted to Dillingham's ultracontemporary floor-through apartment, Brooks saw that Terry had guests. The same two aspiring models from last night's revelry at the Big City Diner now graced the living room divan. Nobody looked as though they'd slept since Troy last left them.

"Hey, ladies!" Dillingham called from the door. "Look who's here!" Terry seemed to be feeling little pain, a lack of sleep notwithstanding. There was a near-empty fifth of Jameson and a full bottle of Tanqueray on the coffee table next to a mirror dusted with the residue of an extended snort-a-thon. "Go ahead. Ask him. He'll tell you straight." Troy's pal closed the door behind them as he spoke and followed Brooks into the room. "They were arguing about who's got the hotter rep as a fashion photographer right now, Bruce Weber or Steve Meisel."

Troy took Dillingham by the elbow and drew him close. "See you in your bedroom a sec, amigo?"

Terry frowned for just a tick of the clock before focusing on his visitor's eyes. "Sure, buddy." He dug into his jacket pocket to withdraw a near-depleted sandwich bag of the main course and dumped another half gram onto the mirror. Before turning away from the women, he waved a hand over the mirror and gestured with great magnanimity. "Go ahead. Do yourselves. I'll convince Troy to join us for dinner, so think about what you want to eat. I'm feeling festive tonight."

No sooner did Dillingham have his bedroom door shut, isolating them, than he all but embraced Brooks in relief. "Jesus, am I glad to see *you*! Talk about a bad case of blue ball. I'll never score with *either* of these bitches unless you help split them up. They're hoovering me out of house and home."

Brooks's disgust was evident as he made a wry face. "You're a sap, compadre. If it was my whiff I'd take it back and tell them, they want more they've got to suck my dick for it."

Dillingham grimaced. "You're such a class act. If I wanted to *pay* for it I'd drive downtown a few blocks and throw twenty bucks."

"C'mon," Brooks remonstrated. "You're already paying for it—and a lot more than twenty bucks. First they snort up an eight ball and then you take them out somewhere expensive to eat. That your idea of *free* love?"

Dillingham grabbed at Troy's sleeve again. "Help me out, buddy. Ride shotgun."

Brooks withdrew an envelope from his inside jacket pocket. "Maybe later, amigo. Not right now. If they're still with you after dinner, we'll meet up. I've got business to take care of and I need you to hold something for me." He handed the envelope across. "In a safe place."

Dillingham took the envelope. "What is it?"

A self-satisfied grin spread across Troy's face. "You remember those pictures I told you about? Bingo, compadre. Bingo in the *main hall*. I've still got a couple of loose ends need tying up. That's why I've got to run." He watched Terry eye the envelope knowingly before tucking it beneath the socks in his top dresser drawer.

As they started from the room, Dillingham stepped close to whisper in Troy's ear. "You won't let me down tonight, right buddy? The brunette? Stacy? She's nice. You'll like her. And Tiffany makes me hard in places I didn't know could *get* hard. You take a good look at her?"

"Sure," Brooks drawled. "A world class ass and hooters from here to Sheboygan."

"So let the business wait a few hours. Strike while the iron is hot and bothered."

Troy snickered. "While I'm gone I want you to splash a little cold water in your face and look again. You still want it that bad, fine, but trust me—it ain't worth what you're paying. No way."

Chief Gus Lieberman was preparing to depart One Police Plaza after a long, pressure-filled day when Dante called him from downstairs, saying he was on his way up. It was little consolation knowing Joey had been at it as long and hard as he had. Still, dinner and a drink could wait. Right now Gus was hungrier for a development—*any* development—in the Davis homicide.

Dante entered with his overcoat slung over one arm and his tie loosened, an unexpected eagerness in his step. "Call Lydia and tell her don't wait dinner. You aren't gonna believe this."

Lieberman watched the coat go over one chair back as Dante took a seat alongside. There was something Gus always saw in his ace bloodhound when the man caught a scent. He was seeing it now. No amount of exhaustion could suppress it.

"I'll bet I've heard it all," Gus replied. "At one time or another. Try me."

"Yeah?" Dante let the mystery of the moment dangle out there like bait on a hook.

"What I *ain't* gonna do is play twenty questions with you, hotshot."

"Okay. Try this on for size. Senator Lyle Mitchell's beautiful young wife is Randy Logan's ex-girlfriend. Better yet, the two of them fucked yesterday in our homicide-scene suite."

"What?!"

Joey held up a hand. "Wait a minute. I'm not finished

yet." He went on to describe how Logan was followed upstairs by a scandal-peddling photographer named Brooks, and how Brooks subsequently hatched an extortion scheme. "I just talked to the owner of the restaurant the two of them met in this morning. He was there, Gus. He recognized Logan and says Randy had words with some heavyset guy in one of the back booths. Logan's claiming he told Brooks to go fuck himself."

Gus reached for the pack of smokes on the corner of his blotter. It helped calm him to pull a cloud of low-tar smoke deep into his lungs, but not as much as one of his old Lucky Strikes might. "I can't fucking believe Logan told you all this. So just answer me one question. How much of it do you *buy*?"

Dante made a face implying anything he said on the subject was still clouded with doubt. "He's in a tight spot if he *doesn't* tell me, Gus. And really, how bad could any publicity actually hurt him? I'm sure this isn't his first infidelity. His wife probably already has plenty on him, so why give in to Brooks on that count?"

"In other words, what's the threat here?"

"Exactly. Brooks made several assumptions that bear little or no relevance."

"And what about Mrs. Mitchell?" Gus asked. "So far as Logan knows, she ain't been approached?"

Joey nodded. "Not before he saw her today. He says she begged him to keep his mouth shut, give her time to figure her next move. Once I showed up and shook his tree, he decided that keeping a lid on it wasn't in his best interest."

"More evidence that chivalry *is* dead." Lieberman was glad Logan had talked to Dante, while the part of him that was still a kid from the old Bronx neighborhood hated an opportunist rat. He could see the tabloid headlines. A star entertainer like Logan was expected to get into trouble. Senator Lyle Mitchell had publicly indicted Logan and his ilk for undermining the foundations of American life. Logan screwing Lyndelle Mitchell would have the media licking their chops from coast to coast. Now, as Gus reviewed everything he'd been told, he kept running up against the same conclusion.

"You think Mrs. Mitchell's a suspect."

"USDA *prime*, boss." Dante's face became more animated as he leaned forward. "You're Lyndelle Mitchell, you've just finished fucking your old flame in the suite you're sharing with your husband's staunchest political ally. The old flame leaves and seconds later the staunch ally wanders in having witnessed the flame's exit."

"Be awkward," Gus admitted.

"No shit. Cora Davis was famous for her confrontations. Her type'll jump to a conclusion just to see what effect it has."

"Mrs. Mitchell panics," Gus finished it for him. "Whacks her with the handiest heavy object. The adrenaline's up and she makes sure she's done the whole job with a pair of the dead lady's panty hose. Motive. Opportunity. No evidence of forced entry because both parties had keys." He paused to think back over what he'd just said, a heavy foreboding now sitting tight across his temples. He reached to massage the area, the gesture having little effect on a sudden, fierce headache. "It's kinda convenient how Logan's managed to remove himself from the equation so nice and neat. It only works if you're willing to buy his story first."

"He's not exactly running away, Gus. Before I left Logan's loft I asked him to phone Brooks and invite him over there at eight o'clock for a little powwow. That means Brooks won't be *home* at eight." Dante shot a glance at his watch. "We've got less than two hours to get a search warrant."

Gus considered where Dante was headed and decided it was time to tap the brakes. "A word of warning here, Joey." It was spoken slowly. "I don't care if this broad is guilty as sin itself. She's a United States senator's wife. You smear shit on her and can't make it stick, it's more than your tin that Tony Mintoff'll want. He'll cut your dick off."

"Duly noted, boss. I'd be more than happy to see you

drop this particular bone in Wayne McKillip's lap, turn around, and walk away.''

Lieberman pulled in more smoke and let it back out in concert with a slow, head-shaking sigh. ''I don't think so. Wayne gets a wild hair growing sideways, I'm never a hundred percent sure he won't pick it in public. Officially, it's still gonna be his case. That'll keep you outta the media spotlight. Meanwhile, I'm gonna form a task force on the Q.T. We'll find you some desks downstairs in Special Investigations. Command-wise, you'll run it directly outta this office.''

''Okay. Let's say we manage to get hold of the evidence this photographer has. What next?''

Gus had already given that some thought. ''Extortion ain't murder, but it's still a felony rap. He'll cooperate if you can catch him cold. What other choice has he got? Sell his story to the *Enquirer* and sit in jail five years watching his interest grow?''

''So what are we waiting for?'' Dante heaved himself to his feet and grabbed his coat. ''If Brooks is willing to cut a deal, maybe we can set up some sort of sting. Rather than go straight at Mrs. Mitchell, we dangle bait and see how she plays it.''

''One step at a time, hotshot. First I call the judge.''

''Wrong, boss,'' Joey corrected him. ''First you call Lydia. *Then* you call the judge.''

With a half hour to spare before his scheduled meeting with Kagoshima, Billy Beaumont called Lyndelle Mitchell, asking her to meet with him in his room. He insisted the matter was urgent when she tried to beg off, claiming exhaustion. It amused him to see the petulant set of her mouth when she knocked, minutes later.

''What's so urgent that it can't wait until morning?'' she demanded. ''I thought you had important business.''

Beaumont held up an envelope with the flap torn. ''*This* is important business. I opened it by mistake; didn't notice who it was addressed to.'' In his work as the senator's chief of staff, Beaumont opened Lyle's mail routinely. Like it or not, Lyndelle had to buy his explanation as plausible.

She reached to snatch it from his hand, and as she read what was typewritten across its face, Billy watched her reaction.

''This is addressed to *me*.''

Trespass or no trespass, Billy occupied the high ground here. Rather than defend himself, he forged directly ahead. ''Read it.''

She opened the envelope while glaring at him and extracted its contents. God, he loved her high-strung thoroughbred quality. She was her Memphis-doctor daddy's girl through and through; all beautiful lines and spirited arrogance, just like the flat trackers he bred.

A brief letter accompanied two snapshot-size photographs. One glance at the pictures was enough to explain. Lyndelle was caught on the threshold of the suite she shared with Cora Davis. She was kissing a man unknown to Beaumont, full on the mouth. Mortified, Lyndelle looked up to confront Billy's frozen sneer.

''Who is he?'' the staff chief demanded.

Lyndelle proceeded to tear the photographs into small pieces and drop them fluttering to the carpet. Her posture assumed a pathetic defiance, shoulders squaring and eyes trying but failing to blaze. ''It's none of your goddamn business.''

Billy reached into the side pocket of his jacket to bring forth two more photos. He held these out of reach. ''I'll ask nicely, one more time, princess. Then I'll pick up the phone and call Guam.'' He gave that a few beats; time enough for it to sink all the way in. ''So. Who's the man you're kissing, and who took the pictures? I hate it when an artist doesn't sign his work.''

Lyndelle stared at the photographs in Billy's hand, her lower lip beginning to quiver. She was trapped and knew it.

"Troy Brooks." The name was spoken faintly, barely audible.

"Who? The guy with your hand on his ass?"

She shook her head, eyes squeezed shut. "The photographer. He's one of those people who makes his living taking pictures of the stars."

"*Both* names, princess."

Her eyes remained closed, and now she reached to pinch the bridge of her nose. "Can't we leave him out of this?"

"Sorry. A cardinal rule of crisis management demands I make a frank assessment of all factors. Accent on all. Who is he, Lyn?"

"Randy Logan."

The name stunned Beaumont. "Jesus *Christ*!"

Her eyes opened, her expression mocking now. "Lyle wouldn't approve of your using the Lord's name in vain like that, Billy."

"Fuck Lyle. He was thinking with his dick when he married you. Now look where it's gotten him."

Lyndelle had never seen this side of Billy, had never heard him talk like this to anyone, let alone her. He watched her eyes go wide, the rules of this combat suddenly clear. "How dare you!"

"Not quite enough vehemence in it, princess. And the way I'm looking at it, how dare *you*?" He prodded the scraps of paper littering the floor with the toe of one shoe. "The price he's asking is awfully high, with no mention made of turning over the negatives. I'd better handle these negotiations." He looked up. "How healthy's your bank balance?"

Her mouth opened and closed. No words came out. He smiled.

"I didn't *think* you could afford that heavy a hit. That means I'm gonna have to help you somehow, doesn't it."

When she stood there, speechless, his smile widened. Cruelty turned up its edges. "I didn't fit anyone with a pair of horns, lady. Like they say, you made your own bed."

Her chin started quivering, and her pale green eyes welled

with tears. Billy shook his head in disgust. "Crying's the cheapest female trick in the book, princess. Go work your wiles on some other sap." He stuffed his photographs back into his pocket and checked the time. "I don't know what plans you've got for tonight, but I strongly suggest you cancel them. Read the Good Book. Think about the error of your ways. I've got this circle-jerk with the Japs to dispense with and then I need some time to think. I should be back by midnight. Then you and I are going to talk again. Meet me here."

She'd gotten control of her tears but not her anger. "Read the Good Book? Coming from you, that's priceless."

He leaned close, the urge to slap her strong. For two years now she'd treated him like Lyle's lackey, but not anymore. "The Word doesn't strike your fancy, then try this: Try thinking of just one good reason I shouldn't make that call to Lyle."

Now *she* smiled. "One? I already have, Billy. We're both on this boat together. It's as much in your interest to play ball with this creep as it is in mine."

Beaumont stood his ground, his face just inches from hers. "How far can I fall, princess? I'm not a senator or a senator's wife. I've got an apartment in the District, a house on the Chesapeake, and a forty-six-foot sailboat, all paid for. I've got the cash to save your beautiful backside and a fair amount more, squirreled away all safe and dry." He showed her his teeth, all perfectly straight and bonded pearly white. His eyes held hers with a knowledge so dead certain there was no escaping it. "So let's get something straight between us, right here at the get-go, Mrs. Mitchell. You want to go *on* playing a senator's wife, you're *my* meat now."

TEN

As Troy Brooks's cab made the turn into Duane Street off Hudson, he was busy psyching himself up for the meeting ahead. Logan had caught him by surprise that morning, but he wouldn't do it twice. Troy had the goods. Troy had this egomaniac rocker and his girlfriend by the short hairs. He couldn't afford to let himself forget that.

"The one on the west corner," he told the cabbie.

The building he indicated was typical of those in the triangle below Canal Street and west of the Civic Center. Prior to 1970, most of them were homes to light manufacturing and small warehouse enterprises, handsome four and five story structures sitting squat beneath the looming spires of the financial district. Brooks knew that exterior appearances in this neighborhood often disguised interior realities. During the eighties, the young turks of Wall Street discovered they could live in spacious digs within walking distance of work while rubbing shoulders with fashion, art, and film-star neighbors. The money flooded in, a host of pricey restaurants sprang up, and living downtown became the hip thing to do.

Once he rang Logan's bell, Brooks was admitted to the lobby via an electronically controlled street door. The elevator car awaited him there on the ground floor, but as was typical in many of these setups, Troy had to wait for Logan to release the car from upstairs. The car itself was a beautifully restored old Deco job, its mahogany panels polished to a gleaming luster, the burnished stainless ornamentation scoured spotless. Troy was not surprised when, rather than opening onto a landing at Logan's floor, the door rolled back to reveal the interior of the rock star's loft.

"Wipe your feet, fuckhead." Logan, still dressed casually in rumpled chinos and work shirt, faced Troy directly from fifteen feet back of the threshold. The sprawling living room surrounding was hung with contemporary art. The floors were covered with expensive carpets, and a multitude of museum cases were laden with primitive ceramics. Brooks was not the least bit surprised by such trappings. Any media star worth his Jaeger–le Coultre wristwatch had an environmental cause he championed and collected art from at least one pricey period. Often several.

Troy was not intimidated, either by the greeting or the setting. Treasures of this sort were once his as well. He would have them again. Right now he had the upper hand. "Not to worry, amigo. You visit a man who shits on his own doorstep, you always wipe your feet."

Logan continued to glower. "That's good. I bet you keep all your loser friends in stitches."

Brooks sidestepped Logan with hands-in-pockets nonchalance to stand with his back to him while examining a moody suburban backyard scene by Eric Fischl. "*You* called *me*, Randy. And I'm breathless with anticipation."

Logan moved behind him, and Troy heard the squeak of leather as Randy took a seat, shifting to get comfortable. All the furniture in that part of the room was buttery-soft Italian stuff, cream colored and slick chic.

"I'll bet you think I've had a change of heart."

Troy turned, impatient to get past all this posturing and down to business. "If you asked me here just to jerk my chain, I'm gone as quick as I got here."

Logan had the gall to grin at him. To leer, in fact. "You're the only one jerking anything, Troy. Joke that it is. You were sucker enough to come when I called, and that's the second mistake you made today. The first was picking me to mess with.'' Randy stretched out his legs, crossed them at the ankles, and locked his fingers behind his head. ''No change of heart, amigo. I called you here as a favor to a Detective Lieutenant Dante, NYPD. He and a whole bunch of New York's finest should be arriving on St. Mark's Place right about now—to tear your apartment apart.''

Brooks cursed himself as his heart rate jumped involuntarily. The son of a bitch was baiting him. ''Bullshit, Randy. You want me to believe you called the cops?''

''Nope.'' Logan's voice was low and smug. ''The lieutenant called *me*. My calling you, inviting you here? *His* idea.''

A wave of confusion threatened to knock Troy's confidence on its backside. What sort of game was this guy playing?

Logan clicked his tongue and wagged his head in disgust. ''I'm afraid you assumed too much, Brooks. You assumed you were the only one who saw me upstairs at the Park View yesterday, and you assumed wrong.''

This was a ruse of some sort. It had to be. A desperation ploy. Troy knew he shouldn't be so easily put on the defensive. He reminded himself again that the high ground was his. ''I'm quaking like a leaf in a breeze, Randy. Let me guess. You told this cop everything—that you screwed the senator's wife and that I'm putting the squeeze on you. Oh, and of course . . .'' He snapped his fingers. ''You don't know fuck-all about who killed the congresswoman.''

Logan slid even lower into the sofa and lifted one leg to hook a heel over the edge of the cocktail table. ''Close enough. I bet you were a whiz with grade school arithmetic.''

Troy's anger, smoldering until now, suddenly burned bright. He took a threatening step toward Logan, his face gone hot with rage. ''You think you can blow me off this easily, you're mistaken, pal! How fucking stupid do you think I am? You make up some bullshit story around some cop's name you got off the news and expect me to *swallow* that shit? Nice try, asshole! For you, the price just went up a hundred grand.''

As Brooks started for the elevator, Logan swung his feet around to plant them and clicked his tongue in disapproval. ''You're *sure* it's bullshit? Absolutely sure? Because I know for a fact that Lieutenant Dante is tearing your place apart right now. Why not call home and see who picks up?'' He dug into his pocket for a quarter and flipped it in Troy's direction. ''There's a booth on the corner of Duane and Hudson. Now get the fuck outta here. I'm sick of looking at you.''

While Troy, his confidence being rapidly devoured by doubt, stepped onto the threshold of the elevator car, Randy reached to key the release. Brooks wasn't watching, but stared instead at the quarter he'd caught involuntarily. The surprise of a sudden movement to his left caught him flat-footed. He instinctively raised an arm to cover up against a blind-side sucker punch, but to no avail. The lead hand was a feint. Randy guessed Troy's reaction perfectly and put all the shoulder he could muster behind his other fist. It landed on Brooks's wide-open midsection with an audible thud, the muscles beneath the area of impact caught relaxed. Troy was forced a step backward, the wind pushed abruptly from his lungs. Only the jamb of the elevator door prevented him from going all the way down. Instead, he managed to keep his feet beneath him and parry a right cross aimed at his head.

A red haze filmed Troy's vision, but surprisingly, he found himself thinking with adrenaline-sharpened clarity. He twisted away from the elevator entrance, still sucking hard for air, and backpedaled clumsily for a piece of open room. With the success of his initial attack, Logan couldn't resist pressing the advantage. He had Troy on the ropes, and right now Troy knew he couldn't sustain another shot like that first one. Pure animal instinct decided his strategy. He was bigger than Logan by at least three inches and forty pounds. He was in pretty fair shape. As Randy moved in, Troy gave up his panicked quest for air, shook his head hard to clear his vision, and came on throwing haymakers.

Logan wasn't expecting a sudden change in the tide of battle. In pressing his advantage he left himself wide open to a counteroffensive and caught a solid right hand to the temple. The force of impact sent a sharp, stabbing pain clear to Troy's elbow, but he was on automatic pilot now. He'd staggered Logan enough to affect his concentration. It allowed him to slip a second punch past Randy's guard. This time, as he buried a fist deep into Logan's belly, he could smell the panic set in. Randy doubled up while trying desperately to cover against a crushing right thrown at his sternum. Troy slipped Logan's guard and landed that punch square. It straightened Randy back up and sent him crashing into a museum case crammed with pre-Columbian ceramics. Now, as Brooks hurried forward in pursuit, his wind came rushing back. He suddenly felt invincible.

The boot heel Logan threw was a lucky, fluke shot. It smashed Troy's shin, the pain of it blinding. It didn't seem possible that Logan could have much fight left, but in a surprising show of resilience, Randy was suddenly on his feet. He circled free of the display case debris, his face alight with pleasure as he watched Troy limp in pursuit.

"No more surprises, fuckhead," Logan growled. "Just you and me, straight up. You wanted this shot for ten years, right? So come on. Take it."

To assist him in conducting the search of the extortionist's East Village residence, Dante requested Gus Lieberman assign him four detectives from his former Major Case Squad command. All four had left the Big Building by the time the call went out. There were hundreds of other detectives already at work on the four-to-midnight throughout the five boroughs and available, but Joe had handpicked these people for Special Investigations after poring over a mountain of files. The brass in the P.C.'s office would no doubt see taking so many bodies out of one unit as disturbingly unorthodox.

Then again, the mayor was making this case the Job's number one priority, and it was Dante's baby now. He wanted the best. All day, Gus Lieberman had been fielding media, Big Building brass, and City Hall heat. On this particular evening he would have given his task force whip the moon and stars.

Dante had the duplex apartment on St. Mark's Place divided up into sectors, with each pair of partners taking an equal share of the load. Detective Sergeants Donald Grover and Rusty Heckman were currently at work in the suspect's upstairs office. Just across the way from them, Detectives Melissa Busby and Guy Napier were tearing apart the master bedroom. Joe and Jumbo Richardson had the makeshift darkroom in the downstairs bath. Their search warrant permitted the confiscation of certain materials, and rather than sort through thousands of negatives in the photographer's files, the partners loaded them into boxes for future scrutiny. That task complete, Beasley was left to search through loose items on the darkroom shelves and hunt for hiding places. Meanwhile, Joe departed to check in with the others.

Napier and Melissa were both on their hands and knees examining the underside lip of a huge pedestal bed when Dante arrived upstairs. The Op Desk had located them at their Queens gym, and they were still dressed in workout clothes. Melissa had a tendency to carry weight, and Dante was impressed with how much leaner and harder she looked since Guy had coaxed her into joining him in his daily workouts. Today she was a bona fide gym rat.

"No luck, huh?" he asked.

"Check out that closet," Napier's muffled voice suggested.

Nicknamed "Boy Wonder," the baby-faced redhead was just twenty-eight years old and by far the youngest detective assigned to Special Investigations. He was also huge, at six foot six and weighing two hundred twenty pounds. His head now emerged from beneath the side rail of the bed. "What I want to know is how some clown on a free-lance photographer's income got a wardrobe like that."

Dante turned to the meticulously organized contents of a closet running the length of one entire wall. The triple by-passing doors were all pushed to the left, revealing an expanse of hi-lo closet poles, a couple of dozen pairs of shoes on racks, a short span of full-length hanging space, shirt and sweater cubbies, and a tie rack hung with a plethora of garish neckwear.

"Man seems to like his threads," he observed.

Napier heaved himself to his feet and crossed to remove a cream-colored suit from the upper rack. "Not just any threads, Lou. In high school, I worked in the stockroom at Barney's. Over two years, I developed something of an eye for threads like these—not that I thought I'd ever be able to *afford* them. Valentino. Gieves and fucking Hawkes. *Three* Burberry raincoats. Missoni sweaters. A dozen Hermes ties and at least that many more Armanis. And the fucking shoes! Beltrami, for Christ's sake. Gucci loafers. The leather in the shoe rack alone set this mutt back twenty-five, thirty large."

Dante lifted a pair of oxblood Tanio Crisci loafers from the rack and noticed the degree of wear sustained by the soles and heels. Several scuffs in the toes had been polished over and buffed. Other pairs of shoes were in much the same condition, all a bit down at the heels. Then he realized how few of the ties hung on the rack reflected current trends. He took a closer look at the suit Napier held in one hand and saw the streamlined cut of the lapels. Each year European designers subtly changed the cut of their clothes: lapel widths, vent configurations, and jacket lengths. Dante didn't have the benefit of Napier's stockroom experience, but he did have enough of an eye to know most of Troy Brooks's wardrobe was at least five years out of date.

"It fits with what Logan told me about this guy," he concluded. "Ten years ago he was this wunderkind writer who made a lot of money and later saw his career go down the shitter. Wrote some unpublishable garbage that got him in hot water. The entire industry blackballed him. Logan says that when Brooks's wife filed for divorce she took what was left of him to the cleaners.''

Melissa crawled out from her inspection of the pedestal bed to join them. Together, they let their eyes wander the room. As her attention returned to Joe, she nodded knowingly. "I knew there was something struck me as odd when I walked in here. Now I know what it is. I feel like I've taken a ride back eight years in a time machine. The clothes, the chrome-and-glass furniture, king-size pedestal bed, monster sound system, swivel-base television, everything color coordinated clear down to the fabric wallpaper and matching bath towels. It's investment-banker chic, circa 1985.''

"We went through the pockets of every garment in that closet," Napier reported. "Checked the toilet tank in the bath, the medicine cabinet, bedclothes and mattress, behind outlet covers, you name it. Where next?''

"I want you two in the kitchen," Dante directed. "Same drill. I'll see what Don and Rusty are up to.''

As they started from the room, Melissa paused ahead of Joe to glance around one last time. "That first book he wrote? *Lip Service?* I *liked* it.''

"Only saw the movie," Dante admitted.

They parted company at the top of the stairs, with Joe starting down the hall toward the suspect's office.

Troy Brooks, his body aching and face swollen after the brawl with Randy Logan, decided not to assist Terry Dillingham in the seduction of his models. There was nothing further from his mind than sex right now. All he wanted was a tumbler of Stoly over ice and a long, hot soak in the tub.

It was squalling tiny bits of hard-frozen snow as Troy's cab eased up out front of his building on St. Mark's Place. Alerted to the possibility of a police presence, he elected to play his approach cautiously. For all he knew, Logan had lured him away from him to enable his own B & E man to search the premises. From the interior of his cab, Troy craned his aching neck to inspect the windows on both floors upstairs. He'd left the place dark, save for a single lamp burning in the entry hall, and now he found it ablaze with light. Adjacent to the front stoop he spotted three sedans of a similar make and model double-parked along the curb. Damn. Logan *hadn't* been bullshitting him!

"Uh, pull up another hundred feet, will you?" he asked the driver.

Per earlier instruction, the cabbie hadn't come to a complete stop or shut off his meter. He let it glide another two doors down, where Brooks had to struggle to wedge his bruised carcass out onto the pavement. His hands shook while collecting his change and stuffing it into his wallet. As he started stiffly down the row of cars parked curbside he gave himself a pep talk, trying to convince himself that the shakes were generated by residual adrenaline from the fight and not fear.

The wind blew accumulated ice crystals into crescent patterns across the pavement and bit at Troy's ears as he tugged up the collar of his coat. Pretending to check traffic, he stepped into the street and drew abreast of the first double-parked sedan. Just as he suspected, the car contained an under-dash mounted radio with handset. The floorboards were littered with paper cups. Straightening, he continued on across to the opposite curb to loiter and scrutinize the facade of his building. After a minute or two of observing the shadows of movement behind drawn shades on both floors, he decided that—battered condition notwithstanding—hooking up with Dillingham would be preferable to returning home right now. He could claim he'd been mugged; maybe generate enough sympathy to get some help ministering to his wounds.

The idea of Terry's models helping Troy into a tub evoked an involuntary chuckle. He wished it hadn't. His ribs, down low on the right side, screamed in protest. "Fat chance," he muttered into the night.

ELEVEN

Delmonico's, situated just two blocks east of the Park View on Park Avenue, was only half-full that Wednesday night. Nancy Hillman was grateful for the privacy this circumstance afforded her and Jerry Davis. Jerry rarely consumed alcoholic beverages in public, but in his current state he deemed a therapeutic glass of wine or two appropriate. Nancy agreed. Davis was having a terrible time dealing with his wife's passing. He needed to stop wallowing in self-deprecation and seek out a healthier perspective on his grief. If the wine helped him toward that end, she fully intended to order a second bottle.

Nancy had known Jerry and Cora for all of her ten years in politics. Cora Davis was her first client when she quit her job as a twenty-five-year-old advertising whiz kid to create political campaigns. Cora, up against her toughest competition in a decade, was foundering badly in the polls. She'd been looking to clean house, throw open the windows, and benefit from Nancy's very conservative but youthful perspective. Over the years of subsequent collaboration, Nancy was allowed glimpses into the relationship between the congresswoman and her televangelist husband. She knew that not all of it was as rosy as they would have the world imagine.

Nancy believed Jerry had married Cora because he admired her strength. He hoped she might assist him in pursuit of his own purposes—and the purposes of the Lord—with greater vigor. Nancy doubted that Davis had ever been in love with Cora; not in that consensual sense that true lovers take for granted. She knew that Cora found sex distasteful. She also knew that Davis had eventually looked elsewhere for his pleasures of the flesh. It always seemed odd to Nancy that Cora, as obsessed as she was with the evidence of men's carnal transgressions, never seemed to suspect her own husband's extramarital philanderings. Had Cora known and simply chosen not to address it? Or was she so completely asexual that suspicions of that nature never crossed her mind? Nancy suspected that Jerry was being tortured by guilt right now. While alive, Cora's shortcomings were merely a dilemma. Dead, she made any failures between them his. Alone.

"You've gone far away tonight, Jerry."

He looked up from toying with his shrimp appetizer, his face forlorn. "My wife is lying in some anonymous stainless steel drawer with her skull crushed. In the bowels of a building administered by a city she despised."

"Some lunatic did that to her, Jerry. Why are you blaming yourself?"

"Because I wasn't there."

She had no reply. Was he implying that if he'd been in New York yesterday, Cora would still be alive? That was possibly true, but it was academic. Jerry needed to move forward, and that was one of the things she wanted to discuss with him tonight.

Their waiter broke up any awkwardness Nancy saw in steering the conversation away from Jerry's wallowing. He delivered their entrées. Nancy decided that ordering a second bottle of wine wasn't a bad idea after all. She asked to see the list again and surveyed it while the waiter poured out what remained for their first selection. Jerry was allowed no opportunity to dive back into his pool of self-pity once the waiter departed.

"There's something I think you should know about, Jerry." She held her wineglass raised and watched the way candlelight glowed shimmering in the claret's ruby depths. She was a failed Baptist in this one regard. She loved a fine red wine.

"What's that?" His tone was distracted.

"It isn't an altogether pleasant story, and I hate to trouble you with it at a time like this, but I need your advice."

The reverend toyed with a chunk of meat carved from an immense porterhouse steak. He frowned and set his fork down. "Please. You obviously think it's important."

Nancy proceeded to reveal the essence of her conversation with Lyndelle during the limo ride to the airport. Lyn's poor judgment hit home even harder, seeing it reflected in Jerry's expression. It wasn't astonishment she saw on his face so much as disbelief. Confounded, gaping disbelief.

"Her father *is* heavily invested in a breeding syndicate. I know that for a fact, Jerry. It's something Lyle likes to keep swept under the carpet—her father's whole involvement with horses in general and pari-mutuel racing in particular. It was a stupid thing to do, letting that man into her suite, but the premise seems legitimate enough."

Davis sat for an uncomfortably long period of time, his gaze lowered to his plate once again. He toyed with the rim of his wineglass and took several slow, measured breaths. Nancy watched the way those short, beautifully manicured fingers seemed to quiver ever so slightly as they moved. "You're saying you don't believe she had any involvement in Cora's death?"

"Lyn?" Surprise lifted Nancy's voice almost an octave.

"She was in the suite with a strange man. Cora could well have misconstrued the nature of Logan's visit."

"Lyndelle claims they never saw each other. Her story checks with the time the police say Cora left the reception. She *did* have a four o'clock fitting appointment at Bergdorf's and did stop by Harry Winston on the way. I think we're losing track of the point here."

Davis frowned as he looked up again. "Oh? And what *is* the point?"

He obviously couldn't think clearly in his stricken state. Nancy sat hard on a surge of exasperation and moved to lead him there as gently as she could manage. "A photographer took pictures and is threatening to implicate Lyn in the manner you just did. If he's allowed to do so, and the media jumps to all the predictable, sordid conclusions, we've got a crisis on our hands."

"We?"

She nodded, her face frozen as solemn as a burial mask. "Think about it. The people of Tennessee would laugh Lyle Mitchell right out of office. Cora's decency campaign—*your* decency campaign—has no greater champion than Lyle. Any inferred sexual connection between the man your wife debated yesterday and Lyle's wife would put your work and Cora's in very real jeopardy."

Jerry scoffed. "That's quite a stretch, isn't it?"

She remained dead serious. "I don't think so. Guilt by association is as American as General Motors."

Davis picked up his fork and jammed a piece of steak into his mouth. He chewed furiously and swallowed too quickly. "Just what do you propose to do? This extortionist is sure to approach Lyndelle as well. And *then* what? Will you encourage her to pay him?"

Nancy hoped her impatience was evident. She placed her hands on the table and came slightly forward. "I propose we look at the bigger picture, Jerry; that we look for solutions that will endure over the long run. Think about what you and Cora were trying to accomplish. Are you willing to see that effort set back indefinitely?" In the quiet of the restaurant, with only the occasional noise of flatware on china and a muffled laugh to fill the void between them, Nancy waited for his response. When none was forthcoming, she forged ahead. "Your voter association with Cora and your own political history could make you an ideal candidate for governor now, Jerry."

It hit him flush, making him blink as his mouth searched for words. "Me?" was all he could manage.

"Think about it a minute. There's no question that you've got the charisma; that your platform has statewide appeal. There isn't a soul in Tennessee who doesn't know who you are. As chair of the state committee, I'm up against it right now. I've got an election just eleven months away, and last night I lost the only viable name the party had in the hat."

"The loving husband of martyred Congresswoman Cora Davis?" he asked bitterly. "That *is* the sort of campaign you have in mind, correct? It's shameless, Nancy. Vulgar."

"Is it?" She lifted her glass to sip again and hoped their waiter would arrive soon to open the next bottle. Neither she nor Davis had much from the first left anymore. "Why, Jerry? Because you don't really believe in the same decent American ideals Cora embraced? Because you weren't *here* yesterday? Please. You spent eight hours on the phone with congressmen who can either pass or kill Cora's prayer-in-school legislation, and you talk like you were playing golf."

Davis sawed off another chunk of steak, stuffed it into his mouth, and when he spoke, he talked around his food, waving his fork back and forth. "Forget about it, Nancy."

"I can't. The more I think about it, the more I like it."

"There's still another issue on the table. Are you suggesting we impede a murder investigation?"

"I don't know. Am I? I mean, in *fact*?"

"We would be witholding information."

Nancy hated this one thing about him—this dogged, letter-of-the-law persistence. "Maybe we can work a compromise there."

He was instantly suspicious. "And how might we do that? Either we tell the police or we don't."

Nancy saw an opening develop right where she intended. The political animal in her breathed a sigh of relief. Jerry might be resisting, but he wasn't wallowing in self-pity any longer. She'd gotten his mind off a destructive track and onto a worth-affirming one. He knew as well as she did that his work and Cora's work was far from finished. "I still don't believe that Lyn had anything to do with Cora's murder, but you're right. The police should know about her presence in that suite yesterday, along with Mr. Logan's. The problem we're confronted with is *when* we report it.''

Davis drained his wineglass and returned it to the table more violently than he probably intended. Nancy was surprised the stem didn't snap. ''I can see where you're headed, and it's out of the question.''

Nancy kept her tone reasoning, but added urgency now. ''Please, Jerry. Think about it a moment. As long as Lyle remains married to Lyn, she's a liability. Do we let her destroy him, or do we buy the time he'll need to face facts? The election is eleven months away. If the police haven't solved Cora's murder by the time the vote is counted, we can leak what we know to them. By that time you'll be governor-elect and Lyle will have safely distanced himself from Lyndelle.''

It was eleven o'clock when Don Grover and Rusty Heckman got word that Dante was calling off the search of Troy Brooks's apartment. It had been frustrating. While other members of the hastily assembled task force team concentrated on the rest of the duplex layout, Don and Rusty worked their way no farther afield than the suspect's upstairs office. Like the rest of his abode, the office was pin neat, with all the appropriate gear: personal copier, fax machine, console desk phone, IBM PC, daisy wheel printer, black lacquer and chrome desk, matching file cabinets. Beneath the surface, they found chaos. The desk drawers were rats' nests of folders without labels, rubber bands, loose paper clips, various electronic office gadgets—most with dead batteries—and a jumble of photographic proof sheets. The file cabinets contained more of the same: Pendaflex files jammed with papers and proof sheets, in no apparent order.

Grover had given up sorting through the mess in the desk drawers and had spent the better part of two hours running Brooks's computer disk file through the PC. When Guy Napier delivered the word, Don pushed back from the screen and rubbed his face. Rusty dumped a load of files, whole-sale, back into a file cabinet drawer.

"You as disgusted as I am?" Heckman growled. He slammed that drawer and rose holding the small of his back.

"At least."

"Nothing there either?"

Grover motioned toward the open disk file. "Ninety per-cent of these things? Fucking video games. What is it, Rust? Doesn't anybody in this city actually work anymore?"

Heckman gave the question the shrug it deserved and crossed to perch on the corner of the desk. Slowly, he surveyed the terrain they'd just combed over. "Nice tools, though."

"Just peachy. While we're forced to hack out reports on thirty-year-old manuals, this creep plays games on equipment I'd give my left nut for."

Heckman patted the printer at his hip. "Hard to believe a techno-junkie like him never went laser, huh?" The rig was an Okidata daisy wheel unit that had to be ten years old. State-of-the-art technology in that realm was laser-jet now.

Grover scowled at the machine, a fresh sheaf of paper in its feed tray and nothing in the carriage. "Wait a sec," he murmured. "Wait a fucking second here." He came slowly out of the black leather swivel-base chair to lean across and flip open the printer's top access panel. Beneath, the print wheel and ribbon cartridge mechanism sat exposed. "I can't believe it's been right here staring at me, all this time."

"What has?" Heckman demanded. He'd wondered if maybe there was something in the carriage that they'd missed. It was empty.

"The ribbon. It's speculation that he wrote this twist an extortion note, but if he did, he sure as shit didn't *hand* write it. Not with all this gear he's got." Grover paused to smile up at Rusty, his eyes bright with excitement.

"Yeah?" Heckman wasn't following.

"The ribbon is a film," Grover reminded him. There was impatience in his tone now. "This moron types his extortion

117

demand onto his PC, edits it, prints it out, and then wipes the data base clean. All evidence of him having written it is gone, right? *Wrong.* You said it yourself. This old Okidata rig is yesterday's technology.'' He jerked the ribbon cartridge from the carriage, held it up beneath Rusty's nose, and pointed to an inch or so of exposed ribbon film. The portion that hadn't advanced through the impact zone where characters were transferred from print wheel to page was a uniform, flat black. The ribbon beyond bore a parade of characters in negative.

"You're a fucking genius, Donnie," Heckman marveled.

"Maybe, maybe not. Tomorrow morning, once we get enough sleep so we can see straight, we'll tear this sucker apart and transcribe it. Maybe we didn't strike out here after all.''

It was a defeated and slightly drunk Lyndelle Mitchell who knocked on Billy Beaumont's door at quarter past twelve. She knew exactly why Billy demanded that she return at this ungodly hour. All evening she'd searched for some means of escaping this inevitability. Twice before, once as an aspiring model looking for her big break and again as a commercial real estate saleswoman in Memphis, she'd crawled into bed with men for the sole purpose of personal gain. Both of those men had been far less attractive than Billy, at least when she first met him four years ago. It was at a Washington cocktail party, and Billy had seemed almost dashing with his gallant flattery. That was also the night Lyndelle met Lyle and became the object of his obsessive campaign to sweep her off her feet. In the years since, Billy became less and less attractive, wearing his anger and resentment out where she couldn't fail to see it. Her marriage to Lyle was the final affront. She'd rejected Billy's advances and alienated his closest friend's affections.

Billy answered her knock dressed in pajamas and a robe, his expression full of icy impatience. "I thought I said midnight, princess. Where the hell you been?''

She pushed past without answering, shrugged out of her coat, and threw it over the back of the floral print settee. Chin lifted in defiance, she began unbuttoning her blouse. "Kill the lights, will you? They're hell on my stretch marks and cellulite."

Billy went rigid. "Wait a minute. What do you . . ."

"What? Think I'm *doing*?" Her blouse unbuttoned, Lyndelle tugged the tails free of her slacks and stripped it back from her shoulders. She stood facing him in her bra, pants, and boots. Perhaps her shrug was a touch too melodramatic, but to hell with it. There was nothing subtle about this game. "I'm getting ready to fuck you, Billy. That *is* what you want, isn't it? For me to get down on my knees in surrender and suck your dick, right? Fine. Just kill a few of these lights."

He hadn't moved since closing the door. "I asked you where you've been."

She stooped to tug her boots off as she answered. "I went out. What was I supposed to do? Sit cooped up here all night, waiting breathless for you to elaborate on how I'm your meat now? Believe me, I got it, straight up front, Billy." After the boots she began to work out of the slacks, freeing the waistband button, tugging the fly zipper down, and hooking thumbs to wriggle them past her hips and ass. She stepped out of one leg and stared at Beaumont in puzzlement. "What? You're going to stand there like a cigar store Indian all night? You've *won*. For years you've played the loyal schmuck who danced while Lyle tugged the strings, but not anymore. You've got the knife and fork now and I *am* your meat. So let's get this over with."

Lyndelle saw the fury in his eyes as Beaumont ignored the lights and started forward. Maybe she'd pushed him too hard. She stepped free of her trousers and reached to unhook her brassiere.

"Get it *over* with? Sorry, princess. That's a whore trick. I want a hum-job and a handshake, I'll call the friendly, accommodating bell captain." Stopping just short of her, he loosened the sash of his robe and removed it. Then came his

119

pajama shirt. Starting with the bottom button, he worked his way to the top. Lyndelle was swept with a wave of revulsion as he revealed the thick, matted white hair of his broad, exercise fanatic's chest. "You're in this for the slightly longer haul," he assured her. "Over with, my ass. An hour before I'm finished with you, you'll be begging me to stop."

He took a step toward her, one of his thick-fingered hands extended to take a breast in his palm. "Your husband likes to brag about your genuine, world-class titties. Did you know that, princess? Proud as hell of these jugs, he is. I can't say as I blame him." His thumb and forefinger closed around her nipple to caress it, gently at first and then more roughly, until he was pinching it.

"Billy, please," she complained through clenched teeth. "You're hurting me."

"Am I?" He released her breast and let his hand drop once again to his side. Then, without warning or provocation, he drove his fist into her solar plexus, sending her gagging to her knees.

Diaphragm frozen, Lyndelle knelt trying to get her wind with the panicked desperation of a drowning victim, while Billy stooped to whisper into her ear. "Let's get something straight right here at the start. You think you can screw me and mind-fuck me at the same time, you insult my intelligence. You're gonna fuck me all right, but on *my* terms."

Lyndelle's breath came back so suddenly she choked. For what seemed like forever she remained on all fours, her stomach heaving and chest shuddering as she was wracked with a fit of retching. When it finally ceased, she saw that Billy had backed off a few paces. He'd lost his pajama pants now and stood naked before her.

"Right where you are is fine for the time being," he growled. "You got our agenda clear now?"

Lyndelle nodded and began to sob, tears breaking to roll down her cheeks.

"Good." His voice was softer but no less demanding. "Crawl a little closer."

* * *

Toby the cat was too relaxed for having been left alone all day. When Dante entered his half-finished loft from the elevator and slipped out of his coat, the little guy barely glanced up from his nap on the sofa. Once Toby saw it was only the boss dragging ass-weary through his domain, he wedged his head back beneath one paw to continue his slumber. Joe was always surprised to see how little the cat was incapacitated by his deafness. His response to other stimuli made it seem as though Toby could hear—the vibration of the elevator, the rumble of the mesh gate being rolled back, footsteps.

Inspection of the kitchen feeding station solved the mystery of the cat's indifference. Joe's neighbor Diana had been down to make sure there was food in the bowl. When Dante was away for more than his usual shift, she often took the cat upstairs for a few hours. Toby, not yet a year old, had most of his size but was still a kitten at heart. He craved a lot more attention than he'd gotten from the boss these past couple days.

His current state of exhaustion notwithstanding, Dante knew it would be at least an hour before he could unwind enough to fall asleep. He grabbed a beer, slipped one of Jumbo's jazz tapes into the cassette deck, and sat back to contemplate the raw warehouse condition of his living room. The kitchen beyond, like one of the two baths and both bedrooms, had been completed for five months now. Then, back before Christmas, he had taken a long-overdue vacation. Since his return he'd been kept so busy on the Job that he'd had no time to pick up a hammer. At this rate he could be in a walker before construction resumed.

Dante heard the thump of something dropped on the floor overhead. Either someone was breaking in or—more likely—Brennan was working late in his studio. When he dragged the phone close and dialed, the sculptor picked up on the second ring.

"What?"

"Heard you thumping around. Diana still up?"

"Uh-huh. Where the hell'd you disappear to last night?"

"Police business."

"Ah. *That's* what we're calling it now. Hang on."

Dante heard a muffled holler as Brennan called his wife to the phone. Diana picked up almost instantly. "Saw you on the news tonight, copper. I hope you're getting rich, working all that overtime, because it's doing nothing for your boyish good looks."

"Boyish?" He grunted it deadpan. "You got a sec? I need to pick your brain." She'd never mentioned being particularly close to Randy Logan, but the two of them moved in the same world and had known each other back in their bread-without-butter days. Right now, the whole thrust of his investigation was being aimed at Mrs. Lyle Mitchell, based on information Logan had passed along. Dante wanted to know more about his source. Every avenue of inquiry had a front door and a back door. It paid to identify both.

There was an audible sigh from Diana's end of the line. "Just answer me one question first. Why do the dweeby little midgets of the world send me naked pictures of themselves and beg me to have their babies, while men like you are only interested in my mind?"

"That's *two* questions," he replied. "And who says it's only your mind I'm interested in?" The Queen of Beasts vocalist had met Brennan while working as an artist's model. She was Brian's inspiration for a series of high-definition bronze nudes that made his reputation. She had a quirky, interesting face that she thought was plain, and a body that made red-blooded men gape, short and tall alike.

"You want me to come down?" she asked.

"Stay there. I may look like shit on TV, but I can still climb stairs."

Located on the corner of West 27th Street and Eleventh Avenue, the building Dante lived in was something Brennan bought after a divorce six years ago. His ten-thousand-square-foot top floor was divided into work and living spaces, the business end housing drawing and fabrication studios. Joe skipped the elevator and arrived at the back door, finding it left slightly ajar. He pushed his way inside to find his sculptor buddy hunched over a bench vise, the body grinder in his hands sending a shower of sparks falling over the toes of his work boots. Brennan switched off and straightened, lifting his face shield as Dante approached.

"Damn, Joe. You look like . . ."

"I know," Dante cut him off. "Shit. Thanks. Good to see you, too. I'm just tired."

"The queen fed the cat. Didn't know when you'd be home. Any luck catching the crazy who whacked the congresswoman?"

Joe was hit by a yawn that jacked his jaw open as wide as the mouth of the Lincoln Tunnel. He covered up and shook his head. "Your luck's hard to measure until you actually land the prize. Lotta legwork today. Maybe a little headway. Nobody's got his wrists out, begging us to slap on the cuffs."

Diana Webster appeared through the door at the far end of the cavernous fabrication shop. Joe registered surprise as she worked her way around chain hoists, an arc welder, and a plethora of woodworking and machine tools. As usual, she was dressed casually, tonight in baggy gray sweatpants and one of Brennan's faded blue work shirts, the tails knotted at the navel. Now, as she kissed him, Dante marveled at the change that was hidden by last night's Mardi Gras headdress.

"You cut your hair."

"With a weed whacker, by the look of it," Brennan grumbled.

Diana turned up her nose and patted her mop of short, unevenly cut dirty blond hair. "Marcel thinks it highlights the bone structure of my face." She planted palms on the workbench behind her and hoisted herself atop it with an athletic grace. "So what's on your mind, copper? You should be home in bed."

Brennan eyed the near-empty beer bottle in Dante's hand and wandered off to pull two more from the shop fridge. Joe drained his remaining suds, set his empty on the bench beside Diana, and folded his arms. "I met an old friend of yours today—or at least an old acquaintance," he told the singer. "He fed me a story, and I'm trying to assess how much of it I should believe. Randy Logan."

Diana looked confused as she tried to make the connection. Then she brightened. "That's right. The debate."

"Uh-huh. Logan remembers me. He saw you and me together at a gallery opening a few years back."

Diana smiled, her look wistful. "That's about the only place I run into him anymore. On the art scene. Impressive collection he's put together."

"I saw some of it. You two were tighter once, right?"

She nodded.

"You ever meet his wife?"

Another nod. "Lisa? Sure. She's a tough little cookie, that one. You'd never believe she's photographed thousands of famine victims, earthquake disasters, and a dozen wars. Not just by looking at her. She's itty-bitty."

"What about their relationship?" Joe pressed.

Diana hunched forward. All the time she spent in her home gym was evident in the lean, sinewy definition of her wrists and forearms. She shook her head slowly, frowning. "A heavy metal star married to a woman who's gone half the year on assignment? What do you suppose Randy does while she's gone? While he and the boys are on the road? Tie a knot in it? That isn't the story I've heard."

"Lisa—you figure she knows?"

Her eyebrows went up. "What's *your* guess?"

Brian returned with two beers and a seltzer for his wife. As Dante took a slug and savored the way the ice-cold liquid coursed across his tongue and down his throat, Diana made a sweeping gesture with her glass. "Don't get me wrong. Randy isn't your typical get-stoned-and-burn-teenage-girls-with-cigarettes hothead. Everything with him is calculated. I doubt there's much romance left in a marriage like that, but

124

how do I know? There's *some* reason they've stayed together. Hell, they've been married for what now? Six years?''

"How about his other women?" Joe asked. "You remember any of them from the old days? From the time before he hit it big?''

She didn't have to think about it for long. "I remember one. A tall, killer-gorgeous blonde he dated for close to three years. He was nuts about that one.''

"Any idea what happened to her?''

She shrugged. "She did some modeling, but it didn't seem like she had the ambition it takes to go supernova. I saw a few pictures of her in the magazines, but that's about it. Had an accent from down South somewhere and probably went back home. I can't recall. That was what? Almost ten years ago now?''

Dante drank more of his beer while thinking over what he'd just heard. It seemed to jibe with what Logan had told him. If Randy's wife was aware of his occasional infidelities, then how much did he have to lose by Troy Brooks exposing one to the media? Especially *this* particular one. Heavy metal fans all over the country would love news like that.

"Why do you ask?" Diana wondered.

He drained his bottle while shaking the question off. "If anything comes of this I'll spill the beans. I swear it. Right now it's all a lot of wild speculation.''

"Logan saw something," Brennan concluded.

Diana scowled. "It's more than that. Too many questions about his and Lisa's relationship, his fucking around.''

Joe scooped up his other empty and started across the room toward the recycling barrel. He was headed toward the door when Diana changed tack before she lost him.

"What's going on between you and Rosa, copper?''

He wheeled, the accusing finger he pointed contradicted by his failure to suppress a smile. "You set me up.''

"I didn't. I swear to God.''

He shook his head. "It's been a long day in more ways

than you can guess. G'night. Thanks again for feeding the cat.''

Toby was curled up sleeping on the end of the bed when Dante switched on the overhead light. He hadn't bothered to check his answering machine earlier and now saw the indicator bulb was blinking. He pressed the message-retrieval button before stripping out of his shirt and stuffing it in with the dirty laundry. The machine whirred and clicked, rewinding the tape as Joe climbed between the sheets. Relieved of the task of keeping himself upright, he realized how tired he was.

"It's Rosa, Joe. At around six-fifteen. I know you're busy, but give me a call when you get a chance.''

That was it. As Dante rolled over, shifting to get comfortable, he nudged the cat further to one side and tugged the blankets up beneath his chin. Romance. Last night at this time he was afire with it, but right now he was too tired to think anymore about love's muddled picture. He yawned and burrowed deep into his pillow.

TWELVE

Lisa Dodd was stiff and hung over. She'd gotten drunk with a news producer friend Wednesday night and slept on the friend's sofa. Somewhere in the process she decided she didn't really give a damn anymore; that her marriage had been over for years. Never before had she actually walked in on Randy screwing one of his bimbos, but news of his exploits tended to get back to her. There was that incident two years ago in Houston. Some bopper filed suit, claiming Randy had given her herpes. Lisa didn't really care about the particulars of her husband's philandering, but she didn't want to die of AIDS, either. She *did* care about being humiliated, and Randy had gone too far this time. All she wanted now was a divorce from the son of a bitch.

When she emerged from a cab outside her Tribeca loft building, she stood a moment surveying the facade. Yes, she still had her old studio space in the photo district, midtown, but this was her home. She wondered who would get it and who would get the horse farm upstate. She'd spent the first two years of her marriage decorating both places, but this was her first love. Most of the primitive-art collection here was hers, collected in her travels. How did a couple divide up possessions like theirs? He treasured the primitives, too, and some of the costlier purchases were made with his money. But if he had a real passion, other than indulging his ego, Randy loved the upstate farm and his horses more than

127

anything else. He collected the paintings and the sculpture because it demonstrated that a heavy metal rocker could have refined tastes. The horses were something else. He knew their bloodlines and the racing histories of their dams and sires by heart. He would fight hard to keep his horses.

While she entered the building and rode upstairs, Lisa supposed she could let Randy have the farm and horses in a straight-up exchange for this place and the primitive collection. She didn't care so much about the contemporary art. They would probably divide it, give or take a few canvases. She knew how much money he'd paid for those paintings, and if he tried anything cute she would make him bleed.

As the doors of the elevator rolled back, Lisa started out of the car and pulled up short. The living room before her was a shambles, the display case containing her most valuable pre-Columbian ceramics smashed. Her breath caught in her throat as she surveyed the shards of broken pottery strewn across the floor amid fragments of shattered glass.

''Oh my God!'' she gasped. ''Randy?!''

With a tentative step into the room she took stock of the damage: The big Wesselman canvas ripped diagonally, its stretcher frame splintered; a sofa overturned; the glassware from the wet bar swept to the floor. A local rock station played at low volume over the sound system, but Randy was nowhere in sight.

''Randy?'' She called it again as she started with trepidation toward his bedroom. At the doorway she pulled up short and reached for her mouth. Randy was lying on the bed, fully clothed, his eyes bulging and face battered. His dead hands gripped a towel soaked with blood. The bedside phone was off the hook.

Lisa turned to run for the bath across the hall. Failing to make the toilet, she fell to her knees across the threshold and vomited onto the tile floor.

The First Precinct caught the call to the Logan homicide at seven o'clock. Forty-five minutes later, as Dante was en route to an eight A.M. meeting with his task force team, he received notification via radio. Duane Street was situated in relative proximity to the Big Building. Dante's detour was a simple matter of dropping two blocks further south once he reached Greenwich Street past Independence Plaza. The corner of Duane and Staple was already jammed with a dozen parked radio units, unmarkeds, and an EMS ambulance when he arrived. He found a hydrant around the corner on Hudson Street, tossed his vehicle I.D. onto the dash, and hurried on toward the rock star's building at a trot.

The sky had cleared and the mercury jumped ten degrees overnight. The residual slush from last night's storm had been washed away by a subsequent rain. Yesterday, Joe's investigation had uncovered more than most managed in the first twenty-four hours. His team hadn't found negatives to incriminate Troy Brooks last night, but Grover and Heckman had come up with a ribbon cartridge that offered some hope. He'd gotten a decent night's sleep. Forty-five minutes ago he planted his feet on the bedroom floor, ready to go on the attack; drag Brooks in, put the screws to him, and confront Mrs. Mitchell with evidence of her having lied to them. News of Logan's death put a nasty spin on last night's developments. Joe was present when Logan made that phone call to Brooks. The smart money said Troy visited here at eight o'clock. Joe wondered what else he'd done.

Chief Lieberman's sedan pulled up in front of Logan's building simultaneous with Dante's arrival up the sidewalk. Two uniforms were working the downstairs door, screening foot traffic. Joe had his shield case extended for their inspection but waited for Gus to squeeze between parked cars and join him. The two of them proceeded through the checkpoint together.

"What do you think, Joey? Brooks? Retaliation for Logan's ratting him out?"

Dante stepped into the elevator, punching the third-floor button. "I guess that'll depend on the evidence, right? All I've got right now is a radio call."

Lieberman fed him a quick update of how the wife had spent the night with a friend, returned home an hour ago, and found Logan dead on his bed. "She called 911, they notified the local station house. Those guys thought it was a homicide in the course of a robbery. They called in Manhattan South. Once Vic Manley got a look at what he had, he called me. I guess Logan took one hell of a beating."

Like Lieberman, Captain Vic Manley had once spent time commanding the Detective Squad at the Sixth Precinct in Greenwich Village. Over the sixteen years since he was awarded the gold shield, Dante had worked tours at the Sixth under both men's commands. Manley was a tall, trim black man with a unique feel for matching his available personnel. He was first responsible for teaming Joe with Jumbo Richardson. As far as Dante was concerned, Vic was among the best street-level commanders in the Job.

"Who've you brought on board?" Joe asked.

"Rocky Conklin, for continuity's sake. Him and Chip Donnelly's Crime Scene team are on their way. If this is Brooks's handiwork, we'll nail him. He'll cop a plea now for sure."

"Not exactly how I saw it unfolding," Dante murmured. "Logan wasn't Mozart, but his music wasn't hurting anyone, either. I asked him to put himself at risk, and look what's happened." Randy had used poor judgment Tuesday afternoon, and now he'd paid for that mistake with his life. If Joe had put an electronics van downstairs on the street and recorded Logan's meeting with Brooks, this might have been prevented.

When the elevator door rolled back, Dante was stunned by the extent of damage done to the scene he'd visited just fourteen hours earlier. He advanced slowly, Gus at his side. "Jesus," he muttered.

Vic Manley spotted their arrival and broke off a conversation with two of his men. "Chief. Joe. What can you tell me about this? My guys haven't turned a thing. The wife doesn't seem to think anything's missing.''

"This story about where she was last night. You checked it out?'' Dante asked.

"Ironclad—and a hangover to prove it. She looked pretty green and we told her to go lay down. She's in her bedroom.''

"With the corpse?'' Gus asked.

Manley couldn't prevent a slight smile. "Negative. His is the first one down the hall and hers is the second, diagonally across.''

Dante nodded in that direction. "How bad's the damage?''

"Not pretty, but you've seen worse. Take a look?'' He led them past conversations conducted in low tones and enveloped in dense clouds of cigarette smoke. Several of the uniforms on the scene—young guys—drifted like tourists, absorbing evidence of the rock star's life-style.

The dead man's bedroom lights were on with the shades drawn. This was just the kind of scene the tabloid photographers fought over. Unless the investigation wanted full-color photographs of the corpse on the cover of next week's *Globe*, they had to keep the lid screwed on tight. A guy with the right film and lens would hang by his knees from helicopter skids if he thought he could get a shot through Logan's window.

"The wife says this is just how she found him,'' Manley reported. "Judging from the amount of blood soaking that towel and the front of his shirt, it looks like he bled out through the mouth. God knows how much more he's got filling his belly.''

Dante and Gus stepped to the victim's bedside.

"Looks like he fought the battle royal,'' Lieberman observed. "I ain't just talking about his face. Look at them knuckles.''

Logan barely looked like the man Dante had questioned yesterday evening. The bulging eyes made his features appear grotesque, while the battering he'd taken altered the shape of the face itself. The condition of the hands indicated Logan had given back some of what he got. The knuckles were torn and scabbed black with dried blood.

"You move him at all?" Joe asked Manley.

"Just to check him for back and occipital head wounds. He's clean of anything but bruises. It looks like he managed to get himself to bed after the fight and tried to call somebody . . . probably for help."

As Dante picked up one of Logan's hands for a closer look, he watched Gus from the corner of his eye. The chief, a thirty-year veteran, went through his self-distracting routine of patting his pockets for cigarettes. Manley didn't smoke, but stepped away to examine several framed photographs set atop the dresser. Gus lit his smoke and addressed Vic's back.

"We know he was alive at six o'clock last night. That's when Joey talked with him, right out there in that living room. Before Joey left, Logan made an appointment with a mutt who was giving him problems. The mutt's an extortionist. He was set to meet Logan here at eight o'clock."

There was confusion in Manley's expression when he turned. "This is connected in some way to the Cora Davis homicide? The two of them debate, then she's dead and now him."

Lieberman filled the Homicide commander in as best he could. He described how Troy Brooks had followed Logan and Senator Mitchell's wife upstairs at the Park View; how he'd taken what were understood to be compromising photographs. "Joey picked up the trail yesterday. He did a lot of good work and maybe even got a little lucky. Logan looked like the missing piece that would tie the puzzle together."

"That call to the radio station?" Manley asked. "Bull-shit?"

"Can't say for sure until McKillip finds him." Gus's impatience was evident in the way he sucked in a quick lungful of smoke and forced it right back out again. "I'd be a fool to pull him off it before he's run it all the way out, but I know it stinks and so does he. They're putting more faith in trying to match names with faces in the rabble outside the hotel. For that, they've teamed up with the Bureau.'' He grunted in disgust. ''From what I've heard, they have about a mile of news footage of the event and a list of nut cases as long as the Jersey Turnpike.''

''Hung over or not, I'd like to talk with the wife,'' Dante told them. ''And once Rocky gets here and can establish a ballpark time of death, we'll probably want to issue an APB for Brooks. I assume he never returned home last night?'' He directed this question at Gus. After his task force left St. Mark's Place last night, he'd asked Lieberman to order a surveillance of the extortionist's apartment.

''Not a sign of him,'' Gus replied. ''You go talk to the wife. I'll check in, see if anything's changed. Much as I hate to, I've gotta touch base with Big Tony.''

While the chief headed off to call his office and confer with the P.C., Manley led Dante down the hall to a closed door. Opening it, he spoke gently. ''Ms. Dodd? Someone here wants a word with you.''

Lisa Dodd lay atop the coverlet on her bed, eyes searching the ceiling above. Gleaming tracks of tears ran back into her short-cropped dark hair. She made no move to acknowledge Joe's presence as he entered and crossed to stand by the edge of the bed.

''I realize this is rough for you, Ms. Dodd. I'm sorry to bother you, but it's necessary.''

She remained in her same removed attitude, eyes still on the ceiling when she spoke. Her words came slowly and were harsh with anger. ''Rough? You've got no idea, mister.''

Dante took a seat on the dressing-table chair, leaned forward, and planted his elbows on his knees. ''Maybe I do. You're gone almost a month and walk in here yesterday to find your husband with another woman. You have all night to think about it—get good and mad—then come back here to find him dead.''

The photojournalist came upright like she'd been jerked. "Who *are* you? How do you know that?"

Focused directly at him now, the heat in her eyes surprised him. They were a deep, sapphire blue and dominated her otherwise ordinary facial features. He saw now that she was tiny, just as Diana had described her. Her slight bone structure made her appear frail, but this was a woman who'd just returned from slogging around the Vietnamese jungle looking at twenty-year-old plane wrecks.

"Lieutenant Joe Dante," he replied. "I'm investigating the Cora Davis homicide. I saw your husband here last night. Around six. He had a lot on his mind and was, uh, *candid*."

Confusion killed some of the heat in her gaze. Her brow furrowed and mouth softened now. Even in that subdued light, Dante could see how burned dark she was by the tropical sun. "You're investigating another murder and you spoke with Randy about it? Here?" She let that sink in for a few beats. "What am I missing?"

"I understand you spent the night elsewhere, Ms. Dodd. Where was that? And after you left yesterday afternoon, you never returned here again until this morning?" He knew it was a question Vic would have already asked, but he wanted to see her reaction for himself. He needed to know what she knew about Randy's dilemma.

"Whoa, Lieutenant. I've already got a question on the floor. You don't think *I* had anything to do with this?" Incredulity. Real or manufactured, it had the right bite.

"No," Dante admitted. "I don't. But this isn't about what I believe; not yet anyway. I'm afraid it isn't a dialogue, either. I've asked you a question and I'd like an answer. Please."

He watched her mull over the idea of digging in her heels. Everywhere her thoughts turned, they ran into walls. "I hit a bar where an old friend works," she said at length. "A shoulder to cry on, I guess. After that I hooked up with another friend. Her husband is out of town. She cooked me dinner, I got shit-faced drunk and spent the night on her sofa."

"Did you know Randy tried to find you?"

She sighed, eyes tearing up again as she shook her head. "It doesn't surprise me, but no."

"Can you tell me what happened when you came home yesterday? I'm guessing those were your cases I saw stacked outside the elevator."

She focused hard on Dante now, the spark of new interest come alive. "You know who she is, don't you?"

"I'm asking the questions here, remember?"

The two of them sat stalemated while seconds ticked slowly by.

"This is a homicide investigation, Ms. Dodd. You've been around the block. You know what that means. Someone was here with him, am I right? Can you describe her?"

"No, I can't. She screamed and dove for the floor the second I stepped off the elevator. I didn't see her face."

"Hair color?" Joe pressed.

"Blond. Lots of it."

"Heavy? Slight?"

That evoked a faint, bitter smile. "Slender, I assure you. Randy wouldn't give a fat woman the time of day, let alone fuck her."

Dante was interested to see how different this woman was from Lyndelle Mitchell; different physical type, different psychology. He remembered what Diana told him last night about the sexual side of Lisa and Logan's relationship.

"I've met enough cops in my work, Lieutenant. You all like to act inscrutable. It's my nature to dig until I expose raw ends. I will, you know."

"I expect so."

"Then save the little bitch the trouble of my embarrassing her. She's connected to all this or you wouldn't be asking me about her."

Dante rose to go. He could see how she'd be good at her work. The pure, raw aggression she embodied intimidated more often than not. "Thank you for your time, Ms. Dodd." He reached for the doorknob.

"Wait a minute, you bastard! We're not finished here."

"We are, Ms. Dodd. At least for the moment." Joe closed the door behind him.

On days like this, Gus Lieberman wondered why he didn't just put in his papers. He had thirty-two years on the Job, had distinguished himself, and was getting too old for all these unpleasant surprises. Back in the days when he first donned the blue and started walking a beat, the C of D could expect to be called to the scene of a homicide maybe once a month. Certainly no more than twice. The rest were routine, the results of family and street disputes. Today the city was gone mad. Criminals were crazed on wonderful new drugs. Decent, law-abiding New Yorkers were fleeing in droves, further eroding a tax base that kept the forces of order in place. Most of the ex-cops Gus knew had retired to Florida or the Carolinas, but unlike them, he couldn't find it in his heart to turn his back. He and three generations of Liebermans had prospered in New York. His wife's family had amassed a fortune on Wall Street. Gus loved this town. Watching the rabble tear it limb from limb made his heart ache.

Right now, Gus saw the wheels threatening to come off his investigation. Yesterday he had one noted personality wearing a toe tag. Today he had two. Already this Thursday morning he'd exchanged calls twice with Tony Mintoff. The P.C. was getting an earful from the mayor and passing it directly down the chain of command. Tony wanted his chief of detectives and the new task force commander on the carpet in his office at eleven o'clock. High-profile murders were bad publicity. They hurt tourism. Tourist and convention traffic meant substantial tax revenues. Logan's corpse was barely cool, and already Mintoff was sighting along his index digit, ready to finger subordinates with the blame.

Pathologist Rocky Conklin had arrived and was in the bedroom with the dead man. He had Logan's shirt stripped from his torso to examine bruises. Logan's pants were down around his thighs to allow insertion of a rectal thermometer. Dante and the recently arrived Beasley Richardson looked on while Rocky murmured something to Joey in low tones.

"This guy was alive when the man who did this to him left, cowboy." As Conklin made this pronouncement, he noticed Lieberman's arrival and nodded. "Chief."

"Why do you say that?" Joey asked. "Because he's here? In bed?"

Rocky rolled the corpse facedown to remove the thermometer. "That's part of it. I think he got the shit beat out of him in a good old-fashioned donnybrook, started feeling sick as a dog, and when he puked blood into that towel, he got scared and tried to call an ambulance. Probably died before he could dial." He lifted the thermometer to the light and turned it, squinting to read the mercury. He then turned away to scribble in a notebook open on the bed. "You say you saw this man alive at six?"

Dante didn't bother answering.

"We'll have to haul him in; cut him open," Conklin continued. "But his temp is straight *room* temp. It'll take a body a good ten, twelve hours to cool that far down in this sort of atmosphere. Let's be generous. He was dead by ten, definitely. If you saw him alive at six, that gives us a window of four hours."

Dante digested this information and put it together with what he already knew. "Brooks shows up here last night, and Logan tells him he's gone to the cops. Brooks gets mad. Something triggers a brawl. Troy leaves, and when he shows up outside his place he finds it crawling with cops."

"So he goes to ground," Gus concluded.

Dante nodded. "Wouldn't you? Especially knowing that we won't find anything, that you've already gotten it out of there? Anything Logan told us is hearsay."

"I'd get *my* ass on ice," Jumbo agreed. "Wait to see how it all shakes out."

Gus told Joey about the P.C. wanting them both in his office for an eleven o'clock meeting. "I'll have Operations

137

get right on the Brooks APB,'' he concluded. ''Where you headed?''

''To meet with my team. Vic can handle the wrap-up here. I doubt our pal Troy will just swim into the net. We'll need to do some fishing.''

THIRTEEN

Billy Beaumont slept only a handful of hours before rising at six o'clock Thursday morning to take his usual 10K run. It was convenient that the hotel was situated directly across Fifth Avenue from Central Park. It made getting exercise in the godforsaken confines of New York a good deal more palatable. By the time nine o'clock rolled around and Beaumont strolled into the downstairs dining room, he was ready for whatever the day cared to throw his way.

Already awaiting Beaumont's arrival at their table, Nancy had company. To Billy's eye, the Reverend Jerry Davis looked a lot better this morning than he did yesterday afternoon. The puffiness around his eyes was gone. He actually smiled while offering to shake hands. Once Billy was seated, his napkin laid across his lap, he returned a breezy but otherwise noncommittal smile.

"No offense, Reverend, but I thought this was supposed to be a business breakfast. Me feeding Nancy the particulars of last night's negotiations. How you feeling, by the way? You *look* better."

Before Davis could respond, Nancy reached over to touch his arm, stopping him. "This *is* a business breakfast, Mr. Beaumont. Since last night, the reverend has become part of that business. A very important part." The state Republican chair set her professional demeanor at full power—an impassive seriousness accented by her carefully planned appear-

139

ance. There was nothing flashy or overstated, just a hint of eyeliner and single strand of pearls to set off her fresh-scrubbed good looks. Her suit was pearl gray, the jacket worn over a simple white silk blouse. Billy gave her credit where it was due. While appropriately conservative, her look exuded confidence and competence.

"Do tell," he urged. "It *sounds* important."

"I've convinced the Reverend Davis to declare for governor in Cora's stead."

Just like that. Billy didn't even bother trying to mask his surprise. He had his water glass halfway to his lips. That's all the further it got. "*You* did that?" The Tennessee state machine was Lyle Mitchell's machine. Nobody who wanted to ride aboard it said boo without first obtaining Lyle's blessing. Cora Davis, before throwing her hat into the ring, had come to Mitchell first.

"Nancy made the suggestion," Davis corrected. "But the decision was all mine. Your tone suggests she may have overstepped her bounds. I don't think so. It's her *job* to ferret out qualified, viable candidates. Once she laid out the particulars, I needed very little actual convincing."

Beaumont elected to skirt the issue of methodology, at least for the moment. Lyle could handle dressing them down for their presumption. "But isn't this just a tad obvious? Your wife is dead barely a day. If I didn't know better I might think you were trying to capitalize on the way she was killed."

Davis stiffened. "I don't like your implication, sir. Need I remind you that I held the seventh congressional district seat for three years before your boss ever ran for the Senate? That I campaigned diligently on his behalf and delivered my district?"

"He's baiting you, Jerry," Nancy warned. "Ignore it. He knows your bona fides better than most."

"I won't have him speak to me that way," Davis argued. "*He's* the one who needs friends rather than enemies, not me. It isn't my credibility that's at risk right now."

Billy nearly pulled muscles trying to keep his face straight. "I'm afraid I'm at a disadvantage here," he murmured. "You two gonna leave me out in the dark?"

"Something's come up," Nancy replied. "Something that may put Lyle in an awkward position. That's what Jerry means about needing friends." As Beaumont listened, Nancy outlined the basics of her conversation with Lyndelle on their way to LaGuardia the previous day. He nearly choked on the story Nancy had apparently swallowed about horse-breeding syndicates. What alarmed him was the fact that Lyndelle had not only told Nancy this story, but that Nancy had passed it along to Davis. In light of how Jerry was choosing to interpret it, this was the worst sort of news.

"Just so you understand," Nancy concluded. "Protecting your boss's reputation is every bit as important to me as it is to you. I'm sure Reverend Davis feels the same way. If Lyle Mitchell is brought down by scandal involving his wife, even if it's based on lies, we will all be damaged. I will no doubt find myself cast out into the cold same as you, Billy. What Jerry is offering is an opportunity to *strengthen* the party's position in Tennessee, not weaken it. His integrity, like Cora's, is unimpeachable."

Billy clenched the hand in his lap into a fist, still struggling to maintain his composure. It wasn't the notion of Jerry Davis as a gubernatorial candidate that irked him; it was the breakdown of the state machine's command structure. Nancy Hillman was a mere functionary, and here she was presuming to create policy. The self-righteous little bitch had gotten her hands on one dirty secret and now saw herself as a kingmaker. Yes, Lyle Mitchell's position was threatened, but he had seen Lyle threatened before. He also knew his job and was already at work designing a defense.

As the waiter arrived to take their orders, Beaumont continued to study his opposition. He decided that if Nancy wanted to believe that she and Davis were his allies in protecting the senator, that would be preferable to him alienating them. The best way to smooth any ruffled feathers would be to give Nancy what she thought she wanted. He would have a word with Lyndelle about her failure at full disclosure sometime later in the day. Right now, he still had a leak or two in the dike demanding his immediate attention. Once the waiter cleared off, he leaned forward, his manner conciliatory.

"Suppose this fella who took the photographs *does* approach Mrs. Mitchell? We've got to assume that's a probability. You've got some plan of action?"

In the aftermath of his challenging her, Nancy's confidence hadn't slipped an iota. She was still all business as she set her coffee cup down and nodded. "I'm thinking in terms of a long-range strategy; of keeping this extortionist strung along until a time when his information is not so damaging."

"String him along." Billy kept it deadpan. "How?"

She regarded him as though he were dim. "*Pay* him, of course. Not all at once, like I'm sure he'd prefer, but enough now to whet his appetite. Keep him on a leash by paying him in dribs and drabs."

"Toward what end?" This was perfect. It was similar to the plan he'd proposed to Lyndelle himself.

"Toward buying ourselves the time we need." There was exasperation in Nancy's tone. "Time to get the Reverend Davis elected governor. Time to present Senator Mitchell with the dilemma Lyn presents and let him face facts. I'm very fond of Lyn, but she's a liability. First there were all the vicious rumors out of Washington and now this mess. Once Lyle sees the whole picture, I believe he'll make the right decision."

Billy wondered. Without that extortion demand and those photographs, he doubted Lyle's infatuation with his wife could be disrupted. Nancy wouldn't be the one who decided when and if Lyle was presented the whole picture. If it ever came to that, it would be Billy's pleasure, and his alone.

The rest of Dante's task force team was hard at work when he and Jumbo Richardson entered the de facto squad room on the Big Building's eleventh floor. To isolate themselves from the rest of Special Investigations, they'd dragged over several freestanding partitions to section off one isolated corner. Inside, they'd arranged four battered metal desks in a line and commandeered an empty file cabinet, a chalkboard, two typewriters, a desktop computer terminal, and half a dozen chairs. Don Grover and Rusty Heckman were seated face-to-face across one desk and were endeavoring to transcribe the text hidden on the cartridge ribbon recovered during the previous night's search. Melissa Busby and Guy Napier were busy working the phones.

Napier dropped his receiver into the cradle and made a note as Dante threw his coat at a chair. "We decided to try and hunt Brooks down through his business contacts first," Guy announced. "You know, the magazines he sold his work to, shit like that."

"Any luck?" Joe asked.

"Not yet, but it's early. Most of the supermarket tabloids all have head offices down in Florida, so we've made them our lowest priority. So far I've talked to worker-bee types at *People* and *Us*. They all know who Brooks is, but not much else. None of the fat cats are at their desks yet."

Across the desk from her partner, Melissa banged her receiver down. As she collapsed back in her squeaking chair and blew a wisp of stray hair from her eyes, she groaned. "No wonder the economy sucks. Nobody who knows anything starts work before ten o'clock." She picked distractedly at the chipped paint of the desk edge as she spoke. "We're in the wrong racket, gents. Not only doesn't crime pay—the hours suck. I've tried *Vanity Fair*, *Rolling Stone*, and *Spy*. The last guy I talked to barely knows what day it is. Not date; *day*."

"How about downstairs?" Dante asked. "You try anybody in the pool?" He was referring to the Big Building's press pool housed on the mezzanine floor.

Melissa pried a good-size chunk of olive-drab paint loose and flicked it away between thumb and middle finger. "You

kidding? They all raced over to Duane Street the minute the
call came in. Dead heavy metal stars are big news.''

Dante encouraged them to keep at it and turned to the
ribbon-cartridge project. He'd been skeptical last night but
hoped now that he was just too tired to share Don and Rusty's
optimism.

''Find anything interesting?''

''Not yet,'' Grover reported. He pointed to a legal pad
covered with neat lines of evenly spaced letters. Some lines
at the top of the page already had lines between them, divid-
ing them into word groups. ''We just finished transcribing
back ten feet onto the take-up spool. Now we're figuring the
breaks.''

Dante leaned close and read:

in/Mexico./Pat/said/something/to/the/effect/of/siete/
anos./Drag/city./Next/time/I'm/down/south/I'm/definite-
lycruisinginformyneedlesession.Thecholeraisgetting
closerbythemin . . .

''Drag *city*?'' he queried.

''This is going quickly now,'' Heckman told him. ''We
should know in another ten minutes whether we're wasting
our time here.''

The phone at Rusty's elbow rang, and he reached to pick
up. ''Task force. Sergeant Heckman. Yeah. Hang on.'' Rusty
handed the receiver over. ''For you, Lou. Op Desk.''

Joe jammed the receiver between shoulder and cheek as
he continued to peer down at the letters on the work sheet.
''Yeah. Dante.''

''Sergeant Lewis, Lou. Got something for you on that
Brooks APB.''

''C'mon, Phil. It only just went out.''

''All the same. The squad at the Ninth picked it up. Seems
a citizen on her way to work this morning was cutting through
Tompkins Square when she stumbled across a John Doe homicide. A search of the area turned a wallet an hour ago. No

money or credit cards, but a driver's license picture matched their stiff. When that APB came over the wire, they got excited. License identifies their dead guy as Troy Bendix Brooks. Gunshot. One in the head.''

Dante fought off a dizzying wave of despair, the wreckage of yesterday's progress now strewn all over the runway. ''Get Rocky Conklin from the M.E.'s office, Phil. He left the Logan scene same time I did. Tell him I'm rolling, that I'll meet him in Tompkins Square.'' He handed the phone back to Heckman, told the rest of the team what was happening, and hurried to scoop up his jacket. The wall clock told him he had seventy minutes before his meeting upstairs. Not much time. He caught Melissa's eye as he reached for the doorknob. ''Get on the horn to the morgue and order a residue scrape of Logan's hands. Somebody else get hold of Vic Manley at the Logan scene. We're looking for a weapon and evidence that Logan fired it. Recently.''

Seconds later, as Dante and Richardson rushed toward the elevators, Beasley voiced a question that was also on Joe's mind. ''The condition Logan was in, you really think he'd be capable of chasing Brooks all the way to the East Village? Whack him, drag ass back home to die in his own bed?''

Dante jabbed impatiently at the down button between the pair of elevators. Maligned since the day the Big Building opened, the elevators at One Police Plaza were notorious for their lack of speed.

''It's a long shot, but what's the alternative?''

''Mrs. Mitchell.''

''Exactly.''

Beasley shrugged. ''If she is our perp, we're gonna have one hell of a time tying her in now. Everyone who can connect her is gone.''

''But not every *thing*,'' Joe muttered. ''Unless Brooks had those negatives with him when he died.''

Terry Dillingham was feeling awkward and ornery this morning. It was nearly ten o'clock, and he was still wide awake, the euphoric coke high now long gone, but the residual stimulant effect keeping him too jacked up to sleep. His toes twitched madly, and his heart raced. Even more frustrating, his bedmate had fallen into deep slumber without any apparent difficulty. Hours ago. She lay stretched alongside, her light snoring driving him to distraction. The *wrong* bedmate.

He should have known he was in trouble during dinner at the Mesa Grill. His models liked the fact that people recognized and stared at him, but neither understood or even cared what his celebrity was about. Theirs was a world where Linda Evangelista, Norman Mailer, and Bo Jackson each generated equal amounts of excitement at the same cocktail gala. A star was a star was a star. They'd returned to his place to snort more of his coke, showing no more interest in him as an object than they had before leaving. Sometime around two A.M., Dillingham finally opted to take Troy's advice. Brooks was still a no-show, and Terry's stash was running perilously low. He announced that fact and told them he had just enough dust left to do him and *one* of them, the idea being to divide and conquer. Tiffany told him to go fuck himself and asked Stacy if she was ready to ditch this creep. Stacy eyed those two grams remaining in Dillingham's bag and said she didn't think so. Not quite yet.

When he finally did get her into the sack, Stacy proved little more exciting than beached flounder. When he tried to kiss her he got no response. When he ran his tongue over her breasts, she betrayed no evidence of having felt a thing. He'd started in on her like a bull on a business trip but soon found himself wilting. Fast. Before he lost it completely he did manage to bring himself off, but even that was an embarrassingly one-sided effort. When he finished, she rolled over without a word and drifted immediately off to sleep.

That was two hours ago. Irritated by the occasional pang of self-loathing, he was trying to convince himself that he didn't give a damn when the phone rang. Startled out of his reverie, he dragged the instrument to his ear.

"Huh?"

It was greeted by a brief silence, followed by a click and dial tone. So much the better. He was in no mood to chat. As he hung up he realized Stacy hadn't so much as twitched.

Tompkins Square, located between Avenues A and B on the Lower East Side, was the scene of recent confrontations between homeless squatters and NYPD. Several of those confrontations had turned ugly, generating charges of police brutality. Those incidents, and the coverage they received in the media, were still a sore spot with many of New York's finest. It had been over a year now since the last tent city was dismantled, the stench of raw sewage washed away, and the mountains of garbage hauled off. Still, as Beasley Richardson entered the park on foot it seemed haunted to him. There was no excuse for a cop losing control in the line of duty, but it had been years since Jumbo worked the streets in uniform. For today's beat cop, New York was a whole different world. He wondered how he might have responded, a young baby face in blues. Would he have kept *his* cool?

With Dante walking alongside, Jumbo reached a spot toward the upper middle of the square where an ornate monument rose. The monument's two columned limbs reached to embrace the heart of the park, and the area within its reach was crowded with Job vehicles and personnel. The immediate scene was cordoned off with the usual yellow plastic tape. Like Joey, Jumbo had his shield case tucked into the breast pocket of his jacket as he lifted the tape to pass beneath. With the warm turn of the weather, they walked with jackets unbuttoned and Jumbo had left his sweater behind in the car.

Dante spotted the whip of the Ninth's Detective Squad and led the way across the cobbles to check in with him. The big, florid-faced man saw them coming and stepped their way. He stood with hands in pockets, pinning the fronts of both his coat and jacket behind his substantial hips.

"Lieutenant Sopchak?" Joey asked. "I'm Dante. This is

147

Sergeant Richardson." He lifted his chin in the direction of the blanket-covered mound at the foot of one monument pillar. "We take a look?"

"Be my guest. It's gotta be the one to the head that killed him, but he had the living shit kicked outta him first. The picture and description on his license was enough to I.D. him, but just barely. I'll be with you over there in a sec. I had the duty cap fly in some extra uniforms. Maybe we'll get lucky, find the weapon."

Jumbo approached the corpse and watched as Joey squatted to lift the blanket. Neither of them had ever seen Brooks before. The face around that focal-point bullet wound, midforehead, was puffy and bruised. Thankfully, he was sprawled on his back, obscuring the damage done as the bullet made its exit. There was a lot of blood on the ground, not all of it yet dry.

"*Big* son of a bitch," Jumbo observed. "Ain't no wonder Logan was so messed up."

Joey pulled the blanket back further to lift one of the dead man's hands, examining the backs of the knuckles. They, like Logan's, were badly contused.

Sopchak approached carrying a plastic evidence bag. Sealed inside was a handkerchief, twisted and soaked with blood. "We found this close to the body," he reported. "Thought maybe he used it as a sorta bandage. Wrapped around a hand, maybe."

"We'll want Rocky to do fingernail scrapings," Dante told Jumbo. He set the hand he held to rest on the pavement. "See if we get tissue and blood to match Randy's. The powder burns around that forehead would say he got it pointblank." After redeploying the blanket he heaved himself to his feet.

Jumbo let his thoughts roam back over the past thirty-six hours. He was wondering where Mrs. Mitchell went after he paid her that visit last night at the Park View. There was little chance she'd helped administer a beating like the one Brooks had suffered, but even an eight year old could pull a trigger.

148

"You think there could be more to that lost-key story than she's admitting?" he asked. "That maybe Logan wasn't telling the whole truth about how he wound up in her room? Could be they had it planned all along; that my questioning her about the lost key set her off."

Sopchak, loitering nearby, scowled in confusion. "Who's *her*? You think a *broad* mighta done this?"

Joey held up a cautioning hand. "You never heard a word the sergeant just said, Lou. Right now, we don't know *what* we think." He paused to let his gaze roam over the surrounding activity. "I'm going to get the Crime Scene Unit here, ASAP. Meanwhile, I've got a meeting in the P.C.'s office. Any help you can give Sergeant Richardson, I'd appreciate it. When our friends from the Fourth Estate show up, we don't know shit. This guy's still a John Doe."

While Jumbo started away with Dante, he noticed that curiosity seekers were beginning to assemble in force outside the yellow tape.

"I think you hit the nail on the head," Joey murmured. He kept his head tucked and in tight, his lips just inches from Jumbo's right ear. "It's the one part of Logan's story I had a lot of trouble with. He claimed he never knew his old girlfriend was in the congresswoman's entourage until she walked up to him at the reception. How likely is that?"

"She slips Logan the key and then reports hers lost," Richardson concluded. "That note she handed him—if she *did* hand him a note—was just word that the coast was clear. I like it. For all we know, she's got a key to his place, too."

"Yep. She panics after you talk to her; rushes downtown to tell Logan what we've uncovered and finds him dead. Randy's already told her who Brooks is and where he lives."

Jumbo let it all sink in. He tried to make the tall, elegant blonde he'd met fit the scenario. "I'm having trouble with the how, Joey. This is a U.S. senator's wife. From Tennessee, of all places. You really think she'd be capable of hunting this dude down on the mean streets of New York and putting one between his eyes?"

"Don't forget where she used to live," Dante reminded him. "Right here in the neighborhood. Great Jones Street off the Bowery, only a block from the men's shelter."

"And the weapon?"

Dante shrugged. "For all we know she carries a little light-frame lady's gun in her bag. Wealthy, good-looking country girl travels to the big city protected. I wouldn't be surprised." He checked the time. "Listen. I've gotta get out of here."

"What you gonna tell them?" Jumbo asked. "Big Tony finds out the one person him and hizoner want us to avoid like dirty needles has emerged as our number-one suspect, he's gonna shit bricks."

Joey grimaced. "I'll say we think it was dope. That Brooks returned home hurting after his fight and headed over here to score something. Help ease his pain. In his condition, he was an easy mark."

"Amazing," Beasley marveled. "You've finally gotten some sense in your old age."

Terry Dillingham didn't know how much time had elapsed since the phone rang, but he must have finally dozed off. He came back to consciousness too abruptly, a chunk of time missing in there somewhere, brought around by an insistent knocking at his front door. He pulled the pillow over his head and tried to ignore it. No luck. Stacy stirred beside him, showing signs of awakening. He wasn't ready to face her yet. Instead, he hauled it out and tugged on a pair of briefs. Anger fueled him as he crossed the living room. Evidence of the previous day's excess was still strewn everywhere; empty glasses and bottles, the smudged mirror, a razor blade, and a tightly rolled bill were still out in plain sight on the coffee table. Guilt hit him again, an avalanche of it this time. He had a publisher's deadline coming up in three weeks, and the book was nowhere near completion.

"Who is it?" he demanded.

"Brooks," a muffled voice replied. "I need that thing I left with you."

Troy, the bastard. If Troy hadn't left him in the lurch last night, Terry wouldn't be feeling like this. He threw the dead bolt and grabbed the doorknob, ready to give Brooks hell.

The nature of last night's action was more familiar to Billy Beaumont than this current one was. Last night he'd lurked in the bushes off the well-worn jungle path and waited for his target to come into view, to come to him. Troy Brooks had been no different than some battle-weary slant; a foot soldier laden with logistical data crucial to the success of Billy's overall operation. Once ambushed and subjected to the correct degree of duress, Brooks had been acceptably forthcoming. Before the cold gunmetal probing the flesh between his eyebrows dissolved him, he'd revealed where he'd hidden his negatives and with whom. Then he'd broken down blubbering and whining, and it wasn't long before Billy put a bullet in him just to buy some peace.

But this morning's action was altogether different, and Billy had hoped he wouldn't find this Dillingham at home. B & E was a whole other territory from ambush, a terrain on which he didn't feel quite so much at ease. He had no idea what Dillingham did for a living and wasn't pleased when the man answered the phone. It complicated matters. Still, paying him a visit now was a risk that had to be taken. Dillingham might hear news of his friend's murder, put it together with what Brooks had asked him to hold in safekeeping, and go to the cops.

As soon as he heard the dead bolt thrown and saw the knob turn, Billy hit the door with a force that recalled his playing days as a fullback at the Citadel. The panel exploded inward to hit Dillingham flush in the face, hard enough to poleax him. Dressed only in his jockey shorts, Dillingham straightened, eyes rolling back in his head. Then his knees buckled. The impact sent him toppling backward to sprawl onto the entry foyer parquet. The back of his head hit with the sickening thud of a melon falling off a truck. Billy moved to slip inside as the fallen man's body began to thrash spasmodically. He stared in surprise. These deadbeat artist types were fragile.

Brooks had reported watching Dillingham hide the negatives in the top drawer of his dresser. Beaumont started toward a short hallway diagonally across the expensively appointed living room, moving around a coffee table littered with an empty gin bottle, half a fifth of Jameson, empty glasses and a mirror smeared with the residue of a recent drug orgy. One wall was graced with a framed photograph by that queer photographer, Mapplethorpe. Some fag with a rod-on, hanging there like it was something normal you put on your wall.

The first doorway off the hall led to a powder room. The room beyond was set up as an office, complete with IBM PC, personal copier, fax machine, and a desk fashioned from an inch-thick slab of plate glass. The master bedroom lay behind the third door he opened.

Billy stepped inside and was scanning the big highboy set opposite when he realized he had company. Slumbering amid a chaos of twisted bedclothes, a dark-haired, long-legged beauty of a girl was oblivious to his presence. The face was glossy-magazine pretty, with pouting lips and sharp, angular bones. What he could see of her body protruding from a blanket drawn across her hips was all sleek lines. A dancer, maybe? He felt his body flush with heat, his cock stirring in its confinement as he edged around toward the target dresser.

Business would have to come first, but by God he was sorely tempted. Slip the muzzle of one gun between her lips and the other between her legs. Watch the fear register in her eyes. Feel her go rigid and smell the cold sweat of terror on her. His cock no longer stirred against its confinement now. It strained taut and eager.

There were two top dresser drawers in the highboy. As Beaumont opened the first, the glides let out a shrill, high-pitched squeal. The girl in the bed came awake with a start, palms planted on the mattress to push herself upright and eyes wide, searching frantically to orient. Billy, with one hand feeling beneath the socks stuffing the drawer, snaked his free hand to his waistband and jerked the compact little .32 Smith and Wesson. The woman focused, realized he wasn't Dillingham, and gasped. Billy thumbed back the hammer as she grabbed for the sheet. Then his fingers found the edges of the envelope at the bottom of the drawer.

The girl opened her mouth to scream just as Billy launched. This had to be done quickly. One hand clamped over her mouth to muffle the scream beneath. His weight bore her backward onto the mattress. He grabbed a pillow, stuffing it into her face. The bark of the gun's discharge was muffled, but still loud enough for a neighbor to hear. He was on his feet again almost as quickly as he'd lunged onto the bed. He dug the envelope out of the drawer and checked it without looking back. It contained copies of the same four photographs he saw yesterday, and a cluster of negatives paper-clipped together.

FOURTEEN

As Dante suspected, Commissioner Anton Mintoff was in no mood for rational discourse this morning. The man had his back to the wall and knew it. For the past hour his phone had rung nonstop. His staff was fielding enquiries from more than just the national news organizations now. Randy Logan was a huge star in both Europe and Japan. They had everyone from the biggest Tokyo daily to "Entertainment Tonight" jamming the lines.

"Ain't no way it's a fucking coincidence," Mintoff ranted. "And where does that leave us?" He punctuated the question with an accusing glare at Chief Lieberman, letting it burn there awhile. "Looking about as dumb as buck privates during short-arm inspection—our dicks dangling in the fucking breeze!"

"We've got reason to believe it isn't political," Gus reported. He kept it dead dry; a refusal to play into the excitable P.C.'s hand.

Mintoff waited for more. When it wasn't forthcoming, he slapped his desk top with an open palm, his impatience ready to burst seams. "What the fuck does that *mean*? I'm sitting here with my nuts in a vise and that's all you've got for me? Jesus *Christ*, Gus. *What* reasons? *Why?*"

Joe watched his old friend's face and wondered just how much Gus was prepared to divulge. Technically, he had a responsibility to tell all. Withholding information now could mean your head on a platter tomorrow.

"Hang onto your seat, Tony."

Mintoff hated this display of familiarity in Dante's presence. His jaw muscles tightened. He hated it almost as much as he hated Dante's heading up Lieberman's new Davis homicide task force. Joe knew that his record in the field and Gus Lieberman were the only two things preventing his assignment to the Personnel Safety Desk at Staff Services.

"Randy Logan and Senator Mitchell's wife were together in that suite Tuesday," Gus continued. "Doing the mystery dance in her bedroom. There's a chance the congresswoman either discovered them there or spotted Logan leaving."

Mintoff gaped. "Fucking? Mrs. Mitchell and *Logan*?"

Gus didn't bother to nod. His face was impassive.

"You know this for a fact?" Mintoff demanded.

Dante jumped in. "We've got strong evidence that suggests it, sir. Logan himself admitted it to me last night. He also told me he was being blackmailed. If Mrs. Davis caught him playing games—which is something we can only guess at now—she wasn't the only one. He was followed upstairs by a reporter."

Mintoff, in all his tailored and perfectly coiffed splendor, sagged, his face gone pale. "Who?" he rasped. "I'll rip the fucker's eyes out, personally."

"That won't be necessary, sir," Dante replied. "This particular mutt's name was Troy Brooks. *Was*, because right now he's on his way to the morgue."

The commissioner jerked open his bottom desk drawer and began rummaging through its contents. He produced an economy-size bottle of Maalox tablets, unscrewed the lid, and shook three out into the palm of his hand. They were swallowed without the aid of liquid. "Back up a little, Lieutenant." His voice regained some of the hard edge to which Joe was accustomed. "I want it from jump street, and it better be good."

* * *

155

Lyndelle Mitchell had a history of sporadic bouts with insomnia. They never persisted for more than a few days but could be annoying when her social schedule demanded she be up and perky. Her doctor had prescribed the sleep-inducing drug Halcion. Last night, after returning to her suite from Billy Beaumont's room, she'd taken twice the recommended dosage. The drug enveloped her in a heavy, pain-obscuring cloud of oblivion, and held her suspended there for nine dreamless hours.

No sooner did Lyndelle awaken at ten-fifteen Thursday morning than a wave of nausea swept over her. With it, the jagged-edged shards of recollection sliced into her consciousness. Another wave of nausea broke over her, and she lurched from her bed, fleeing toward the bath. There, she collapsed to the floor, hunched over the toilet, and vomited until bile burned her throat.

A half hour later she'd showered and moved listlessly through the task of dressing herself in a simple black skirt and bulky gray sweater. She wasn't at all hungry but knew she had to get out of the hotel. Part of her wanted to see Randy, while another part told her he had problems of his own now. She tied back her hair and applied makeup to her reddened eyes and puffy face with zombielike precision. In the hope that music might help distract her, she switched on the bedside radio.

The station she'd tuned in yesterday played mostly blues and jazz. It brought back memories of her early twenties; that time spent here in New York when everything had seemed so alive and vibrant. In New York she'd discovered Zydeco, rockabilly, salsa, and all that old New Wave stuff that had rocked the late-night club scene. Down home, everything was top-forty country and easy listening. Her husband believed opera was for faggots and jazz for nigger lovers. As Lyndelle applied eyeliner with shaky hands she listened to a wailing, heart-tearing old blues ballad by L. C. Robinson. The emotion in his song and the way he could make his guitar cry matched her mood perfectly.

"Time for a news update here at the top of the hour," the WKCR disc jockey announced. "First, right here in New York, the city—rocked just yesterday by news of Congresswoman Cora Davis's murder in her suite at the Park View hotel—wakes up today to word that metal rocker Randy Logan was found dead this morning in his Tribeca loft. Logan, the political-activist bad-boy singer from the band Crucifixion, was the dead congresswoman's opponent in a much-publicized debate Tuesday afternoon. Police haven't yet revealed whether they believe there is a connection."

Lyndelle, numb, sat staring at her reflection in the dressing table mirror. "Billy," she murmured. "Oh my God."

"In another corner of Manhattan this morning, a pedestrian on her way to work discovered Troy Bendix Brooks shot to death in Tompkins Square Park. Brooks, author of the 1980 counterculture hit *Lip Service*, fell on hard times five years ago after publication of his critically denounced second novel, *Angel of Death*. The shooting is believed to be drug related."

Lyndelle shut the radio off in passing as she rushed to her closet. She'd witnessed Billy's ruthlessness in the past, in the way he ran Lyle's office and handled his adversaries. Last night's savage sexual onslaught only confirmed it. Lyle and Beaumont had run long-range reconnaissance patrols into Laos and Cambodia during the Vietnam conflict. From the stories she'd heard, the methods of those Special Forces teams were often inexorable. Confronted with the problems presented by Randy and the photographer, Billy might naturally see quick elimination as his first and best option.

She had to get out of there. Now. After dragging her garment bag onto the bed, she stripped clothes at random from the closet and packed.

Twenty minutes into their meeting, Dante and Gus had laid all the cards before them on the table. Like it or not, Dante had surrendered everything. Mrs. Lyle Mitchell was his prime suspect. Last night's search of the Brooks apartment turned up nothing to support Randy Logan's allegations. Mintoff was incensed that Dante had allowed Logan to lure Brooks away from St. Mark's Place. He believed that Joe may well have gotten Logan killed. This possibility was not hot news to Dante. Joe didn't know how the fight between Randy and Brooks got started, but the fact that Logan had walked—or at least crawled—away might mean that Brooks hadn't intended to kill him. Still, Logan was dead, and Dante had put him at risk.

"And I suppose you believe that crawling up Mrs. Mitchell's ass is your next move, right *Lieutenant*?" Mintoff leaned on that last word as if he were crushing a bug into his blotter with his thumb. "Where's your evidence that Mrs. Mitchell was in any way involved? Not hearsay, mister. Something I can throw at a window and expect to break glass. What the fuck's the word of some squirrelly, pelvis-gyrating punk worth?"

"The two subsequent homicides seem to bear it out, Tony," Gus reasoned. "Logan is approached and refuses to pay Brooks's demand. To Mrs. Mitchell, Logan's refusal to pay makes him a liability. So where was she last night? Is it possible she showed at Logan's place, found him in bad shape, and decided to let nature take its course?" He shrugged dramatically. "I don't know. Maybe we should ask her. And maybe we should ask her where she was later. Maybe we should start talking to cabbies who worked that area last night; see if any of them carried a good-looking blonde from Tribeca to the East Village."

Dante watched Mintoff's face as Gus spoke. The P.C.'s jaw remained set, his eyes darting nervously about the room. He picked at invisible lint, first from his sleeve and then from one pant leg.

"Not without your man bringing you something concrete, Chief."

Ah, Dante thought. More distance. Gus was *Chief* now.

"You can talk to cabbies 'til you're blue in the face and whatever they tell you won't mean shit as far as I'm concerned. Not without hard evidence that ties Mrs. Mitchell to all this. Her, specifically.''

A knock came at the commissioner's door, and his exec poked his head inside. ''Sorry to interrupt you like this, sir. There's a Sergeant Grover out here, insisting he talk to the lieutenant. He says it's urgent.''

Dante didn't ask to be excused. He was on his feet and headed for the door with his excitement level on the rise. Don Grover stood in the P.C.'s outer office holding a creased sheet torn from a legal pad. As Dante approached, Grover handed the piece of paper across.

''We knew you wouldn't want us to wait on this, Joe.'' The detective sergeant wore a self-satisfied smile. ''Bingo.''

Dante unfolded the sheet and read the message typewritten across it:

Mrs. Mitchell,

Enclosed photographs for your examination and approval. Your boyfriend doesn't seem to appreciate your situation. He tried to blow me off. Maybe he thinks a quarter mil is too high a price to pay for them. I don't. Talk it over with him. I'll be in touch.

Short and sweet. Unsigned. Dante was tempted to throw his arms around Grover's neck and kiss him. ''I was chin deep in shit and going down fast in there, buddy. You just threw me a lifeline. I owe you one.''

Grover scowled. ''Bullshit.'' He eyed the P.C.'s inner-sanctum door. ''Rough time, huh?''

Dante lowered his voice to a whisper. ''Man's so scared this'll blow in his face, he's trying to hog-tie us.'' He tapped the creased edge of the sheet against his open palm. ''But not anymore.''

Melissa Busby and Guy Napier finally hit paydirt when Guy phoned the *Village Voice*. A woman there told him that

Troy Brooks and the novelist Terrence Dillingham had been pals since bursting almost simultaneously onto the New York literary scene. That was over ten years ago, and while the rest of that world had since turned its back on Brooks, he and Dillingham remained tight.

Napier had the wheel this morning. After parking he sat staring at the front of the impeccably maintained East 36th Street brownstone where Terrence Dillingham lived. "You think the Brooks homicide has hit the news yet?" he asked.

"Good chance."

"Wonder if he's heard."

Melissa turned to face him, and Guy guessed what was going through her mind. They'd been partners for two years now and lovers for nearly that long. Mel seemed as though she could read his thoughts sometimes. She knew facets of his personality that he'd never felt comfortable revealing to his male counterparts. Sometimes, he felt her knowledge compromised their working relationship. Other times, like now, he was glad she understood. This part of the job was the hardest for him—informing friends and loved ones of a death.

"If he hasn't, *I'll* tell him," she offered. "C'mon. The more you think about it, the worse it gets."

Melissa was out of the car and across the sidewalk before Napier emerged to slam his door. He watched the way she charged the stoop and smiled. The fact that he stood a solid foot taller and outweighed her by nearly a hundred pounds in no way made her less his equal. It was something he liked about their dynamics. Their sex, size, and age differences weren't areas of conflict.

There were only three names and buttons on the building intercom panel. A label bearing the name *Dillingham* occupied the center position. Once he rang, Guy stepped back out into the sunshine while Mel shaded the sides of her face to peer in through the door glass. Almost instantly, the door opened inward. Guy had seen pictures of Dillingham in magazines over the years. The man who stood holding the door and squinting against the glare wasn't him.

"You the police?"

"Yes sir," Melissa replied.

"Jesus. What the hell took you? I called at least twenty minutes ago."

It caught Mel off guard. "I'm sorry?"

"You're *sorry*? You just told me you were the police, didn't you?"

Guy stepped up to join Mel on the threshold. "We're not responding to any call," he told the man. "What's the problem?"

Tall, thin, and patrician in his bearing, the man peered at Napier over his tortoiseshell half frames, his mouth open in a gape of disbelief. "I'm not hearing this. I called nine-eleven nearly half an hour ago after hearing what sounded like a gunshot coming from upstairs. I phoned up there to see what was going on, heard a door slam, and got no answer. Then I called you people, for all the good *that* did anyone."

Napier's receptors were wide open now. "Upstairs. Which apartment?"

"Dillingham's. *Terrence* Dillingham. The writer."

Melissa was already past him. She ignored the elevator and mounted the stairs, taking them two at a time.

"Who else has a key to his place?" Guy asked.

"The super. He lives in a basement apartment, two buildings west of here."

"Forget it!" Melissa hollered it down the stairwell. "The front door is open."

Guy sprinted for the landing above and found Mel in the elevator lobby beyond. A door separating the lobby from the stairwell service area stood ajar. Mel had the apartment's front door open a foot and was peering into the room behind it.

"Mr. Dillingham?" she called out. "Police officers."

"You found it that way?" Guy asked.

"Nuh-uh. Closed but not locked."

They waited a moment for an occupant to respond and heard nothing. Napier took a deep breath. "Noise of a gunshot? I think that constitutes reasonable grounds."

Melissa pushed the door all the way open.

When the telephone console on P.C. Mintoff's desk emitted a subdued chirp, he stabbed at the intercom button and leaned forward, anger twisting his face. "Goddammit, Captain, I thought I said no calls!"

"Sorry, sir. Op Desk has an emergency communication for Lieutenant Dante from two of his task force team in the field."

Mintoff switched on the unit's speakerphone. "This is Commissioner Mintoff, Op Desk. Patch them through."

As Dante waited, he hoped to God it wasn't one of his people dicking around, calling to find out what sort of sandwich he wanted for lunch.

"Sir? Detective Busby. Davis homicide task force. Is Lieutenant Dante with you?"

"He can hear you, Busby. We're in a meeting here."

"Yes, sir. Joe?"

"Yeah, Mel," Dante spoke up. "Go ahead."

"I'm with Napier in an apartment at 127 East 36th. Troy Brooks's best friend Terrence Dillingham lived here. We found him on the floor inside the front door. He's dead."

Dante's stomach did a backflip. "Shit!"

"There's more, Joe. A young woman in Dillingham's bed. No I.D. in her handbag; not even credit cards. It's going to be hard to get a positive unless friends or family come forward. She's missing most of her face."

"Sit tight, Mel. I'm on my way." Dante was already on his feet as he said it. He'd left his jacket three floors down in the squad and needed to collect it. As he started for the door, he turned to Gus. "Get hold of my guys for me, will you, boss? Tell them to contact Conklin and Chip Donnelly. Say I'm on my way down.'' He next addressed Mintoff. ''That note to Mrs. Mitchell wasn't *enough* to prove those photographs exist, sir? How about this?''

FIFTEEN

A hectic schedule that morning kept Nancy Hillman oblivious to anything beyond her immediate attention. From her breakfast meeting with the Reverend Davis and Billy Beaumont, she accompanied Jerry to his meeting with the funeral director on Lexington Avenue. Once Cora's body was released Friday morning, Jerry wanted it shipped to Nashville as quickly as possible. Nancy and the reverend returned to the Park View at eleven-thirty. She entered her suite and immediately sensed something had changed. Lyn's bedroom door stood open, but there was no sign of her. When Nancy left two hours ago to meet with the undertaker, Lyn hadn't yet risen. Now, when Nancy poked her head into the empty bedroom she saw the bathroom door standing ajar and an open closet stripped of all but a few garments. The shoe rack was empty. There were two small pieces of luggage on the closet floor, but Nancy failed to locate Lyndelle's garment bag. While the dressing table was still littered with cosmetics, it otherwise appeared as though Lyn had beat a hasty retreat.

Nancy advanced into the room to confirm her suspicions. She stood contemplating one of the several garments left behind in the closet when the phone rang. Lyn was on the other end of the line.

"Nance? God, where have you *been*? I've been trying to get you for almost an hour."

164

"Never mind where I've been," Nancy countered. "What's going on? Your closet is almost empty."

"What's going *on*?" There was a mixture of panic and incredulity in Lyndelle's tone. "You're kidding, right? The man's a maniac. He's on a murdering *rampage*!"

Confused concern became alarm. "Slow down, hon. What are you talking about? *Who* is on a rampage?"

"Billy! For the love of Christ, Nance! You remember what I told you yesterday? What do *you* think?"

"I wish you wouldn't take the Lord's name like that, Lyn. And I don't know what you're asking me. Of course I remember what you told me. There's hardly been another thing on my mind."

"Good God. You haven't heard the news."

"What news, Lyn? I've been terribly busy."

"Randy Logan is *dead*, Nance. And the extortionist I told you about? The one trying to blackmail Randy with the pictures he took? He's dead, too."

Nancy suddenly felt ill.

"I didn't tell you quite everything," Lyndelle confessed. "Randy and I were kissing in those pictures. He and I were old friends. Lovers, actually."

Now Nancy was convinced Lyn was talking gibberish. It simply wasn't possible. Randy Logan? The foulmouthed Antichrist? "Lyn, please. Just tell me where you are. Have you been drinking? Something's obviously upset you."

"You haven't been listening," Lyndelle snapped. "That extortionist tried to blackmail *me*, Nance." She hurried into a description of Beaumont's interception, ending with the evidence of his subsequent activity as reported in that morning's news. "You don't believe me, turn on the goddamn news!"

Nancy had been slow on the uptake, but she wasn't stupid. The information suddenly congealed. She understood. Her slightly sick feeling became acute nausea. "Billy." Her voice was low and hollow.

"Yes!" Lyn fairly shouted it.

Nancy recalled her breakfast meeting with Beaumont and how smugly he'd played it, never betraying his position. She'd always known him to be a cool customer, but right now she felt like a fool.

"Where are you, Lyn?" Her voice struggled to find calm. "You can't just run away. You're a senator's wife."

"I told the hotel desk there's been a family emergency. I'd rather run than stick around and accidentally slip in the tub. Billy's out of control, Nance. I need time. I made a mistake, I admit it, but I shouldn't have to die for it."

Nancy was scrambling now. "How can I reach you? What if Lyle calls?"

"That's my problem, isn't it? Anyway, don't worry. I'll be in touch." Before Nancy could get in another word, Lyndelle broke the connection.

It was a full thirty seconds before the state chairwoman could move. Billy Beaumont was fiercely loyal to his old friend and boss, but was he arrogant enough to believe that protecting the senator's reputation justified murder? It was hard for her to believe he'd sat there at breakfast listening to her own less-drastic solution with a straight face. Nancy didn't know what to believe. How much, if any, of Lyn's story was true? She needed a news update, fast. Then she needed to weigh what she learned with what she already knew; to determine who had the most to gain by the conclusion she reached, and who the most to lose.

After half an hour at the Dillingham scene, Dante decided he'd seen enough. His feelings of helplessness and anger weren't leading him any closer to their source. It was just half past noon, and already he'd witnessed the aftermaths of four homicides. These last two were the worst of them; a successful young writer with his face caved in and a shapely young woman with hardly any face at all. In less than twenty-four hours, every witness Joe could connect to Mrs. Mitchell's philandering had turned up dead. No forensic proof existed connecting these homicides—not yet, anyway—but Dante knew the connection was there. Ballistics tests would show that the bullets killing Brooks and the young Jane Doe in Dillingham's bed were fired from the same gun. It was hard for him to imagine how the elegant, reserved woman he'd interviewed Tuesday night could do what had been done to Terrence Dillingham's face. But Dillingham was a pudgy, dissipated specimen. Evidence suggested he'd ingested some amount of cocaine and alcohol. Mrs. Mitchell looked to be in better-than-fair condition and was tall enough to generate some good leverage. Joe remembered that Congresswoman Davis was killed by a single blow to the head. Blunt object. A little practice could hone a killer's skill.

At 12:35, Dante and Richardson departed the East 36th Street address to take Mrs. Mitchell into custody for questioning. The rest of the task force team was left behind to mop up. Joe had the wheel and guided them uptown along Park Avenue through early lunchtime traffic as Jumbo put words to what they both were thinking.

"Brooks thinks he's hit the jackpot with the pictures he took, but Logan blows him off. One minute Logan is telling him to shove his scam up his ass, and the next he calls back and invites him over. If I were Brooks, I'd be a little paranoid. I'd want to get the goods hidden away someplace safe."

"But," Dante continued the train of thought. "It's after banking hours, so if he's got a safe-deposit box, he's got no access. He doesn't feel safe, waiting until morning, so he turns to his best friend." A cab cut diagonally in front of them to get to the curb, and Joe swerved to avoid him. "Asshole."

"You think Mrs. Mitchell mighta gone back there?" Jumbo asked. "Been there last night when Brooks showed?"

"And left Randy there to bleed to death while she headed off in hot pursuit?"

Jumbo shrugged. "It's possible, ain't it? How could she know how bad he was hurt? He'd gotten the shit beat outta him, but he wasn't cut or shot. Could be she followed Brooks to the East Village, got the drop on him, and put a gun to his head. Under circumstances like those, most people spill the beans. He would have told her where he hid the goods.''

Dante went left at East 61st Street. Two blocks west, he drew up out front of the Park View's side entrance. Thirty-six hours after the congresswoman's murder, everything looked business-as-usual out there on the sidewalk. Various well-dressed men and women pushed in and out through revolving doors. A doorman hailed a cab for a patron, while bellmen unloaded luggage from the trunk of a limousine onto a cart. As long as the Davis homicide garnered headlines, there would be a steady trickle of curiosity seekers drifting through the hotel lobby and lingering out front to stare at the building's facade. After twenty-one years on the Job, Joe still wondered why they were drawn and what they hoped to see. Maybe some part of the human nature stirred certain souls to participate, however remotely, in the tragedy of others.

Passing the front desk on his way to the elevators, Dante noticed lobby traffic seemed lighter than it had the day before. Perhaps his perception was amplified by the darkness of his mood, but the atmosphere seemed heavy today.

''Looks like people been reading the news,'' Jumbo commented. ''Place is like a fucking ghost town.''

So much for Dante's overactive imagination. When the doors of an elevator parted, they found Dom Ricci on duty inside. Yesterday's most helpful witness nodded hello and once the doors closed, isolating them, he lowered his voice to a stage whisper. ''Jesus, Lieutenant. I heard the news about the rock star on the radio during my break. What gives? This ain't no coincidence, right?''

Dante lifted a finger to his lips. ''Any reporters come snooping around, you don't know shit, right paisano?''

Ricci flashed a conspiratorial grin. ''Fuck 'em, Lieutenant. Floor?'' He sat on his stool with hand poised on the control lever.

''Seventeen.''

Ricci started upstairs, his eye on the floor indicator. ''Ain't none of you guys been up to the scene all day. I was wondering when you'd show back up.''

''Any unusual comings or goings?'' Joe asked. He kept his tone conversational. Mrs. Mitchell may have betrayed herself by not covering her movements that morning. Rocky Conklin's examination of the corpses at the Dillingham scene, combined with the neighbor's hearing that gunshot, put the times of death right around ten o'clock.

The operator thought about the question for a second or two before lighting up. ''The senator's wife headed outta here like she had a real bug up her ass. I thought maybe she was sick or something.'' He paused to frown. ''Funny, though. She didn't call for no help with her bag.''

''Bag?'' Beasley beat Joe to it.

''Yeah. A garment bag. Louis Vuitton, Gucci . . . I see so mucha that designer crap it all starts looking the same.''

Dante glanced at Jumbo. ''You're saying she checked out?'' he asked Ricci.

''Either that or she zipped off somewhere for an overnight.''

''What about Miss Hillman?'' Joe pressed him. ''The dark-haired woman sharing Mrs. Mitchell's suite.''

''Oh. She rode downstairs with that reverend fella, fifteen minutes ago. The congresswoman's husband.''

The car arrived at the seventeenth floor and Joe asked Ricci to wait a moment while he jogged down the hall to pound on the door of suite 1706. He didn't wait long for a response but pressed an ear to the panel, listening for sounds of activity within. Less than a minute later he returned and asked for the lobby.

The front desk staff was busy processing several new guests. Joe and Beasley waited a moment before approaching. A tall, efficient-looking woman with prematurely gray hair caught Joe's idle attention. He was drawn closer by her unmistakable accent. She had the same tonal inflections as both Nancy Hillman and Lyndelle Mitchell.

''Checked *out*? There must be some mistake. I spoke with

the senator's office just an hour ago. They assured me that Mrs. Mitchell will be here until at least tomorrow.''

Dante nudged Richardson, nodding in that direction. Jumbo was listening, too, as the clerk started to explain.

"I'm sorry, ma'am. Mrs. Mitchell wasn't scheduled to leave. I believe there was a family emergency. She checked out nearly an hour ago.''

Dante leaned close to Jumbo's ear. "Grab her as soon as she steps away,'' he murmured. "Find out what her interest is.''

Jumbo nodded and drifted back from the desk as his subject turned aside, clearing the way for Dante's inquiry. Joe had his shield case out as he crossed to question the clerk whom he'd just overheard. Dressed like one of the models used in *Town and Country* spreads, she was younger than many of the staff here but typical of the Park View image. The prim, dignified way she squared her shoulders and lifted her chin to greet him suggested to Dante that she took her job very seriously.

"Yes, sir. May I help you?''

Dante eased his shield case into view and tipped his head toward the woman just departed. "Lieutenant Dante. Davis homicide task force. I couldn't help overhear the conversation you just had.'' Her prim dignity went a little soft in the presence of a gold shield. It made her nervous, and probably for no reason. "I heard you say that Mrs. Mitchell checked out. Something about a family emergency?''

"Yes, sir. That's correct. About an hour ago.''

"Did she have you call her a limousine or a cab . . . or happen to say where she was going?''

The clerk shook her head. One delicate hand reached nervously, fingers tugging at the blunt-cut ends of her shoulder-length hair. "No, sir. She didn't do any of those things. I offered to have a bellman help her with her bag. She told me she could handle it, no problem.'' She stopped, lips parting slightly and eyes widening. "Oh. Wait a moment. She *did* say something. Not where she was going specifically, but that she had a plane to catch. She didn't have time to pack some of her things. She said Miss Hillman would deal with sending the rest of her luggage on to Washington."

"Could you leave a message for Miss Hillman?"

"Certainly, sir." The clerk snatched up a pen, obviously relieved to have something to do with her hands.

"Ask her to call me at this number as soon as she gets in." He handed the woman a card. "That's the chief of detectives' office. They can reach me anywhere."

Shortly before leaving the hotel for the mortician's that morning, Jerry Davis had suggested lunch at Tavern-on-the-Green. Now, under the circumstances, Nancy didn't think so open a venue was appropriate. She waited until their cab dropped them out front of the Tavern's awning to stop the evangelist from proceeding inside, touching his elbow and shaking her head.

"Something's come up," she announced. "I think we should take a walk."

Davis looked around him, bewildered. They were in the middle of Central Park. "It's lunchtime, Nancy. You saw what I ate for breakfast. I'm famished."

"You won't be. Come on, Reverend. A little fresh air will do us both good."

She didn't wait for him to comply, but moved ahead on her own. Davis stood fast beneath the Tavern awning until Nancy was halfway across the parking lot. Once he realized she was serious and not coming back, he eased into gear. Her behavior was puzzling. It wasn't at all like her. Nancy most often got her way by mixing equal parts flattery and clarity. Her interests were everyone's interests. Her means to an end were those that cut the cleanest path. The fact that she was so physically appealing didn't hurt either. He very much enjoyed her company and the attentions of handsome women in general, but Nancy in particular. She was acting disturbingly out of character, and that confounded him.

"Wait for me, Nancy. Please." Davis hurried across the

parking lot after her. He finally caught up as she was turning north along West Drive, moving at a brisk pace. No sooner had he pulled alongside, his breathing labored, than she started to speak.

"Lyn checked out of the hotel this morning, Jerry. She called me half an hour ago. I've got no idea where she is."

"She did *what*?" A jogger passed, twenty feet away, followed by two women in full bicycle gear. Otherwise, they were alone out there, the city having blocked the road to traffic as was customary weekdays between ten and three.

Nancy quickly related the basics of what she knew. As he listened, the picture drawn for him became increasingly unsettling. Jerry could only conclude that Lyndelle had a hand in killing his wife. Beyond that, either Lyndelle had elected to eliminate anyone who might bear witness to her crime, or Billy Beaumont had done so in order to protect Lyle Mitchell's position. Either way, his world was suddenly tipped on its ear. Everything they'd discussed at breakfast was moot now.

"This is insanity," he blurted. "She and that mangy rock-and-roll hoodlum? It's beyond belief."

Nancy closed her eyes, her expression pained. "I didn't want to believe it either, Jerry."

"But what about Beaumont? Could he have lost his mind? We had an agreement. All he's accomplished is to dig the hole deeper than it already was." Davis allowed his gaze to linger on Nancy's profile as he spoke. Only God knew how often he'd wanted to touch that face; to penetrate the barrier of decorum between them without making a fool of himself. She was the most desirable creature he'd ever laid eyes on, a mixture of physical charms and ambition that was near perfection.

"We don't know he's involved for a fact," Nancy cautioned. "We know where Billy was for a good part of last evening. But where was Lyn?"

Davis was having a hard time visualizing it. Lyndelle Mitchell raising a lamp over Cora's head and crushing her skull. Lyndelle shooting a man. He stood there at a loss for words.

When Nancy continued, it was almost as if she could read his mind. "You don't want to believe it any more than I do, I know. A beautiful woman with money and her social station. But we have to look at it from her perspective; to think about what she had to lose."

It was much easier for Jerry to believe that Randy Logan had killed Cora, and that Billy Beaumont had killed both Logan and the extortionist. He knew Lyndelle capable of calculation, but only the sort aimed at increasing her pleasure. Like Nancy, she was a creature to be desired, loved, and pampered. Unwilling to concede otherwise, he voiced his misgivings. "If she was responsible for any or all of those three deaths, her running makes no sense. Not before the inquiry tomorrow morning. When she fails to show up, one question is sure to lead to another. Why wouldn't she sit tight once all the leaks were plugged? Billy, too. No one outside our circle knows of Logan's involvement *or* of the extortion attempt."

Nancy hunched her shoulders and frowned at the pavement out front of her as she walked. She was no longer striding purposefully ahead, but going slowly now, deep in thought. "Maybe she's not thinking as clearly as that. Maybe from where she stands, she believes it's already gone too far for turning back."

"So what do *we* do now?" Jerry asked. "Go to the police with what we know and let them sort it out?"

"And give them license to charge ahead like bulls in a china shop? I'm not ready to admit defeat on quite that scale, Jerry. The scandal would destroy a lot of lives and careers, mine included."

Davis felt the tug of his own newborn ambitions at war with the lawfully right thing to do. "It's a shame, you know. The more I thought about running for governor, the more intriguing the notion became. I spent a good portion of my sleepless night last night considering how beneficial my platform could be to the whole moral reconstruction movement. I suppose I should be thankful we've said nothing to the press yet.''

He stopped to look her directly in the eye. For some time now he'd guessed that Nancy knew more about what drove him than she openly admitted. She had to suspect the limitations imposed by Cora and that he had strayed to satisfy his hungers. It didn't stop her from offering him the governorship—a fact that not only flattered his public persona, but also sent a flush of sexual heat through his loins. He had a power that Nancy found desirable.

''I don't think we should give any of those ambitions up until we're forced to,'' she argued. ''I may be a bit overwhelmed right now, but I haven't rolled over.''

It was charming to hear her say it, even though he believed it was posturing. ''And if the police come asking questions? They're sure to if they learn Lyndelle has left the hotel.''

''She called it a family emergency,'' Nancy replied. ''What connection could the police make? That Cora and Logan debated each other? How far can they get if that's all they have? The way I see it, we've got until that inquiry tomorrow to figure out how we'll proceed with this.''

SIXTEEN

While following his subject away from the Park View front desk and across the lobby, Beasley Richardson tried to learn something by studying her appearance. The walk was all business, head held high over rounded shoulders, each foot planted with purpose, her ample hips rotating precisely and with little or no sway. The wash-and-wear cut of her hair was as no-frills as her loden green pantsuit. Businesslike, yes, and more concerned with neat comfort than high fashion. Jumbo was sure she fancied herself a worthy adversary. A tough customer. He gave up studying her demeanor and moved to intercept as she approached the main revolving door.

"Excuse me, ma'am. Sergeant Richardson, Davis homicide task force. Talk to you a minute? I heard you back at the front desk."

She turned to see he had his shield case out for her inspection. The suddenness of his appearance threw her off her game a moment, giving her pause before she nodded. "Certainly, Sergeant." She extended a hand to shake. "Mildred Sipe. Memphis *Commercial Appeal*. Maybe we can make this a dialogue?"

A reporter. He was slipping. "You want to get coffee or something? There's gotta be someplace around here."

She shook her head. "I'm fine, Sergeant. I just had lunch."

Indicating the several furniture groupings, midlobby, she started in that direction. "Anywhere here is okay by me."

Now that he was up close he could see that gray hair notwithstanding, she couldn't have been much over thirty-five. He also noticed that her speech was distinctly different from Mrs. Mitchell's; more easygoing. It told him that while the two women were roughly the same age and spoke with the same gentle twang, they came from different worlds. Once he was settled in a chair set at an angle to hers, he removed his notebook and uncapped his pen.

"Sorry," he apologized. "The *Commercial Appeal*. That's a newspaper?"

She smiled. "Not the *Times*, maybe, but a circulation of nearly a quarter million. I'm an investigative reporter. Political intrigue, white-collar crime, influence peddling; that sort of thing."

He was being buttered for a frank and equal exchange and didn't figure she'd continue to be this forthcoming for long. For the moment he thought it best to steer clear of Mrs. Mitchell and see if he could learn something through the back door. "This is sorta a stroke of luck then, me running into you like this. There's a lot we're still trying to piece together about the congresswoman's power base back home. Who her friends and enemies were. What sorta battles she was fighting on her home turf. Where the beefs and gripes all stood the day she was killed. The New York media are fixated on the wacko angle. We can't afford to narrow ourselves that way. Not yet, at any rate."

"You mind me asking just where you *are* focusing, Sergeant?"

This was the dialogue part. She was supposed to give a little and get something back. "There was a call claiming credit made to one of the big rock radio stations yesterday," he replied. "We're still running that one out, but between you and me, I ain't holding out much hope there. Call came too late and the caller had too much prior information. We've got another team working with the Bureau, combing through the news footage we managed to collect. Amazing what they can do with that stuff now. I'm sure it'll produce some interesting leads.''

''In other words, you're telling me that thirty-six hours into your investigation you're where you were when you started.''

He shrugged. ''You know the game, Ms. Sipe. We dig them out and chase them down. What I'm looking for right now is a sorta primer; the kind I can't get reading a Republican party press guide. How 'bout it?''

She grimaced, adjusting her position impatiently so she had a better view of front-desk traffic. If nothing else, she'd kill the downtime constructively. ''The *real* dirt, right Sergeant? Okay. Cora Davis was a nobody before she met her husband Jerry. Sure, she'd won a Nashville City Council seat running on a platform of righteous indignation, but without the good reverend, that's as far as she was ever going to go.'' Jumbo watched her pause there to consider what she'd said. One who weighed her words. Good. Apparently satisfied, she continued. ''Jerry Davis is immensely popular with the fundamentalist Protestant constituency Cora represented. Over the past few years, the reverend's message from the pulpit has become increasingly political in tone. Cora was the perfect champion for Jerry's causes in Congress. They worked as a team.''

''Sounds like a marriage made in heaven,'' Beasley observed.

She caught the dryness in his tone and grinned. ''You'd think so, wouldn't you? But lately there've been some rumors flying. There are people in the know who say Jerry Davis had misgivings about his wife running for governor. In the press, Davis denied those misgivings. Adamantly.''

Richardson saw a thread of potential intrigue emerging. They'd been assuming that the perp responsible for the Davis homicide was the same one responsible for the subsequent killings. What if they were two separate sets of crimes? The fact that Logan and Lyndelle Mitchell were observed in a compromising position by Troy Brooks did not necessarily mean that either of them had killed the congresswoman. He felt his pulse rate climb as he leaned forward, his hands extended as though prepared to receive a pass from center.

"Help me out here. Why would he have misgivings? The same man who worked as hard as he did to get his wife where she was? Wouldn't being governor give her more power and prestige than being a congresswoman?"

Mildred Sipe's expression was patronizing. "Precisely the problem, Sergeant. Man of God or not, the Reverend Davis is still a man. Like most other men down home, Reverend Davis was no doubt raised to believe it's the man of the family who wears the pants."

"Ah." He couldn't help but grin as he said it. "Being a congresswoman put her on a sorta helpful parallel, but governor would be a whole other ball game. A lot more threatening."

"How enlightened, Sergeant. You give me hope. As a congresswoman championing the same causes her husband preached from the pulpit, Cora Davis was seen as her husband's helpmate. Once the party started courting Cora for the governorship, keen observers noticed a certain flagging of the good reverend's enthusiasm."

"What were her chances?" Beasley pressed. "How much did Reverend Davis really have to fear?"

Another shrug. "If Cora were still alive? If the election were held tomorrow? There's a good chance she would have cleaned the current incumbent's clock, Sergeant. He's embroiled in a banking scandal, and every day it looks worse. Tennessee is an old Democratic stronghold—has been since before the Civil War—but corruption in some quarters is starting to stink so bad it can't be ignored."

"What about enemies?" he asked. "There must be other people who want that job as much as she did. Or some faction particularly outspoken in opposing her? The other day, during that debate, we had close to five hundred people worked themselves into a pretty good lather outside this hotel."

When Mildred Sipe smiled, Beasley saw an edge of malice in it. "I, for one, loathed the woman's politics, Sergeant. So did most of the people in my circle. Not *everyone* from Tennessee is a throwback to the Pleistocene age. But hate her politics enough to murder her? That takes a crazy person."

Richardson liked the woman's candor. He knew enough about Cora Davis's politics to have formed his own opinions. He imagined he and Mildred Sipe were not all that far apart there.

"If I needed to get in touch with you again, how would I do that, Ms. Sipe? You'll be in town for another couple days?"

"That sounds like a dismissal, Sergeant. I've hardly gotten started here."

Beasley smiled warmly. "Me neither, but that's my partner over there." He pointed to where Joey had emerged from a door behind the desk and now stood conversing with the hotel's security chief. "He just gave me the high sign. I'm afraid I've gotta run."

The reporter rose with Jumbo. "I'll trade, Sergeant. You give me your reach number and I'll give you mine. Fair enough?"

He dug into the side pocket of his jacket and handed her a card. "I'm on a beeper. You call that number, they'll find me."

She glanced the card over and nodded. "I'm at the Algonquin. For the moment, I'm booked through Sunday."

As Richardson started in Joey's direction, he mentally sketched a scenario for the Davis homicide with a motive that hadn't previously occurred to him. Envy was the oldest motive in the book. It made him wonder what had kept the Reverend Jerry Davis so conveniently in Washington Tuesday afternoon.

On his return to the hotel late that morning, Billy Beaumont asked the front desk to hold all his calls before heading upstairs for a much-needed nap. When the phone woke him,

Beaumont's bedside clock told him he'd been asleep for less than an hour. He waited until the fifth ring to answer, his anger peaking.

"I thought I asked you people to hold my calls!" he snarled.

"And I thought we had an agreement this morning, mister!" It wasn't a switchboard operator's voice, but Nancy Hillman's, icy with her own rage. "I don't know what you're up to right now, but I suggest you get yourself presentable in a hurry. I'm going to come knocking in about two minutes. You don't answer your door, I'll call the police and wash my hands of you."

Before Billy could reply, the line went dead. As he replaced the receiver in its cradle he tried to imagine what had set off Miss Goody-Two-Shoes. She and the princess were tight. It would be just like Lyndelle to run sobbing to an old friend and soak a shoulder.

True to her word, Nancy arrived at Billy's door while he was splashing water into his face and finger-combing his crew cut. He was surprised to find her accompanied by Jerry Davis when he answered the door. This had nothing to do with Davis. It irritated him to see her complicating matters by dragging that sanctimonious gasbag into it. Leaving the door ajar, he turned away abruptly to open the window curtain, flooding the room with light.

"You mind telling me what the hell this is all about?" he demanded.

"About?" an angry Davis retorted. "It's *about* two murders. I don't know how you were able to keep a straight face this morning, Beaumont." Davis had advanced into the room while Nancy shut the door behind them. He confronted Billy directly now, nearly toe-to-toe. "And if you *are* responsible, I'd like to know one good reason why we shouldn't throw you to the wolves."

So that was it. They'd heard about Brooks. But what was this about *two* murders? Had the Dillingham news aired already? And if it had, he'd killed two people in that apartment.

180

Something didn't add. Billy pushed a smug, narrow-eyed smile back in the good reverend's direction.

"Just what is it you're afraid of, Jerry? This morning you told me how you plan to win the governorship. The one stumbling block was the man you planned to string along. Now he's *not* a problem. Not anymore. I've got his negatives, and the police believe they've got the victim of a dope deal gone south. Nobody's the wiser but us three." He let his grin widen and winked. "Oh, right. Us three and the offending third party. Hell, good buddy. You should be *thanking* me."

Davis turned to gape at Nancy. "I can't believe this. He freely admits killing people in cold blood."

Standing there in his stocking feet, Beaumont loomed a good four inches taller than Davis. Increasing the differential by coming forward on the balls of his feet, Billy peered down at the top of the evangelist's balding head. *Bald* head. Those strands of hair plastered meticulously across his dome were pathetic. "You listen to me, you self-righteous little prick! You think I did it for *me*? You come to me this morning with some half-assed plan to outsmart a guy who can wreck the entire Tennessee state machine and are *still* naive enough to think it might have worked? That kid was a hustler, not some fucking dummy. He had the *goods*, Reverend! Here. Take a look!" Billy crossed to dig into his briefcase for the envelope. He removed two photographs from it and thrust them in Jerry's direction. "Those don't put *me* in jeopardy, Reverend. They put *you* there. You wouldn't have a snowball's chance in hell of being elected governor with Lyle Mitchell destroyed. Wake up and smell the coffee. Ask your champion here what the *real* score is. She'll tell you. Her ass is on the line, too."

"I wish you wouldn't use language like that, Mr. Beaumont. It may work in the back rooms of Washington, but neither Miss Hillman nor I appreciate it."

Billy couldn't believe this guy. "Who are you kidding, Jerry? You don't like the way I talk to you? Tough shit. You're on board for the ride here, same as I am."

Outraged, Davis's eyes shot daggers. "You're mistaken, Mr. Beaumont. I don't *need* to be governor. And I won't sit by here. You've gone too far. I won't condone murder."

Beaumont edged in close and laughed in Jerry's face. Wincing, Jerry backed away a pace, swallowing hard. "Sure you will, Jerry. Let me try a couple of names on you. Kristie Knotts? Mrs. *Gordon* Knotts? Just in case there's any confusion, she's the Kristie Knotts who sings second soprano in your Belle Meade Pavilion choir."

Davis paled visibly, the muscles supporting his scowl sagging as his eyes fell to the floor.

"Or how about Alline Oldham? I can't say Mrs. Knotts is really my type, but Alline? Now there's a set of knockers a man could get down and *wallow* between." Davis looked like he might retch. "I've got another two or three names besides those. In light of them, I'd say that lofty position of yours starts looking a damn sight precarious, wouldn't you?"

It was hard to imagine Nancy didn't understand Beaumont's threat perfectly. Still, she showed no sign of backing off. "We've got a problem of which I doubt you're aware, Billy," she told him. Stepping around the stricken Davis, she picked up one of the photographs Jerry had dropped to the carpet. As she straightened, she stared at it. "Lyn has checked out of the hotel. She heard about Logan and Brooks on the news and thinks she might be next on your hit list."

Beaumont scowled. "Wait a minute. *Logan* and Brooks? Who said anything about Logan?"

Nancy's look told him she was in no mood for games. "I thought we were onto more pressing issues."

Understanding washed over the political infighter like water dumped from a bucket. The condition Brooks was in when he found him last night. When the kid arrived outside his East Village apartment building to find it crawling with cops, he'd emerged from his cab moving stiffly. Billy had confronted him during his retreat from the scene and found his face puffy and bruised, the knuckles of his hands all torn up and bloodied. Billy had his own agenda and hadn't bothered to ask Brooks how he came to get so beat up.

"I didn't touch Logan. Brooks killed him. So what's this bullshit you're feeding me about Lyndelle?"

Nancy shook her head. "She was gone when Jerry and I returned from the funeral director's. I'd just discovered her empty closet when she called. She was hysterical."

"Called from where?" Beaumont demanded.

"She wouldn't say. She fabricated a story about a family emergency and checked out; claimed she had to catch a plane. I think we'd better find her before the coroner's inquiry tomorrow morning; calm her down and try to talk some sense into her."

Billy forced his analytical processes into overdrive. New York was a big city, and the planes out of its airports flew to a lot of destinations. Still, it would be difficult for an amateur to get very far without leaving a trail. Lyndelle's panic would work in his favor. Everyone made mistakes. He gestured impatiently in the Reverend Davis's direction while his focus remained on Nancy.

"Get him out of here and try to impress on him just what the stakes of this game are. If you hear anything from Lyndelle, I want to know about it the minute it happens. Go on; clear off. I've got work to do."

With the disappearance of his prime suspect, Dante called his task force team back to the squad room. Rather than break for lunch, they sent out for sandwiches. Gus was summoned to sit in. Once everyone was assembled, Joe took up position before the blackboard, half a turkey on whole wheat in one hand and a piece of chalk in the other.

"Okay, people. You've heard the news. It looks like we spent the morning scraping shit off fan blades, only to have our suspect give us the slip. That's how it *looks*, anyway. Beasley floated a fly in the soup while we were on our way down here from the hotel. You'd all better have a listen." He nodded in Richardson's direction.

Jumbo wiped his mouth and tossed his napkin onto the desk top before him. "It's something this lady reporter from a paper down in Memphis said to me. She told me that the congresswoman's husband was showing signs of jealousy. Cora Davis's party was planning to run her in the upcoming race for governor, and this reporter thinks the TV preacher was worried about being upstaged if his wife won. That don't mean he had her killed, but it got me thinking. Why are we assuming it's just one perp we're after? What if it ain't?"

"Room access," Napier replied. "Murder weapon. Location of the corpse inside the suite. No evidence of struggle. They all point to someone the victim knew—i.e., Mrs. Mitchell."

"I agree. And all that shit between Mrs. Mitchell and Logan would give her motive . . . *if* the congresswoman stumbled on them together. But what if she didn't? What if Logan and Mrs. Mitchell did their business and only the photographer caught them at it? They'd still have plenty of reason for wanting to see *him* dead. Yeah, the congresswoman was whacked in that same suite, and Logan's presence there tends to implicate them, but one thing we learned yesterday doesn't fit." He stopped, waiting for someone else to make the connection, too. Fifteen seconds ticked by.

"Okay," Napier growled. "You're fishing and I'm hungry. Hook me."

"The congresswoman was called away from that reception to answer a phone call," Jumbo reminded them. "Later, she told the elevator operator taking her to her floor that she'd been summoned upstairs by security. When they arrived there was no one in the hall outside her room, waiting for her. When we asked the security chief about that call, he denied making it; neither him nor anyone on his staff."

"So many things have happened in the past eighteen hours, I'd forgotten all about that call," Dante confessed.

"We all had," Jumbo admitted. "But then while I'm talking to that reporter, she mentions the husband's jealousy and it popped back, front and center. There ain't a reason I can think of why Mrs. Mitchell would make that call, or why the shutterbug would either. So I got to ask myself: Who did?''

"There you have it," Joe told them. "Beasley's fly, our soup. I think it justifies some further probing in that direction. We wonder why, for instance, Reverend Davis didn't appear in New York until late Tuesday evening. It could be there's some legitimate reason. He mentioned something to me about editing a newsletter. We'll check it out." He turned to face the chalkboard, where he'd sketched a very rough map of the greater metro area and inscribed a circle around it. "Meanwhile, Lyndelle Mitchell remains a primary concern. The desk clerk at the Park View tells us Mrs. Mitchell checked out of the hotel at eleven-fifteen this morning. She refused their offer to call her a cab and left some of her luggage behind. That suggests she's traveling light and wants to avoid leaving a trail. If she intends to leave the city by plane, she's had barely two hours to reach an airport, purchase a ticket, and get aboard. It's been thirty minutes now since Chief Lieberman requested Operations set up a liaison with the FBI, FAA, and airport security at LaGuardia, Kennedy, Newark, and Westchester. They're putting together a command center at LaGuardia and establishing a computer link to call up passenger manifests for all departing flights." He turned away from the board, his eyes falling now on Grover and Heckman. "I want you two guys on the scene, ASAP. We're talking about a two-hour window that's growing every second. Any inconsistencies you run across, chase them down." He turned in Melissa's direction next. "The *Times* faxed a recent photo of Mrs. Mitchell to Printing Section. I want you and the Boy Wonder to collect the dupes. Chief of department's got uniforms en route to Grand Central, Penn Station, and both Port Authority terminals. Let's get those fliers distributed and establish contact with the C.O. at each location. Even if she's already given us the slip, somebody might remember seeing her. She stands out in a crowd."

"What about the Hillman woman?" Melissa asked.

185

"Didn't you say she and Mrs. Mitchell have been friends since college? If they're that close, maybe she knows something."

A yawn escaped Dante's mouth, surprising him. All that good sleep he'd gotten last night was already wearing thin. "She was out to lunch. I left word for her to call and haven't heard back, but Beasley and I are headed back there now." He shoved the last of his sandwich into his mouth, chewed hurriedly, and swallowed. "Okay people. Those are your marching orders. Time's wasting. Call me with good news."

SEVENTEEN

When a cellular call to the Park View found Nancy Hillman returned from lunch, Dante requested she remain accessible for the next hour. As he and Jumbo arrived at the hotel for the second time that afternoon, Dante wondered how many more times they would go through these motions. From the cognizant nods of doormen on Fifth Avenue, to the smiles of acknowledgment flashed by lobby staff, they were becoming regulars.

On his way toward the elevators, Joe recognized a clerk recently come on duty as the same one he'd spoken to yesterday about Mrs. Mitchell's lost room key. He caught his partner's eye and veered to approach the desk. Before he could dig out his shield case and present it, he realized he needn't bother.

"Good afternoon, Lieutenant. Sergeant."

Dante thought this woman seemed a trifle less upbeat than she'd been yesterday. Recent events were starting to ever-so-subtly fray nerve ends. "I was wondering," he asked. "Did Mrs. Mitchell's lost key ever turn up?"

She shook her head. "I told my supervisor that you were interested. She asked everyone to keep an eye out. I'm working a split today and asked about it when I came on after lunch. Maybe it *did* fall down that grate."

"Maybe," Joe agreed. He turned to go when something else occurred to him. He glanced over at the message cubbies

187

set into the wall behind the clerk. "Tell me something. If somebody wanted to deliver a message to a guest—by messenger, let's say—does the messenger take it up to the room or leave it here at the desk?"

"We don't allow messengers upstairs, Lieutenant. The elevator operators are supposed to screen them out. Generally, hand-delivered mail is left here at the desk. We call the room to advise a guest that a delivery was made. They have the option of either collecting it personally or having a bellman bring it up."

There was no way that the extortion note discovered by Don and Rusty had made its way to Mrs. Mitchell via the regular mails. Not enough time had elapsed to allow delivery. Joe was assuming Mrs. Mitchell *had* received it, but now confronted the possibility that she hadn't. She knew from Randy Logan what the extortionist's intentions were. It was conceivable, then, that the letter might still be sitting in Mrs. Mitchell's box. He peered at the tiny numbers until he found suite 1706. The box was set high enough to prevent him from seeing anything lying flat on the bottom of it.

"Who else has access to guest mail?" he asked. "Do they have to collect everything personally, or can someone else pick it up?"

The clerk frowned, trying to figure where he was going. "We don't generally have a problem with theft, if that's what you're asking. But unless it's marked personal or there are other specific instructions, another guest could collect mail for a friend or associate. That often happens when a business group books a block of rooms, say."

Jumbo was following the direction of Dante's inquiry. He pointed to the 1706 box. "Anything on the bottom of Mrs. Mitchell's cubby there?"

The clerk started to turn and stopped, shaking her head. "Miss Hillman would have collected it along with any other messages. There were a number of them when she stopped here half an hour ago; including one from you, I believe."

"Were any for Mrs. Mitchell that you remember?" he pressed.

She frowned, thinking back. "Not today. No. Not any mail for either of them. Just phone messages."

"What about yesterday?" Dante asked. "You seem to have a pretty good memory. I'm wondering if there were any messenger deliveries for Mrs. Mitchell. Specifically." He remembered Logan telling him that Lyndelle Mitchell hadn't yet been approached by Brooks when she arrived downtown at Randy's Tribeca loft. That was late morning. She didn't leave Logan's until sometime early afternoon. This same clerk was on duty that shift, too.

"Not that I received. No sir." She scowled, seeming to recall something lurking almost out of reach. "Wait a moment. There was one envelope addressed to Mrs. Mitchell in the box when I came on. I remember it specifically because Mr. Beaumont collected it for her when he checked in."

The senator's chief of staff. So much had happened in the past eighteen hours that Beaumont's arrival to handle the Japanese negotiations had become seemingly irrelevant. "When was that?" Joe asked.

"Late yesterday afternoon, sir. Around four. He arrived on the Delta shuttle and both Mrs. Mitchell and Miss Hillman collected him from the airport."

"And *he* collected the envelope addressed to Mrs. Mitchell."

"That's correct. Along with quite a lot of other mail."

If only the switchboard operator they'd interrogated yesterday morning had the same attention to detail. Joe had been struggling with what could have provided the impetus to turn a woman of Mrs. Mitchell's station and demeanor to murder. By the time she returned to the hotel yesterday afternoon, she would certainly have been on edge with the knowledge of the Brooks extortion scheme. The thought of those photographs accidentally falling into third-party hands could have been the push she needed, what had set her off.

"Mr. Beaumont?" he asked. "What room is he in?"

The clerk tapped a few keys on her computer and scanned the monitor screen. So she was mortal, after all. She didn't remember *everything*.

"Seventeen-eleven, Lieutenant. Would you like me to call upstairs? See if he's in?"

"Not necessary. We're on our way up to see Miss Hillman anyway. We'll stop by."

Thirty-five years ago Billy Beaumont had pledged a fraternity at the Citadel. In the years since, he had joined half a dozen other fraternal organizations. It was commonly held that such organizations were useful networking tools in business—a common bond shared by men of similar social position, political interests, and ambitions. For Billy's money, the bonding strengths of clubs and organizations took a backseat to the bonding strength of war. In his life there was no stronger bond than the one that welded him and other Special Forces personnel of the Vietnam era together. Many Green Beret officers, commissioned and noncommissioned alike, had stayed in touch since the conflict. Some had embarked on business ventures together. Others, like Billy and his former C.O. Lyle Mitchell, had forged political alliances. When compared statistically, he believed that closely knit commands like the Special Forces would prove to have produced more men who rose to positions of power and responsibility than any other segment of the armed forces. That was the nature of the interdependence and cooperation such units fostered.

Clyde Vaughn, a senior administrator at the Federal Aviation Administration's Department of Transportation headquarters in Washington was one such Special Forces product. A former major who'd served briefly under Lyle Mitchell, Vaughn had seen his career at FAA given a leg up once Mitchell was elected to the senate. He'd moved from the obscurity of a regional safety-inspection office in Kansas City to directing the agency's effort to monitor aircraft manufacturing specifications worldwide. Billy Beaumont had helped bring Vaughn's situation in Kansas City to Lyle Mitchell's attention. A subsequent series of rapid promotions resulted in an annual salary increase of nearly forty thousand dollars and side benefits worth twice that much.

"Billy!" Vaughn roared when reached at his DOT office. "You don't call, you don't write. How the hell you been, buddy? You getting any, or should I even ask?"

"A little here and there," Beaumont admitted. He had his tie loosened and was slouching in one of the room's big, comfortable chairs. The top sheet of a pad propped in his lap was scribbled with notes. Vaughn was the last of a half-dozen calls he'd made. After this contact, all he need do was sit and wait for Lyndelle to fall into his net. "Listen, Clyde. I've got a little favor I need you to do me."

"You name it, buddy."

"This means something we've got to keep on the Q.T. Just between us," Billy explained. "You ain't been living under any bushel baskets, so I imagine you've heard some of the things being said about Lyle's new wife." He let it hang out there and waited for Clyde to come to it.

"Yeaaah." Slow and carefully drawn out. "I always thought a piece of ass that good looking was *too* good to be true. What's the trouble?"

"Don't know that there is any. Just looking to play it on the safe side. She flew up to New York this week with Cora Davis, and in the wake of *that* mess, she's dropped outta sight. She told Lyle she intended to spend some of the time with old friends, but never said anything about checking out of her hotel. He's off on Guam and asked me to keep an eye out. This move caught me by surprise."

"Any idea where she went?"

"That's my problem," Beaumont admitted. "She could be anywhere. I've got no idea what she's up to, but if she's using all that craziness as cover to fly off with some scuba instructor, I want to know who and where."

"I read you, good buddy. Consider all exits covered. She

set foot in a ticket line anywhere in the northeast over the past two days, I've got her nailed cold. Damn shame the old man had to fall for a package like that. You don't *marry* bitches like her.''

"This is just between you and me, Clyde-boy. I'm on my way to National to catch the shuttle now. You get lucky, leave me a message at the Park View.''

"I get lucky with the lights out. This be too easy to call luck.''

As Vaughn said it, a knock came at Beaumont's door. He told Clyde he had to go, racked the receiver, and hauled himself from his chair to answer. While reaching for the doorknob he mentally retraced the progress made over the past forty-five minutes. He could see no gaps in his coverage. Now it was a waiting game.

Billy discovered two plainclothes cops on the other side of his door. He didn't really need to see the shield cases they held in their hands, having dealt with enough cops over the years to believe he'd know one naked. The tall white guy with the lean, pro-athlete's build and the beautiful tweed jacket might have been tough to pin alone, but coupled with the black guy beside him, the pair of them reeked law.

"Afternoon, officers. What can I do for you?''

The white guy introduced himself as Dante, a lieutenant and commander of a task force investigating Cora's murder. The spook was a sergeant named Richardson. Dante asked if it was okay for them to come in for a few minutes. Billy didn't see why not.

As the two of them entered, each taking in the interior of the room with its rumpled bedclothes and the briefcase opened atop them, Beaumont was careful to observe and catalog. He was skilled there, trained as a soldier to break a subject down into its component parts, evaluating each in turn. He took the task force commander first and within seconds noticed the condition of the man's hands. He'd seen hands like those before, for the first time on a hand-to-hand combat instructor on loan to Special Forces from the South

Korean army. That R.O.K. army sergeant's specialty was silent killing with knife, garrot, or bare hands. Billy judged this man to be in his late thirties or early forties; young to have drawn such important duty. This was not an adversary to be underestimated.

"I understand you're Senator Mitchell's chief of staff," Dante opened. "Mind if we sit?"

"Please," Billy invited. He indicated the empty settee and chairs. "You understand right. In light of what's happened here, I thought it best I come up to monitor the situation firsthand. The congresswoman was scheduled to conclude some delicate negotiations on this trip . . . with potential foreign investors in our state. It's fallen to me to carry that ball now, too."

"Uh-huh." Dante made a note in the book he'd withdrawn from an inside jacket pocket. "Those negotiations were of interest to us until Miss Hillman assured us the deal was all but signed and sealed. Was it? You make it sound like less of a sure thing."

"Naw. It's just that these folks are a skittish lot. That's all. No deal is ever a sure thing until there's ink on the dotted line."

Another note got jotted. Billy wondered what the hell he could be writing and figured it for theatrics. Cop theatrics.

"We understand Mrs. Mitchell has checked out of the hotel, Mr. Beaumont. Something about a family emergency. What can you tell us about that?"

Point-blank. Just one softening salvo and then right to the heart of the target. Billy hadn't anticipated it coming quite so soon in their conversation, but he *had* anticipated it. He let his expression go just a hint sheepish and heaved a sigh. "I suppose, with the coroner's inquiry set for tomorrow morning, that you view her departure as being problematic. Correct, Lieutenant?"

"The inquiry is part of the problem," Dante agreed. "But only if she doesn't show. More immediately, we have some questions we'd like her to answer."

"Maybe I can help you with them," Billy offered. "Or Miss Hillman."

There was no hint of camaraderie in the lieutenant's expression; just a deadpan stare with slightly raised eyebrows. "Nice try, Mr. Beaumont. Where is she?"

Billy eased back in his chair and shook his head. There wasn't much maneuvering room here, but the club he carried still had a lot of clout in it. These guys were two municipal flat feet and he was a U.S. senator's mouthpiece. "The truth, Lieutenant? Mrs. Mitchell's known to have a mind of her own. I haven't the foggiest. I was up half the night with this Jap business and up early again this morning meeting with Miss Hillman to talk changes on the Tennessee political scene. I took me a little nap around noontime—or at least tried—before Nancy shows up at my door all panicked with news that Mrs. Mitchell's checked out. I've got a theory or two on the subject, but most everything in my mental oven is sorta half-baked."

"You mind letting us peek inside?" Dante pried. "See if anything's burning?"

So the guy was a wiseass, too. "Yeah. I *do* mind. You've got to understand the delicacy of my situation here, Lieutenant. It's my responsibility to protect the standing and reputation of a United States senator. I'd be talking out of school if I was to speculate on his wife's behavior."

"It sounds to me like you've got a question or two of your own about it." The spook sergeant made this observation.

"That's saying something I haven't, Sarge." The spook looked formidable in his own right. He was about the same height and build as Billy, quite a bit thicker through the chest and middle but by no means a fat man. There was nothing handsome about the face. The white cop was saved from being too good looking by a rugged, tough-guy chin and a couple of nasty scars etched along his jaw and neck. This other looked just plain mean; a straight-ahead, battering-ram type of mean. "What I'm saying is that you two need to understand *my* responsibilities. Maybe you don't read the tabloids, but what they've got to say about the senator's young wife ain't all nice. I'll be damned if I'll help fan those flames.''

"Then let me put it to you as plainly as I can," Dante suggested. "For the moment, anyway, Mrs. Mitchell is our prime suspect in the murder of Cora Davis. That's all I'm at liberty to tell you, but it should be enough to help *you* understand what *my* responsibilities are. You want to protect Senator Mitchell, I suggest you play ball.''

Beaumont's heart started an involuntary trip-hammering against his sternum. "She's *what*?!" Damn the bitch's eyes. How had he screwed up? Sources in Washington told him that NYPD's forensic people had struck out. What were they hanging their suspicions on? Something they'd found in Logan's possession? And what could *that* be? If they'd found one of Brooks's photographs, Lyndelle would be a suspect in more than just Cora's murder.

"You heard me, Mr. Beaumont." The white cop's voice was cold as cutlass steel.

Billy met the man's stare, cool for cool. "So what is it you want from me, Lieutenant? An admission that there *is* no family emergency? You know that anyway. You want me to embarrass Lyle Mitchell by taking a shot in the dark at where his wife might be? I won't do that. I don't believe she killed Cora Davis. Why would she?''

The spook sergeant answered that question. "What do you know about the contents of a letter addressed to Mrs. Mitchell here at the hotel, Mr. Beaumont? One you picked up from the desk yesterday.''

Billy never saw it coming. Jesus. They knew everything. He sat hard on a sudden surge of panic and was sure his face betrayed him. He shrugged, maybe a hair too dramatically. "Nothing. Why? Was it something important?''

Dante didn't reply as he heaved himself to his feet, followed by his partner. "I bet you think we're jerking your chain here, Mr. Beaumont; trying to jar something loose. I wish I were. If you hear from Mrs. Mitchell, I hope you're smart enough to let us know.'' He started for the door.

Billy couldn't believe this guy's arrogance. Who did he think he was talking to? He was on his feet and following as Dante got the door open and started through into the hall. ''And I hope *you're* smart enough to give the wife of a United States senator the benefit of the doubt, Lieutenant. Mrs. Mitchell's behavior is due to nothing more than her high-strung nature. I'll bet money on it. Maybe I should remind you that Lyle Mitchell is a senior member of the Senate Appropriations Committee. A city that's in as sorry shape as New York can't afford to piss off anyone in his position.''

Dante stopped in the hall and turned back to face Beaumont square-on. ''That sounds like a threat, Mr. Beaumont. You want to go on record with it? I can have a court stenographer here inside half an hour.''

Before moving across the hall to Nancy Hillman's suite, Dante dragged Richardson back into the privacy of the elevator alcove to compare a few notes.

''Confident bastard, ain't he?'' Jumbo observed.

''He knows more than he's telling,'' Dante replied. ''Or at least suspects it. I'm wondering if he doesn't have Mrs. Mitchell stashed somewhere, hoping we'll stumble onto something that takes the heat off her.''

''He's a damn fool if he does. I think he was assuming a couple of things that we just shot out from under him. His poker face flinched back there. Twice. If he's hidden her, he had to know we'd tied it to her somehow. But *prime* suspect? That rocked him.''

''It did,'' Dante agreed. ''That, and mention of the letter. How much you want to bet that the senator is on his way back from the Pacific, even as we speak? That before Mrs. Mitchell shows up at any inquiry tomorrow, they've got him in their corner?'' As he asked it, Dante checked the time. It seemed like it had to be later in the day than only two-thirty.

"Once Mitchell shows up, ours becomes the center act in a three ring circus. We need to find her, Beasley. Soon."

"So let's get authorization to hang a wire on this bastard's phone. There's reasonable cause by the shit-load. Suspicion of sheltering the prime suspect in four fucking homicides? I don't care *who* the son of a bitch works for. Ain't a judge in New York who'd deny us."

Dante jerked his head in the direction of Suite 1706. "Let's hit the Hillman woman first; see how her ignorance matches up. Who you want to be?"

"You kidding?" Jumbo asked. "Big ugly nigger like me is tailor-made for this job."

Dante grinned. "Okay, but not *too* bad. Just the specter of mean, held in check on a flimsy-looking leash."

"No sweat. I can tell us black folk make her sorta nervous anyway. That leash'll look like fucking kite string."

EIGHTEEN

For all Nancy Hillman knew, Lyn was now on a plane for Nassau or Caracas. Two and a half hours after Lyn called, Nancy returned to her suite to find no further messages. A short time later, the detective lieutenant reached her to say he was on his way. Nancy could guess what was on his mind. Any minute now he would trigger a massive manhunt. Disaster loomed for Lyle Mitchell, Nancy, and the entire Tennessee Republican machine. It was only a matter of time before the world knew Lyn was a fugitive, and Nancy was in a near panic to figure some way of stalling that inevitability. She needed to buy herself at least twelve hours; time to patch the boat Billy had shot full of holes. As far as she was concerned, Lyle Mitchell had already toppled overboard, but Jerry and the governorship were another matter. If Nancy could make the public see Cora Davis as a martyr—a victim of the moral decline she and her husband waged war against—Jerry might yet rise phoenixlike from the fire of Lyn Mitchell's sins.

Nancy was so deep in her reverie when Lieutenant Dante's knock came that it startled her. When she answered she found the lieutenant accompanied by his heavyset negro partner. She wasn't quite sure why, but once again she sensed that this latter man looked on her with disdain as he entered. Maybe it was because she was a young, relatively affluent white woman from the South. That would make her an obvious target. In her experience, men like Sergeant Richardson often harbored bitterness.

"Gentlemen. Please have seats. Can I get you anything? Coffee? Your message sounded urgent."

Neither detective was wearing or carrying an overcoat, and as they sat, declining her offer of a beverage, Nancy made mention of the lieutenant's unusual jacket. "What a beautiful tweed, Lieutenant. Where is it from? Do you know?"

"Ireland. Donegal," he replied. "I took a trip there this past fall. What's going on with Mrs. Mitchell, Miss Hillman? We stopped here to ask her some questions around noontime and learned from the front desk that she's checked out."

"It's funny," Richardson added, "but when we talked to Mr. Beaumont just now, he pretty much admitted there ain't no family emergency."

They'd talked to Billy. Nancy had to force a pragmatic calm into her tone as she replied. "I'm afraid this could get a little sticky, gentlemen. Mr. Beaumont no doubt tried to be diplomatic, and I'm not sure how much I should say, either. Like Mr. Beaumont, I'm concerned with protecting Mrs. Mitchell's husband."

"Protect him from what?" Richardson pressed.

Nancy took a deep breath and smoothed her skirt down over her knees. Some fast thinking had gotten her onto the right track. Of course Billy wouldn't say anything. His loyalty to Lyle made him predictable in that regard. "If you're worried about Lyn failing to appear at that inquiry tomorrow morning, I think you can put your minds at rest. I received her assurance that she'll be there. You need to understand how incompatible her life-style is with the sort of scrutiny she's been under these past two days." She watched the sergeant shoot a confused glance in his partner's direction. The lieutenant, too, seemed perplexed.

"I'm afraid I *don't* understand, Miss Hillman. You're saying she's hiding? Why?"

Nancy pushed herself to her feet and wandered to the window overlooking Central Park. Bright sunshine reflected off the windshields of cars streaming down Fifth Avenue. With the warm turn of the weather, pedestrians strolled with surprising profusion along the sidewalks. "Lyn Mitchell has been my friend for a long time, Lieutenant. She's a beautiful young woman married to a much older man. I'm afraid she has certain . . . well . . . *appetites* that society believes a good girl shouldn't indulge. Frankly, I think it was living here in New York those several years that changed her." She turned back to her guests, her face a touch sad at having to say these things. "I blame myself for introducing her to Lyle. I didn't honestly know the whole truth behind who she'd become. It's such a shame."

Richardson's brows knit over brooding dark eyes as he spoke. "So where is she?"

"That I don't know."

"Ah. And you expect us to believe that?" It dripped sarcasm.

Nancy walked toward Lyn's open bedroom door and stood looking in. "You tell me how far she's gone, Sergeant. Come over and take a look. Half her luggage is still here, along with most of her makeup." Thank goodness for that. Nancy saw it giving her the traction she needed to bear down a little—to put *them* on the defensive. "What is it you want with her, anyway? Other than to pry into the peculiarities of her private life?"

Dante suddenly changed direction. "What do you know about a letter Mrs. Mitchell received yesterday afternoon, Miss Hillman? Did she mention it to you?"

"Letter? From whom, Lieutenant?"

Dante rose and tucked his notebook back inside his jacket. "If you hear from Mrs. Mitchell, we'd like you to let us know. You've still got the card I left for you at the desk?"

She nodded.

"Please, Miss Hillman. It's important."

Nancy followed him as he started away. "What's this all about, Lieutenant? If she's assured me you'll see her at the coroner's inquiry, why is finding her now so important?"

"She's our prime suspect in the Davis homicide," Dante replied. "If she's innocent, it's in her best interest to get in touch. Right now there's some pretty strong evidence mounted against her."

Three cab rides, one broken heel, and three hours spent in a strange hotel room after leaving the Park View, Lyndelle Mitchell was a wreck. The room was on the fifth floor of the Grand Hyatt on 42nd Street at Park Avenue. Shortly after arriving there, after phoning Nancy and ordering a room-service lunch, Lyndelle turned on the television to watch the local news. The latest breaking story to make the noon broadcast was a report on the murder of novelist Terrence Dillingham and an unidentified woman in his East 36th Street apartment. When the reporter mentioned the possible connection of this incident with the murder of Dillingham's best friend that morning, Lyn lost her appetite for her lunch. That best friend was Troy Brooks. The media still hadn't connected Brooks to Randy, but she believed it was now only a matter of time.

Convinced that she was next on Beaumont's list, Lyndelle could see no way to go back from here. Billy and Lyle were much better friends than she and Lyle could ever be. If Lyle had to choose between them, there really wasn't any choice. She was an object, and Billy was a blooded war buddy. The best thing to do was run. If she could get herself safely hidden away from Billy, sooner or later the police would figure out who killed Cora. The murder of a congresswoman wasn't the sort of thing cops gave up on. She had some mad money socked away in an account back home in Memphis. Not a lot, but enough to carry her for six or seven months. By that time, all this craziness would have blown over. She wouldn't be able to go back to her life with Lyle, but at least she'd be alive.

Her most immediate problem was a shortage of ready cash. She'd not been thinking all that clearly when she bolted from the Park View. She'd forgotten her makeup. Some clarity had returned now as she formulated a basic plan. Dressed down in slacks, her gray sweater, and flats, hair tied back and sunglasses, there was little chance of being spotted on the crowded streets of midtown. Her AMEX card was good for a thousand bucks. She could get another five hundred each with her VISA, Master, and automated-teller cards. Twenty-five hundred dollars wasn't a lot of money, but it would be a start. It and an airline ticket charged to one of her cards would easily get her to Mexico—there was a remote stretch of beach on the west coast that she knew—and keep her until her money from Memphis arrived.

Beasley and Joe were back in the elevator alcove, Jumbo leaning against a wall while Dante paced tight circles, his head bent in thought.

"I'm wondering if *she's* the one who has her hidden," Joey mused. "And that Beaumont knows it but doesn't know where."

"So how do you think Davis fits in? Him and the Hillman woman traveled up here together Tuesday evening on the train. Why then and why together, other than the fact they're two peas from the same fucking pod? She's such a tight-ass she nearly squeaks when she walks. You think maybe she turns tiger with her skirt over her head?"

Dante snorted. "Now *that* would be an interesting development, wouldn't it? Those two working together at one end and Beaumont working alone at the other?"

"Couldn't hurt to dig a little more," Jumbo supposed. "I'm not quite as fired up over the jealous-spouse angle as I was a couple hours ago, but I'd still like to know why he waited until so late in the day to come up here."

Dante led the way from the alcove into the hall. "So let's go ask him."

Jerry Davis suspected that Tuesday night's heavy sedation had adversely affected his sleep cycle. He'd slept poorly last night. After his walk in the park with Nancy and their con-

fronting Beaumont, he'd felt suddenly exhausted. On returning to his room he'd kicked off his shoes, stripped down to
his skivvies, and stretched out to close his eyes for an hour
or so. For the past forty minutes, he'd had no luck finding
slumber. Instead, images of Alline Oldham's breasts and
Kristie Knotts's ample thighs persisted in flaunting themselves before his mind's eye; Alline's breasts, Kristie's thighs,
and Nancy Hillman's face.

Over the past two days, Jerry had spent more time in Nancy's company than he had over the past year. It made him
more acutely aware of his desire for her than he thought he
could stand, but rather than destroy their rapport with a
clumsy advance, he was still seeking the right moment to
declare himself. He'd thought the time might come during
their romantic lunch in the park, but events had conspired
against him. Oh, how they had conspired. He could still see
the look of hurt on Nancy's face as she absorbed Billy Beaumont's threats. In his weakness for the flesh, Jerry had betrayed her and betrayed God. He stood compromised in the
Lord's eyes, and in her eyes, too. Now, as he searched desperately for some means of redeeming himself, he wondered
how soon the throbbing ache in his loins would overwhelm
him. Just as he reached a point of total immersion in the pain
of his desire, the illusion was shattered by a knock at his
door.

"Who *is* it!" he all but snarled.

"Lieutenant Dante, Reverend. Can I speak with you a
minute?"

With the detective's muffled voice, the spell was broken.
Davis scrambled from bed, his erection wilting rapidly as he
hurried to the closet for his robe. "Just a moment, please.
I'll be right with you."

Davis stepped into the bath, ran the tap, and carefully
brushed the lank strands of hair dangling down over his right
ear back across the crown of his head. He splashed water
into his face and patted it dry before crossing to answer the

door. He found Lieutenant Dante and that black sergeant, Richardson, on his threshold.

"You might have done me the courtesy of calling first," he snapped. "I was *trying* to take a nap."

"Sorry, Reverend," Dante apologized. "Can we come in?"

Davis stepped back with reluctance. "I hope this is regarding some breakthrough you've made, Lieutenant. I find all this waiting around with no word from you people extremely frustrating."

Dante and his partner eased past and stood waiting for Davis to offer them seats. Instead of doing so, Davis stepped over to lean back against the windowsill, arms folded.

"I'm afraid the only development is Mrs. Mitchell's disappearance," Dante replied. "Are you aware that she's checked out of the hotel?"

Jerry watched the lieutenant closely in an attempt to determine what he already knew. The man was giving nothing away. "You spoke with Miss Hillman?" he asked.

"Did Mrs. Mitchell say anything to you before she left, Reverend? Anything to indicate why?"

"No sir. She did not. Surely you don't believe *she* had anything to do with my wife's death."

Again, Dante veered off onto new ground. "We haven't really had a chance to follow up our conversation of yesterday, Reverend. Have you had any new thoughts? We're still trying to assemble a list of all your wife's enemies."

Davis let himself relax a bit. He took a deep breath, closed his eyes, and pinched the bridge of his nose while shaking his head. "Don't think I haven't given it plenty of consideration, Lieutenant. I've hardly thought of anything else. No, I'm afraid I *haven't* come up with anything new, I'm sorry to say."

"You just asked me if I've spoken with Miss Hillman. I assume that means you have?"

Jerry focused on his interrogator with new curiosity. The way the man bobbed and weaved with his questions was irritating. "Miss Hillman has been most supportive these past two days, Lieutenant. I've spoken with her any number of times. Yes."

"You had lunch with her today, correct?"

"We decided to skip lunch and take a walk in the park instead. I haven't really regained my appetite, and it turned into such a nice day."

"She told you about Mrs. Mitchell's checking out then?"

Jerry frowned and nodded. "She did. I'm afraid I've been so preoccupied with my own problems that I hadn't noticed Mrs. Mitchell's behavior. Nancy seemed to think Lyndelle might profit from my having a heartfelt chat with her. I didn't realize the urgency of it was so pressing."

"Does Miss Hillman know where Mrs. Mitchell is, Reverend?" Sergeant Richardson asked.

Davis shook his head. He didn't like the sergeant's manner. While Dante was a bit slippery with his questions, but otherwise pleasant, Richardson was coarse and abrupt. "I have no idea what Miss Hillman knows, Sergeant."

"But wouldn't she tell you if she *did* know, Reverend? You two are pretty close, ain't you?"

"Just what does that mean?" Jerry snapped. He'd lost his patience. He wanted these two men out of his room.

"It means that you and Miss Hillman traveled here on the train together Tuesday night; that you and her had a appointment together with the funeral director who's shipping your wife's body home. You've shared a couple meals together. That would indicate to me that you're pretty close friends. Am I mistaken?"

Davis came away from the windowsill to draw his robe tighter around him, the picture of indignation. "My relationship with Miss Hillman is purely professional, Sergeant. In her capacity as chair of our state's Republican Committee she became a good, loyal friend of Cora's and a friend of mine as well. I don't like what you seem to be suggesting."

Richardson threw Dante a look of helplessness and spread his hands in a gesture of apology. "Listen, Reverend, I ain't implying nothing. I said it looked like you two were friends. Good friends. And you just confirmed it.''

"That's not how I read it,'' Davis shot back. "I . . .''

"Gentlemen!'' Dante interrupted. "Can we move on?'' He paused, waiting as Jerry glowered at Richardson. "The matter of your arriving here so late Tuesday is something we touched on yesterday.'' The lieutenant referred briefly to his notebook. "You said you were at home in your wife's Washington apartment all Tuesday afternoon; that you edited a newsletter of some sort and made some phone calls. That you had lunch out.'' The notebook snapped closed. "I had the impression your wife's debate was a pretty big deal. I'd think you'd want to attend.''

Davis stiffened. "Of course there's a reason I couldn't accompany Cora. Otherwise, I would have.''

"You mind explaining that reason?''

Jerry's lower lip began trembling. "How dare you! My wife is killed in this godforsaken city of yours, and you're asking *me* where *I* was Tuesday? Washington is over two hundred miles away, Lieutenant.''

"I'm aware of that, Reverend.'' The man was irritatingly calm. "It's standard procedure to determine where the husband of a murder victim was at the time she was killed; where he was and why.''

"I don't believe this!'' Davis sputtered. "You're asking me to detail my *alibi*? You people have no shame!''

"Simple question, Reverend. You were in Washington Tuesday afternoon. This newsletter had some sort of deadline? What?''

"I was *lobbying*, damn you! For legislation Cora authored to see the name of God allowed back into the public-school curriculum. The vote is scheduled for Monday, and both of us were to be out of town for the rest of the week. Cora thought the matter every bit as important as I did. It demanded my full attention.''

Dante refused to relent. "So those were the phone calls you made? To other congressmen or whatever?''

"That's right. To other congressmen, to organizations sympathetic to our cause. You want names, I'll give you names."

The lieutenant had the audacity to flash him a cool, bland smile. "Thank you, Reverend. I appreciate the offer. When do you remember making your last call?"

"I believe the last call was one I took, not one I made. It was from Miss Hillman, telling me she'd gotten hung up. She was scheduled to collect me at five-fifteen to catch our six o'clock train. She didn't believe she could make it and had already called ahead to rebook us for seven."

"Hung up where, Reverend?"

"Miss Hillman? She was doing demographics research at the Library of Congress. In the microform room."

"And when did she call?" Dante pressed.

"Sometime after four. It may have been as late as half past. It would be difficult for me to take that call and be in New York killing my wife, don't you think?" His sarcasm dripped like honey from a spoon.

Dante tucked his notebook away. "Thank you, Reverend. You have our condolences. There are days when I think this is a godforsaken city, too. Today's been one of them."

In the hall outside the Reverend Davis's room, Dante touched Beasley lightly on the sleeve as they started toward the elevators.

"Get on the horn to Mel and Napier. Those phone records ought to be easy enough to check. If he took a call from the Library of Congress there might be a record. Nobody with an expense account uses quarters anymore. They've all got phone cards."

Richardson's curiosity antennae went up. "You see something in there that I missed?"

Joe shook his head. "Not really, but what sort of fools would we look like if it turned out she *didn't* make that call; that he's bullshitting us and we failed to check it out? How long does a shuttle flight between here and D.C. take? Half an hour?''

Jumbo wiggled his eyebrows. ''You *do* like my jealous spouse angle.''

''I don't know what I like,'' Dante confessed. ''Mrs. Mitchell, standing out there all alone like that, is too fucking pat.''

NINETEEN

Billy Beaumont displayed some decent reflexes and good speed when the phone rang just out of reach. He got to it before it finished that first ring. It was only thirty minutes since he'd spoken to Clyde Vaughn, but nearly three hours now since Lyndelle had vanished.

"Beaumont," he barked.

"Billy? What's going on back there?" Senator Lyle Mitchell demanded. "I didn't hear from Lyndelle at the usual time last night, and I haven't been able to reach her yet today. The front desk is telling me she's gone and checked out."

Billy had wondered when this call would come. He'd learned years ago that Lyle rarely sat around waiting for answers to come to him. He liked the feeling of always being on top of his world, not buried by its confusions. "I don't *know* what's going on, Colonel. Fact is, she did check out. Where she's gotten off to, I've no idea."

"Well tell me what you *do* know. I can't say I like the sound of this."

"That makes two of us, Lyle. She didn't take Cora's killing very well. It hit her pretty hard; the fact that they'd been sharing the same suite and all. Sometime this morning, she just dropped off the map."

Lyle's tone of voice became more strained with each utterance, even carried a distance of twelve thousand miles.

"You must have *some* idea why she left. Didn't she say anything?"

"The police are asking questions, Colonel. I'd rather not go into it; not long-distance like this. I know that sounds awful, and I don't want you to go getting all riled up. I'm sure she's fine, wherever she is."

"I asked you what it's about, damn it!" It wasn't like Lyle to curse unless he was seized by fury.

Beaumont sighed and steeled himself. "She's the investigation's prime suspect right now, Colonel. She was in her part of that suite with another man around the time Cora left the reception to head upstairs."

When the silence on the line wasn't punctuated by the noise of a loud crash, Billy felt it safe to assume Lyle hadn't stroked out. "Colonel?" He said it softly.

"I'm here." It was weak with absorbed pain. "But I'm on the next air force flight out, Sergeant. I'm counting on you to hold the fort until I get there."

Billy had started to tell the senator he would do what he could when Lyle broke the connection.

Located between 49th and 50th Streets on Fifth Avenue, Saks was less than ten blocks uptown from the Grand Hyatt. Dressed down the way she was, Lyndelle felt completely at ease in the late-afternoon shopping crowd drifting through the department store's main floor. She appreciated the opportunity to get out and walk, finding it had helped clear her mind.

Her first stop was the Clinique counter, where she selected cream blush, a clarifying lotion, liquid foundation, and lipstick. She would make stops at other counters to purchase eye makeup, nail polish, and a few other shades of lipstick. These initial purchases came to a hundred forty dollars and change, for which she handed the clerk her AMEX card before stepping over to inspect a display of new spring blush colors. The one she'd purchased was her standard, but she was about to embark on a new life. Maybe it was time to break out of the Republican-matron rut; go for something with a little zip in it. There was one spring bronze shade she found appealing. She busied herself before a mirror, taking a tiny dab on a middle finger and stroking it back along one cheek.

Several minutes elapsed before she looked up, wondering what was taking the clerk so long. There were several other women in Clinique lab smocks, but her clerk wasn't among them. As Lyndelle started back along the counter she noticed two clerks huddled together like a pair of neighbors gossiping over a backyard fence. One of them covered her mouth with a hand and whispered to the other.

Something was wrong. Lyndelle backed slowly out into the center of the aisle so she could see around the corners at both ends of the counter. Her clerk had vanished and every alarm in her system was going off. Almost as a reflex, she slipped out of the light coat she wore and pulled the tie from her hair.

She was melting away into the crowd when she finally spotted the woman who'd waited on her. The clerk was weaving her way up a main aisle from the back of the store, accompanied by a tall, olive-complected man in a navy blazer and pale gray slacks. A uniformed security guard caught up with them. He and the tall man walked with heads bent in conversation. Something in the latter's right hand caught the light as he raised it. Panic surged through Lyndelle. The man was holding a platinum AMEX card. *Her* AMEX card.

Across the floor to the west, two more security guards converged on the scene. Lyndelle draped her coat over a stool at the Elizabeth Arden counter and worked her way toward the 50th Street side entrance. The instant she hit the sidewalk she started east toward Madison Avenue at a brisk but controlled clip. It was everything she could do to keep herself from running.

Don Grover and Rusty Heckman had huddled with an airport security administrator and a deputy inspector from Central Investigations for over an hour at the LaGuardia Airport command post. In that time, teams of detectives were dispatched throughout all three major metro airports and the large regional facility up in Westchester. Computer linkage was established with every carrier operating departing flights, and passenger manifests were spewing out of three print terminals faster than a twelve-man team could scan them. All the big airlines were on-line by the time the partners stepped outside the mobile communications unit to grab a breath of fresh air. It wasn't quite four o'clock, and already the sun rode low on the Manhattan skyline. As shadows grew longer, the air had cooled enough for Heckman to turn up the collar of his jacket.

"She's still in the city, Donnie. I can feel it."

"Either that or she had enough cash on hand to buy a ticket under an assumed name. Maybe we oughta start flagging them entries. The cash purchases. How many could there be? Nobody pays cash for anything anymore."

The phone rang for a third time within the hour as Nancy was preparing to take a shower and dress for the evening. The first two calls were from Jerry and Billy. She'd tried to mollify the former in the wake of the visit he'd received from Lieutenant Dante. They agreed to talk further over the dinner they had planned at Smith and Wollensky. The second call came from a considerably cooler Billy, wondering if she'd heard Lieutenant Dante's latest bombshell explode. He reported having heard no word yet on Lyn's whereabouts and wondered if Nancy had received another call. After what seemed like an eternity, Lyn finally reported in.

"Nance?"

"Lyn!" Nancy had to restrain herself to keep from shouting it. "I've been beside myself all afternoon. I thought you were going to call."

"I *am* calling," Lyn replied. "Who canceled my fucking credit cards?"

"Please, Lyn. Why do you insist on using that language? It isn't like you."

"You'd be surprised. It was Billy, wasn't it?"

"I really don't know what you're talking about. We need to talk, Lyn. The police have been here again. They're saying terrible things about you. I've been going crazy wondering where you are."

"Not far enough away," Lyndelle snapped. "The son of a bitch has trapped me, Nance. I haven't got any money and I can't move. I just tried to buy a few essentials with my American Express card and nearly got arrested. I need you to get me some cash and a plane ticket."

"Plane ticket to where? How can running solve anything, Lyn?" Nancy refused to be swept up in Lyndelle's panic. Her best bet was to be the voice of reason. "Lyle is on his way to New York. If you need a good lawyer, I'm sure he'll get you the best money can buy."

"Who are you kidding?" Lyndelle mocked. "If Lyle thinks he can save his own political skin by throwing me to the wolves, I'm history and you know it. Stop thinking like a politician for a minute. I'm asking you as a friend."

"The police are calling you the prime suspect in Cora's murder, Lyn. Even if I did get you a plane ticket, I'm sure they're watching all the airports."

"Make up a name and pay cash. I'll take my chances with them recognizing me. I want to go to either Houston or Phoenix, whichever flight leaves earliest."

"Really, Lyn. Lyle is your husband. He adores you. I'm your best friend. We'll help you through this."

"Do *you* think I killed Cora?" Lyndelle demanded.

"I don't know what to think, Lyn. Did you?"

"Of course I didn't. I swear to God. I'll need a couple thousand dollars, too. Don't worry. I'll pay you back."

Nancy checked the clock beside her bed. "Do you realize what time it is? Most of the banks are already closed."

"There's an American Express office three blocks away from you on Lexington Avenue. It's open until six."

"How far can you run on two thousand dollars, Lyn? And for how long?"

"You're wasting time, Nance. The longer I stay in this city, the worse my chances are of getting clear. I need that ticket tonight."

"Okay," Nancy relented. "I'll do what I can. Even if I get it, I won't be able to deliver it until late this evening. I've got a five o'clock meeting with Billy and an eight o'clock dinner with Jerry. If I cancel on either of them, they'll ask questions. The best I can do is get away from dinner as soon as I can."

"Thanks, Nance." Lyndelle's voice had softened. "I won't forget this."

"Where do you want it delivered? If I'm going to make my meeting with Billy, I've got to get moving."

An edge of caution crept back into Lyndelle's voice. "Can you be back there by ten o'clock? I'll call you. We can set something up."

Nancy started to protest and stopped herself. Lyndelle was running scared. If this was the way she wanted it, it was probably best to play along. "All right. Ten o'clock. Meanwhile, I want you to think about what you're doing, Lyn. I still say it's crazy."

Nancy heard a click at the other end of the line. Then she heard dial tone.

Dante was back in the squad reviewing the forensics and M.E.'s reports on that morning's plethora of homicides. Gus Lieberman had authorized pursuing an eavesdropping warrant for William Beaumont's hotel room, and at four o'clock Beasley had departed with an attorney from the department advocate's office to take the request before a judge. Grover and Heckman were still out at LaGuardia. They'd recently called in to report their current focus on ticket purchasers who'd paid cash. It appeared, at least initially, that the list of such names would be mercifully short. They were having a problem authenticating purchasers' names without the paper trail a credit card or check left behind.

Guy Napier and Melissa Busby had returned from delivering fliers with Lyndelle Mitchell's picture on them to the city's bus and train stations. Guy was put to work contacting the phone company in Washington and requesting a record of toll calls made to and from the Davis apartment, Tuesday afternoon. Melissa was working alongside Joe, digging through that stack of new reports. Both were searching for some pattern or common element they'd been too busy earlier in the day to see.

"Something fishy here, Lou." Napier announced it from his seat at the far end of the desk island. Minutes ago he'd received a fax transmission from the District of Columbia's Chesapeake & Potomac Telephone Company. After working in Joe's former command for over a year, the Boy Wonder still couldn't bring himself to address the whip by his name. "Either she dropped a quarter after all, or she made that call to Davis from Brooklyn."

Dante looked up from the file he was scanning and frowned. "What are you saying?"

"I'm not quite sure." Napier held up the sheet in his hand and pointed to it with his pen. "Davis made calls to Baton Rouge, Mobile, Tallahassee, Wittier, and Charleston between three and four. Then there's no activity again until four thirty-three: a call made from the 718 area code. That's the last toll call listed Tuesday, either made *or* received."

Melissa had set the file she was reading down to focus on what her partner was saying. "How big a coincidence is that? Reverend Davis talking to someone on the phone in New York within half an hour or so of his wife's getting whacked? Maybe Jumbo's jealous-spouse angle holds more water than we thought."

Dante continued to frown as he tried to make sense of Napier's new information. "Nothing from the Library of Congress?"

Napier shook his head. "Negative. At least, not charged to any account."

Joe pointed to the phone at Napier's elbow. "Let's get on the horn to New York Tel; see who that 718 listing belongs to. I'm curious."

Billy Beaumont didn't know what to make of Nancy Hillman when he answered the door at five o'clock. It wasn't the customary business suit she was clad in tonight, but a dress; a short black dress that hugged her waist, hips, and fanny like a second skin. He was surprised to discover the state chairwoman had a pair of slim, shapely legs and was surprised to see how tiny her waist was. While watching him gape, Nancy flashed him an amused smile.

"You're surprised."

He snorted. "Shouldn't I be? This is quite a transformation, little lady."

"Are you going to invite me in or leave me standing out here in the hall?"

Beaumont stood aside and waved her on with a gallant sweep of the hand. "I was just fixing to have myself a little eye-opener before you showed up. Join me?" As he asked it he crossed to the dresser next to the bath and lifted a bottle of Jack Daniel's to uncap it.

Nancy reached to rub the back of her neck. "After the day I've had? I just might join you in two or three. Have you thought any more about Lieutenant Dante's little news flash?"

Beaumont poured a couple of fingers of whiskey into two glasses and splashed water over it. "Yep. I still can't figure how he found out. Not unless that Logan fella left something behind when he died. Maybe a picture of the two of them together in an old scrapbook or something. Ice?"

When Nancy nodded, Billy dropped a cube into one drink and handed it over. He lifted his own, sans ice, and clicked glasses. "I take it she hasn't called?"

"She did. Not quite an hour ago. She still won't tell me

where she is, but she told me one interesting thing. You canceled her credit cards.''

Beaumont listened for accusation in her voice and found none. ''Damn straight, I did. I don't know how much cash she's carrying, but I'm willing to bet it isn't more'n one or two hundred bucks. I've also got an old buddy at the FAA watching every passenger manifest on departing flights from the whole metro area. She's trapped.''

''She was nearly arrested when she tried to buy something at Saks this afternoon. And you're right. It sounds like she doesn't have very much cash. She wants me to get her a plane ticket under an assumed name. It looks like she intends to head south. She wants me to get her a couple of thousand dollars in cash, too. I don't know how far she expects to get on that. Not the way she spends money.''

Billy was suddenly excited. They had her. *He* had her. All he had to do was play this bitch along for a few hours, steal the lead, and land her himself. He knew for a fact that Lyndelle always traveled with a barbiturate the doctor prescribed for sleeplessness. It looked best when a suicide ate pills with his or her own name typed on the bottle.

''How are you supposed to get them to her?'' he asked. ''You arranged to meet somewhere?''

Nancy shook her head. ''Canceling her cards like that really frightened her. I promised I'd be back from dinner by ten. She said she'd call me then.''

''What does the reverend know about all this?''

''Nothing. Not yet. He says he didn't get any sleep last night. I suggested he try to nap for a few hours. That was about ninety minutes ago, and I haven't heard from him since.''

''How about keeping this between just us, Nancy? If I have to play hardball to keep her on ice until Lyle gets here tomorrow morning, I don't want the reverend going soggy on us.''

Nancy shrugged. ''I guess you've got a point. She isn't going to *want* to sit still.''

"Good." Billy drained his glass and set it up to spill himself another. He noticed Nancy was doing a better job with hers than he'd expected and lifted the bottle in question.

"Not quite yet. Thanks."

He set the bottle down and gestured at her dress. "So what's this all about? I do believe it's a side of you I've never seen."

She laughed, sipped a bit more of her whiskey, and resumed kneading the muscles of her shoulder and neck with her free hand. "You've seen what I wanted you and every other Republican from Tennessee to see, Billy. Lately I've been wondering if that was the right choice. Don't think I didn't hear the rumblings from Cora's camp; all those new staffers she hired in Washington trying to convince her to get somebody with-it to run her gubernatorial campaign. They'd all but convinced her to bring that fella from Los Angeles aboard; the one who made those waves in Arizona and Orange County last year with his slick political videos. This is the new Nancy Hillman; the one who's going to get *Jerry* elected Tennessee's next governor."

Billy grinned and pointed at her left hand. "You've got some tightness building there?"

"Building? It's been there since breakfast."

"My mama used to get terrible headaches from tension like that. Have a seat over there." He pointed to one of the chairs.

Billy was a little surprised that she complied, but had other things on his mind as well. While she eased into the indicated armchair, he was trying to figure how she'd learned about Cora's intention to hire Ben Fisher to run her campaign. That was top-secret information—an idea proposed by Lyle himself. The senator knew Nancy's nose would be out of joint, so he insisted it be kept hush-hush until the announcement was actually made. Miss Goody-Two-Shoes was full of surprises this evening.

The view down the front of Nancy's dress once he stepped around behind her was enough to focus Billy's full attention on the task at hand. As he eased his fingers across the smooth white neck, he asked himself how he'd managed to miss seeing her finer attributes all these years; the graceful curve of her jawline where it fell away from her ear, her thick, lustrous hair cut blunt at the nape of her neck. He could also see the faint traces of blue veins in the skin of her breasts where they swelled together.

"Ahhhhnnngh!" She groaned as he eased his thumbs in deep to find the knots of tension along her spine. "Oh my, that feels good."

"Just relax," he coaxed. "Let your head roll forward like there's nothing holding it up. Just let it go." His fingers joined his thumbs now, pulling her shoulders back square while he gently massaged the tightness away. "Tell me where it's the worst."

"Ahhh." She rolled her head from side to side. "Everywhere. I feel like the inside of a golf ball: one huge mess of rubber bands wound tight. Here." She reached to tug the shoulders of her dress down, the straps of her brassiere slipping with them. He swallowed hard, his eyes riveted. Her breasts hardly sagged a bit.

This was outrageous. Billy told himself to be careful, to take it easy. As he worked pushing the tension away along her collarbone, he looked for just the right warm and neutral tone of voice as he spoke. "You're one nasty mess of knots, little lady. If you want, you could stretch out there on the bed and I'll do your whole back. Either that or get the desk to call you a masseuse."

Nancy lifted her head to glance back over her shoulder. "You're doing such a nice job, but I'm sure I'd be imposing. I don't know how I let myself get like this. I'm a wreck."

"Imposing? Not at all. You go ahead and stretch out if you want while I pour myself another drink. How's yours?"

She drained her glass and handed it across to him. Then she unclasped the thin belt at her waist, dropped it into the chair behind and kicked out of her shoes. "You know, I'm not particularly upset with the way you chose to handle things,

Billy. I still think Jerry will make a good candidate, but he doesn't have much stomach for the harder realities. I think my idea to string Mr. Brooks along had its flaws. I admit you were right and I was wrong. It could have blown up in our faces.''

Beaumont stood with his back to her, refilling their glasses. When he turned he found Nancy seated on the edge of his bed, the zipper of her dress tugged down and the shoulders peeled forward to her elbows. As he extended her glass, she slipped one arm free of the garment before reaching to accept it. She then switched hands, freeing the other.

"Thank you." She sipped and closed her eyes, savoring the whiskey as it went down. Holding the bodice of the dress modestly against her breasts, she swung her legs up onto the bed and stretched prostrate.

Billy gulped half his drink in one swallow, set his glass next to hers on the night table, and eased up alongside. When he placed his right hand palm-downward at the narrowest part of her waist, his thumb probing the musculature along her spine, she moaned with contentment.

"Given time, I knew you'd see the error of playing along with an extortionist," he murmured. His tone was kept calm and reassuring. "Problem was, I didn't *have* any time. I had to act quickly and decisively." His left hand joined the right, and together they worked upward along her spine to where the brassiere strap intersected. Without hesitation, his fingers popped the clasp and continued on their way. He waited for her to protest. Instead, she sighed with pleasure and reached to pull her hair up away from her neck. He noticed how well-developed the muscles of her shoulders and upper arms were as she moved.

"You work out, don't you? What? Aerobics or weights?"

"Some aerobics," she murmured, her voice muffled by the bedclothes beneath. "But Nautilus mostly. I do a circuit, four times a week."

"Hasn't hurt you any," he complimented. Women who worked out devotedly at a gym liked it when men recognized the results. "I guess the better shape you're in, the more muscle you've got to tense up in a stress situation. I try to stay stretched out as much as I can, no matter where I am."

"I've been a little distracted," she confessed. Her words came clearer now as she turned her head facing him and opened her eyes. His hands had worked their way to just above her shoulder blades, where his fingers gently massaged tension outward toward her shoulders and arms. "Ummm," she purred. "It looks like we're both a little tense this evening."

Billy was trying to figure how he could persuade her onto her back. He stood alongside the bed, shoulder high with her, and leaned forward to where he could bring good pressure to bear. "How's that?" he asked.

She let her left hand slide flat to the edge of the mattress. There, the tips of her fingers found the inside of his thigh just inches below his crotch. He froze, not realizing he was holding his breath, as her hand slid upward to caress the bulge of his erection.

Releasing him, Nancy rolled languorously onto one hip, making no effort to cover herself. He'd been right about her breasts. They were beautiful, with pert, pale pink nipples tiny as quarters and a ripe fullness that drove him to distraction.

"You're surprised," she observed. "Just as you should be. I wasn't yet twenty-two when I learned that people *do* judge a book by its cover. I've been making my reputation on that discovery, ever since. Packaging is everything."

Billy finally realized he'd been holding his breath and let it out in a whoosh. He felt awkward in the face of her boldness. This was new ground for him. Women just didn't do this. "So. The demure young woman I've known for the past ten years was just a *package*?"

"Sure. Cora Davis needed an advertising whiz to help put her on the map, statewide. I was that whiz. The problem—at least as I saw it—was the fact that I was a fairly decent-looking twenty-five-year-old woman. Nothing scared Cora more than lust, Billy. If I was going to sell myself to her, I had to package myself as a kindred spirit.''

''You did one hell of a job,'' he marveled.

She smiled, her hand back at rest on the bed once again. It lingered less than half a foot away from where Billy hoped he might persuade it to return. ''I did, didn't I? Why don't you make yourself a little more comfortable, Mr. Beaumont? I think you're a trifle overdressed.''

TWENTY

After fifteen minutes of being shuffled up the ranks by cautious New York Telephone employees, Guy Napier finally reached a supervisor who could handle his inquiry at 5:05 that Thursday evening. Napier explained where he'd obtained the number in the 718 area code and what he wanted to know about it. The woman on the other end of the line insisted on confirming his identity by calling back through the SID main desk. She was eventually patched back through, and Guy struggled to keep his usual good nature intact.

"I'm sure you're just trying to do your job, but this matter is pressing," he explained. "We're trying to conduct a *homicide* investigation."

"I'm sorry, Detective. I have guidelines I've got to . . ."

"Just tell me whose damned phone it is."

"It's one of ours, sir." He could hear the strain in her voice as she said it. "A card-activated unit at the LaGuardia Marine Air Terminal."

Not Brooklyn; Queens. Guy could feel his excitement level rise. The Marine Air Terminal was where Delta operated shuttle flights between New York and both Boston and Washington. At 4:33 on Tuesday afternoon, someone had used a pay phone at the LaGuardia shuttle terminal to call Reverend Davis in Washington at his wife's Watergate-complex apartment.

"Card-activated unit. That means the caller *had* to use a phone card, correct?"

"That's right, Detective. Any of the major calling cards."

"And you people have a record of those calls? For billing purposes?"

"Yes, sir. We do."

Napier was excited now. "My record from the Chesapeake & Potomac Telephone Company shows the call from that phone being made to a phone in Washington on Tuesday afternoon." He gave her the exact time and the Davis apartment's number. "Could you run it down for me? I need the name of the person that calling card is issued to."

"I'll have to call you back, Detective. It will take time to access those records."

Napier told her he wasn't going anywhere, thanked her, and hung up. Dante and Melissa were looking at him expectantly as he eased back in his chair and rubbed his face.

"So?" Mel demanded. "Don't make me throttle it out of you."

"Shuttle terminal at LaGuardia. Mrs. Mitchell was in a Bergdorf's fitting room at four-thirty, Tuesday. This was someone else. Could it be the reverend *did* hire someone to whack his wife, after all?"

"What's this?" The surprise in Billy's voice was as clear as the Manhattan skyline on a windy day.

Nancy had watched him get out of his shirt, trousers, and underwear with the agile eagerness of a young boy going for his first summer swim. He slid in next to her and helped peel her the rest of the way out of her dress. No sooner had he pressed his mouth to the nipple of her left breast and reached for the other than he stiffened and pulled back.

"*That* is an augmentation implant, Mr. Beaumont. I'm surprised a man of your experience hasn't run into one before."

"You mean they're not *real*?"

She laughed out loud, her belly heaving beneath the weight

of him. "Of course they're *real*. They're just slightly larger and better shaped than they once were. I haven't spent eight hours a week in a gym and the past ten years watching every calorie I ingest to have a perfect ass and saggy tits."

"Damn, girl.. It feels like there's a rock in there."

Nancy was losing him. After all she'd gone through to get him this far, she wasn't going to let that happen. She bucked hard, flipping him off her and over onto his back. With the quickness of a cat, she was on her knees between his legs. He gasped as she leaned to drag her tongue along the underside of his erection.

"Why don't you just look and let me do the touching, Billy?" She ran her tongue across her lower lip, wetting it while caressing him between thumb and forefinger. "They don't *look* so bad, do they?"

His ardor came back in a rush. He heaved his pelvis, thrusting himself upward against her hand. "You want me to beg, I'll beg," he gasped. "Suck me, damn it! This is torture!"

She uttered a low, earthy chuckle as she lowered her head to engulf him. In the act, she was tempted to clamp her jaws shut as hard as she could before getting control of her revulsion. The temptation passed. She took a deep breath through her nose and tried to generate some semblance of eagerness. All the while, she told herself that this was the price of her ambition. Even the most inspired plans had to be nurtured like a plant. She was the gardener, planting the seed and waiting for it to sprout. Once it did, the ground around it had to be watered. The cultivation of a perfect plan required self-sacrifice and patience.

When the phone at his elbow rang at exactly five-thirty, Guy Napier nearly slipped a disk twisting to grab it. To occupy himself for the past twenty minutes he'd picked up one of the reports Melissa was reviewing and read the dry, Crime Scene Unit documentation of a scene still too vivid in memory. He'd been the first to walk into Dillingham's bedroom and discover the naked young woman shot dead in the bed.

"Detective Napier, Davis task force."

It was the telco supervisor, finally getting back to him. "I'm sorry about the delay, Detective. It's after regular business hours and we're short-staffed. That call was placed on an AT&T calling card. I can give you the account number, but I'm afraid you'll have to contact them to find out who it belongs to."

"You got the number?"

"I do. Yes, sir." She gave him both the account number and the number where he could reach AT&T's calling-card unit. Once he thanked her for her trouble and broke the connection, he punched the AT&T number into the keypad.

"AT&T National Card Calling Center. Miss Jackson speaking. How can I help you?"

Guy told her who he was, what he wanted, and read the account number to her. Once he'd finished, he could hear the click of computer keys down the line before Miss Jackson cleared her throat.

"Yes, Officer. I can confirm that is an active account. It is registered to a Congresswoman Cora Davis, the state of Tennessee's Seventh Congressional District, United States Congress. The account address is listed as room 1205, Rayburn Building, Independence Avenue, Washington, D.C."

"You're *sure* about that?"

"Yes, Officer. It's right here on the computer. The most recent call charged to that account was made last Tuesday at 4:33 P.M."

Napier thanked her, dropped the receiver back into the cradle with a clatter, and sat back to regard Melissa and his boss. "You're not gonna believe this."

"Try me," Dante insisted. The lou looked tired. He had file folders spread all over the surface in front of him, his tie tugged loose, and crumpled sheets of notepaper littering the surrounding floor. Once he sank his teeth he was like a terrier with an old sock.

"It looks like the Reverend Davis received that call from his wife's ghost."

"What?" Both Dante and Mel blurted it simultaneously.

"The account it was made on belongs to Cora Davis. Either your friend at the M.E.'s office is way off base with the time of death, or the perp stole her calling card when he whacked her."

Dante was sitting up a little straighter now. "Wait a minute. Davis claims he got a call from Nancy Hillman sometime between four and four-thirty. She called to tell him she would be late getting away from the Library of Congress. At least that's what *he* claims; that she was doing research in some place called the microform room."

"You sound like you don't necessarily believe it," Melissa observed.

Dante shook his head. "I don't know. Why don't you give a call down there, Mel? Researchers must have to sign for materials or something. Let's see what we can find out." He turned to Guy. "And let's get hold of Chip Donnelly at Crime Scene; find out where they're holding the congresswoman's personal effects. I want to check her handbag and wallet, see what else might be missing."

As the whip issued his directives, he was already reaching for the closest phone. Napier listened as the lou reached the Op Desk and asked to be patched through to the Central Investigations command center at LaGuardia. Once he was connected, he asked to speak with Rusty or Don.

"Donnie? It's Joe. Listen. I want you guys to contact the Delta shuttle service out of the Marine Air Terminal. Check all Tuesday flights between here and Washington. What we're especially interested in is one that departed any time between four-thirty and maybe an hour after that. Let's get our hands on the passenger manifests."

There was a pause while Dante listened to Grover's clarification query.

"Tell you the truth?" the lou replied. "I'm looking for something out of whack. If we've got to, we'll run every name on those manifests through NCIC. Some of the timing bothers me, Donnie. I've got a woman says she's going to be late for a train who calls just about the time somebody called Davis from New York using his wife's calling card. Let me know what you come up with.''

Lieutenant Rosa Losada had left that message for Dante twenty-four hours ago and hadn't heard a word back. At first, when she didn't hear from him late Wednesday or anytime Thursday morning, she told herself he was busy. That morning's developments supported the notion. But now, as she prepared to leave her Public Information office at quarter to six, she wasn't sure how much longer she was willing to accept that excuse. It was Dante who'd said they needed to talk. So why hadn't he returned her call?

Most of the pedestrian traffic was moving in the opposite direction as Rosa stepped off the elevator on the eleventh floor. Several detectives departing the building at the end of shift caught her eye and murmured greetings in passing as she entered the Special Investigations Division. The offices were quiet, with only one plainclothes detective remaining in the area out front of the division commander's office. As she approached him she could hear snippets of conversation down partitioned hallways on her left and right, but for the most part SID was shut down for the day.

''Where's the Davis task force holed up?'' she asked the lone detective.

Balding, with heavy jowls and bags beneath his eyes, the man turned his bloodhound gaze on her at chest level to scan her identification tag. ''Sure, Lou. Down the end there on your left. All the way at the back.''

''You know if Lieutenant Dante is on board?''

He shrugged, his gaze remaining on her breasts quite awhile before finally tearing itself away. ''So far as I know. Him and some'a them others been in there a couple'a hours now.''

She headed away with his eyes burning holes in her backside. The task force's makeshift squad was a cramped room created by partitions and filled with the rudimentaries of Special Investigations police work. There were a half-dozen telephones scattered atop the usual beat-up metal desks, a fax machine, computer console, chalkboard, and file cabinets. In the midst of it, Rosa discovered Joe ensconced with two detectives she recognized from his old Major Case command. All three of them looked up as she appeared in the accessway. Both Guy Napier and Melissa Busby were on telephones, while Dante was scribbling something on a legal pad.

"Got a minute?" she asked.

Dante nodded, tossed the pad onto the surface before him, and hauled himself to his feet. She could see from the way he moved just how tired he was. As she turned to lead the way, she noticed the office diagonally across the hall was empty and headed in that direction.

"Sorry I haven't gotten back to you," Joe apologized. "I've been up to my eyeballs today."

Rosa gained the center of the empty office and turned. She caught the way Joe was visually inspecting her: the conservative, low-heeled pumps, blue-tinted hose, and navy wool suit. As usual, she wore very little jewelry: a pair of tiny gold stud earrings and a thin gold pendant chain at her throat. Those were the things she knew Joe saw; those and other tiny details, like what color eye shadow she was wearing and the color of her nail polish.

"So I've heard." She kept her tone measured. Dispassionate. "I stopped by to see if I could persuade you away for an hour; have a bite to eat. You look like you could use a break."

His eyes flicked to the clock on the office wall. It was six now. "You have anything particular in mind? We were probably going to order in."

"Chinese?" Chinatown was less than a five-minute walk from One Police Plaza. A minute by car. One of their favorite haunts used to be the Golden Unicorn, at the foot of East

Broadway. She could see, watching his expression, that he was tempted.

"We're busy trying to run down some leads," he explained. "I'm waiting for a call from the airport."

"That's why they invented the beeper," she countered. "You've got to eat, Joe, and you need the distraction. Remember how you used to tell me a good detective has to step back periodically during an investigation? See what's being missed and give the loose pieces a chance to fall into place? Isn't this as good a time as any?"

The developing smile twinkled with amusement. "Okay. I'm sold. Give me a sec to huddle up with these two, see if they've learned anything new."

Lyndelle Mitchell studied herself in the bathroom mirror of her Grand Hyatt room and wondered who she thought she was kidding. She'd left the Park View in a panic with eighty-seven dollars in cash. After fleeing arrest at Saks and Nancy's warning that the police were sure to be watching the airports, she'd taken a subway to a huge unisex barbershop in her old East Village neighborhood. There, for the modest sum of sixteen dollars, she had them chop her hair short and decidedly un-Republican. Another ten dollars purchased a nearly black shade of Miss Clairol's Nice'n Easy hair coloring. She'd spent fifteen more precious dollars on cold cream, some Maybelline mascara, a bright, mallow pink lipstick and even brighter pink nail polish. One shocking transformation later, she was left with less than fifty dollars to her name.

Even if Nancy got her that plane ticket and additional cash, Lyndelle knew that without her passport or birth certificate she would have to cross the Mexican border from either Texas or Arizona as a day tourist and make her way south to the Pacific coast by bus. She had no plans once she arrived. Check into a hotel and start ordering room service? Or rent a room in a little pensione and take her meals in local cafés? Either way, how long would her money last? And then what?

No matter how Lyndelle examined her future, she returned to the same conclusion. Sooner or later she would have to face the music. What would she accomplish by running? She might buy herself a month or six weeks of peace, but there would be no peace of mind. Lyle was going to find out about Randy and most likely divorce her. She hadn't killed anyone, and running would only reinforce the impression that she had. If she'd come clean right at the start, she would be in no worse shape than she was right now, and Randy would still be alive. Those other people would still be alive, too.

As she contemplated a face framed by a mop of black hair and painted in desperation, she thought of that tall, confident cop who'd interviewed her and Nancy Tuesday night. No doubt he and the rest of the police were already looking for her. But where else could she turn? If Billy found her first, he would kill her. She didn't know who to trust anymore, and all she wanted was to get out of this alive.

That detective had given her his card. She thought she might still have it in her bag. An Italian name. Could she trust *him*? And what choice did she have? The longer she stood contemplating her stranger's face in the bathroom mirror, the more convinced she became that running was crazy.

As Nancy Hillman lay watching the steady rise and fall of Billy Beaumont's chest, she wondered why sex had such a profoundly opposite effect on men and women's energy levels. Billy had been a very busy boy into the wee hours of last night, but in Nancy's experience men like him tended to nod off after a good romp anyway. The more sensitive ones might struggle to stay awake and cuddle a little, but men with the Tarzan mentality had nothing left on their agendas once their seminal vesicles were milked dry.

It had been fifteen minutes since Beaumont first appeared to fall off to sleep. Five minutes had passed since his sleep patterns deepened enough to trigger light, steady snoring. Nancy felt confident now. She tested the reliability of his current condition by slowly rolling over onto her belly and easing a leg out, lowering a foot to the carpet. All the while, her eyes remained glued to his face. Not a twitch. She planted hands palm downward on the mattress and ever so slowly pushed up until most of her weight was borne by one arm and that foot on the floor. Once she'd centered her balance over the leg, she pushed away. Still not a twitch.

Nancy doubted she'd need the gun in her handbag but drew it out for good measure. The noise of its discharge would ruin everything, but she could take no chances. Now that she'd come this far, there was no turning back.

The lamp plugged into the wall alongside the bed on Billy's right was identical to the one used to kill Cora down the hall. In two prior trips to New York, Nancy had noticed that the furnishings and accessories in each room of the Park View were identical. She'd selected the lamp as her weapon because she liked the heft of it. She liked the heft of this one now as she pulled the plug and lifted it carefully from the nightstand.

Relieved that the gun wouldn't be necessary, Nancy placed it on the bed out of Billy's reach, lifted the lamp high overhead, and brought the base of it crashing down across the bridge of the sleeping man's nose. The force of impact sent blood spattering across her upper arms and naked torso, but she was already moving too quickly to pay it much mind. She snatched up one of Beaumont's over-the-calf socks, wrapped it once around his neck, and hung on as his body began to convulse. His final indignity didn't last longer than thirty or forty seconds. She staggered back, panting, the offal stench of sudden elimination gagging her. It was then that she noticed the blood on her and thought it best to take a quick shower.

TWENTY-ONE

It was six-thirty when Rusty Heckman called the squad. Melissa had her hands full of burrito when the phone rang, and Napier dropped his plastic fork to pick up. In the process, he dragged his sleeve through a paper tub of hot sauce. He dabbed at the sleeve with a napkin while lifting the receiver to his ear. Rank did seem to have its privileges. While Dante dined out with Lieutenant Losada, Guy and Melissa were relegated to ordering in Mexican and waiting for the contents of the congresswoman's handbag to be delivered from the forensics lab's property room. On the Library of Congress front, the Job's FBI liaison had asked the Bureau to make the inquiry for them. All they'd learned so far was that the facility's microform room was open to congressional researchers until 9:30 P.M.

"It's Rusty, Guy. Speak to the boss?"

"Out to eat," Napier replied. "You need him paged?"

"You tell me. Donnie and I were already working on the cash-purchase angle, so it made it easy to dig there first. Delta's the only outfit running shuttle flights out of the Marine Air Terminal. Every hour on the half hour. There was only one flight in the time frame we're talking about. Six passengers wrote checks and three paid cash."

"Fast work," Napier complimented him. "Any of those names ring bells?"

"We're still digging there. Almost a hundred percent of

233

those passengers were flying one leg or the other of round-trip tickets. We concentrated on the return legs of any earlier D.C.–New York flights first. Of the check and cash names we isolated, six of them were on return legs; two of the three cash payers.''

Napier dragged a cheese-gooey nacho over and lifted it gingerly to his mouth. ''You fownsum'n.''

''Huh?''

He swallowed hard, clearing his tongue. ''Sorry. Eating dinner. You found something, right?''

''One of the two cash people, a woman, arrived at one-thirty Tuesday afternoon. That puts her on a one o'clock flight out of Washington National. She had a reservation on the four-thirty return and just missed it; had to reschedule for the next flight out, an hour later.''

Guy had Rusty's drift. ''She only intended to stay in New York a total of three hours. I guess business types do that sort of thing all the time, but if she'd made that earlier flight, she would've been back in D.C. with plenty of time to catch a six o'clock train back out.''

''Only she wasn't,'' Heckman concluded. ''Our friend Miss Hillman fucked up.''

Nancy Hillman emerged from Billy's shower using a washcloth to wipe down every surface she might have touched. Before leaving the bath she hung the wet cloth over the door knob and dressed hurriedly. While running a comb through her hair, she surveyed the image she cut. As frightened as Jerry was, tonight was the night he would take the plunge. Of that she was sure. Once she engineered a brilliant campaign for him and he was elected governor, it would be perfectly appropriate that he marry his attractive campaign manager. Their age difference might bother some, but she had cultivated the perfect image. It was a far cry from the one Lyndelle flaunted. Before the year was out, Nancy would be Mrs. Jerry Davis. A Christmas honeymoon in the islands might be nice.

She found the negatives and pictures in Billy's briefcase. It was another ten minutes before she located the .32-caliber Smith and Wesson in the pocket of his trench coat. On the off chance that he travelled with more than one weapon, she broke the cylinder and checked the load. Two of the chambers were empty, a sniff of them suggesting recent discharge.

Before leaving the room, Nancy swept the wet washcloth over the lamp where she'd grabbed it, the plug where she pulled it from the wall, and over the bed coverlet where she'd lain. As an afterthought, she fought her way past the stink of excrement to wash the dead man's penis and area surrounding it. Once she slipped back into her shoes and rinsed the washcloth thoroughly under the bathroom tap, she left it hanging over one of the shower knobs. At six thirty-five she checked the security peephole in the door for traffic before letting herself into the hall outside.

Prior to departing the Big Building for Chinatown, Dante checked with Beasley to make sure no snags were hit in obtaining the warrant to hang a wire on William Beaumont's room phone. After that, he spoke briefly with Gus, explaining where the investigation stood and promising to update him as soon as anything broke loose. Now he sat across from Rosa in the third-floor dining room of the Golden Unicorn. She drank vodka while he sipped green tea.

"This case is making you crazy," she observed. There was a hint of real sympathy in her tone.

"You can't imagine by half," he replied. "I've got an idea now what it feels like to be hit by an avalanche. The mayor and P.C. are going to know it, too, once the media starts digging a little deeper."

She reached across the table to cover his right hand with hers. "You're being careful where you step? You know how much Tony Mintoff would like to see you buried in the rubble, right along with everything else."

He sighed while meeting her gaze and tried to put the distractions of a thousand intersecting impulses from his mind; to break free of the day's events. "As careful as I can. This one's got a mind of its own." He held up both hands. "So far, I've still got all my fingers and toes."

"I had fun Tuesday night, Joe. Surprised the hell out of myself, but I did have fun."

"Me too."

"Tonight isn't good, but we need to talk about it sooner or later . . . unless you want to leave it where it is."

He lifted his teacup to his lips and sipped slowly. "Funny, isn't it?"

"What's that?"

"How neither of us got what we thought we wanted out of a relationship. Me? A wife, kids, and beer in the burbs. You and your one-woman-island independence. Yeah, we should talk."

Their waiter arrived with a platter of sizzling deep-fried oysters on skewers. Dante watched the precise way Rosa's hands worked an oyster free, her manner unmistakably feminine while avoiding dainty. The noise of his beeper startled them both.

"Damn," he growled. Switching off, he checked the message window to find the Op Desk's call-back number. "I'll be right back."

"Wait," Rosa stopped him. She reached to retrieve her handbag from between her feet and dug out a compact, flip-up cellular phone. "You've got your leash and I've got mine. Here. It's the city's dime anyway."

Dante accepted the unit gratefully, punched the Op Desk number into the keypad, and lifted the thing to his ear.

"Operations. Lieutenant Crowell."

"It's Dante, Dick. What's up?"

"I've got some dame said you gave her your card Tuesday night. Claims you been looking for her all day. She wouldn't give me a number and wouldn't hold, but was willing to call back in five. Says she thinks you definitely want to talk to her."

Tuesday night. Looking for her all day. "I think she's

probably right, Dick. I'll hold.'' Dante covered the mouthpiece with a finger and spoke over the top of it. ''Sorry about this, but I may have just hit pay dirt.''

Rosa waved the apology away, stabbed at another oyster with her chopsticks, and extended it toward him across the table. He leaned to take it and chewed slowly, savoring its delicate flavor.

''Joe. You still there? I've got her back.''

''Yeah, Dick. Go ahead.''

There was a pause and a click. Dante was sure the connection was accidentally broken. Then: ''Hello?'' It was hesitant, female, and about the right pitch for Lyndelle Mitchell's voice.

''I'm here, Mrs. Mitchell. You're a hard one to track down.''

''Believe me or not, I didn't kill anyone, Lieutenant. I'm probably crazy to think I can get you to believe me, but it's time I try. I'm afraid for my life.''

''I don't think this is the best way to do it, Mrs. Mitchell. I'm on an open cellular line. Do you want to come in on your own?''

There was a long hesitation on the line before she replied. ''Maybe you should come here. All I want is your assurance that there won't be a horde of media people following you.''

''You've got my word. I'll be alone. Where's here?''

''The Grand Hyatt. Room 516.''

''Okay. I'll be there within the half hour.'' Dante flipped the unit closed and handed it back across the table. ''Hate to say this, but I've gotta run.''

Rosa set her chopsticks down atop her plate and wiped her fingers in her napkin. ''Mrs. Mitchell wants to talk. Maybe turn herself in, right? I couldn't help overhear. Could it hurt to have a woman along?''

Joe was prepared to reject the notion out of hand when he saw the look of calm, reasoned logic on Rosa's face. It made him stop and think. Yes, he'd told Mrs. Mitchell he would come alone, but maybe Rosa's presence would be a calming influence.

"Okay." He dug his wallet out, threw a fifty onto the table, and started to rise. "You settle up here, I'll run back for the car and meet you downstairs."

At 7:05 P.M. the FBI liaison called Melissa Busby back with word from Washington. Within three minutes of completing that exchange, Melissa was connected to Dante via the Op Desk. The lieutenant was in his car, the strength of the cellular signal from Rosa's borrowed phone unsteady as he spoke.

"Yeah, Mel. What's up?"

"I thought you were going to dinner."

"I made it as far as the appetizer. We've located Mrs. Mitchell. You've got news for me?"

"Maybe." Melissa sat with one foot up in Napier's lap, her shoes on the floor beside her chair. She'd been on her feet all day, and the Boy Wonder was massaging them with that strong, sure touch of his. Right now she couldn't imagine anything feeling better. Like the rest of the team, she was exhausted. "It's all circumstantial, but we may have hit on something."

She went on to relate what they'd learned from Grover and Heckman at the airport. "If that woman is our perp, the timing of the call charged to the congresswoman's card is consistent with her missing the four-thirty flight. *Just* missing it."

"You ran the name?"

"Phyllis Sherwood. If it's legit, it didn't ring any NCIC bells. But get this, boss. The Bureau sent a man over to the Library of Congress to check Tuesday's records at the microform room. Nancy Hillman was there, but her last information request was made at eleven-thirty that morning. There's no other record, past the time when she turned that material back in, twenty minutes later."

Melissa heard horn honks and the squeal of tire rubber on

pavement. Dante muttered something suitably obscene. Across from her, Guy tapped the one foot and beckoned for the other.

"You say this Phyllis Sherwood took a one o'clock out of National?"

"That's what the record reflects."

"If Nancy Hillman turned that stuff back in at eleven-fifty, she had plenty of time to make that flight."

"That's what we were thinking, boss. Too much of it fits."

Lyndelle Mitchell hadn't bitten her fingernails since she was in her early teens. Now, as she sat perched on the edge of her hotel-room bed and stared out the window at building lights across 42nd Street, she realized she'd destroyed the nails on her left hand. Suddenly, calling a cop she didn't know and trusting him with her fate seemed like a lapse of sanity. Her bag remained packed, there on the baggage stand by the door. Twenty minutes had elapsed since she called. Maybe she had time to change her mind; time to run.

A gentle knock at her door set her heart thundering in her breast. Too late for any last-minute changes of it. She sat frozen for a moment, unable to do anything but examine the pink polish on her nails where she'd picked at it. The color was hideous.

Her worst fears were confirmed when she answered the door. The lieutenant had lied to her and not come alone. He was accompanied by a handsome dark-haired woman in a suit and heels. Flushed with anger, she let loose with it.

"You gave me your word!" She tried to keep her voice low and it came out a hoarse, rasped whisper.

"Calm down, Mrs. Mitchell. This is Lieutenant Losada. We were having dinner together when you called. She thought you might be more comfortable with a policewoman on hand."

Who was he kidding? This lady was too well dressed and much too good looking to be a cop. Lyndelle focused her attention in the woman's direction, eyes still narrowed accusingly. "You want to arrest me? Fine, Lieutenant. But I'll be damned if some network *bimbo* you want to fuck is getting exclusive access. I'm not saying another word."

The lady at Dante's side smiled, opened her purse, and withdrew an oxblood leather case. She opened it and held out a gold lieutenant's shield and identification for Lyndelle's inspection. "I'm the deputy commissioner of Public Information's executive officer, Mrs. Mitchell. Not a reporter. It was my suggestion that Lieutenant Dante bring me along. He wants to help you."

The heat of color flushed Lyndelle's cheeks. The photo I.D. picture matched the woman standing before her. It said she *was* a Lieutenant Rosa Losada. Five feet eight inches tall, dark brown hair and brown eyes. Her speech was precise and her confidence suggested she got results with substance rather than style.

"I'm sorry," she apologized. "Please come in."

"That's quite a disguise," Dante commented as he passed. "It just might have worked."

Lyndelle blushed a second time while reaching self-consciously to touch her short-cropped hair. "I was planning to run for Mexico. There's a stretch of beach south of Zihuatanejo where I thought I could disappear for a while."

"But not forever, right?"

She sighed and nodded. "But not forever. I don't have my passport with me. Someone has canceled my bank and credit cards."

Dante's interest was piqued. He turned to face Lyndelle where she stood with her back to the closed door. "Any idea who?"

She folded her arms beneath her breasts, hugging herself, and wandered toward the bed. "Billy Beaumont. My husband's chief of staff."

"You told me on the phone that you didn't kill anyone, Mrs. Mitchell. Then why run and hide? I don't understand."

She let her hands drop to her sides and lifted her chin in defiance. "I know I'm your main suspect in Cora's murder,

Lieutenant. You undoubtedly think *that's* why I'd want to run.'' She shook her head. "It isn't. I'm afraid for my life."

Dante frowned. "Maybe you should explain. I'm missing something here."

Lyndelle took a deep breath and went on to tell how Troy Brooks had followed her and Randy Logan upstairs from the debate reception, Tuesday afternoon; that Brooks had taken pictures and later used them in an attempt to blackmail both his subjects. She explained how she and Logan had been lovers while living on Manhattan's Lower East Side a decade ago.

"I never received the extortion attempt, Lieutenant. At least not directly. Brooks left it for me at the front desk and Billy—Mr. Beaumont—collected it and opened it first. Yes, I was in the suite Tuesday afternoon with Randy, but I swear to you I never even saw Cora, let alone killed her. When I told you about stopping at Harry Winston on my way to Bergdorf's? That's the truth. By the time Randy left, I was already running late. I took a quick shower, dressed, and got out of there."

When she stopped, Dante beckoned broadly, encouraging her onward. "You say that Beaumont intercepted whatever it was that Brooks sent you. What happened then? Did he confront you with it?"

Lyndelle squeezed her eyes shut as the memory of it came flooding back. She nodded, unable to move or open her eyes. As she stood there, she felt a hand on the back of her forearm, the touch unmistakably feminine.

"What happened, Mrs. Mitchell?" Rosa Losada asked. "We're not here to hurt you."

Lyndelle shuddered, wracked with uncontrolled revulsion. "He decided he would blackmail *me*."

"Mr. Beaumont did?" Rosa asked gently.

Lyndelle set her jaw as she opened her eyes and nodded. She looked back to Dante while fighting the quaver in her voice. "You ask me why I fear for my life, Lieutenant? Billy Beaumont decided that what he found in that envelope made

241

me his now. Sexually. You've got to understand that my husband is Billy's employer and one of his oldest friends. This morning when I woke up to news that both Randy and Brooks were dead, I knew who was responsible. Billy Beaumont would just as soon kill me as fuck me if he thought he had to.''

Moving to take a seat on the edge of the bed, she looked first to Dante and then to Lieutenant Losada, trying to gauge her story's impact. He'd said the two of them were having dinner together when she called. They seemed comfortable in each other's company, accustomed to sharing the same space. He was a detective investigating a murder, and she was some sort of administrator. It made her wonder just what their relationship was.

"How much does your friend Nancy know of this, Mrs. Mitchell?" Dante asked.

Lyndelle was confused by this sudden change of direction. "What do you mean, Lieutenant?"

"I'm asking what she knows of the discovery Troy Brooks made and of your suspicions concerning Beaumont's intervention."

Lyndelle shook her head. "Nancy's been a good friend to me for a lot of years, Lieutenant. I don't want to drag her into this.''

She watched his face as he took a step backwards and eased his hands into his pockets. He was betraying nothing. "Indulge me, please. When I interviewed Miss Hillman this afternoon I got the distinct impression she'd spoken to you. Is that true?"

She had nothing to hide anymore. If she was innocent, then Nancy was also innocent of any wrongdoing in helping cover for her. "Yes, it is.''

"When?" Dante pressed.

"Twice, actually. First around noon, and then again after I was almost arrested at Saks. That's how I discovered my cards were canceled. I called asking her to get me some money and buy me a plane ticket.''

"And she agreed to that?"

Lyndelle had her hackles up now. "I didn't kill anyone, Lieutenant. She's one of my closest friends. She *believed* me. I only wanted her to help me stay alive."

"You told her your suspicions about Beaumont?"

"Of course I did."

Dante's hands were back out of his pockets and spread in a gesture of supplication. "If Miss Hillman cared about helping you stay alive, why didn't she tell *us* about your suspicions?"

Lyndelle rolled her eyes in impatience. "And do what? Destroy herself *instead* of me? Her entire career is tied directly to my husband's. His political fate is hers as well. If he is destroyed by a scandal involving murder and my affair with a rock star, her life blows up in her face."

She watched Dante's face register disbelief. "Her *career*? We're talking about murder, Mrs. Mitchell. Five human beings are *dead*."

Lyndelle dug her heels in, already knowing full well what his words implied. "You might be able to blame me, Lieutenant, but not her. I don't see how Nancy could have stopped any of that."

Gus Lieberman was at home with Lydia, the two of them finishing dinner when Dante called. It had been a long day of leaning on special units to rush reports, trying to keep abreast of fast-breaking developments, and putting out political flare-ups before they became infernos. Gus was whipped. He could only guess how his task force commander felt.

"Yeah, Joey. Make an old man happy and tell him you're set to call it a night."

"Sorry, Chief. No can do."

Gus extended his empty wineglass in Lydia's direction, an imploring look of desperation begging her for a refill. "*Ooo-kaay*. The floor's yours, hotshot. You find me sprawled in the middle of it, feel free to step over."

"I want Jumbo to pick up Senator Mitchell's chief of staff

for questioning. I need you to call downtown and get the issuance of a bench warrant to search Beaumont's room. Mel and the Boy Wonder are standing by in the squad. They can pick up the paper two minutes after you signal the all clear.''

''Whoa,'' Lieberman stopped him. ''One thing at a time. Do you know what you're asking?''

''Mrs. Mitchell turned herself in to me a few minutes ago, Gus. Parts of her story are hard to believe, but a lot of it seems to add. She claims she doesn't know why Cora Davis got it, or who gave it to her.''

''That's a pretty big missing piece, ain't it? C'mon, Joey. You sure she ain't pulling your pud?''

''There's one hell of a set of coincidences my people spent the afternoon developing, Gus. *They* say she isn't. That phone call the congresswoman took? The one the desk staff thought was from security? We think Nancy Hillman made it.''

''From where? Washington?''

''From right here in New York. Probably from a phone somewhere in the hotel. The weather was miserable Tuesday. Everyone was wearing heavy coats and hats. She could have walked right through the lobby without anyone recognizing her.''

Gus obviously needed a lot more information. ''*Why*, Joey? Nancy Hillman? Why *would* she?''

''I'm still piecing it together, Gus. But try this on for size.'' Joey went on to describe Jumbo's conversation with the reporter from Memphis earlier that day; the rumored misgivings Reverend Davis was having about his wife's run for governor. He then related his own conversation with Davis; how Davis claimed he was home all Tuesday lobbying for one of his wife's bills. ''He says the last call he received that day was one made by Nancy Hillman from the Library of Congress. We checked his phone records on the off chance she used a card and might confirm his alibi. There's no record of Nancy Hillman calling from the Library of Congress and no record of her being there after eleven-fifty that morning. The only toll call made to the Davis apartment after four o'clock was a credit-card call made from a pay phone at LaGuardia's Marine Air Terminal. I'll let you guess whose card it was charged to."

Gus was incredulous. "C'mon, Joey. You expect me to believe she was *that* fucking stupid?"

"Not Nancy Hillman, Gus. Cora Davis."

"What?"

"Yep. And given the T.O.D. that Rocky's established, the call was made while she was lying on her bedroom floor at the Park View with her skull crushed."

Lydia appeared with a full wineglass and watched with surprise as Gus drained it in several gulps. "Jesus, Joey. So you think the TV preacher might be in on this, too?"

"I'm just giving you what we've managed to put together so far, boss. We need to get a picture of the Hillman woman; circulate it among the flight crews of the planes we think she took." He explained the Grover and Heckman discovery of the mysterious Phyllis Sherwood and how her flight times dovetailed with the Cora Davis time of death. "I've got two things on my agenda now. I want to haul Beaumont in, toss his room, and see how the Hillman woman reacts to knowing we're closing in. The other thing I want to do is keep Mrs. Mitchell on ice awhile longer. She asked her friend Nancy to get her some money and a plane ticket. I'm toying with letting them play it out."

Gus set his empty glass down and threw his head back to contemplate the ceiling. Drag a U.S. senator's staff chief in for questioning? Tear his room apart in search of a murder weapon? He could hear the mayor's circuits blowing all the way out here in College Point, Queens. It was the sort of decision that could make or break the remainder of a brass hat's career.

He took a deep breath and sighed, that wine hitting him all at once and harder than expected. "What the hell, Joey? Maybe *this* is the way they'll get me out the door. You're sure this bimbo ain't yanking your dick?"

"She's *married* to Lyle Mitchell, Gus. Think about it a

minute. No matter what happens from here, she's out on the street with the shirt on her back and a change of lingerie. It's not any secret she slept with Logan. Not anymore. Trying to *keep* it a secret is why Beaumont went on his rampage.''

"You call Beasley," Gus relented. "I'll call the judge."

TWENTY-TWO

TWENTY-TWO

Dante fully intended it that Lyndelle Mitchell overhear his conversation with Gus Lieberman. As he hung up the phone in the Grand Hyatt hotel room he turned to face the senator's wife, his expression impassive. With her radical new haircut, the darkening job, and the gaudy makeup, there wasn't a cop in the city who would have spotted her boarding a plane or bus. Joe doubted her own husband would recognize her.

"What's this about Nancy?" she demanded. "You think *she* killed Cora? Why, for godsake?"

"You heard what I told the chief," Dante replied. "We can't prove she was here in New York Tuesday afternoon— not yet, anyway—but the smart money is betting she was. You know her better than we do. You tell me."

Lyndelle bit down hard on her right thumbnail and shook her head in disbelief. Joe noticed that the nails of her other hand were chewed to the quick, the garish pink polish on them badly chipped. "I can't even guess, Lieutenant. My whole world's gone crazy. Nancy always had a politically ruthless side, sure. But murder?" She paused, her eyes going far away. "It could only be about one thing."

When she let it hang out there, incomplete, Dante pounced. "*What* one thing?"

Lyndelle's eyes maintained their focus on something distant. "Ambition. When we were in college together, everyone thought I was the ambitious one. Fact is, I fell into most

247

everything that happened to me. Not Nancy. She always created her luck.''

"Can you give us an example?" Rosa asked it from across the room. "Anything aberrant that might indicate this sort of turn?"

Lyndelle's focus returned to the room. She smiled sadly. "The way she remade herself to land her first job in politics. She was fairly conservative, even when we were in school, but she had a sexy little body and masses of wonderful dark hair. She loved the attentions of men, and that was one area where she wasn't the least bit conservative. Sure, her dates were all going to be doctors and lawyers, but she went through them like some women go through a department store sale rack.''

Rosa looked to Joe. "You've met her and I haven't.''

"No masses of hair anymore," he replied. "And not somebody you'd figure for a party girl.'' He thought about what Lyndelle had said and nodded toward her own hair and face. "When you say she remade herself, you're talking about more than buying a few conservative suits, am I right?''

Mrs. Mitchell stared at the ruined thumbnail of her right hand and stood, suddenly agitated. "Everything, Lieutenant. She was an acknowledged rising star in Nashville advertising circles, and she wanted to run political campaigns. Cora Davis was another rising star on the local scene, and Nancy figured the best way to get somewhere fast was to hitch her wagon. That meant making herself nonthreatening to Cora. You saw the way she acts. Not a hair or word out of place.''

"So what are her ambitions now?" Rosa asked. "Why kill a woman you intend to run for governor?''

The more Dante watched Lyndelle, the more trouble he had imagining her married to the Mouth of the South. This was a woman at odds with her self and her world.

"I honest to God can't say," she replied. "She must have some hidden agenda. The only risks she ever takes are calculated ones.''

"I want you to make that ten o'clock call to her," he said. "Make it appear as though you still plan to run. If you'll agree, I want to have our Electronics Section videotape the meeting. Your conversation may force an incriminating admission." He checked the time. It was nearly eight o'clock. With any luck, Beasley was moving on Beaumont and a judge would soon be signing a search warrant. "We've got two hours to talk about what you'll say to her."

Lyndelle had stopped pacing. She stood regarding him with obvious fear and doubt. "And what if it doesn't work? What if she just hands over the money and the ticket, wishes me luck, and leaves?"

Joe shrugged. "Welcome to the exciting world of police work, Mrs. Mitchell."

For three hours that Thursday evening, Jumbo Richardson sat with a surveillance technician in the basement of the Park View monitoring William Beaumont's lack of phone traffic. Three incoming calls had gone unanswered, leading Jumbo to believe that Beaumont was not in his room. He was bored to distraction when Gus Lieberman contacted him saying two detectives would be arriving shortly to help take Mr. Beaumont into custody. Jumbo figured they might have to cool their heels awhile before they could accomplish that, but he was grateful for any excuse to stretch his legs. At 7:55 P.M., he called the chief back.

"Something odd going on, Gus. When are Mel and Napier due to show with that search warrant?"

"It could be awhile. The judge ain't convinced Mrs. Mitchell's hearsay is reasonable grounds. Why? What's up?"

"I don't know exactly. Man ain't answered his phone in three hours, but there's a 'do not disturb' sign hanging on his doorknob. Joey and I talked to him midafternoon, and the elevator operators don't remember seeing him leave."

"You beat on his door?"

"Yep. *Hammered* on it, and not a peep."

"Sounds like reasonable cause for concern, don't you

think? Grounds to have management open that door up for you?''

''*Without* the warrant?''

''I'd think so,'' Gus replied. ''The hotel has a responsibility to protect itself in the face of a medical emergency. You tell them what you just told me and then watch. In *this* sue-happy society? They'll break that door down if they can't find a key.''

Fifteen minutes later, at 8:10 P.M., Jumbo and two squad detectives from the 19th watched the Park View security chief and a nervous night manager open the door to room 1711. Once he'd inserted the key and turned the knob, the security man stepped back and let the manager do the talking.

''Mr. Beaumont? Hotel management. I'm sorry. We tried to ring your room and you didn't answer.'' All this was said with the door cracked open a bare inch and a half. When it elicited no response, the manager frowned down at the privacy sign now in his hands and shrugged eyebrows at the assembled company.

''Go ahead and open it up,'' Jumbo advised. ''Man could be dyin' of a heart attack in there.''

The security man eased the manager aside and pushed the door wide, with Jumbo peering into the room over his shoulder. It was dark in there, with the curtains drawn and only the light flooding in from the hall providing illumination. The unmistakable odor of excrement reached Richardson's nose as he followed that stark beam of light across the carpet, up onto the bed, and across an inert human foot, bare of shoe and sock.

''Mr. Beaumont?'' The night manager called it louder this time.

In the month after Cora Davis accepted the League of Women Voters' invitation to debate Randall Logan at the Park View, Nancy Hillman had been over the parameters of her plan until she knew every element by heart. Or so she thought. Schedules, timetables, itineraries—all committed to memory. Three weeks ago she flew to Philadelphia for a long weekend and took the train to New York. She checked into the Park View as Phyllis Sherwood to confirm certain layout details. When she arrived Tuesday afternoon, she'd been surprised to find Cora booked into a two-bedroom suite, but that proved less a problem than missing her flight back out of LaGuardia. She'd timed her exit to allow certain leeway, but an accident on the BQE proved her undoing. It delayed her arrival at the airport by twenty minutes. She'd been forced to scramble to put her scheme back on track, and she'd been scrambling ever since.

Tomorrow morning when she alerted hotel management that Billy Beaumont had missed his breakfast meeting with her and wasn't answering his door or phone, the discovery of his body would lead the police to certain inescapable conclusions. Nancy was careful to leave Troy Brooks's negatives and photographs in a place Lyn could easily have overlooked in a hasty search of Billy's room. Those items would raise questions the police would want Lyn to answer. And by tomorrow morning, Lyn would be long gone.

Nancy wished she had a picture of Jerry's face when she answered her door to him an hour ago. Her little black dress was proving quite a hit. No one had ever passed through the doors of Smith and Wollensky a prouder man than Jerry was with her on his arm. She caught him watching to see who might be looking at them; quick glances, smug in knowing it was his date other men were ogling. Each time she let her attention stray to her plate, or to her glass as she raised it, she could feel his eyes undressing her. The heat of his desire radiated in waves through the atmosphere between them.

"Where did you go just then?" Jerry asked. His expression was quizzical. "You looked so far removed. Is something troubling you?"

She swallowed quickly and shook her head. "I was just thinking of how hard these past few days have been for you, Jerry. Of what a nightmare this all must be."

"They've been a nightmare for you, too," he protested.

"How must you feel, knowing the police consider your best friend to be their prime suspect?"

Better than you'll ever know, Nancy thought. "Lyn and I have drifted so far apart these past ten years, Jerry. I can't say I really know her the way I once did. Of course I feel sorry, but the empathy I thought I would feel for her is missing. She's become someone else."

Davis sighed. "It's such a tragedy; for Lyle, for everyone around them. I might understand killing in an uncontrolled fit of anger, but premeditated murder? That belongs to the realm of Satan."

Nancy reached for her wineglass and fed him a look of deep understanding over its rim. "You haven't told me what you think of my dress, Jerry. I realize it's something of a departure, but don't you think it's sort of—I don't know— fun?"

Davis swallowed hard, a quick smile trying to mask the color rising in his cheeks. "It surprised me. I'll admit it. But I think it's very complimentary. Uh, flattering. Yes. Very flattering."

She let her voice become a hint saucy. "There's talk in some circles of me not being enough of a political infighter to handle the governor's campaign. Not a hard enough edge. Not the savvy. This is the new Nancy Hillman you're seeing tonight, Jerry. I hope you approve of the direction."

Davis chuckled outright as he lifted his glass to click it with hers in toast. "I pity my opponent, Miss Hillman. Correction. *Our* opponent. I think you look positively stunning tonight. As far as your having the savvy required to win us the governor's race? I haven't a shadow of doubt."

Joe Dante and pathologist Rocky Conklin arrived simultaneously at the scene of the William Beaumont homicide. As they rode upstairs together in the elevator, the ill-humored Conklin peeled the wrapper from a lesser brand of cigar. Joe knew Rocky wouldn't waste a good cigar while analyzing the grizzlier details of forensic medicine; that while at work in the field, Conklin always smoked throwaways. He saved those Cubans for the quiet refuge of home or his basement office.

"It ain't like I'm keeping actual count, cowboy, but ain't this some kinda record? Five stiffs in one twenty-four hour period? It's gotta take *some* prize."

Dante was too preoccupied to engage the good doctor in idle chatter. After taking Jumbo's call, Joe decided to take no chances that his cellular-phone conversation with Mrs. Mitchell might have been overheard. He asked Rosa to take the senator's wife to her place. It was another half hour before he got Mrs. Mitchell checked out of the Grand Hyatt and delivered to Rosa's Upper West Side building.

"I want the T.O.D. as fast as you can pin it, Rock. Any second now, this case is gonna blow. Me? I'm digging in as deep as I can get, and I want to be damned sure my ass is covered."

Conklin grunted, his mouth working the unlit cigar from side to side while impatience knit his brow. "What the fuck is going on here, cowboy? You sound like you've got a line on it."

"Can't say yet, Rock. And if I did, you'd wonder what I've been smoking."

The elevator doors opened onto the seventeenth floor, and the scene Dante encountered there was hauntingly familiar. Some of tonight's faces were different than those from forty-five hours ago, but the subdued atmosphere was identical. As Joe and Rocky advanced down the hall toward 1711, uniformed cops and several detectives stood in small knots, choking the air with their cigarettes. Several nervous guests looked on from open doorways.

They found Jumbo huddled in conference with Gus Lieberman, P.C. Tony Mintoff, and hizoner himself. Neither the Randy Logan homicide nor Terrence Dillingham's had been enough to lure the P.C. and mayor from their lairs, but a United States senator's chief of staff? The media, primed by the earlier killings, was starting to make connections. Tying Dillingham to Brooks was easy enough, lack of motive notwithstanding. Logan and Cora Davis was a slightly longer leap, but that didn't prevent the first rumblings of speculation. No leap was required to tie Beaumont to Cora Davis.

As soon as Joe appeared at the door, Gus spotted him and signaled him over. Joe hadn't yet joined him when Mintoff took a step into the center of their circle to point an accusing finger in Dante's direction.

"Where is she, mister?"

"Easy, Tony," Gus tried to calm him. He turned to Joe, eyes begging him to be cool. "Search of the room failed to turn what you were hoping for, but it did turn something else. Mel found pictures and negatives zipped into the lining of Beaumont's trench coat."

Both Troy Brooks and the woman in Dillingham's bed were killed with bullets from the same .32-caliber gun. Ballistics had determined that much. Joe hoped to find the gun somewhere in this room. "Same pictures we were looking for last night, right?"

"You got it."

"I asked him a question, Gus," Mintoff snarled. "Where the fuck is she?"

"In a safe place," Joe replied. "She didn't do this, sir." As he said it, Dante glanced over to the bed where Beaumont's corpse lay, a sheet draping it. Some thoughtful early arrival had cut loose with a good blast of industrial-strength air freshener in there. It mixed with tobacco smoke to provide fair cover for the odor of human excrement, but the stink of it still crept through.

"I asked *where*, Lieutenant."

"In an apartment on the Upper West Side, sir," Dante turned quickly to Gus. "Beasley tells me the modus looks the same, boss. Table lamp and one of the victim's own socks. When the congresswoman got it, we kept the lid screwed tight. Nobody knows the details but us and the perp."

Lieberman mulled this as he shook a fresh nail from his pack and stuffed it between his lips. "Only difference is that Beaumont got it from the front, not the back of the head.

Other than that, it's an exact copy. What are you saying? That this other broad you got your eye on *wants* us to believe the same perp did it?''

"You've lost me," Mintoff complained. "*What* other broad?"

Gus glanced around the room at the half-dozen police personnel present and shook his head. "This ain't a good place to talk particulars, Tony. Dante's people have turned some inconsistencies. Gimme a sec, then we'll lock ourselves in the bathroom and I'll bring you up to speed."

"Why isn't the senator's wife in custody?" Mintoff demanded. "What's this bullshit about her being in some apartment?"

"We don't think she did this; but she may be able to help us catch who did," Gus explained.

"Help you *what*?!" Dante thought Big Tony might pop an artery. "First you float the idea that the wife of Lyle Mitchell is a homicidal fucking maniac. Now you tell me she's probably innocent, but you want to use her to help catch whoever *is* a homicidal fucking maniac. Have you taken leave of your *senses*?"

Right now Dante didn't care if Mintoff could have him shipped off to Siberia or marooned on a South Atlantic sand spit. He was too damned close to let Big Tony or anyone else screw it up for him without a fight. "Did you look at any of the pictures in that envelope, sir? If you didn't, don't bother. I'll *tell* you what's in them. They're pictures of Randy Logan with his tongue down Lyndelle Mitchell's throat. She admits fucking Logan Tuesday afternoon, and last night I had his own admission backing hers up. When I left her just now she was talking about her marriage to Senator Mitchell in the past tense. If he ever gets an eyeful of those pictures, he'll dump her sure as I drink coffee in the morning." He stopped, giving it a second to sink in. "So who do you want to protect here, *sir*? Lyle Mitchell and his soon-to-be-ex wife, or the city of New York's homicide investigation?"

The mayor had remained in the background, absorbing

information and holding his own counsel. Now, when Mintoff looked furtively in his direction, hizoner sighed in surrender. "You let the lieutenant run this investigation even though you don't like him much, Tony. Why? Because Chief Lieberman thinks he's the best man for the job. The die is cast. If you don't let him have his head now, what *other* choice have you got?"

Dante had never seen the commissioner look more helpless. The mayor was challenging him to shit or get off the pot. Joe wasted no time in pressing the advantage.

"I was talking to Pete Shore at Intelligence Division a couple weeks back. He mentioned a room they were using at the Skyline Motel for a sting op; fiber-optic mini-cams, every square inch wired for sound. I want authorization to use it tonight. It and enough technical people to run it."

"What the hell for?" Mintoff snapped.

"Maybe this ain't the place to talk about that either," Gus cautioned. He turned to Dante. "This is about that phone call you want the lady to make, right?"

Joe nodded. "I want to let them play it out; catch our suspect stepping in it. Get it all on tape."

Across the room, Rocky Conklin had donned gloves and pulled the sheet back from the corpse to begin the unpleasant task of examining William Beaumont's remains. Ignoring the stench, he worked with deft, practiced precision to examine the dead man's facial wound and the bruises around his neck. Jumbo had joined Rocky to confer in low tones.

"Maybe now's a good time for you and the commissioner to have that secured talk," Joe suggested to Gus. He nodded toward the bed. "I'd like to be in on this."

"Go ahead," Gus told him. "Your Honor? Tony? Let's leave the lieutenant to his work."

As Dante joined his partner and the pathologist, he steeled himself out of habit and was grateful he had. The bridge of Beaumont's nose was driven down level with his eyeballs, the sockets filled with dried and blackened blood. Joe held his breath as he leaned down to have a closer look at the bruise marks around the dead man's neck.

"These look more pronounced than the ones we found on the congresswoman, Rock. What's the difference here?"

Conklin shrugged. "Most likely? Where he was hit. On her it was a straight shot to the brain-stem area. Here we've got sharp bone and cartilage fragments shoved into the fore-brain. The penetration is what killed him, but it took a minute or two longer."

As Rocky spoke he gingerly plucked out the rectal ther-mometer, squinted at the mercury, and made a note of the reading. He then flipped back a dozen pages in his notebook, flipped forward again, and began to scribble. A calculator came out of his equipment case, but rather than use it to reach his conclusion, he employed it to check himself. Dante had never noticed that particular quirk.

"I'm using the same temperature constant I got from the manager the other night, so until we verify it, this is just ballpark. I'd say he got it somewhere between four and six. Pressed to narrow it, I'd feel comfortable cutting a half hour off each end."

"You got a sec, Lou?" It came from Napier, across the room where he and Melissa were examining the contents of Beaumont's closet. Dante broke off to approach their position.

"Nice work finding those negatives," he complimented them. "You got something else?"

"Just these." Napier handed Dante a shoe box. "Brand new pair of six-eyelet lace-ups. Check out those soles. Hardly a scratch on them."

"So?" Joe asked.

"The Boy Wonder's got an eye for shit like that," Melissa explained. "He noticed it about the trench coat first." She reached to pluck a suit from the pole. "Then about this suit, two new dress shirts, and a couple pairs of socks."

Dante took the suit to examine it, handing back the shoes.

"That suit's never been worn," Napier explained. "Smell

it. Never been to a dry cleaner. As far as we can tell he's got two complete changes of business attire, and half those duds are new, including his only coat."

Dante saw where they were headed. As a former member of an elite Special Forces command, William "Billy" Beaumont would know all about the paraffin residue from a weapon's "blow-back." He probably even knew a smattering about forensic science. He'd no doubt worn gloves while pulling the trigger on Troy Brooks and Terry Dillingham's bedmate, but he knew that once he left those scenes his clothing carried evidence of the crimes with them. He'd gotten rid of them and bought new clothes.

TWENTY-THREE

Nancy Hillman, approaching the Park View from the east with Jerry Davis at her side, was alarmed to see 62nd Street crowded with police vehicles. An ambulance was backed up to the side entrance, its rear doors swung wide. While a handful of uniformed patrolmen kept onlookers at bay, two attendants wheeled a stretcher across the sidewalk. None of their actions carried any sense of urgency, and no wonder. The cargo strapped to the stretcher was enveloped by a black rubber body bag. Nancy looked over at Davis. He had paled visibly.

"What now?" Jerry groaned. "I'm not sure I can take any more of this. Has the world gone mad?"

Nancy took his hand to pat it. "A guest probably had a heart attack." Inside, she was anything but calm. A sudden panic had seized her. It was quarter of ten o'clock, and in another fifteen minutes Lyn was scheduled to make her call. There were too many police cars parked out here. While she knew they must have discovered Billy, she failed to understand how. Had someone he deployed to search for Lyndelle called the hotel and insisted he be disturbed? That was the only possibility that made sense.

"Fifty policemen don't respond to a heart attack," Jerry replied. His tone asked how she could be so naive. "Maybe we should walk back around the corner. To the Regency or someplace. Have a brandy. I've had my fill of policemen and their questions for one day.''

"I can't, Jerry. I still have calls to make. It's a bother, I know. The time we spent together at dinner? It's the best I've felt in days, but it's nearly nine o'clock back home. I really can't let it wait any longer.''

"Later then," Davis pressed. "I had a terrible time getting to sleep last night. Join me for a nightcap.''

She saw his eyes stray to her body. He'd taken the hook and was ready to be reeled in with no fight at all. She had planned to seduce him tonight, but now, after two hours of his drooling on her, she questioned the wisdom of that plan. No doubt Alline Oldham and Kristie Knotts had jerked him straight into the boat. But that would destroy any sport. A man's attention span was short once his basic nature got its way. No pay dirt tonight, Jerry boy. Or tomorrow night, either. Maybe a kiss goodnight at the door, where she'd let her body linger up against his. Play him awhile. Buy a couple more dresses like this one; make his balls really ache.

Nancy got another jolt as the heavyset Sergeant Richardson appeared on the sidewalk, dead ahead. He glanced up and down the street, surveying the scene. She watched his eyes travel past her and then jerk back in recognition.

"Oh, gosh," she murmured. "Here we go again.''

Jerry followed the direction of her gaze. Richardson was making his way through the thin throng of bystanders to approach.

"Evening, Miss Hillman; Reverend. We tried to reach you. The desk told us you were out to dinner." Richardson's eyes strayed briefly to Nancy's body.

"Tried to reach *us*?" Jerry asked. "Why, Sergeant?''

Richardson sighed. "It's your friend Mr. Beaumont, Reverend. May I ask where you and Miss Hillman were between four and six tonight?''

"What *about* Mr. Beaumont?" Davis demanded. "What's happened to him?''

"That was him they just rolled out of here. Afraid I can't tell you much more. You mind answering my question?"

Nancy gasped. "Oh my gosh. Billy?"

She saw Jerry reacting with the same sort of shock and reached to clutch his arm. "We were in our rooms, Sergeant. The reverend had a terrible time sleeping last night. Those sedatives the doctor gave him Tuesday threw him for quite a loop. He took a nap, and I can vouch for it. I'm the one who called to wake him up." She looked toward the departing ambulance. "Dead? How, Sergeant? What on earth is going on here? Senator Mitchell is due to arrive at nine o'clock tomorrow morning. He and Mr. Beaumont have been close friends for over thirty years."

Richardson ignored her questions. "Speaking of the senator, you haven't heard further word from Mrs. Mitchell?"

Nancy feigned preoccupation, shaking her head absently and letting her gaze wander off up the block. "No. Not again. No." She dragged her attention back with what hopefully seemed like effort, like Lyn was the farthest thing from her mind. "I'm sorry, Sergeant. I half expected to hear from her again before dinner. She sounded so frightened when she called."

"There's a three state APB out for her now, ma'am. If she does call you, we need to hear about it right away. See if you can get her to call you back in, say . . . an hour. If you can do that, maybe we can get a trace."

Nancy assured him she would make every effort to cooperate and moved to lead Jerry away into the lobby. Her hand hooked into the crook of his arm, she steered him through the side door with only five minutes to spare before Lyn was scheduled to make that call. She needed to get the reverend upstairs in a hurry, calm herself, and get focused. It was almost showtime.

Dante watched Lyndelle Mitchell as he escorted her and Rosa into room 210 on the second floor of the Skyline Motel.

Don Grover and Rusty Heckman, fitted with headsets, were visible moving around inside the bath. Melissa and Napier were doing the same thing in the room proper, making sure that the five fiber-optic camera lenses were all functioning and able to pick up movement in every sector. All were conversing with technicians manning the electronic monitoring equipment installed in the room next door.

Joe performed introductions as Rosa zipped Mrs. Mitchell's bag open on the bed and began hanging the contents in the closet. The senator's wife took a seat in the one available armchair, her face sober with the reality of what she was about to do.

"Second thoughts?" Dante asked. Facing her directly, he squatted on his heels. Before leaving Rosa's apartment, Mrs. Mitchell had spent time removing her garish makeup. Only the severity of her haircut and the dye job remained.

She shook her head, raising her eyes from folded hands. "Not second thoughts. No. I'm still trying to come to grips with the idea of Nancy as cold-blooded murderer. You don't know how hard that is for me to accept."

"What about facing her alone in this room?" Joe asked. "I've got to know that you understand exactly what we're asking you to do. If we're right, she *is* a cold-blooded killer. Whether you accept it or not, you'll be putting yourself directly in harm's way."

"I know that, Lieutenant." She drew herself up a little straighter as she said it. "And Cora's death may not be my fault, but I still believe Randy and those other people would be alive if I'd done the honorable thing. I hope what I do tonight will make living with that a little easier." She stopped, obviously trying to cope as best she could. "Besides, I won't really be alone. You people will be all around me."

Dante tapped the crystal of his watch. "It's ten o'clock. Let's make that call."

* * *

Nancy had just returned to her room and hardly had time to hang her coat before the phone rang. When she answered, Lyn sounded rushed, almost breathless.

"You got the ticket?"

"To Phoenix tomorrow morning on American," Nancy replied. "Six forty-three. I tried for something earlier. Sorry. There was nothing with space available tonight."

"How about the money?"

"That wasn't as easy. AMEX would only give me a thousand in cash. They insist the rest be in traveler's checks. I didn't know how I could work that, so I got another five hundred for you with my cash card. It's the best I could do."

Lyn let a silence hang and then murmured, "God. I'm really doing this, aren't I? I haven't done a goddamn thing other than be in the wrong place at the wrong time, and I'm running away an accused murderer."

"I know how crazy it sounds," Nancy soothed. "But the more time I've had to think about it, the more sense it makes." As she said it, Nancy wondered how long she could hope Lyn wouldn't hear news of Billy's death. Sitting around bored in a hotel room, Lyn had too much time on her hands. There weren't many distractions other than magazines and television. The eleven o'clock reports would splash the news all over the airwaves. "It's bound to blow over sooner or later," she continued. "I think it's a good idea to give Lyle some time to cool off."

"Blow over?" Lyn demanded. Finally, some of the spark Nancy expected. "Murder accusations don't *blow over*, Nance. If I stay, I'm screwed. Running gives me a chance. People walk into the woodwork and disappear all the time."

"You need a good night's sleep, Lyn," Nancy advised. "The sooner I deliver your ticket and money, the sooner you can get to bed. Can I bring you anything else? Did you remember your Halcion?"

"My Halcion I've got, but I forgot my makeup case. Just dump everything on the dressing table into it. I'll straighten it out later."

"And bring it where?"

"Oh. I'm at a place called the Skyline Motel. It's on the corner of West Fiftieth and Tenth Avenue. The neighborhood isn't the greatest, so have your cab drop you right out front. I'm upstairs on the second floor. Room two-ten."

By the time Nancy stepped into the hall ten minutes later, the police had sealed the door to the room diagonally across the way and left the scene. The usual quiet had returned while the heavy, stale odor of cigarette smoke lingered. Tomorrow morning an army of maintenance staff would be steam-cleaning the hall carpet and dispensing buckets of air deodorizer. By the weekend, the seal on Billy's door—the second, in addition to the one on Cora's suite—would be the only remaining evidence of the week's tragedies. Nancy carried Lyn's makeup case past that door, humming to herself. After an elevator ride to the lobby, she walked out the 62nd Street side entrance, hurried the short block to Park Avenue, and hailed a cab.

Rosa Losada was sealed into the surveillance room next door to 210 with most of Joe's task force and a cadre of electronics technicians. Beside her, Melissa Busby was now equipped with a headset and conducting a final test of communication links. As Melissa spoke in low but distinct tones into her mouthpiece, Rosa watched the bank of monitors before her. The five cameras were deployed two in the bath and three in the motel room itself. Technicians manipulated knobs as each monitor was brought into the sharpest possible focus. Three caught Mrs. Mitchell, sitting alone on the bed, from distinctly different angles. One produced an overhead view of the entire room. Another was aimed past the foot of the bed toward the closet and its sliding doors. One of those doors, pushed partially aside, allowed a glimpse into the closet interior. There on a standard single closet pole, Rosa could see the garments she'd hung on hangers and Mrs. Mitchell's empty bag set atop a luggage stand. The last two monitors revealed the bathroom from opposite directions, its white porcelain fixtures and fiberglass tub-shower gleaming in the harsh glare of fluorescents.

Rosa felt a tingling in the pit of her stomach, a sensation specific to work on the street side of the Job. In the three years since quitting the street to work in Public Information, she'd forgotten that sensation. It was the pure, palpable extract of risk. Until tonight, she hadn't realized how much she missed that surge of excitement. She looked down self-consciously at her suit and heels. Seated beside her in wool slacks and a sweater, the woman all the guys called Mel made Rosa feel like someone's prissy kid sister. It wasn't Mel's fault, either. She wore the clothes of a detective and did the work real cops did. Rosa didn't like confronting that realization, no matter how she tried to justify the choices she'd made.

Guy Napier couldn't see a damned thing and had to rely on Mel's voice, soft in his ear, to help him visualize the room outside the closet. The fact that he was six foot six inches tall didn't make his situation any more bearable. He'd drawn this duty because he was the youngest member of the team and could, theoretically, stand the most time in tight confinement. He and Dante were also judged to have the best reflexes. Should the demand for physical intervention arise, they were thought most capable of effective response. Otherwise, he lay scrunched on the floor of the closet to provide Mrs. Mitchell with much-needed moral support. His muscles were knotting up on him something fierce, and Mel's word pictures did little to soothe a growing claustrophobia.

The fact that the whole damned hotel was hellishly overheated didn't help matters. As Mel droned on about how nervous Mrs. Mitchell looked and how she hoped the woman would get her fidgeting under control, Guy was more concerned with the sweat trickling from his hairline toward his eyes. A drop of sweat had just worked its way through his eyebrow to run stinging into one eye. He was shifting as noiselessly as possible, trying to get the back of a finger up to where he could wipe the worst of it away, when a soft knock came at the hall door.

Nancy Hillman felt a perverse amusement at finding Lyndelle in no-star accommodations like these. The Lyn with the short black hair who answered the door looked haggard and drawn; the same Lyn who'd had all the best things in life handed to her as homage to her beauty and charm.

"You okay?" Nancy stepped up to throw her arms around Lyndelle's neck and hug her with unashamed fierceness. "You look tired, baby." Breaking the hug, she stepped back, hands on Lyn's shoulders. She wanted to remember this for a long time: her glamorous ex–beauty queen, ex–fashion model friend dressed in rumpled slacks and a hideous, baggy sweater, her luxuriant blond tresses hacked off and dyed. "My goodness. What have you done to yourself?"

Without waiting for an answer, she released Lyn and glided into the room. Her fingers worked idly at the knot of her coat belt as Lyn closed the door behind. The room surrounding them earned a slow, pitying shake of the head.

"Not exactly my style, is it?" Lyn commented. It seemed forced; a failed attempt at brightness.

"The truth?" Nancy asked. "It beats jail." She worked her belt loose to unbutton the coat. As she shrugged it off and dropped it casually across the bed, she kept Lyn's face in view. Lyn stared at her impassively.

"Yeah, I guess it does. What sort of trouble did you have getting the ticket?"

Almost deadpan. Anger surged through Nancy. This was her moment; her new image. How dare Lyndelle refuse to notice?

"What?" Nancy hadn't heard Lyn's question.

"I asked if you had any trouble getting the ticket. What's wrong, Nance? You look sick." Lyn snapped her fingers as soon as she asked it. "I know. It's so beastly hot in here. I'll open the window."

"I'm fine," Nancy replied. Lyn crossed to tug the window

open a foot anyway. "And no. I had no trouble at all. As long as you charge a ticket to your own account, you can have them write it to any name you choose." As she said it, she reached into her bag to produce an airline-ticket folder. Handing it across, she shook her head. She couldn't resist voicing her disappointment. "You didn't notice my new dress."

"Oh, I noticed it," Lyn replied distractedly. She had the folder open and was examining the ticket within. "Don't you think it's a little much? I mean, for *your* image?"

Lyndelle never looked up as she said it. Averting her face to hide her anger, Nancy stepped to the window to catch some of the breeze circulating to cut the heat. The contrast between the air coming in that window and the interior atmosphere was marked enough to give her gooseflesh.

"I thought maybe it was time for a change."

Directly outside, the lip of the first floor roof ran out another ten feet toward the Tenth Avenue sidewalk. Its surface was dotted with stainless exhaust-vent caps. When Nancy caught a whiff of frying grease, she pulled away from watching traffic and activity in a tiny Hispanic grocery across the avenue. She found Lyn eyeing her expectantly.

"The money?"

"Oh." Nancy dug an envelope out of her purse and handed it over. "Mind if I use the bathroom?"

"Please. And thanks, Nance. I'll pay you back. I swear it."

TWENTY-FOUR

Try as he might to prevent it, sweat was now flowing into Guy Napier's eyes at a furious rate. When Mrs. Mitchell answered the door and Nancy Hillman entered, he was forced to lie with his right hand cradling his weapon and left gripping an ankle to hold his feet from view. His shirt was plastered to his torso. He'd squeezed his eyes shut to relieve their burning and was praying Mrs. Mitchell wouldn't need his assistance. He feared that when he opened them he might be temporarily incapacitated.

"The Hillman woman has entered the bath," Melissa informed him. "She's closed the door and is opening her purse. She's taking something out wrapped in what looks like newspaper . . . turning on the sink tap . . . lowering the commode lid and unwrapping the package on top of it. Oh God, she's got a pair of rubber gloves and a plastic bag with a gun in it."

Napier released his ankle and hastily reached to wipe his eyes. God, they burned.

"Wait a sec. She's got the gun out of the baggie and is *hiding* it. Inside one of the towels folded and tucked into the wire rack. Now she's flushing the john and taking the gloves off."

Jumbo Richardson, left in command of the monitoring center, cut in. "What about it, Joey? You want to drop the net now or play it out?"

Dante had established a prearranged code using the Morse button of his hand-held radio. One long beep meant let it roll. Two meant shut it down, throw the cuffs on her.

"That's one beep, Boy Wonder," Jumbo advised. "Keep a tight butt hole awhile longer. Let's see what Mrs. Mitchell can squeeze outta her."

"I was wondering if you could spare me a few Halcion, Lyn?"

Nancy asked it as she stepped from the bathroom, the harsh fluorescent light behind giving her a garish outline as she advanced.

"Since when?" Lyndelle asked. "You've always slept like a baby."

"Not this week, I haven't. Please. You never go anywhere without a full bottle. Just two or three."

Lyndelle shrugged and crossed to where she'd set her handbag beside the bed. While digging out the bottle and lining up the arrows of the child-proof cap, she turned back to face her old friend. "I know Billy's dead, Nance. I saw it forty minutes ago on the ten o'clock news."

Nancy had her own pocketbook open and was reaching inside when she froze. "I was afraid of that."

"You know I didn't kill him, Nance; just like you know I didn't kill Cora."

"How could I know that?"

Lyndelle pried the cap off the bottle and shook two Halcion into the palm of her hand. "Who else would know, Nance? Jerry? I don't think so. I saw him Tuesday night, too. No one was ever more shocked."

"I was in Washington all day Tuesday, Lyn."

"So you say. How does Jerry like your new image, Nance? Have you fucked him yet, or are you still leading him on?"

Nancy was jolted to the core. Her eyes glazed, her face suddenly a frozen mask of hatred. "You've got a filthy mind and a filthy mouth, Lyn Jennings. Why didn't you tell me Cora was going to hire that show business Jew from Los

Angeles? You call yourself my friend? If it wasn't for me, you'd still be back in Memphis, nothing but a has-been beauty queen.''

Lyndelle's fingers clenched the two pills in one hand while she flung the rest of the bottle at Nancy with the other. The bottle missed its target by a good yard, hit the wall opposite and scattered its contents all over the carpet. ''Show business *Jew*? Careful, Nance. Your up-the-holler roots are showing.''

''You know who I'm talking about,'' Nancy snarled.

Lyndelle shook her head. ''No dear. I'm afraid I haven't the foggiest.''

''The bigshot campaign strategist and video packager. The one Cora planned to use instead of me. Don't pretend you know nothing about it. It was Lyle's idea.''

''You're ranting, Nance. You know Lyle never talked politics with me.''

Nancy started for the door, but on reaching it turned, cutting off Lyndelle's only avenue of escape. The hand that was in her bag now brandished a compact, short-barreled automatic pistol. She gestured toward the floor with it. ''Pick up the pills, Lyn. All of them. Then go into the bathroom and draw yourself a glass of water.''

The instant Nancy Hillman's hand emerged from her purse with the weapon, Beasley Richardson's voice cut through Melissa's word picture.

''Jesus, Joey. Go! She's got another gun!''

Dante was starting to freeze his ass off, flattened to the building outside the open motel room window. He'd put himself out there and Napier in the closet so if necessary, he could create a diversion at the window while Guy got the drop from his concealment. The man he'd left calling the shots was saying go. One instant Joe was trying to relax his muscles against the cold, and the next he dropped into a crouch and launched himself at the half-open window.

* * *

Guy Napier pivoted on his downside hip the second he heard the word. His free hand came up to chest level to meet his gun hand as he lashed out at the sliding doors with both feet. He felt something pop in the back of his left thigh as the pair of doors exploded from their tracks. It was followed by a knife-thrust of pain as the room before him was engulfed in a maelstrom of shattering glass.

In the few seconds after Nancy pulled that gun—seconds that seemed to stretch out for an eternity—Lyndelle was sure she was a dead woman. Lieutenant Dante, with all his protective precautions, had abandoned her. And then it seemed as though a bomb had gone off. As Nancy insisted Lyndelle pick up the scattered Halcion tablets, Lieutenant Dante crashed headlong through the window, his shoulder catching the aluminum sash and caving it inward. It sent shattering glass flying in all directions. Nancy swung her gun in a wild arc and fired blindly into the blank hole where the window had hung. The look of surprise on her face would remain etched in Lyndelle's memory for the rest of her life.

Dante was already on the floor, his upraised forearms tucking in an attempted shoulder roll, when the closet doors came down. Lyndelle, frozen in place, watched as the huge young detective hidden inside the closet blinked furiously while drawing bead. Nancy was seized by indecision for a heartbeat as she jerked her weapon from one eruption of chaos to the other. Dante, coming at her fast as he completed his roll, seemed the most immediate threat. He was up on one knee and leveling his gun when she shot him point-blank in the chest. From inside the closet, Napier's .357 Smith and Wesson barked twice in quick succession. Nancy was flung backward to collide with the door, the thud of impact as harsh and final as the slamming of a coffin lid.

With Dante writhing on his back beside her, Nancy collapsed in a pool of crimson gore and began to convulse. Napier struggled to rise, tried to put weight on his left leg, and toppled with a grunt. The cowering Lyndelle was the only one standing as Detectives Grover and Heckman burst into the room behind drawn guns.

"Joe's down!" Grover snapped into the mouthpiece of his headset. "Get us an ambulance. STAT!" He advanced, dropping to one knee beside the fallen lieutenant as Sergeant Richardson, Melissa Busby, and Lieutenant Losada rushed onto the scene.

"Gaahhhd *damn* it!" Dante roared. It was part pain, part fury, and not at all the utterance of a dying man.

"Where, Joe?" Rosa asked. She was on her knees beside him, one of his hands in hers.

"Dead fucking center," Dante muttered through clenched teeth. "Shit, that hurts."

"Beats hell out of a head shot," Grover consoled. "Vest or no vest, your luck runs out when they start shooting for your brains or your balls."

"Thanks, Donnie. You're a regular angel of fucking mercy." Dante fought through his pain, forced himself to focus, and turned his head to find Lyndelle. "Is Mrs. Mitchell okay?"

Numb with shock, Lyndelle managed to step forward into his field of view and nod. Dante looked back to Rosa before squeezing his eyes shut and swallowing.

"Get her out of here for me, will you? When the news hounds hear a ten-thirteen EMS call, they swarm like flies to shit."

Rosa looked doubtful.

"I'm fine, babe," he assured her. "Go on. Catch up with me at the hospital."

As Lieutenant Losada led her from the scene, Lyndelle's eyes fell on Nancy one last time. Both of Detective Napier's shots had hit her. The resulting carnage splattered a dozen feet in either direction along the wall behind, across the ceiling overhead and the carpet beneath. Nancy's body, soaked a gleaming crimson and her eyes still wide with surprise, lay faceup in a growing pool of blood.

EPILOGUE

Aside from some minor cuts sustained when landing on broken glass, and an ugly purple welt midchest the size and shape of Iceland, Dante had escaped reasonably intact. Two of his cuts required a total of twenty-eight stitches; by no means a personal best. Two hours of monitoring his blood pressure determined there were no internal injuries, while an x-ray series turned up a hairline fracture along his sternum. He was going to have a lot of trouble sleeping for the next five or six weeks. After some argument he was pronounced fit enough to leave the St. Clare's Hospital emergency room at 1:15 A.M. He'd lost track of how many times in his career he'd been forced off the job on medical leave, but right now the idea sounded good to him. He was beat. His loft renovation project had ground to a standstill. His cat was starting to treat him like a stranger. For the next few weeks he would gladly say to hell with the mutts and the slime.

Once Joe was released, Gus Lieberman walked with him down a brightly lit corridor toward the street. The chief had spent the first part of the past hour finishing a news conference conducted out front of the Skyline Motel. When he arrived, he found Dante champing at the bit. The hospital wanted to keep him for twelve hours' observation. Joe's hatred of hospitals was legend, and he was having none of it. Guessing who would win out in the end, Gus had offered his old friend a ride home.

"Big Tony is shitting bricks that you allowed Senator Mitchell's wife to be put in that kinda jeopardy, Joey. I told him she *wanted* to do it, but he's threatening to have you hauled before a review board."

"Tell him he can kiss my ass."

Gus chuckled. "The light of a new day'll bring him around. He and the city are in the clear; the congresswoman imported her own brand of trouble from outta town. All you did was put out the fire."

"Where'd Rosa take her?" Joe asked. "Last I saw, she was pretty shaken."

"Back up to her apartment along with Mel and the Boy Wonder. The big guy fucked up one of his hamstrings when he kicked them doors down. He pulled it pretty good and wanted to get ice on it as fast as he could. Midtown North has ice, but Rosa was offering drinks, too. You mind me asking what she was doing there? I thought you two were ancient history."

Dante slipped his boss an irritated scowl. "Yeah. I *do* mind. It's a long fucking story, and I'm not sure of the particulars myself."

"I see." There was something odd in Gus's tone. Dante glanced up. He followed the direction of his rabbi's gaze out through the double glass doors dead ahead. Double-parked in the street, Rosa stood leaning against the front fender of Dante's Job-issue sedan.

"Looks like you already got a ride home."

"C'mon, boss," Dante protested. "Whatever happened to age before beauty? You want the privilege, I'm sure she'll understand."

Rosa Losada watched Joe and the chief emerge onto the 51st Street sidewalk as she advanced to the curb. For a guy who'd taken a .38 slug in the chest less than three hours ago, Dante seemed surprisingly spry. He was actually smiling and joking with Gus as he emerged into the night air.

"I've been ordered to mind my own fucking business, so

I will," Lieberman announced. "He's all yours, Lieutenant." As he said it, he peered into the backseat of the parked sedan. "Where's your charge?"

"I left her with Melissa and Napier. They know where the liquor and sheets for the sofa bed are. She'll be fine. She was so exhausted the only thing keeping her eyes open was good manners."

Gus extended his hand to Joe. "Thanks, hotshot. You done good."

Rosa watched Joe's expression sober. "Too many stiff ones, Gus. The last place this city needs full employment is at the fucking morgue. Keep me posted, yeah?"

Dante turned and started for the car. On reaching it, he paused to look quizzically in Rosa's direction.

"That's right," she told him. "I'm driving. Once I get you home I can catch a cab back downtown. I left my car in the garage, remember?"

"That was tonight?" he marveled. "It seems like a week ago."

They got underway and headed south toward Dante's West 27th Street digs. Gus had told Joe that the Reverend Davis was denying any knowledge of Nancy Hillman's Tuesday afternoon trip to New York. There was a polygraph test scheduled to see how his story would hold up. Gus also reported that Senator Lyle Mitchell would land at Stewart Air Force Base up the Hudson in Newburgh in about eight hours' time.

"You think he'll throw her out on the street?" he asked. "Mrs. Mitchell? You got a chance to know her better than I did."

With hands loosely gripping the wheel, Rosa surveyed the near-empty avenue and shook her head. "I doubt he'll get the chance. While you were off at the Beaumont scene, we had a lot of time to talk. She's thought quite a bit about what motivated her to sleep with Randy Logan. She thinks she was trying to recapture something she lost . . . or maybe a better way to put it would be sold—to the highest bidder."

"That's funny. When I first met her, Tuesday night, I thought she looked every inch the part. Nobody could have been more surprised than I was when Randy Logan told me he'd taken a roll with her."

"She says her husband courted her like no one ever courted her before; that he spent money on jewelry and flowers and took her places that made her feel important. She had no idea what the downside would be until after she married him. She knows a dozen other women who made similar choices and have no trouble handling the limitations. The problem is that *she* couldn't."

"What could they possibly have in common?" As Dante asked it, he shifted a little in his seat. A quick intake of breath suggested the move had cost him.

"Not much," Rosa agreed. "Lyle Mitchell wanted an object who'd look wonderful on his arm at Washington functions. Lyndelle thought the respect and power that came with being a senator's wife would be enough."

"So where's she go from here?"

"Good question. I asked it, too. She's talking about moving back here; seeing if her old friends in the fashion business can help her find something."

"Wonderful," he groaned. "Why am I afraid No Excuses just found themselves a new spokesmodel?"

They reached Dante's block, and as Rosa pulled up to park in front of his building, Joe tugged his coat closed around him. "What ever happened to that conversation we were going to have over dinner? You want to take a rain check?"

Rosa shut off the ignition and removed the keys. "How about inviting me upstairs for a nightcap?"

He seemed surprised by the suggestion. "Look at me, Rosa. I'm a wreck. I've been on my feet since yesterday morning and I'm loaded up with painkillers. What sort of company can I be?"

Rosa laughed, lifted the flap of her handbag and dropped the keys inside. "I think I can be the judge of that, mister. The first time we ever made love, you had worse cuts and more broken bones than you've got right now. More rest, maybe, but these things tend to balance out.''

He stared down at his lap to hide a grin and shook his head while fumbling for the door handle. ''At least I'm consistent, right? Come on. It's cold out here.'' He heaved open the door and swung his legs around with another gasp of pain. ''What a job,'' he muttered. ''You gotta love it.''

Don't miss
a single heart-pounding moment
in these thrillers by
CHRISTOPHER NEWMAN

Available in your local bookstore.
Published by Fawcett Books.